UNCOMMON COMFORT

"What's wrong with you?" Vonn growled at Winters. "I've got an impeccably solid psych rating. My Xenophobe Potential rating is so low they don't even list it on my profile. So when *It's Mister Bob!* comes out of his cabin to greet us, I go into this hyper overload, this fear that I've never felt before in my life. And you sit there with a Psych 13 rating—you shouldn't even be on the same ship with those aliens—and you're talking to that thing like it's your long-lost brother. I just don't get it."

"I guess I'm just not scared of him," Winters said plainly.

"Why? What do you have that I don't?"

Winters shrugged. "misterbob reminds me of something I used to eat."

By Joe Clifford Faust
Published by Ballantine Books:

A DEATH OF HONOR

THE COMPANY MAN

Angel's Luck
  Book One: DESPERATE MEASURES
  Book Two: PRECIOUS CARGO
  Book Three: THE ESSENCE OF EVIL*

*Forthcoming

PRECIOUS CARGO

Book Two of
Angel's Luck

Joe Clifford Faust

A Del Rey Book
BALLANTINE BOOKS • NEW YORK

A Del Rey Book
Published by Ballantine Books

Copyright © 1989 by Joe Clifford Faust

Library of Congress Catalog Card Number: 89-91800

ISBN 0-345-36088-5

Manufactured in the United States of America

First Edition: January 1990

Cover Art by David B. Mattingly

For two bold adventurers:
the fathers of Nip, Bink, Tuck, Hoover, Eyelash, and the
twins Damascus and Rapunzel

ONE

"On behalf of the United Terran Empire Fleet, I'd like to welcome you aboard the Hergest Ridge . . ."

Dorienne Junnell had to say it twice to be heard over the insistent ringing of the alarm. "I've done all I can with this situation. Ensign Tesla, fetch the commander."

And Ensign Revel Tesla, fresh out of Ordinance School on Y'lred 1, saluted and left the bridge, bouncing down the halls in the weak gravity of the *Hergest Ridge*. He would have much preferred a full gee, but there was reason to keep it low. There were Arcolians on board.

Tesla slipped into a grav drain conduit, snapped a latch, and was pulled a hundred meters down into the ship. His feet hit metal, and he crouched, turned, and pushed off, a not-quite-perfect catfall for a not-altogether-pressing emergency.

He made his way through the halls by instinct, not bothering to look at the signs. He liked to run errands in that part of the ship. Space was at less of a premium there, and the halls were wide and spacious. If he was planetside, he would have likened it to a walk in the outdoors.

The alarm still fresh in his mind, he found the hatchway marked POLONDO SUITE, opened it, and stepped through. He immediately felt out of place. His standard-duty uniform looked cheap and felt worse as he wove between people wrapped in K'perian silks, the shifting shades of pseudofelt made only on Mehnra 4, and the exquisitely engineered furs of the Nimrev Company.

After a moment to stop and look things over, Tesla found what he was looking for—a round table in a corner, covered with the remnants of what must have been a wonderful meal, the celebrants sipping cognac out of crystal lo-grav goblets. They were all laughing as they listened to a story being told by an old gentleman in a United Terran Empire uniform.

"Excuse me," Tesla said after waiting for a pause in the story. "I need to speak with Commander O'Hearn."

The uniformed man stood and extended his hand. "Maggie," he said.

A woman in a blue zipsuit of exotic design took his hand and rose. She nodded graciously at the others at the table. "Forgive me," she replied, "but duty calls."

She followed Tesla out through the suite, politely acknowledging those who hailed her but firmly staying behind the ensign, who cleared a path for her. He deftly took her through the crowds, and when at last they made the hatch, he held it for her, tactfully fending off well-wishers.

"Well, Ensign," she said, smoothing out the lines of her dress uniform. "What is it that brings me away from the well-crafted fictions of Admiral Studebaker?"

"First Officer Junnell requested that I bring you to the bridge," he said. "We're having some difficulty with the Outboard Systems Repulsion Net."

The commander's hands went to her hips, the movement causing the holographic *UTE Fleet* logo above her right breast to dance in the light. "Have you checked orbital forecasts for migratory asteroids?"

"Yes, ma'am," Tesla replied. "And we've checked hull polarity for stability. There's less than one-tenth of one one-hundredth of a percent of error, which doesn't begin to account for the polarization we're seeing."

"Wait a minute," Margaret O'Hearn said. "You're picking up *processed* metals on the net?"

"More than that," Tesla said apologetically. "We're getting a large amount of ionization."

"Why didn't you tell me?" she said, and started down the corridor. "How long have you been getting the readings?"

"First trace of processed metals came in about twenty minutes ago," Tesla informed her as he tagged behind. "It seemed like a singular occurrence, so we didn't think about it until ten minutes later when the reading jumped. That's when we started to see the ionization."

"What kind of intersect were the readings coming in on?"

Tesla opened the grav drain conduit for her. "That's the reason I was asked to summon you, ma'am. They don't appear to be on an intersect. They're on a direct line with this route."

O'Hearn grabbed the handrail and jumped feet first into the conduit. She aimed her legs straight, released the bar, and was sucked in and carried a hundred meters. She hit metal and bounced out of another hatch near the bridge. Tesla was right behind her.

"This is your first time out, isn't it, Ensign?" she asked, starting down the cramped hall.

"Yes, ma'am."

"Have you ever worked with an Outboard Systems Net before?"

"They had one at the academy—"

"Not a simulation," O'Hearn said. "An actual, functioning net running short space options?"

"Not until today," he said sheepishly.

"The OBSYNE operates differently in short space," she told him. "When a particle hits the net there's a shift in the spectrograph readings that must be compensated for."

"Begging the commander's pardon," Tesla said politely, "but we've been seeing some pretty large particles. The system deflected one that was ten meters long."

"Ten meters?" O'Hearn looked worried. "And there's no report of migratory asteroids along this path?"

"None, ma'am." They stopped at the bridge hatch. It hissed open, and O'Hearn led the way in. She winced at the alarms and motioned for a bridge officer to cut them off.

"Mr. Junnell," she said. "Status report."

The first officer looked up from her console. "The OB-SYNE is vaporizing and deflecting large pieces of radioactive processed metals on this route. Spectrograph readings indicate titanium, platinum, molybdenum . . ."

O'Hearn moved to the console and studied the readouts. "What are these?" she asked, tapping a column of multi-colored bars.

"The nearest I can tell, plastics," Junnell said. "And here, some organic material."

"Ensign Tesla, will you please check this route schedule and see if there are any vehicles that have been reported missing along it?"

"None, ma'am," Tesla replied smartly. He had been expecting the question.

"Very good. What do you make of this, then?"

"I wouldn't know, ma'am," said the ensign. "That's why we sent for you."

"Do we shift down, ma'am?" Junnell asked.

O'Hearn shook her head. "There's no reason for us to throw this ship off schedule other than the fact that we're running into some heavy metals."

"How about the salvors, ma'am?" Tesla suggested.

"Junnell. Amounts?"

"Not enough to justify the stop, Commander."

O'Hearn shrugged. "For this I missed Studebaker's account of how he single-handedly forced the Arcolian Accord."

Junnell laughed.

O'Hearn turned to the ensign. "Don't worry. You did the right thing, especially since the readings were on a direct line."

"Excuse me, Commander," Junnell said. "The readings are coming in on a path intersect."

"But the ensign told me . . ."

"I took another set of readings after dispatching him. There's been a marked shift in the relative angle of intersect. They're coming at us from off this route."

O'Hearn stepped away from the console. "That's more like it. Are we near an intersect with any other routes?"

Tesla checked a projection of a star map. "The nearest," he said, "is an old route from Garland Outpost to Jubilo 3."

"What are the intersect coordinates?"

"Relative angle would give us a forty-five/forty intersect. The main path is twelve minutes off core."

"Very good. Mr. Junnell, does this coincide with what the OBSYNE is telling us?"

"Yes, ma'am. These particles could very well have come from the Garland–Jubilo route."

"Are any ships missing on that route?"

Tesla hit a key, and the screen in front of him filled with information. "Three reported, ma'am, all within twenty-one standard days."

"Three?" O'Hearn said.

"The *Roko Marie*, a dreadnought based out of Cosen 3; the *Preambulator*, an independent light cruiser; and a small merchant ship called *Angel's Luck*."

"Angel's Luck," O'Hearn echoed.

"Total number of persons believed missing with these ships comes to eight hundred and nine."

"How does the Vasac read?"

"Nothing within our range except more metals, varying in size," Junnell said, "but there's nothing ship-sized in the immediate vicinity."

"That's not saying that there might not be something nearby."

"Half a day to look?" Tesla suggested.

"There could be something along the Jubilo route," Junnell advised.

"Notify the salvage team," O'Hearn said. "Take us back into real space and plot a course that'll put us onto the Jubilo route core. Ensign Tesla, I'd like you to notify the passengers via All Call and then put out a bulletin on AFA for ships in the vicinity."

Tesla started for the communications board.

"Begging the commander's pardon," Junnell said, clearing her throat, "but what about our guests?"

O'Hearn smiled at her first officer. "No pardon needed, mister. They should be notified in person. Belay that last order, Ensign. I need to do a formal notification first."

"The xenos?" Tesla asked.

"Arcolians," O'Hearn corrected. "Have you met them, Ensign?"

Tesla flushed and looked around the bridge. "No, ma'am, but—"

"Very well. You may escort me to their quarters."

"Ma'am—" Tesla cleared his throat and looked her in the eye. She had given him a polite order. "Yes, ma'am." With a nod, he stepped in front of her and led her to the door.

"Mr. Junnell," O'Hearn said. "Ensign Tesla will ring you once we have spoken with the Arcolian delegation. After that you may make a general announcement."

"Yes, ma'am," Junnell said, turning back to her console.

O'Hearn followed Tesla out of the bridge to a larger gravity conduit and waited while the junior office opened the hatch for her. She thanked him and boosted herself into the well. Peering down the hole, Tesla waited for the commander to clear before stepping in himself. His landing on the inner deck was a little sloppy, but O'Hearn said nothing about it. Instead, she allowed him to take the lead down the corridor.

"Are you afraid?" she asked.

"Yes ma'am."

"Thank you for not lying, Ensign. To tell you the truth, they still make me a little nervous."

"Sir? Uh—ma'am?"

"I grew up hearing about the great xeno menace, so I had all of the predetermined notions and fears. Most of it was propaganda—you know, how they ate their own young and all of that."

"But they did do the spiking," Tesla said thinly. "It's been documented a number of times."

"They did," O'Hearn admitted. "And some of the things we did to them were atrocious, too. It's another aspect of the war that made it so ridiculous."

Tesla cracked a knuckle. The sound echoed loudly as they walked.

"Relax, Ensign."

"I've heard they're rather hideous by our standards, ma'am."

"That depends on which type you're looking at," she said. "You're going to be meeting E-forms. They've been specifically trained to interact with humans."

Tesla nodded. They stopped before a sealed door flanked by two guards in light armor.

"We're stopping the ship to make a salvage recon," she told them. "The ensign and I will be notifying the Arcolians."

One guard nodded, and the door hissed open. O'Hearn and Tesla stepped into a short hall capped by another door, the words AMBASSADORIAL SUITE laser-etched across it in an exotic font.

"Anything else before we go in, Ensign?"

Tesla swallowed. "Do they really smell, ma'am?"

"Better than a dog. That's why you shouldn't be scared—"

"Ma'am," he said quickly. "I mean *their* scent—"

"Always changes," she advised. "It's how they communicate. Very powerful, very sophisticated. Just stay calm. No matter what you sense, keep your wits about you and it'll pass. And remember, you might not smell so pleasant to them, either."

He smiled. "Yes, ma'am."

O'Hearn thumbed a switch next to the door and paused. A bass rattle cracked from the other side.

"Commander O'Hearn here to speak to the delegation," she said.

Crr-aaaack. The sound reminded Tesla of old naturevids he had seen of bullfrogs singing after a rain.

"One other thing. They're still working on their voices. It'll take you a while to get used to them."

O'Hearn put her hand on Tesla's shoulder. It seemed to comfort him. He was going to ask her what she meant by "get used to them," but by then the door had opened and his nostrils were filled with the essence of fresh roses.

"Their way of welcoming us," O'Hearn whispered.

The ensign nodded and followed his commander into the room. The floral scent became overpowering, and his throat started to close. He started to bite his lip, and suddenly the presence lifted and became a background fragrance.

Then he realized: There they are. There were five of them, each a shade of red that looked as if it had been baked to darkness. Dressed in flowing purple robes, they were standing in a semicircle, the tallest of them barely a hundred centimeters in height. Their football-shaped heads bobbed up and down on short, broad bodies, as if in approval.

Tesla felt their eyes on him. Eyes or eye? he wondered. It was a single, oblong organ with two vertical slits for pupils. It mimicked the kind of look done on portraits so that the subject appeared to be staring at the viewer no matter where in the room the viewer stood.

"Greetings," O'Hearn said.

The Arcolian closest to them started to accelerate its head-bobbing, and from the empty bottom of the face, a slit appeared.

Crrrr—rrrrrrrk!

"And I'm pleased to be here." O'Hearn smiled. "With

me is Ensign Revel Tesla. He's new to the *Hergest Ridge* and a newcomer to being in space.''

The lead Arcolian's head bobbed more. Tesla's breath scooted from his lungs. It actually looked . . . pleased. He forced himself to smile back, and the scent in his nose changed. What is it? Baby powder?

"The ambassador is trying to make you feel comfortable," O'Hearn said.

"Thank you," Tesla replied nervously.

And then the Arcolian's slit reappeared. Tesla could see a shimmer of white inside, a single white bone on top, and a thick black muscle on bottom.

Crrr—

Of course! It made a deep oscillation somewhere in that massive cavity behind the head—

—rrrrraaaaa—

—and ran it through that approximation of a human mouth to shape it into words.

—kkkck!

"And you're his first Arcolian." O'Hearn laughed.

The head stopped bobbing and the croak came again. Tesla stared at its mouth, watching, and in one glorious moment, he understood.

"It's my first year in space, too."

Tesla laughed. The scent changed again: cold beer and barbecue. He felt immediately at ease. "The problem is," he said, "I'm told it takes eighteen months to get used to it all."

The Arcolian's head bobbed again, faster. "Yes," it said. "Very good, very good."

Tesla looked at his commander, pleased with himself. He had amused an alien.

"I should introduce you now," O'Hearn said. "This is the delegation that we are taking to Council 5 as official representatives of the Arcolus system. You're speaking with misterbob.''

"Mr. Bob?" Tesla asked. "Are—''

"I'll explain it later," she said quietly.

misterbob raised one of its hands, and without thinking, Tesla moved to shake it. On contact, he broke into goose-flesh. Not only was the hand cold and chitinous, but his own hand was being gripped on each side. He looked down at the Arcolian's hand. It was made up of two facing palms, each with four fingers, joined at what would have been the wrist.

"I'm—" Tesla swallowed and caught his breath. "I'm very pleased to meet you. Really." He started to gently shake the ambassador's hand. misterbob gripped his hand on both sides and pumped hard. Tesla tightened his own grip and smiled.

Rrrrrrrrr, the Arcolian rattled.

"The ambassador is laughing," O'Hearn explained.

Tesla laughed, too. "Ambassador misterbob," he said.

"misterbob to you," it said.

"misterbob," Tesla repeated, and the Arcolian bobbed its head.

"Next to misterbob is his assistant, redbutler."

Tesla politely stepped to the next Arcolian and shook its hand. The grip still made his flesh crawl, but he ignored it. "redbutler," he repeated. "The pleasure is mine."

redbutler's mouth did not open, but a low cracking came from its throat. *Nnnnnnnnnnnnnn—*

"redbutler is not quite used to meeting chitinless Sapients," misterbob apologized.

"Sapients?" Tesla whispered to the commander. "But aren't they sapient also?"

"Yes," she replied. "That's their—the only way to describe it really is a pet name . . . for us."

"Indeed," misterbob said.

O'Hearn extended a hand to the third Arcolian. "laceylane."

"Pleased," Tesla said.

"laceylane is what we would call a xenologist. Likewise am I, but this study is more to her function."

"I hope you enjoy your stay among us."

"You are such fascinating creatures," laceylane replied.

Commander O'Hearn paused before the fourth Arcolian, brow knit as if she were trying to suppress something. "This," she said slowly, "is killerjoe."

The urge to snicker flashed across Tesla's face. He fought it back and shook hands with the alien. "killer—" The urge had to be pushed back again. "—joe."

There was motion from under killerjoe's robe, a quick flutter from its upper chest. A glance around showed that the other Arcolians were doing the same.

"You are amused?" killerjoe asked.

They know, Tesla thought. They could smell it. "Yes." He smiled. "I am quite amused."

Rrrrrrrr, it rattled. "Very good. Very good."

"killerjoe is the assistant to the other ambassador. Ensign Tesla, I'd like you to meet Ambassador leighbrand."

Tesla's mouth fell open. "leigh—"

"brand," O'Hearn finished.

"You scent of surprise," leighbrand croaked. "Does this please you?"

The ensign flushed. Of course, they would be able to smell his changes of emotion. "I am very surprised, Ambassador—"

It raised an arm. "leighbrand," it said. "Please. We take names like Homo sapiens so you will feel comfortable among us." The baby-powder smell returned.

"The pleasure is mine, leighbrand," Tesla said, fighting his feelings of uncertainty. "I'm sure that we have much to learn from each other."

"Indeed." leighbrand's head nodded as misterbob's had. The Arcolian seemed pleased. The scent it was giving off was—sawdust?

"The reason Ensign Tesla has escorted me here," O'Hearn said, "is so I could inform you of a change in the ship's schedule."

Nnnnnnn, redbutler cracked.

"Ah," misterbob said. "You are not having problems with malefactors again, are you, margarethearn?"

"No," she replied. "Most of the factions who were in protest of the Accord have come to accept it. We are changing schedule because we may have come across the wreckage of a missing ship. Our course takes us near another commercial route. Because of the proximity of the two, this is called an intersect."

"Intersect," laceylane buzzed. "Small, pestlike brother—"

"That's another word," O'Hearn said gently. "*Insect*. An intersect is a meeting of two paths."

"And you must stop along this intersect," killerjoe said.

"I am not required to stop," O'Hearn explained. "But I desire to stop."

"Because you value The Life in others," laceylane said.

"Yes."

"A most interesting behavior," misterbob rattled. "It intrigues me. A behavior I must study more."

"We will be powering down and changing course to check out the intersect area. If there are materials worth salvaging—recycling—then we will be in the area for approximately one standard day as we—" She stopped for a moment, trying to think of the phrase.

"Make harvest," leighbrand said.

"Exactly." O'Hearn smiled.

The chests of the Arcolians fluttered.

"You scent of pleasure," killerjoe said.

"Yes," she answered. "It pleases me to be able to communicate with you."

"Indeed," misterbob said.

leighbrand and laceylane echoed the sentiment.

"I merely wanted to notify you of this change as a courtesy. If this will cause any problems with your arrival on Council 5 . . ."

"No," leighbrand said. "We are as guest to you. We are not to spoil your hoard."

killerjoe's hands shook. "No, leighbrand. Not hoard. We

do not wish to . . . to . . ." It looked around the room. "Assist, laceylane."

"We do not wish to hinder your gathering," laceylane said.

Commander O'Hearn nodded politely.

"And we wish to observe your behaviors," misterbob added.

"As always," O'Hearn said, "you have freedom to scent out on my ship. I merely ask that you have some of my chitinous ones accompany you."

Their heads bobbed amid the crackling noises, and the changing scents in the air made both O'Hearn and Tesla dizzy.

"Indeed, indeed . . ."

The commander took a polite step backward. "If you will excuse me, I must return to duty."

"Of course." misterbob raised up from the floor and shuffled toward her, looking every bit like a hunchback clothed in royal finery. The right arm raised, and its hand surrounded O'Hearn's. "Your duty does well to us."

A shiver ran up Tesla's spine, and the scent of roses returned.

"And you, Ensign."

Tesla managed a military bow. "The pleasure belongs to me," he said. "Thank you all for being patient with me."

There was more of that pleased rattling and a chorus of "indeed."

Nnnnnnnn, redbutler said.

The ensign opened the door for his commander, and they left the suite. As they passed the guards, O'Hearn took a chronometer from her pocket and checked the time.

"The dinner will be over by now," she said.

"My apologies, ma'am," he answered.

"Nonsense. You did the right thing." She pocketed the timepiece. "As soon as you notify Mr. Junnell that the Arcolians have been contacted, you may finish your watch."

"Yes, ma'am. Thank you, ma'am."

She dismissed the ensign. He started to leave but stopped abruptly and turned back to her.

"Ma'am?"

"Yes, Ensign?"

"Thank you for having me accompany you. I needed that, and I suspect you knew it all along."

She nodded curtly. "You're welcome, Ensign. Remember this day."

Tesla saluted. "Yes, ma'am." He vanished down the corridor.

It worked out right, Margaret O'Hearn thought with a sigh. I only hope the harvest runs as well.

2

"Can you hear me?" specialist Peter Chiba asked.

Junnell's voice crackled in his headset. "Reading strong."

"All right. I'm heading out. The ionization levels might play hell with the comfreq, so if you start losing me, give me a red light on the substandard."

"Absolute."

Chiba glanced at his copilot. "Ready, Zack?"

Zack nodded.

"Let's see what we can find."

Zack pulled a lever, and the tug shuddered as it disengaged from the outer hull of the *Hergest Ridge*. "We're away."

Chiba spoke into his mouthpiece. "*Ridge*, this is *Jamming Jenny*. We'll be heading out toward the Jubilo route core and see what kind of action we get on the Vasac."

"Absolute," Junnell said.

He took the tug away from the liner. "Don't get your hopes up. From the readings you showed me, it looks like this stuff is going to be too hot to save."

"That won't stop some people," Zack said. He studied the screen on his panel. "I'm showing something on the Vasac."

A loud clang reverberated through the *Jamming Jenny*.

Chiba swore. "What was that?"

Zack pointed out the portal. A metal rectangle was spinning away from them. "Inner hatch door."

"Keep your eyes on the Vasac, dammit. Don't let anything hit us again."

"Sorry."

Chiba keyed his mike. "Mr. Junnell? You said there was a battleship missing out here?"

"A dreadnought."

"Then there must have been one hell of a big explosion. We just spotted an inner hatch door that was totally out of its mounting."

"Can you bring it in?"

Chiba looked at Zack, who tapped the colorgraph unit. "Only if she wants something that glows in the dark."

"Negative," Chiba said. "It's—"

Zack dove for the board and slapped a palm switch. The inside of the tug hummed.

"Repeat that," Junnell said. "You were cut off."

"We had to use the OBSYNE," Chiba said. "Something was about to hit us."

"Organic," Zack said, studying the colorgraph.

"A body," Chiba said, looking out the window. "You getting much action on your Net?"

"All kinds of it," Junnell replied. "From the aft section."

Chiba nodded. "We're in front of the path," he told Zack. "Let's get turned around."

He leaned forward in the webbing and stabbed at the controls through the thick gloves of his EVA suit. The tug rattled as the maneuver thruster fired.

"Now I know why you call this thing *Jamming Jenny*," Zack said.

"No, you don't," Chiba answered. "I named it after an old girlfriend."

"No kidding." Zack palmed up the OBSYNE, and a twisted girder ricocheted off the tug's hull, putting them off course. Chiba fought the control yoke, and the craft protested even more.

"This is how the bed used to shake," Chiba said.

"Mother Mercy." Zack whistled. "Will you look at that."

Looking out the window, the underside of the *Hergest Ridge* looked like the horizon of a planet stretched out before them. Above it were hundreds of shimmering projectiles that ranged in size from tiny bolts to charred plates of hull armor. The scene was lit with showers of blue spark and fire as debris hit the mother ship's Outboard Systems Net.

"I've never seen anything like this in my whole life," Zack said. He poised his hand above the palm switch.

"Screw that," Peter Chiba said. "Just turn it on. We'll never dodge all of this."

"What's wrong?' First Officer Junnell asked.

The *Jenny* shuddered as a medicouch hit the OBSYNE. Chiba grappled the controls to keep it on course.

"We've got all sorts of shit out here," Zack said. "It's unbelievable."

"Clean the frequency," Junnell snapped.

Chiba guided the tug as best as he could past the larger pieces of shorn metals and the bodies—he had never seen so many bodies, charred, exploded, and quick frozen . . .

"What have you got?" Junnell asked.

"You name it," Chiba said. "If there's a battleship missing in this area, we've found it."

"Anything worth taking?"

"Negative," Zack said. "If we didn't have a passenger manifest, no problem. But it's all hot. We'd have to have special facilities." He studied the SysOps board for a moment, then looked at Chiba.

"Problems?"

Zack nodded, bumping his head on the inside of his helmet. "All this radioactive stuff hitting the Net is putting a strain on the power plant. It'll be rough getting back if we're in this much longer."

Chiba pulled back on the yoke, and the horizon of the

mother ship disappeared. "*Ridge*, we're requesting permission to disengage. There's nothing we can do out here but get pounded."

"Stand by," Junnell said.

The two salvors watched the storm below them, the shifting colors as metals and plastics and organics hit the field protecting the luxury liner.

"This is a hell of a mess," Zack said.

"Sucker must have kissed a nuke," Chiba replied. He took the tug perpendicular to the path of the oncoming debris, and when they appeared to be outside the worst of it, he stopped and turned back toward the *Ridge*.

"That's better," Zack said, checking the power plant levels.

Chiba tried to stretch in his seat. There was no room in the small tug for comfort, and whenever he had to wait for an executive decision, his idle mind became slowly claustrophobic. Stars have mercy, he thought, if I should ever get trapped inside this thing. He drummed his fingers on the armrest of his seat.

"Chiba?" It was Junnell.

He sat straight up. "Go ahead, *Ridge*."

"I've got an okay to clear the debris field, but we need a couple more things before you come in. First, we have been asked to confirm the source of the wreckage as the dreadnought *Roko Marie* out of Cosen 3."

Chiba looked at his partner and mouthed an obscenity. "That'll take hours."

"No, it won't," Zack said. "Just give your *Yueh-sheng* cousins a call . . ."

"Shut up," Chiba added, glaring, "or I'll sic them on you."

"Second," Junnell went on, "we've just made Vasac contact with a large object that seems to be moving along the core route. It could be the merchant-sized vessel that was reported missing in this same area, so we'd like you to investigate."

The specialist wiggled into his seat and keyed his mike. "Absolute, Mr. Junnell. We'll check out the Unidentified first. Dump the coordinates when ready." He started to power up the tug, then punched a key on the console beside him and cleared his throat. "CHRIS, are you listening?"

A smooth female voice came over their headsets. "Yes, Peter."

"We're going to be getting some vector coordinates from the mother system. I want you to put us on a direct intersect."

"Whatever you say, love."

Zack laughed. "Junnell will have you skinned alive if she finds out you've modified the CHRIS."

Chiba angled the tug back toward the debris field and started to run parallel with it. "But she won't find out. I've got this CHRIS set on a dual mode. Crisp and businesslike to anyone but me."

"Not a good idea." Zack tied the Vasac in with the tug's personality.

The *Hergest Ridge* vanished behind them, its aft battery of lights sparkling off the remains of the dreadnought. The two salvors stared at what was still there, in disbelief that there was so much left behind. What they saw was the stuff of everyday lives from a ship whose complement had once numbered six hundred: zipbeds and brainstim units, vidscreens and food processors, fitness equipment and pharmaceutical chests . . .

"Peter, dear," the CHRIS said. "I've received the coordinates for the intercept."

Chiba released the control yoke. "Take us there," he said. "And give me an audible when we make primary Vasac."

"Certainly."

Chiba continued his scrutiny of the litter. Besides the smaller stuff, there were sections of bulkheads, staircases, rails, shorn bits of gravity wells and lifts, boilerplates, armor—

"Look," Zack said quickly. He grabbed a handle and

rotated one of the outer lights to shine on a section of battered armor. A gash had been melted through a section of it, and the plate itself had been blown off by whatever had caused the disaster. "Those are plasma burns. They were in a fight with someone."

Chiba looked at him. "A merchant?"

"The complete report advises that a light cruiser is also missing along this route," the CHRIS advised.

"Look!" Zack had almost shouted, gripping the handle and throwing light across the armor. "We've hit the jackpot."

Stenciled across the plate was ROKO MARIE 262112A.

Zack called the number in to the *Hergest Ridge* while Chiba moved out of the plate's way and continued to survey the wreckage. There was a gravball game, a host of organics jars from the biosystem, a commode, and what looked like an intact transgear system.

"There's a fortune to be made out here," Chiba said as the field began to thin.

"If only it wasn't so hot," Zack said.

Chiba looked at him. "That's right." He keyed the *Hergest Ridge* frequency. "Mr. Junnell, you there?"

"Go ahead, Peter."

"Requesting that you calculate and redmark the route this stuff is taking. It's extremely radioactive, and I'd hate to see pieces of it end up as part of somebody's sleeping quarters."

"Absolute," Junnell said. "And thanks."

"She likes you." Zack grinned.

There was a rubbery-sounding tone.

"Vasac range," Zack said.

Chiba squinted and leaned forward against the webbing. "I can't see a thing." His fingers walked down the armrest, and the forward lights of the tug aimed out into the darkness.

Pong, came the tone.

"See anything?"

Zack shook his head.

"CHRIS, what do you make of this?" Chiba asked.

"Well, dearest—"

"Suppress."

"This craft has engaged in Vasac-to-hull contact with what is approximately a merchant-sized vessel of unknown origin. Corroborating with the mother system, I have determined that the craft is moving on inertial power with no signs of thrust since the initial sighting. It has not been the source of any transmissions and is operating in a subshift phase."

"That's comforting," Zack grumbled.

The tone was beginning to come in faster.

"We're closing," Chiba said. "Do you see it?"

"Of course," CHRIS said.

"Zack," he said, exasperated.

"Looking," Zack answered, taking his light in slow sweeps, trying to get a reflection.

The odd tone was coming in slow and steady, like a heartbeat.

"It sounds like we're on top of the damn thing," Zack said.

"CHRIS, put us on collision avoidance—"

"That won't be necessary," CHRIS snapped.

"Hell," Zack said. "Now you've gone and made her mad."

Then Chiba's eyes caught it, a speck of gray amid the darkness. "Belay that request," he told the CHRIS. "I've got visual contact."

The tone had grown even faster, becoming an incessant rattle. Chiba gave the order to silence it, then took the tug from the CHRIS's intercept course, guiding it on with the control yoke.

Zack stared into a screen and brought up an image of the vehicle. He enhanced the image until the spot took shape; the edges were rough from cables and connectors, but its shape left no possibility of mistaking it for something else.

"It's a merchant ship, all right," Zack said. "Out here in the middle of nowhere." He shifted uncomfortably in his seat. "You don't suppose it's the *Rough Trade*, do you?"

Chiba looked at him. "The plague ship?"

Zack nodded.

"No," Chiba said decisively. "That's just an old merchant's tale." He strained against his webbing, guiding the tug closer to the derelict ship. It was starting to take shape through the window, and he could see that the hull had been charred and pitted. "I hope it's just an old merchant's tale."

The lights played across the old ship's hull, falling across scratches and into pits and scars on its surface. Chiba eased the yoke back and pivoted the tug so that the upper surface of the ship would pass under them.

"I've spotted the reg number," Zack said into his headset. "Confirmation of identity—merchant vessel is the *Angel's Luck*, three seven four nine one."

"CHRIS, hail the ship on AFA. Let them know we're friendly."

"No need," Zack said. "The bridge is dark. Besides, this thing has been out here for months."

"Looks are deceiving," Chiba said. "The debris field could have caused the damage we're seeing."

"To the crew of the *Angel's Luck*," the CHRIS said, "registration three seven four nine one. We are representatives of the Class A liner *Hergest Ridge* and request appropriate response on any of the Emergency Comm bands. If you are unable to respond, please activate your alert beacon."

Nothing. Chiba took them within a few meters of the ship's surface. Some of the upper hatchways and conduits had pieces of debris tangled around them. "How does this look, Zack?"

"I'm getting radiation, but it looks like it's from the junk around it. The hull is giving off normal residual levels."

"Repeat the message, please," he told the CHRIS.

"This ship has been through hell," Zack said, taking the searchlight across the hull. "Look at those small plasma burns. This thing got sprayed from proximity fire."

"You think it got caught in a fight between the other missing ships?"

"No response on the AFA broadcast," CHRIS said.

"Thank you," Peter Chiba said. The *Angel's Luck* passed under the tug and out of sight. He fired the maneuver thruster and pivoted around. "Let's look at—"

"Mother Mercy!" Zack shouted. "Take a look at that!"

"What's wrong?" Dorienne Junnell asked.

Chiba gave her a running narrative as he closed on the aft section of the merchant ship. All that remained of the engine compartment was an empty shell, its outer rim blackened from retrofire. As the tug closed the distance, they could see that conduits had been severed and power buses ruptured. Zack took the light in a slow scan across the inside of the vacant compartment. Only the emergency power capacitor was left.

"This keeps getting weirder and weirder," he said.

"Assessment," Junnell said.

Chiba sighed into the mike. "You're asking me? We've got a derelict ship near the scene of what could have been a lopsided battle. *Anything* could have happened out here."

"What's the vehicle's status?"

"We'll call it abandoned," Zack said. "We hailed it and got no reply. The bridge is dark, there's no sign of onboard activity—"

"Is it worth salvage?"

Chiba thumbed the mute button and looked at his partner. "In other words, is it worth the cost of the stop?"

"Could be," Zack told her. "Although it would be worth a lot more if it had engines."

There was a long silence. Chiba laughed and told Zack that he had overheated the first officer's frigid brain. Zack replied by suggesting several exercises that could thaw it out again. Their laughter was interrupted by a new transmission.

"Bring it in, boys," she ordered.

"Absolute," Chiba replied.

"Maybe we can find something in the ship's log that'll explain all of this."

"Big mystery," Zack said. "We'll let you know once we're en route."

Chiba boosted the thrusters and overtook the merchant once more. He slowed just short of the bridge, matched velocity with the larger vehicle, then eased the tug's four feet down onto the hull's thick armor. The *Jamming Jenny* swayed as it made contact, and Zack laughed.

"Positive charge on contact surface," Chiba said.

Zack diverted the power plant systems and gave Chiba a green light.

"Let's attach."

The legs of the tug bent at their joints, and it started to squat.

"Give me a gas burst."

Jets set into the flat bottom of the *Jamming Jenny* shot streams of helium against the merchant's hull, clearing the surface of obstructing particles.

"Engage and lock."

The tug continued to squat until the hulls touched. A hum ran through the *Jenny* and its surface polarized, locking it to the *Angel's Luck*.

"We're on."

Chiba unlocked his webbing and leaned across the cabin. "Let's put some thrust out the front and see if we can slow this thing down." He started to come out of his seat when a shock wave passed through the *Jenny*, pitching Zack violently against the restraining surface of the web and flattening Chiba on the floor.

"Son of a *bitch*!"

"What was that?"

Zack cranked his head, trying to work out the knot in his neck. "We're detached," he said thinly. He toggled a switch on the console. "That ship's hull has a negative charge."

"But you told me—"

"It wasn't there when we engaged. You felt it yourself. We were locked on."

"Would this thing have a random protection circuit, changing hull polarity to keep something from attaching?"

Zack shook his head. "The hull was dead to positive the-whole time I monitored it. The only way it could have activated is if—"

"Someone was inside," Chiba said. He picked himself up and settled into his seat, pulling the web tight around him. "And they've got a power source that's big enough to repolarize the hull."

"Obviously someone who does not want to be found," Zack replied.

"I don't know if I'd go that far. Not many people elect to drift through deep space like this."

"Do we take a look, then?"

"Absolute. Arm the grappling bolts and neutralize our hull. They won't bounce us again."

Chiba flexed his hands and closed on the *Angel's Luck*, again ordering the CHRIS to hail the occupants. Once velocities of the two ships were matched, he started his descent. "Fire the hooks at seven meters."

"Absolute," Zack said.

"And let me know if there's anything else out of line."

The tug moved in on the outer hull, the pads of its feet running parallel to the surface. Junnell's voice sounded in the salvor's ears, asking about the situation. Chiba sucked in his breath, playing the yoke, guiding it down.

Zack raised the cover from a switch and flipped it. The tug jolted beneath them and started to gain altitude. Diamondhead spikes shot from four ports on the *Jenny*'s underside and pierced the merchant's hull. Once through, the spikes' heads mushroomed, effectively locking them in place.

"We're anchored," Zack said.

"Reel us in."

Servos hummed inside the tug, and the cables that connected it with the spikes went taut. Slowly the *Jenny* lowered, pulled by the onboard winch mechanism, until it was again flathulled with the merchant ship.

Chiba unlocked the webbing and cautiously pulled out of his seat. "Think they'll try it again?"

"They just did," Zack said. "Their hull just shifted polarity. They must not be running from the bridge, or they'd know we spiked in.''

Chiba made his way to the back of the tug compartment. He produced a molded object from a storage compartment and strapped it onto his back.

"Power pack?'' Zack asked, rising from his seat.

"They've probably cut power to the doors. CHRIS, Zack and I are going to see if we can contact whoever's inside. Would you inform First Officer Junnell of the situation and then continue to hail this ship's occupants?''

"Junnell is a bitch,'' CHRIS said matter-of-factly.

"Suppress,'' Chiba snapped.

"Told you the dual mode would cause problems,'' Zack taunted. He slid a power pack onto his back and plugged it into a laser carbine.

"Whoa,'' Chiba said. "What do you think you're doing with that?''

In the bulk of the suit, Zack's shrug was lost. "Natives might not be friendly.''

"Put it back. If CHRIS is telling them we're friendly and you go in there with a laser, what are they going to think?''

"We might have to use it on the door.''

"If they've frozen the door, we'll let the techs on the *Ridge* worry about opening it. Come on.''

Zack stowed the weapon and followed Chiba to the hatch. It opened without a sound. They inched out of the *Jenny*, fastened safety lines to the tug, and started toward the bridge window.

"Sucker's generating gravity,'' Zack said. He inched up on his toes to prove it.

"They might cut it and hope we fly off,'' Chiba said. "Take up the slack in your line.'' He took a cautious step off the rounded edge of the ship, planting his feet squarely on the thick glass of the bridge window. "Over here.''

Carefully spooling out line, Zack shuffled over to his partner, tapping his feet uncertainly on the reinforced glass surface. He shone his light through the window. Inside, the

bridge looked gutted. Component systems had been removed and stacked, leaving the consoles empty save for spills
of color-coded wires. Scattered across the floor were pieces
of equipment, from electronic measuring devices to pressure
calipers and lasewelders.

"What are they doing in there?" Zack asked. "Repair
work?"

"Looks like," Chiba replied. "Although it's not going to
do them a hell of a lot of good with no engines."

"Maybe they know something we don't."

Chiba studied his partner's face through the reflection on
the faceplate. "Zack, you have an incredible grasp of the
obvious." Turning, he shuffled down the bridge window,
bringing the edge of his safety line down across the surface
of the merchant's hull. Once off the window, he scanned with
his light until he found a hatch in a recess from the downward
slant. He played out more line, then swung over and down
by the hatch works.

"You with me?"

There was no reply.

Chiba looked up toward the bridge and saw Zack still at
the bridge window, hesitantly studying the path he needed to
take. "Get down here."

Zack took one step. "I barely passed academy-level
EVA."

"The truth," Chiba said, "is that you're a coward."

"Cut me some slack, will you?"

"Move your ass, partner." While Zack dealt with the basic problem of movement, Chiba set about the task of opening the outer hatch. He located and dusted off a control panel
bearing the legend ANGEL'S LUCK 37491 and opened it.
Drawing a cord from the pack on his back, he guided his
light across the door's circuits, disconnected them from the
ship's power line, and connected his pack.

Every light on the board came on in red.

"Son of a bitch."

"What's the matter?" Zack asked, puffing and struggling to maintain his balance. "I got here, didn't I?"

"Not you," Chiba growled. "The door circuits are fried."

Zack keyed a circuit test into the board. Nothing changed. "You're sure it's not the pack?"

"If it was, I'd still be back at the ship. It's controlling the line feed and my light."

Pulling a tool from his belt, Zack flopped to his knees and began to pull the screws out of the mechanical access cover. "That's why you wanted me down here, Peter. You give me all the hard stuff." He flicked the loose bolts over his shoulder. Their velocity was enough to carry them away from the merchant's weak gravity.

"You're costing us money," Chiba said.

"It's not our ship yet."

"You're costing someone money."

Pivoting on one heel, Zack flung the cover plate out into space like a disc. "Let them complain. We're saving them." He reached into the compartment and pulled out a bent piece of metal. "You want to do this?"

"When you're doing such a fine job?"

Zack took the handle, fitted it into a slot near the door, and began to crank at a steady pace. The hatch started to rise, and a silent billow of dust emerged from under the door.

"There's something in there," Chiba said. "The lock was pressurized."

Zack said nothing, but continued to crank, grunting and gasping in the close confines of his suit. At one point his breath started to cloud the faceplate, and he stopped to adjust the internal atmosphere of his suit.

Finally the hatch was open enough for them to step through. They disconnected their safety lines and magneted them to the outer hull, then Zack cranked the outer door down from the inside while Chiba accessed the inner control panel and connected the power supply.

"This one's dead, too."

"The hell you say."

"If you don't believe me, bring in the dogs."

Zack thumped Chiba in the shoulder. "We're not supposed to talk like that when there are xenos around."

"We're not supposed to call them xenos, either," Chiba said. He eased down and set about the task of opening the inner maintenance plate. It fell away noiselessly, and Chiba grabbed a small knob. "Pressurizing." With a firm grip, he started to turn it. There was nothing at first, and then, from the outside of his helmet, he could hear a slight hiss.

"We're getting something," Zack told him. He punched keys on the arm of his suit and checked the readout. "Stale," he advised, "but breathable."

"Let's wait." Chiba took the crank from Zack and started on the inner door, watching it rise. "Should have known the hatches would be out"—he grunted—"with the way they had the bridge gutted."

"Could've had them on an indy circuit," Zack said.

Puffing, Chiba stopped to scratch his nose on the rough spot inside his helmet. "So why are they fried?"

Zack said nothing. Chiba could only assume that he had shrugged again. He bent over the crank and started in again.

"Should've let me bring the lay-zer," his partner sang.

"Get off." The door rose another meter and Chiba stopped. "That should be good enough." Pointing his arm, he filled the corridor with light. "Clear," he said, crawling through.

Zack was right behind him, complaining about protocol and the fact that he had been stripped of his weapon. Chiba started down the dark hall, working at the seal around his helmet. "You forget that we're running on the assumption that there are survivors on board. That trick with the magnetics could have been done by a CHRIS."

"Ship's too big for a CHRIS," Zack replied. "This would take a KEVIN or a CHARLES. And without the engines, where would you get the power to run it?"

"Lots of questions," Peter Chiba said. He put his gloved

hands against his helmet and pulled it off. Hanging it at his waist, he shook the sweat from his head.

His earpiece crackled with Zack's voice. "Well?"

Chiba sniffed. The air was heavy with scents: nitrates, sweat, plastics. "Smells like someone's here."

There was a *pop!* and Zack removed his helmet. He choked in mid-inhale. "I'm going to puke."

"Let's see if we can get some answers," Chiba said. He started walking.

Zack followed him, listening to their footsteps echoing through the empty corridor. "Where are we going?"

Chiba studied the walls and ceiling as he went. "I'm not sure. This is an older ship, an off-model. I'm not as familiar with the layout." He stopped for a moment and aimed his light into a coreward tunnel. "That'll take us to the bridge."

"After you," Zack said.

His partner shook his head. "We already know what kind of shape it's in. They're obviously running things from an Emergency Standby. I'm more interested in how they got the power for their magnetics."

Zack sniffed. He was trying to take short breaths to keep from getting too much of the air's sour smell. "What are you saying, then?"

Chiba's light went down the corridor. "I think we should check out their power plant. If we can find the source of energy, I'm sure we'll find them."

Zack extended his hand. "You're the boss."

They took a cautious pace, letting their lights cover the distance ahead of them. This hall, Chiba explained, ran the length of the merchant's underside, and its excessive width allowed it to be loaded from the forward section if such a need should arise. The passing years proved the design to be more novel than practical, and it had not been put on a ve-hicle in over a decade. That was not to underrate the quality of the ship, which had an excellent reputation throughout the galaxy.

The trip across the *Angel's Luck* brought them no new

information. They went past doors—EMERGENCY STANDBY, SUBSTORAGE, ACCESS HATCH, MAINTENANCE WAY—every one of which was frozen. The apertures to structural ducting and wiring looked untouched, as if no attempt had been made to do any repair work on that level of the ship.

"It's dead in here," Zack said. "You sure there are survivors?"

"Let's not start that again," Chiba said.

"Why are we even down here? Why aren't we up checking the cabins? We're wasting our time down here."

"It's never a waste of time," Chiba told him. "We're down here to see what they were carrying. If they're alive, so be it. If not, the *Hergest Ridge* gets salvage rights, and you and I a percentage."

Zack grinned. "I'm beginning to like this business."

A T-intersection loomed up on them. Chiba and Zack stopped before a large door. "The cargo bay is on the other side of that."

"I'm not cranking it," Zack said.

"You don't have to. There's a smaller door." He aimed the light. Not a dozen meters from where they stood, light was falling from an open hatch, bathing the new wing of the corridor in pale light.

Chiba flicked off his search beam. "Let's go."

"What if they're guarding the cargo?"

Chiba looked at his partner. "Aren't you glad you left your laser?"

"No," Zack complained.

"Hello," Chiba called. He stepped into the frame of the hatch and looked into the cargo bay. "Incredible."

"What is it?" Zack was right behind him, gently nudging past for a better view. His mouth dropped open.

Before them stood a large pleasure craft, sleek and streamlined, anchored to the floor of the hold with magnetic bolts. The bridge window was lit, as were the exterior lights, the source of illumination that they had followed from the intersection.

"Some cargo," Chiba said, stepping toward the craft's nose.

"*Reconnez Cherie,*" Zack read from the hull. "Nine seven two one two eight nine."

The salvors skirted around the bottom of the craft, running their hands over its shining hull. Their ears picked up a faint hum, the telltale drone of a power plant.

"At least we know where they got the energy to charge the merchant's hull," Zack said. He rounded the corner to the aft section, where Chiba was waiting by the exhaust vents.

"Hell of a job of engineering," he said, gesturing. Thick conduits ran from inside the yacht and across the hold floor to a feed matrix set into the far wall. "That's power in from the engines," Chiba said. "They must have gone into the empty engine compartment and reduced the flow modulator so they could tie this in as the merchant's power source."

"Took some thought," Zack said. He turned and scanned the rest of the cargo hold. It was an empty cavern.

"Someone's here," Chiba said, "in adequate comfort. They'd have enough power for food synthesis, waste disposal, limited-capacity environmental monitoring—"

"Then where are they?"

"On the yacht?"

Zack smiled. "Let's ask."

They went around the pleasure craft again, stopping where the boarding ramp lowered from the nose. Chiba rapped his knuckles against a landing strut. There was no response.

"That was worthless," he complained.

"I'll knock," Zack said confidently. He stepped over to a scatter of tools on the bay floor and picked up a sizable wrench.

"Don't damage the merchandise," Chiba said.

Zack pulled back his arm to strike, and a metallic *click* filled the bay. The salvors jumped. Servos hummed inside the *Reconnez Cherie*, and the nose began to open like the mouth of a great bird. Jagged teeth appeared, turning into stairs as the jaw lowered and scraped to a halt against the deck.

Chiba and Zack watched as a hatch opened, revealing a haggard-looking woman with tangled hair and dark circles under her eyes. She started down the stairs, oblivious to the presence of the salvors.

"Greetings," Zack said.

She spotted them. "Oh!" she said, and stepped back.

"We mean no harm," Chiba said, stepping onto the stairs. "We're salvors. Did you get our message?"

"No." She smiled. "But you're about to get ours." From inside her zipsuit, she produced a pistol.

Chiba held out his hands and backed down from the first step. "Hold on—"

From Chiba's right came a voice. "Freeze, you Ori bastard."

The lights in the bay came on, and there was another metallic *click*. To the left, between the salvors and the exit, were two bearded men with bloodshot eyes, each brandishing a low-tech automatic weapon. The salvors turned toward the engine compartment and saw two more: one tall, the other enormous, with a childlike face that was straining hard to look mean.

Zack put his hands up. "Laser," he said to Chiba under his breath.

The man to their left spoke again. "What are you doing here? How did you find us?"

Peter Chiba stared at them in disbelief. Which question do you want me to answer first? he thought.

The man pulled back the bolt of his weapon.

"We came in—" Chiba started.

"We know that."

"We're salvors."

"Like hell."

The shorter man on the right pulled back the hammer of his revolver. "How did you know we were out here?"

"We didn't," Chiba said. "Our ship picked up debris

readings from that other ship—'' He started to gesture, but it made his hosts nervous. "So we, uh, stopped to, uh—"

"Investigate," Zack said.

"You did." The speaker was the other man on the left, the one with dark, wild eyes. "And you just happened to be on this route."

"No. We came off the intersect from the Council 5—"

"You were looking for your cousins, weren't you?" The wild man aimed his weapon square at Chiba's face. "Well, let me tell you something. We don't care *what* kind of ship you all came in. We took out the *Roko Marie*, and we can take you out."

"Peter," Zack said, trying to keep calm.

"Shut up," Chiba said urgently.

"We have a problem—"

"Not funny," Chiba hissed.

"You do have a problem," the big one on the left said. His voice matched his appearance: immaturity hidden with a threat. "We're going to kill you."

"Peter, they think you're—"

The big man moved forward. "Should I do it now, Mr. Duke?"

The man beside him shook his head. "Wait."

"Yueh-sheng," Zack stressed.

Chiba dropped his hands. *"What?"*

"Get your hands up," the wild one said, "or I'll fill you with mutiny pills."

"No," Chiba said flatly. "If you're going to kill me, at least let me die with some dignity."

"That could be arranged."

"Don't turn my corpse over to the *Ebitsuka*," Chiba continued, "or you'll be disappointed, you stinking, racist bastard."

The wild man exchanged glances with his partner. "What do you think, May?"

The one called May lowered his weapon. "You're not *Yueh-sheng*?"

"If I was," Chiba shouted, pointing at Zack, "would I be relying on *this* guy to cover my ass?"

"He talks like a brother." The wild one smiled.

"I'm not your frigging brother," Chiba spat.

"I don't like this," the one called Duke said.

"Let him talk," the woman said.

"Or if you don't want to deal with us, you can punish us by making us go back to our ship empty-handed," Chiba snarled.

"Forgive him," Zack said. "We're salvors, and when he gets on a roll—"

"Then you can all just rot in this burned out, stinking, piece of *shit*—"

"This is *my* ship," May said, offended.

"—until the *Yueh-sheng* really does find you. Just don't bunch me with a bunch of cutthroat gangsters because my eyes aren't shaped like yours. I happen to be a *professional*, and I don't have to put up with this."

"I should have warned you," Zack apologized.

There was silence as the captors took that in.

"Are you going to shoot us or what?" Chiba taunted.

"Salvors," Duke said. "Who are you with?"

Chiba was silent.

"The United Terran Empire Fleet," Zack volunteered. "Shipboard division."

"Figures." The wild-eyed one sniffed. "The UTE corporation has to stick their fingers into every little orifice."

May uncocked his weapon and took another step toward them. "Shipboard division, you say?"

Chiba remained tightlipped. Zack nodded quickly.

"Who are you registered with?"

"The *Hergest Ridge*," Zack answered. "Two seven seven one, manifested passenger transport."

"You're letting them stall," Duke said impatiently.

May held up one finger. "Indulge me," he said. "Who do you answer to?"

"Lieutenant Jack Parsons is the chief salvor, and he's under First Officer Dorienne Junnell, who is on-bridge duty officer.''

"Forget that," May said. "Who's in charge of overall operations?''

Zack cleared his throat. "Commander Margaret O'Hearn, GTC Prime Command rated.''

May looked away in thought.

"And the way you found us?" Duke asked.

"We told you," Zack said. "Our ship was picking up large amounts of processed metals on the OBSYNE, and we went off core to investigate.''

"You took a passenger ship off course?" Wild Eyes asked.

"There was a hell of a lot of metal showing up," Zack said. "And it was badly radioactive. What did you do to that ship, nuke it?''

"I believe him," May said. "I think they're on the level.''

Wild Eyes protested.

"Do you want to spend another month on this ship?" May asked. "In this condition? Is it worth it to you? Their story holds up for me; I trust them.''

"I'm with May," the woman said.

Wild Eyes gave her a hard look.

"Sorry, Vonn," she replied. "But you can't imagine how badly I want a hot shower.''

Duke stared at them. "You guys have hot food over there?''

"Tons," Zack nodded.

He lowered his revolver and uncocked it. "I'm with May." He slapped the giant next to him. "How about you, Winters?''

The big man tossed his weapon to the floor. "It stinks in here.''

Vonn sighed in resignation. "All right.''

May dropped his weapon and went to Peter Chiba, hand extended in truce. "I apologize for being a racist bastard. Welcome aboard the *Angel's Luck*.''

3

Two hours later, Chiba and Zack were back in the *Jamming Jenny*, firing its thrusters to slow the merchant ship's speed and bring it into a parallel course with the *Hergest Ridge*. The radio freq had been alive with chatter. O'Hearn was pleased with the rescue and had spoken to them personally. Junnell was ecstatic, gushing at them and prompting crude remarks between the pair on their private channel. Even Admiral Studebaker had come on with a congratulatory speech. Word had it that even the xenos were happy.

The *Angel's Luck* survivors gathered in the main bridge to watch as the distance between the two ships closed. At first, James May was outraged that the salvors had fired tow lugs through the hull, but Vonn pointed out that the bolt was self-sealing, so they would not have to evacuate, and that the salvors' insurance would cover the cost of repairs.

So they watched as the brightest star in view slowly grew into a craft of massive proportions.

"That's big," Winters said.

"It's bigger than the *Yueh-sheng* ship we shitcanned," Vonn replied with a certain amount of pride.

Duke folded his arms and regarded his comrades. His head was aching again, an intense, through-the-temples throb that felt as if his skull would burst. He blinked against the pain and studied them, tired, ragged, and dirty.

"May," he said. "We should talk."

The merchant looked away from his leaning point on the window. "We'll have plenty of time for—"

"About the phials," Duke said, moving through the bridge and plopping down in the copilot's seat. He kicked his legs, and turned to face the others. "What are we going to tell our good rescuers?"

"Not a thing," Vonn said. "If word gets out about what we're carrying, they're going to want a salvor's share."

"I doubt that," May said softly.

"You never know. Even if they don't put in a claim, there

are going to be questions. Our names will be all over the place. They don't need to know any of it."

"Li promised us that we'd be safe," Winters said.

"Li is dead," Vonn replied.

"That alone may satisfy the *Yueh-sheng*." May leaned against the window and duplicated Duke's folded-arm stance. "Remember what he said about them. They don't always settle the score with outsiders, but when it comes to betrayal from within their own ranks, they *always* get their way."

"Then Li committed suicide," Roz said, "by going against his own people."

"Li thought he could beat the odds," May said. "There's always someone who thinks you can do it with enough money."

"They planted a tracking device in his skull," Vonn said loudly. "And a frigging bomb to boot. That's the kind of people we're dealing with."

"But they think we're dead," Winters said solemnly.

"And we should keep it that way."

"Then the general consensus," Duke said, "is that we are to say nothing to anyone about our having the Essence Corporation Phials."

There was a murmur of agreement.

"The only other factor here is that of retaining our anonymity."

"The commander will have to make a Salvage or Rescue report," May said. "It'll go by lase to the UTE Fleet headquarters, who will file it."

"They'll spill it," Vonn shouted. "This is a public relations bonanza for them, free publicity. Salvage operations aren't worth jack unless you've got a major haul, but saving human lives is money in the bank. They'll milk it for all it's worth."

"I'll talk to the commander," May continued. "Perhaps she'll listen to reason and suppress the information until we can collect the reward for the phials and scatter."

"Fat chance."

May took a step toward Vonn. "Don't knock it until I've given it a chance," he barked. "If she doesn't come through for us, then we'll try something else. Otherwise, let's not worry about it until the time comes. Got that?"

Vonn sighed. "You're the boss."

"We say nothing, then," Duke said. "Not until May's spoken with the commander."

"Nothing about the phials to anyone," Vonn amended. He gave Winters a hard stare. "Got that?"

Winters nodded.

"And what about our story?" Roz asked.

The others looked at her.

"They're going to ask how we got into it with a ship the size of the *Roko Marie*," she explained. "And they're going to wonder why we went to the trouble of resisting and destroying them. I don't think they'll believe that the *Yueh-sheng* risked one of their dreadnoughts on a routine act of piracy."

May took a moment to study their faces. "This is going to take some thought. And time."

Vonn raised his gaze to the luxury liner hanging in space. At their distance it appeared no larger than a meter in length.

"We've got awhile," he said.

They had another four hours to get their story straight. The *Jamming Jenny* brought the two ships to within a kilometer of each other, and then two other tugs appeared and attached themselves to the merchant's side. With the CHRIS units from the three tugs tied in with the liner's navigational computer, Dorienne Junnell took control and maneuvered the *Angel's Luck* within meters of a docking platform on the *Ridge*'s underside. The tugs cleared from the merchant's hull, then the platform slowly charged, changing polarity and becoming a huge electromagnet that held firmly on to the merchant ship.

A suited crew came out into the vacuum, unfolding a collapsible evacuation tube. They brought it up to the side of the merchant ship and attached it to one of the outer hatches.

The crew leader signaled May, who had the others waiting in an Emergency Standby near the hatch.

"They're ready for us," he told them. "The drill is fairly simple. They've cut the gravity in the receiving end of the ship so we won't fall and kill ourselves. I'll be cutting the gravity here and opening the airlock. All you have to do is go out into the tube and head for the *Hergest Ridge*. The tube is pressurized, so you can breathe, and soft, so you won't hurt yourselves. The material's tough, so you can kick and grab the edges to move yourselves along without doing any damage. There's no hurry, but the sooner you get down to the ship, the better. There'll be people waiting at the other end to help you out. Got that?"

The others nodded.

"Go to the hatch," May said. "I'll be right there."

Winters left first, flanked by Roz and Duke. Vonn waited until they were gone and then grabbed May's shoulder.

"Where'd you put the phials?"

May smiled. "They won't be found. They're in the soft spot."

"And where is that?"

May shook his head. "You should know better than to ask that."

"What if something happens to you? I'd have to dismantle the ship a plate at a time to find them."

"Nothing is going to happen to me."

Vonn looked out the door of the Emergency Standby. "I don't like this. Duke hasn't been well—"

"I've never told any of my copilots where the soft spot is. Hell, Duke doesn't even know what one is. And I sure didn't tell Winters."

"I don't like this, May."

"It's better this way. They could have a sanitization crew come through this place and they wouldn't find it. The only place safer—"

"There is no safe place," Vonn insisted. He turned and went down the hall.

May cut the gravity and joined the others. Duke had opened the first hatch and was keying in the sequence to open the outer one.

Winters grabbed his arm and squeezed hard. "You're not going to kill us, are you, Mr. Duke?"

Duke smiled. "I saved you from the *Yueh-sheng*, didn't I?"

Winters nodded.

"This is just like going for a ride." He thumbed a switch, and the outer hatch rolled open. On the other side was a ghostly blue tunnel that bent downward. A rush of cold, sweet air rushed into the hall, and as one they closed their eyes and smiled.

"I like that," Winters said.

"I'm not waiting." Roz went to the hatch, grabbed the handle, pushed her legs through, and dropped down with a scream of delight.

"Gang way," Vonn said. He was the next to disappear.

Duke held his hand out to the merchant. "May."

May pointed back. "A captain is always the last to leave the ship."

"You're next then, big guy."

Winters's face cocked into a smile, and he stuck one leg through the hatch.

Duke guided his hands up to the bar. "Hang on here. It'll be easier."

Winters stuck his other leg through and whooped as the cool air surrounded him.

"Now push off."

"I'm a little scared."

"You're going to love this," Duke said. "I promise."

The massive arms flexed and pushed. The hands opened, and Winters dropped.

Duke turned to May and saluted. "See you on the outside."

He grabbed the bar, tucked his knees up to his chest, and kicked them out into the tunnel. Releasing the bar, he shot through the hatch, and his feet sank into the wriggling blue wall, slowing him down. He grabbed one of the thick rings that lined the inside of the tunnel and pulled himself forward, moving down toward the source of the cold air.

Another bend came and he slowed. The wind was rushing in his ears and tossing his hair, but he was sure he heard whimpering. He inched around the bend and found Winters, limbs splayed out and sinking into the sides of the tube, clutching for dear life.

"What's wrong?" Duke asked, pulling himself to a stop.

Winters motioned with his eyes. "I don't want to fall."

Duke followed his gaze. The tube ran another thirty meters and emptied into a gray room. He could see a crowd of people at the bottom, standing and staring up into the tunnel.

"You won't fall," Duke explained. "There's no gravity."

"But they're standing on the ceiling."

"That's their floor. It's all relative." He looked into the big man's eyes. It never did any good to take the technical approach with Winters. "Trust me, big guy. They'll keep you from falling."

Winters peered down the tunnel uncertainly. "You're sure?"

Solemnly putting his hand over his heart, Duke made another in his seemingly endless series of promises to Irvin Winters.

"All right." Winters turned to go headfirst down the tube.

Duke stopped him and instructed him to turn around and go feet first. "Then all you have to do is crouch when your feet hit the floor. It's an easy catfall."

Winters twisted his frame around. "Now what?"

Duke grabbed Winters by the hair and pushed. "Go!"

The big man wailed all the way down the tube and landed with a thump.

"What's the problem here?"

The voice came from over Duke's shoulder. May had joined the queue.

"Just a slight bottleneck." Duke lay flat in the tunnel, facing the relative floor. With a kick he shot straight toward the *Hergest Ridge*, the shimmering blue blurring in his peripheral vision. He cleared the tunnel and in an instant tucked his legs up and turned one hundred eighty degrees. His feet slapped the floor and he crouched quickly, looking for something to grab hold of.

He paled slightly. There was nothing.

The momentum started to throw him out of his crouch. Two uniformed figures stepped in on each side of him and pulled him to a stop.

"Thanks," Duke said.

"Nice catfall," one said.

"Showoff," the other said.

A moment later May's feet dangled from the opening in the ceiling. Slowly he drifted down as the gravity in the room came up.

"Cute," Duke said. "Very cute."

One of the ranking uniforms gathered the survivors into a single-file line. "You will be given ample time to clean up and orient yourself to shiptime," he said, "but first, the commander would like to greet you."

He took them into the next room, which was nothing more than a short corridor. They stopped and stood for a moment, then a uniform at the door snapped to attention.

"Officer on deck!"

The door opened and Margaret O'Hearn, wearing her Working Command uniform, stepped through with Ensign Tesla at her heels. The other uniforms came to attention, and the five survivors felt their backs straighten.

O'Hearn looked down the line of them, stopping with May, the last in line. She stared for a moment, then her lips turned up almost imperceptibly.

"On behalf of the United Terran Empire Fleet, I'd like to welcome you aboard the *Hergest Ridge*. I am Commander Margaret O'Hearn, and this is my aide, Ensign Revel Tesla. We are pleased to be able to assist you, and we'll try to make your stay here as comfortable as possible. Each of you will be provided with the necessities of daily life, and we have five berths waiting for your arrival.''

Vonn took Roz's hand and smiled. "We'll only need four."

O'Hearn glared at him. "We have prepared five berths for you under the guidelines of the Transgalactic Transport Treaty. Due to the size and nature of this ship, your presence will in no way be an imposition on us. Rather, we are delighted to be of service to you."

She began to pace past the line of survivors. Tesla followed them, a tube with a sighting device in his hand. He peered through it at Roz and said, "Smile."

"The ensign will be taking your pictures, and you'll be given complimentary Badges of Passage for our trip to Council 5. They will be good for food, personal items, three changes of clothes, and limited drinks, and may be used at any of our shops and stores. In return we request that you follow the rules and regulations of this ship as if you were a paying passenger with the according contract of liability." She stopped and stared hard at Vonn. "A copy of the contract can be found in your private berth."

All of them nodded.

"Smile," Tesla said. Vonn scowled at him.

O'Hearn looked them over. "Which of you is in command?"

May stepped forward. "James May at your service, ma'am." He made a polite bow.

She nodded. "We will need to discuss your ship's situation, and we will need to work out the details on the salvage negotiation and liability waiver. Because this is a rescue, the UTE Fleet will compensate you for any damage done to your ship that we might have caused."

"Thank you," he said gallantly.

"But that can be done later. In the meantime, I'm sure you all want to find your berths and get cleaned up. Lieutenant Stanns will escort you to the proper section of the ship and see that you each get a proper-sized UTE Fleet uniform—with our compliments.''

"Smile," Tesla said to Winters.

"Mr. May, when you are ready to meet with me, feel free to ring the administrative office and make an appointment."

May touched three fingers to his brow in an informal salute.

"Enjoy your stay," she told them.

She turned and left the room, Tesla rushing to get Duke and May's pictures into his device. He was out of the room a split second after his commander, and the uniform at the door shouted "Dis-*missed*!"

Everyone relaxed.

"I am Lieutenant Stanns," the ranking uniform said. "If you would follow me to your berths, please."

"Gladly," Roz said.

"Incredible," Vonn commented as the party started down the hall. "You're going to try and negotiate terms of salvage with that woman?"

"I think she'll be very reasonable," May said.

"Yeah? What about suppression of certain information?" he whispered.

"The UTE Fleet chooses their commanders based on Officer Presence, Respect, Judgment—"

"I know all of that, but you saw what she was like. She's from the old pike-and-saber crowd. She'll be tough to crack."

"She won't need cracking," May said confidently. "She'll listen to a logical presentation."

"Even if it means bending the rules, huh? Do you have some kind of inside on this Commander O'Hearn?"

"I know her from the academy."

"Really." Vonn laughed. "Well, was she a frigid bitch then, or is that something she learned at command school?"

May's hand shot out and grabbed Vonn by the lapels. He stepped back from the rest of the party and pushed the mercenary against the wall.

"Watch your mouth," he hissed. "Don't you *ever* talk about her like that again."

Vonn's mouth dropped open in shock. "I'm sorry. I didn't know. Was she special to you?"

"She's my ex-wife," James May snapped.

4

"What do you think you're doing here?"

Still vacuuming off water from her lo-grav shower, Roz grabbed a towel to cover herself.

Vonn gave her a crooked smile. He had already showered and shaved and was wearing his dust-blue UTE Fleet uniform. "Why do you think I'm here?"

"No," Roz said flatly. "I'm going to bed."

Vonn reached forward to tug at the towel. "That's what I had in mind, too."

She snapped the fabric out of his grip. "Alone." Her voice was firm. "And don't give me that whipped-puppy look of yours."

He wiped the expression from his face.

"You've got to understand that we've been in very close quarters for the last three weeks and I need a breathing space," she said. "I barely knew you when we left Garland Outpost."

"You know me now."

Roz grabbed her complimentary uniform and retreated into the shower pod. "No offense to you, Vonn, but I need a break. When I got on the *Angel's Luck* with you, I was being chased by the biggest crime syndicate in the galaxy. Now that they're out of the way—"

"They're never out of the way."

She stepped out of the shower pod. She had still been damp when dressing, so the fabric clung to the curve of her body, and her nipples were denting the uniform's bust. Vonn looked at her and simply stopped breathing.

"You know what I mean," Roz said. "They think we're dead. They're no longer looking for us."

"You've known that for—"

"But we were trapped on the *Angel's Luck*. It was a small, sweaty little box, and there was still the distinct possibility that we were going to die. I . . ." She trailed off, eyes searching the room as if looking for the right words. "I needed you then. I needed your strength."

"You're done with me, then?"

She smiled and shook her head. "I just need some time alone, that's all. I have to sort out my thoughts. Now that we're out of danger, I have to figure out how we should rebuild our relationship."

"Rebuild—"

"I still like you." She moved in on him and kissed his cheek. Her hands found his chest and gently pushed. He found himself being inched back. The kiss ended. She stepped away. "I'll give you a call. I promise."

The door to her berth slammed shut. He stared at it with an open mouth. From the other side of the door, he could hear the fabric rustle as she peeled the uniform from her frame.

He smiled. Any second now that door's going to open . . .

After five minutes of trembling in anticipation, he realized that the door was not going to open.

"Hell." He pouted.

Absently he touched the badge fastened to his breast pocket; then he pulled it loose and studied it. Embossed on one side was a bar code and the shifting holo that had been taken by that squirrely little ensign. On the other was the color-coded stripe that showed what funds the UTE Fleet had credited him with until they arrived at the Council system. A reminder was etched below the stripe: FOOD/UNL; PERSONAL/UNL; CLOTHING/3 SETS; DRINK/LIMITED ACCESS.

He stared hard at those last two words. There he was, wounded, and the ship's banking computer would not even let him anesthetize himself. It would probably cut him off after two or three stiff ones.

With a sigh, he started down the hall, stopping to ask directions to the cheapest lounge on board. If there was an actual monetary limit, he might be able to stretch things. He might even be able to find some benevolent soul who would act as patron in his misery-dulling quest. And even if he could not, he could make his own purchases in such a way that, even if he was not totally anesthetized, the pain he felt would certainly be dulled.

5

The next morning, James Theodore May walked into an adjutant's office and announced his appointment with Commander O'Hearn. He was directed through to the next door and told to thumb the pad when he was ready.

May did so, and the door opened. He walked into a comfortable-sized office with subdued lighting. It was the antithesis of the gray corridors in the business end of the *Hergest Ridge*, colored instead with the traditional off-blue that had become the corporate color of the UTE Fleet.

The door closed, and a trim figure rose from the desk. "James. It's good to see you."

He slowly approached the desk, unsure of how to approach the commander. With a smile, she came around to greet him and caught him in a hug. He closed his eyes and wrapped his arms around her, holding her tight.

"Maggie," he said.

She eased out of the hug and stepped back. "I suspected it might have been you when the records listed a merchant ship named *Angel's Luck* as missing in the area of our intersect with the Garland–Jubilo route. But there have been so many ships called that—"

"Not lately." He smiled at her. "I tried to get in touch with you last night—"

O'Hearn took another step back, then returned to her seat at the desk. "I deliberately ignored the calls, James."

He looked hurt. "I thought we were still friends."

Margaret O'Hearn laughed. "We are. I did it for decorum's sake. It wouldn't do to receive a rather scruffy-looking rescuee in my cabin. I must maintain a sense of propriety."

"I did clean up first," May said. "But I understand." He approached the desk and eased down in one of the guest chairs. "It's good to see you."

"I'm glad you're all right," she said, eyes misting.

"I'm glad you're doing well." He swept his hands around the office. "Commander, even. I'm grateful you made the decision to stop."

O'Hearn's features slowly lost their warmth. "What were you doing out there, James?"

May cleared his throat and sat back in his chair. He filled his lungs with air and looked her in the eye. "I refuse to lie to you. I promised I'd never do that again."

"That part of it is over and done with," O'Hearn said. "Just like I should be done with prying into your personal affairs. I'm sorry."

"Don't be. I know you have to file a report with your superiors. Put down that I had catastrophic engine failure and leave it at that."

"And what about the ship registered to the *Yueh-sheng*?"

May drew a quick breath. "What about it?"

She gave him a long stare. "Should I say that you were prospecting with the intent of making a salvage claim?"

A chill ran down May's spine. That was one of the stories they had rejected before leaving the *Angel's Luck*. "In a merchant ship?"

"People have done stupider things," O'Hearn told him matter-of-factly. "We found, as you probably did, that the wreckage of the *Yueh-sheng* ship was too radioactive for amateur salvage efforts. I'd like you to verify this for your standing claim of a finders' percentage against those who do reclaim what's there." She handed him a simfile. "Your thumbprint, please."

May squirmed in his seat. "I won't lie to you anymore, Maggie. This thing with the salvage operation—"

"Is just crazy enough to be true." Their gazes crossed. May stared into the violet haze of her eyes, and for a moment he was back with her, studying astronav at the academy and not doing a good job of reading to her from the text, then looking up at her and seeing that she was looking right back at him.

"Maggie," he said slowly.

"Yes."

He blinked. The haze disappeared. "How much do you know?"

O'Hearn was taken aback by the question. Her face showed confusion. "What?"

"How much do you know about my current situation?"

Her face flushed, and she pulled another simfile from a storage slot. "Well," she said, trying to sound businesslike, "we did a routine systems check of your retinal prints."

He rose from the chair. "What? When did you manage to get those?"

"When my ensign took the holo for the badge. We're using a new lasecam for making ID's. We can blow up details, render a profile from face-on—"

"You had no right to do that!"

O'Hearn slapped her hands on the desk and rose to meet May's glare. "I had every right to do that, mister. The company has put me in charge of this ship, and it's up to me to care for the cargo and watch out for the welfare of its passengers. I may have rescued a handful of people from a derelict ship, but I still should know whether or not they're a bunch of gun-toting hooligans."

"They're not a bunch of gun-toting hooligans," May assured her.

She opened the file. "Maurice Vonn, age twenty-nine. Trade, Mercenary. Recent ports of call: Bering's Gate, the

Pegasus system, Darkwind, Solina 8. If you keep up with the news you'll recognize most of those as galactic hot spots. The record file shows he's been marked by eight different systems. Accused of but never convicted for Sabotage, Arson, Murder-as-Act-of-War, Theft, and Smuggling. Accused but never tried of Possession of Illegal Weapons, Possession of Restricted Weapons, Smuggling, Arson, and Escape. Convicted but never sentenced for Sabotage, Kidnapping, Escape—''

"I get the idea." May sighed. "He's no angel."

O'Hearn tapped the file and the screen changed. "Irvin Winters. Exact age unknown; approximate age thirty-five. He has the maturity and intelligence level of a twelve-year-old. Recent ports of call include Harvest Home, Cypress 13, Solina 8—''

"Spare me."

"Rosalind Cain, age twenty-two, missing from Garland Outpost, suspected Foul Play." She tapped the file again. "William Wesley Arbor, age twenty-three, also known as Duke. Wanted in the Tetros system for two counts of misdemeanor Abandonment, felony Embezzlement, and felony Theft. Like his other friends, there's nothing indictable but enough to make me suspicious."

Exasperated, May sat. "I can explain."

"And what have *you* been up to, James? The *Angel's Luck* had been put on the watch list. Somebody named Hiro had filed charges of Piracy, dropped them, filed again with charges of malicious assault, later added Deliberate Insolvency and Piracy, dropped everything a week later and was filed as deceased shortly after that."

May stared at the floor. "I got into a little trouble."

"Watch it, James. You said you were through lying to me."

"I had a copilot mess up my finances—''

"Do I want to hear this?"

"—and my ship got repossessed."

She glared at him, color rising in her face. "You did *what*?"

"Malaysia Prime has gotten really hard-nosed since we signed the finance papers, Maggie."

"You got our ship taken away?"

"You signed over your share with the divorce," May reminded her.

"Yes, but we worked so hard—"

"But I got it back. It's just a little battered. I met Vonn when I was down and out, and he was on to this little scheme that would have brought in enough money to pay it off."

"Your salvage scheme," O'Hearn said. "I knew under normal circumstances you'd be smarter than that."

"You're putting words in my mouth," May muttered.

O'Hearn looked back at the file. "Wait a minute. Now this makes sense. Hiro, he's that little Oriental man who was our loan officer."

"Hiro," May said, "was Malaysia Prime."

"And he tried to take the *Angel's Luck*. Naturally you were so stubborn that you took off on this salvage thing. That explains the Piracy and Deliberate Insolvency."

"Maggie—" He stood.

"But Malicious Assault? What did you do to get the ship?"

"*Maggie!*" he shouted. "You're doing it again! You're so damned anxious to get to the core of things that you've left me out of the picture! What are you trying to do, get this over with so you can be rid of me?"

Her mouth dropped open. "Oh, James. I am sorry."

He pulled the chair close to the desk and sat. "I'm sorry, too. I know this isn't easy."

"I certainly don't want to get rid of you. Believe it or not, I'm actually glad you're here. This is a high-pressure trip for me."

He smiled. "I understand."

"I've made this run dozens of times, but the Arcolians are making things a little tense."

"It's only natural that—" He broke off. "*Arcolians?*"

"A diplomatic delegation headed for Council 5. Naturally, there are a lot of mixed feelings about this. I've had to step up security, everyone on the ship has been cleared, but that's not saying that something won't be waiting for us in the Council system."

May reached out and touched her face. "Don't worry about it. I'll make it easy for you and keep out of your way."

She took his hand. "But you can't do that. The Arcolians would like to meet you."

May gasped. The room felt as if it was closing in. "What for?"

"They don't understand the value we put on our own lives, or the lengths we go to in assisting others. They think you're special in some way, since we initiated a rescue operation. They want to meet you and make sure you're . . . normal."

He fought for air. "Well. Uh . . . I think . . ."

"If any of your party is xenophobic, I'll understand if they don't come. But you should be there. And Roz, if she can handle it. They seem to be very curious about women."

"This is incredible," he said. "All those years of calling them a menace."

"Takes some getting used to, doesn't it?"

"When?"

"We're planning a reception so they can meet some of the passengers. We'll let you know."

"All right." He put his hand to his chest. His heart was finally beginning to slow. Those damned phials in his ship were more of a burden than he thought.

"James." She was up from her seat and was escorting him to the door. "I do need your assistance."

He nodded.

"If there's anything you need to tell me—"

His throat closed.

"—about anyone with you, if they're a threat to the Arcolians, I'll have to know."

He swallowed and forced himself to nod.

"I cannot—repeat, can*not*—have anything go wrong."

"I understand."

They stopped at the door. The commander reached for the pad, and suddenly May's will collapsed. The anguish of the last month and the threat of the phials needed an outlet, and Margaret Faith O'Hearn had always listened and kept him going.

He grabbed her hand. "Maggie."

She looked at him blankly.

"There's something I've got to tell you."

"What is it?"

"I think—" His eyes caught hers again and gazed into the shining violet. As he turned away, he saw their fellow merchant cadets, lining the halls of the chapel, their sabers drawn and crossed into an arch of honor for them to walk down, their gravcar waiting in the midday heat.

"James."

Back in her office, he looked at his ex-wife. She had the command she had initially given up. She had the ship—one of the biggest in the UTE Fleet. She had the Arcolians and the mixed emotions of the galaxy to contend with. And in a moment, she would have the Essence Phials, as well.

"Maggie, I—"

He could not do it. Not yet. Not now.

He wrapped his arms around her, pulled her close, and kissed her hard. She offered no resistance.

6

A few minutes later, May plopped down in the chair in his berth and took the bottle of Tresell vodka out of its box. He had used up his entire drink allotment on it, and the expenditure had not made him feel any better.

"Scum," he grunted.

He opened the bottle and had a long drink. It did not help.

"You're no better than Vonn."

He took a series of long pulls. They did not help either.

"You bastard. You mercenary bastard."

He capped the bottle and put it on the floor, then sat slumped forward in the chair, his head in his hands.

7

"*Damn it!*"

Margaret O'Hearn cursed in the solitude of her office. They were coming, she could feel them, and there was nothing she could do about it.

"Why did he have to show up? *Why?*"

She drew a deep breath and bit her lip. She had loved him, but she had given up too much. The path back to her abandoned career had been long and strewn with frustration. And she had always fought the one thing, her one weakness, the flaw that would have kept her out of the office in which she stood, had the powers-that-be at UTE Fleet known about it.

"Damn him. *Damn him!*"

O'Hearn drew another breath, walked to her desk, and thumbed a pad.

"Yes, ma'am?"

"Sergeant Pryce, I'm going to be busy reconciling the salvage rights presented by our recent stop. Please see that I'm not disturbed until further notice."

"Yes, ma'am."

She keyed another pad, and the office filled with a rush of white noise, rising and falling like pounding surf. Bringing the volume up to mask any sound to those outside the office, she sat heavily in her chair and succumbed to tears of rage.

TWO

"You didn't just make a scene. No. Scandal is a more appropriate word."

"This is your limit. You understand that?"

"Yes," Vonn said, chin resting on his hand.

His card appeared from inside a slot. He pulled it out and clipped it to his breast pocket. As he watched, a door opened in the chest of the robot that was waiting on him, and three shot glasses rolled onto the countertop in front of him. One of the arms raised, and liquid issued from a nozzle set into it, filling each glass in turn with bourbon.

"No more this evening," the robot's speaker repeated. "You have reached your permitted limit."

"I know, dammit," Vonn barked. "Now leave me alone."

The robot wheeled away to aggravate another customer. In quick succession, Vonn picked up the glasses and swallowed their contents. With a grunt, he slapped the last glass down and wiped his mouth with the back of his hand.

Then he waited for something to happen.

Nothing did.

He still saw one of two things: Roz, standing in the doorway of her berth, the uniform clinging to her in all the right places; or Anders, in the hall of the *Angel's Luck*, turning around in slow motion after emptying a clip of ammo into the security guard who had ambushed them. The weapon fell to the ground, his hands clutched his stomach, and he leaned against the wall.

"I don't feel too good."

Too slowly, Vonn stood. Winters had pushed him down—none of it made sense. He turned and stepped over Bear, who no longer had a face.

Anders turned so his back was against the wall and started to slide down. Blood streaked the wall as he did.

"Anders. *Anders—*"

"Vonn," Anders said. "Promise me something. Don't go under. All right?"

Vonn was still reaching and had not had the chance to answer when Anders turned away and let blood gush from between his lips. Then he closed his eyes, and his heart stopped.

The three glasses sat lined before the mercenary, a symbol of a promise he did not have time to make.

He cursed under his breath. "How can I go under when they won't give me enough stuff to do it with?"

The bourbon rolled in his stomach, and he belched. The robot was coming his way. It shone a light in Vonn's eyes to check his retinas.

"Had enough," it told him. "You've reached your purchase limit."

"Go stand in the rain," Vonn snarled.

The robot stopped in front of him.

"Look, I told you . . ."

"What'll you have, sir?"

Vonn turned. Someone had taken the stool next to him. The newcomer stuck his ID into the robot and ordered two doubles of Maltese bourbon. The mercenary turned to leave, but the stranger laid a hand on his shoulder.

"Just a moment."

The robot returned the card, filled two shot glasses, and trundled off.

The stranger slid one of the glasses to Vonn. "This one's for you."

Vonn looked suspiciously at the glass. "I've reached my limit," he said.

The man lifted his glass and took a sip. "The 'bot checks your credit standing, not your blood-alcohol level."

Vonn took the glass in his hand. "This is very generous of you."

"Not as much as you think. They don't care if you get plastered on this ship, but if you're walking around on their money, they watch how much you spend." He flashed his ID. "I have no restrictions on my card."

Vonn lifted his glass in a toast. "To what do I owe the privilege?"

"I hate to drink alone." The stranger returned the toast, and the two men swallowed their drinks.

"My name is Vonn." He extended his hand.

"Bachman." The stranger's hand closed on the mercenary's to shake but twisted to grab his thumb. Vonn returned the gesture.

"Maybe I should call you 'brother.' " Vonn smiled.

"Bachman will do," the other man said. "For now."

"What brings you over here?"

Bachman keyed the button to summon the robot. "You've been in here every night for the last week. You buy three rounds, take them all down fast, stare at the wall for a while, and then leave. I figured you were a brother-in-arms who was having problems."

"You don't want to hear my problems," Vonn said.

"Try me."

Vonn shrugged. "Nothing big. Just a woman."

"Liar," Bachman said.

"She's an unwilling stringer. We had something going, but I got in too deep on a job and had to pull her with me.

We were doing all right until we got rescued by this damn ship. She won't have a thing to do with me now. Says she needs time to breathe, some excuse like that.''

"You're one of those who got rescued from that derelict merchant ship, right?'' Bachman asked.

"Yeah.'' Vonn sighed.

The robot appeared and scanned Bachman's eyes. Bachman put in a repeat of the last order. "Aren't you supposed to be at some big party tonight? Meet all the well-to-dos on board and shake claws with the xenos?''

"Piss on 'em,'' Vonn said. "That's what I told them.''

"You're not a 'phobe, are you?''

"Of course not. I just don't have any interest in going to meet a bunch of society types who want nothing to do with me.''

"That's it?''

Vonn put his hand on his heart. "Bring in the dogs if you don't believe me.''

Laughing, Bachman took the two new drinks. "If I did bring them in, they'd be more interested in the xenos. You'd just smell like a drunk.''

"Not yet.'' Vonn knocked back the drink. "But I'm working on it.''

Bachman held up his glass and stared at the amber liquid inside. "My friend, you are a victim of a battlefield romance. When the pressure's on, complete opposites can fall into each other's arms. When it's over, you're left stripped clean with a bad romantic hangover.''

Vonn drummed his fingers on the countertop. "Tell me about it. I got a kid that way, supposedly. Never seen him, though. It was strange. Until that night we were dug in, his mom was just a brother to me. Of course, when she found she was knocked up, she got all crazy in the head, abandoned the unit, disappeared.'' He could feel his throat harden and his eyes getting moist. "Why did I have to go and think about that?''

"You've had too much to drink," Bachman said, taking a reflective sip.

Vonn patted the man on the shoulder. "Thanks for the hospitality," he said, "but I should leave."

Bachman grabbed his hand.

"Let go," Vonn said.

"I heard your problems," he said quietly. "Do you think you've got a moment to hear mine?"

Vonn took a deep breath. "I'm told there's lots of available strange on the ship. You don't need me."

"It's not sexual. It's financial."

Vonn turned his pockets inside out. "Can't help. I'm strapped."

"I've got too much money," Bachman said, "and I need to unload some cash. I'm willing to share it with a man of the right talents."

Vonn's head shook loosely. "No, thanks. I've got plenty. I'm coming off of the worst job in my life, I lost my best friend—"

"Then why are you on a restricted access card, friend?"

"The money's on the lase—"

Bachman grabbed his arm and pulled him back to the stool. "You and I both know that's one of the three biggest lies in the galaxy. Why don't you get real and admit you've been screwed?"

"I haven't—"

"Get real. Word gets around. It doesn't take a rocket scientist to figure out what's happened to you."

Vonn's stomach tightened. "You think so?"

"I know so. Salvage is a screwy business, one that you can't go out and do half-cocked. You get a lead on a debris field from a big ship and run out in the first crate you can get. But if that ship's a merchant, you're not going to have the equipment or the proper shielding for deep-space operations. And when the debris turns out to be highly radioactive, it can interfere with your computer systems and strand you in the middle of nowhere. You end up beat, broke, and with insolvents owing you money.''

Vonn nodded slowly. The story was all wrong, but the end result was identical. "Yeah," he sighed. "You pegged it.''

"Are you interested, then?"

"Depends. What's the action?"

Bachman wagged a finger as the BarBot trundled past. It stopped and served up two more drinks. "That, my friend, will be determined by your skills.''

"I can do anything. Demolitions, Forward Observation, Discreet Sanctions—''

"Not here," Bachman said quietly. He turned around on the stool to face the door.

"What's wrong?" Vonn laughed. "Too much riffraff in here?"

"Walls have ears," Bachman said solemnly.

Vonn stared at the two new drinks longingly. "Tell you what. You get the cloak-and-dagger business out of the way and then come looking for me. You'll know where to find me.''

"Of course," Bachman said. He slid from the stool. "Tomorrow night then, or the night after. I'll need a chance to check out your credentials.''

"You don't even know me."

"I can find out."

"And what if you don't show, tomorrow night, or the night after?''

Bachman gave a wry smile. "Then you've no problem. Your money's on the lase.'' He looked toward the door and walked away, not even giving Vonn the comfort of a last glance back his way.

"Whatever you say," the mercenary grumbled under his breath. He turned to the bar and saw the two shots of Maltese bourbon. With a look over his shoulder to make certain that his mysterious patron was not coming back, he took them both and nursed them down, and the long-awaited numbness started to creep in.

2

May tugged at Duke's collar and straightened his lapel. "There," he said, dusting a mote of lint from the shoulder of the dress uniform. "You look like a million credits."

"I still feel uncomfortable," Duke said. "The last time I wore a uniform, we were in big trouble."

"Be calm. These are called informal dress blues, and it's perfectly legal for civilians to be wearing them. Besides—" He elbowed his protégé in the ribs. "We're the guests of honor."

Duke flexed his shoulders, and they strained against the suit. "I don't know about this. These are important people, and I'm just a farm boy from Tetros."

"When word gets out about the Essence Phials," May assured him, "every one of the folks in there will wish they knew you personally." He slapped Duke on the back and steered him toward the door of the Polondo Suite.

There was a shout from behind them, and they turned. Roz was heading their way, fastening her hair up with a magnetic bauble.

"Wait up, and we can make a big entrance," she said.

"Where's Vonn?" Duke asked.

"Do I look like his mother?" It came out in a snarl. "Sorry," she said sheepishly. "I guess he's off pouting somewhere. I told him I wanted some time to myself, and he let himself get all torn up over it."

"As long as he doesn't get in trouble."

Roz dropped her hands, and a small silver satellite began to orbit the stacked bun of hair. "How about Winters?"

"He's at the arcade as a guest of Commander O'Hearn," May said. "His profile came back Psych 13."

Roz and Duke looked at him with blank stares.

"Don't tell me you're too young to remember Psych 13," he complained.

Duke shrugged. "Sorry."

"Remember that little test they gave us this morning? It

renders a profile of psychological tendencies for an individual's personality. Winters's scores indicated distinct xenophobic leanings, so he was tactfully diverted from this evening's entertainment. The last thing we need here is to have a big scene over the Arcolians."

"He'd be bored anyway," Roz suggested.

"I'm not exactly looking forward to this myself," Duke said.

"Nonsense." May began to shepherd them to the door. "This is going to be a night we'll all remember."

The door to the suite hissed open, and the three of them stepped into an atmosphere of pure affluence. It was bright to the point where it almost hurt their eyes.

Three meters into the suite, Duke and Roz and May were entreated to stop while there was a polite round of applause directed at their having survived a truly bad situation, and then those already present queued up to meet them.

"What's all this?" Duke said out of the corner of his mouth to May.

"Reception line," he answered. "We're V.I.P.'s, second only to the Arcolians on this trip."

Commander Margaret O'Hearn was the first to shake their hands, and she again officially greeted them aboard the *Hergest Ridge* for the benefit of the other guests. May thanked her, then gallantly scooped up her hand and kissed it. A pleased sigh went through the crowd, followed by more applause.

Next came Admiral Studebaker, and Duke's eyes bugged out. With a trembling hand he shook with the retired commander of the entire Spaceborne Military Fleet. The admiral almost crushed the Tetran's hand, smiling and laughing. "I hope this doesn't put you off space flight, son. We need more boys with your fighting spirit."

Duke flushed and, on the spur of the moment, gave him the two-fingered civilian salute. There was more gracious applause.

But from there, things went downhill. There were minor

military leaders and inventors and holostars; owners of casinos and shipbuilding complexes and entire stellar systems; and lots of bored, bloated women whose entire fortunes seem to have materialized out of nowhere. Face after smiling face presented themselves, bringing limp handshakes and words of concern that never failed to ring hollow.

"We're *soooo* glad they were able to pull you off of that ship. We bet it was *soooo* frightening to be in such a position. We wouldn't have been able to take it for *soooo* long. Your story is *soooo* exciting—you should sell it to one of the holonets."

"Why do I feel like we're the evening's entertainment?" Duke mumbled to Roz.

"Because we are," she said through a clenched-tooth smile. "This is their big chance to see how the other ninety-five percent lives."

"Slumming," Duke said with a smile.

Somehow, they survived the parade of opulence: the glittering of exotic gemstones; the intoxicating scents of pheromonal perfumes that cost more per dram than any cargo that had ever been stored inside the *Angel's Luck*; the gold and platinum and diamond implants that augmented or replaced eye and tooth; the painfully exotic furs, each of which carried the guarantee that it had cost the Nimrev Company at least one human life to bring into civilized space.

"Delvin Miguel," said an overly fat man who crushed Duke's hand as they shook.

"William Arbor," he returned with a grimace.

"That's Miguel as in the Miguel Systems Harmonic Processing System."

Duke nodded his head emptily. "I'm sorry. Should that mean something to me?"

The man laughed loudly. "It should if you've ever pulled a transgear, son. My HPS wrote the book on *all* the new transgear specs."

His breath reached Duke's nose. It was a strange combination of garlic and clove and foul, dark smoke. It made Duke's eyes water and blink.

"The next time you pull a transgear, son, you tell your friends that you met *me*—"

Duke's nose felt strangely numb, and a sharp spike of pain shot through the little finger on his right hand. "You make the Miguel HPS?" he asked, sweat beading on his upper lip.

Another hearty laugh. "Son, my family *is* the Miguel HPS."

Duke gave him a hard stare. "So you're the son of a bitch."

The man's look soured.

"Duke—" May blurted.

"What did you say?" Miguel protested.

"You've never run one of your machines, have you?" Duke asked.

"They're tested in my factory—"

"By robots under ideal conditions. Never under real conditions." Duke's little finger flopped lifelessly against the palm of his hand, which he brought up back out to show Miguel. To the fat man, it looked as if there was a finger missing.

Sputtering, Miguel stepped out of the receiving line and retreated.

"Duke!" May grabbed his upper arm and hissed in his ear. "What the hell was that all about?"

Duke looked at him innocuously. "What was what all about?"

"Dammit, quit the funny business. We've got to put up with this until they open the buffet, and then we can get revenge. One plateful of the right canapés and a glass of the proper drink will run these stuffed shirts more money than beef on the *Saint Vrain*."

Roz started to laugh, and the two looked at her. She was talking to a grade-B holostar who was displaying a set of breasts in the light gravity.

"My dear, of *course* you've seen me as a man—these detach for *that* kind of role!"

"Don't let it stroke your palm," May whispered.

Duke absently rubbed feeling into his little finger and turned back to the reception line. He deftly avoided contact with the grade-B switch-hitter and tried to show some interest in the causes that the other gawkers brought with them. After an only moderately painful forty-five minutes, the line ended and the atmosphere dissolved into a lighter fare of socialization. May put his hand on Duke's shoulder and steered him toward the food.

"Off the record," he said, "I wished I'd been the one who told off that pig Miguel. I nearly lost my damn arm in one of his machines." A wry chuckle followed.

Duke watched with wide eyes as May steered him around the cliques of money and position, who, having done their patronly duty of wishing well to them, were conspicuously avoiding the *Angel's Luck* survivors. "You know something, May? You meet a better caliber of people at Doctor Bombay's," he said, referring to the bar on Tetros where he and May had met.

May stopped in front of the food and handed Duke a thick plate. "Don't let the weight of that fool you. In this gravity, you have more of a tendency to spill things. They cut little slots in the base to keep things from jostling around."

"I mean it, May. Doctor Bombay's was a real serpent's pit by Tetran standards. You had traders and mercenaries and thieves and whores, but you know something? Any one of those people had a heart of gold and would give you the shirt off their back if you were hurting."

May brought a spoonful of Cesslian Cheese Powder to his nostrils and inhaled it. "Ah." He smiled. "That just cost someone a couple of hundred credits."

Duke grabbed May's hand before he could indulge in seconds. "Have you heard a word I've said?"

May's head bobbed. "These people also have money, and money, Duke, can do a lot more good than somebody's shirt. I plan on networking anyone who'll give me the time of day."

"Well, I wouldn't take their money," Duke said indignantly. "They'd look down their nose as they made out the check, smiling because they think they're being charitable."

May held a spoonful of cheese to Duke's nose. "Have some."

Duke pushed it away, leaving a dab of black powder at the tip of his nose. "I'm not hungry."

"Tolerate it," May told him. "We know what most of these folk are really like. It'll be our little joke, all right? Relax. Have a drink. You might find one of the three people in this room besides ourselves who are really sincere."

"A drink." Duke scratched at his nose and was a little alarmed at the color he found on the tip of his fingers. "I will." He smiled, then slapped the merchant on the back and wandered through the suite, stopping to express his appreciation to Margaret O'Hearn. She smiled pleasantly at him—one of the sincere, he told himself—and dabbed the remaining powder from his nose with her kerchief. He thanked her, and she pecked him on the cheek. Walking away, he wondered what she would have been like as his mother.

Duke sidled up to an expensive-looking fountain and pointed to a stack of cocktail napkins. The barman handed him one, and Duke brought it to his nose and sneezed. The jerk from his muscles brought his feet off the ground; he lightly touched down.

"I can't believe what people will eat in the name of food," he said as his sinuses plugged.

"How about drink in the name of a good time?" The barman smiled. "You name it, I've got it, from every quadrant of the galaxy."

Duke sank the soiled napkin into his pocket. "Back home," he said, "I used to get this beer called Dooley's—"

"Potatoes and rice," the barman said, raising his finger. "No pretensions."

"A beer for drinking," Duke said, finishing the slogan.

"I don't have that, but I've got the next best thing. Let me whip some up for you." He turned back to a row of bottles.

"Beer?" a loud voice questioned.

Duke pulled the napkin from his pocket and sneezed. His eyes were watering again.

"Beer," the voice repeated. "Pretty tame stuff for a salvor, isn't it?"

He slowly turned to see a man of his height, hair in a multistory flat-top, Cateye implants over his irises, and a nasal cannula delivering wisps of blue smoke from a source hidden in his breast pocket.

"A beer for drinking." Duke shrugged. "You're the explorer, aren't you?"

"Explorer nothing," the man said indignantly, smoke venting from his lips. "I'm a *discoverer*."

"That's right." Duke turned back to watch the barman carefully mixing from two different bottles of beer. A hand turned him back to the discoverer.

"Twelve fringe systems bear my name and elements of my ID code," the man said importantly.

"When I get back to Tetros," Duke said calmly, "two teenage girls will bear my last name and elements of my genetic code."

The barman set the mug before Duke and gave the discoverer a nervous look. "Come on, Stin. We all know about you."

Stin shrugged his shoulders as if the remark was rolling off of his back. Duke sipped his beer.

"What I want to know," Stin continued, "is how do you rate? I mean, what did you do in comparison to me to win the goodwill of this ship?"

"Tell you what." Duke raised his mug in a toast. "You can have my share. All right?"

"You little slime—"

Duke wagged a finger at the barman. "Buy this hero a drink for me, would you?"

The barman stepped back.

Stin stabbed a finger at him. "Freeze. I'm not having *beer*." Blue smoke curled into the air.

"What'll you have, then?" Duke asked, not looking at him.

"A man's drink."

Pain shot through Duke's little finger. He winced.

"What's wrong?" Stin laughed. "You some kind of quick-change artist? You can't join me in manly communion?"

Blue smoke stung Duke's eyes, and the image of Stin became hazy. The "discoverer" was no longer brightly attired and wildly offensive—he was just another guy, tired and weary, decked in a tattered green uniform, streaked and smeared with transgear conduction fluid.

"I could." Duke smiled, showing his teeth. "But why should I lower myself?"

Stin slapped his hand on the bar. Beer shot from Duke's mug into the air. "You low-classed little—"

Duke looked at Stin's crotch and shook his head. "I don't think you're packing enough gear to join me in a drink, *son*."

"You think—"

"A hero's drink." Duke turned to the barman and spoke in a low voice. "If you please. Two shots of Aiaagan gin."

Stin laughed as the barman complied. "Some cheap shitwater vacuumed out of a sty on—"

"Don't knock it." Duke picked up his glass and held it up in challenge.

Stin grabbed his glass and raised it to his lips.

Duke raised a finger. "But first, savor the bouquet." Nose over the glass, he sniffed.

She's late.

"Oh, no." The voice sounded far away and came from a disjointed figure that was a strange combination of a weary transgear puller and an arrogant bastard. "You're not getting me like that. You first, *hero*."

Duke put the glass to his lips and downed it with one gulp. It burned with liquid fire, and his tongue was coated with the thick sensation of metallic fish oil. His lips turned—*she's late she's never been this late before*—up.

The figure before him raised his glass.

Duke reached over and hooked a finger around the arrogant bastard's nasal cannula and snapped it off. "Bouquet," he said.

The weary transgear puller sniffed and smiled and downed the drink. The arrogant bastard, in his place now, froze for an instant.

Duke's empty glass clattered on the bar. "Another."

The barman dutifully filled it.

The glass came up again. Duke watched the arrogant bastard pause. "Two."

The gin hit his throat *never, ever, been this late before. Something's happened. Something bad, like he had seen happen to the others.*

The gin went down with a loud swallow, but something was wrong. The weary transgear puller drinking with him was instead some arrogant bastard who was mulling over the shot of gin he had just bought him, lingering over its scent.

The glass hit the bar again. "Three." Liquid splashed in what little gravity they had. "What's wrong, smartass? Have to think about it?" He threw the drink back, thick and satisfying. "Hell, I've had three in the time it's taken you to think about it, and you still haven't made your mind up."

The arrogant bastard looked at him grimly, then studied the crowd of people that had gathered around him. Determination set his features as smoke leaked from his broken cannula. He opened his mouth and tipped up the glass.

"Congratulations. Now you're a real hero."

The bastard's surgically altered eyes squinted, and the muscles in his jaw froze.

"Of course," he observed, "you've got to swallow it."

Tears leaked from the corners of the bastard's eyes.

"C'mon," he taunted. "You're not a hero yet." He moved in close and grabbed the bastard's groin. "Swallow it and show me you've got a pair."

A grunt came from the knotted muscles in the bastard's throat.

"Down the hatch," he urged.

The grunt became a rumble.

"Showtime!" He loosed his grip on the bastard and spun him away just as the man's lips spewed gin and half-digested food and blue smoke. He staggered away from the bar and fell to his knees, then was surrounded by a shocked crowd of patrons.

"All right. True colors at last." He slapped the glass down on the bar and pointed to it with two fingers.

"I'm sorry."

He looked up. The damnedest thing had happened. That weary transgear puller had become the bartender.

"I think you've had enough."

"Yeah," he said, trying to keep his voice down. "Maybe you're right. But dammit, she's late."

"I'm sorry," the weary bartender repeated.

He gave him a two-fingered salute of respect. "It's not your fault, son." He looked back to where the bastard had fallen. "I see this type all over. They act like terminally horny plebes until someone drains their fuel valves."

Turning away, he started through the bar. It was full of strange, unfamiliar patrons. He caught a glimpse of Admiral Studebaker and tried to have a word with Old Ironjaw, but when he saw him, the man was impossibly old. He tagged someone in a commander's uniform on the shoulder and it turned out to be a woman, someone he was not looking for at all, someone who looked like his mother might have, had she lived . . .

The air in his lungs became stale and was putting pressure on his chest. A turn back toward the bar showed the transgear bartender sadly shaking his head. Another turn showed a door; he began to claw through the crowd toward it.

He was intercepted by a short, uniformed man who grabbed the front of his uniform.

"Duke! Duke, what the hell's wrong with you?"

He knocked the man's hands clear. "Damn your eyes, Captain, you know better than to lay your hands on someone of superior rank!"

"Are you all right?" the captain asked.

"Why does everyone look at me as if I'm diseased?" he shouted. *"I've had my inoculations. Do I look that wilted?"*

The captain pulled him close. "I've got to get you out of here—"

He knocked the captain back. "You'll do no such thing! I will, however, forgive the fact that you dared lay hands on me if you will be so good as to get me a bottle of gin—"

"No," the captain said, closing ranks. *"You've had enough."*

He took a quick step back, looking at the host of indignant faces. "Damn your eyes!" he shouted. "You're all just a bunch of fucking toadies and that's all you'll ever be!"

He spun back on the captain, hand reaching for his baton. By the thundering stars, he'd show this young maggot a lesson—

But the baton was not there.

He looked up in sheer panic. A fist was heading straight for him. His arm jumped to block, too late. There was a black explosion in his brain, and then swimming yellow stars.

He could identify some by their constellations. Arcolus, Bettendorf, Lazarus, Bering's Gate . . .

3

Vonn's gait was uncertain but not unsteady. His smile was of extreme contentment. The elusive Mr. Bachman's gift had worked wonders on the mercenary's morale. He had achieved the blissful state of not giving a damn.

Instead of going straight to his cabin, he wandered the lower decks of the *Hergest Ridge*, trying to take the longest possible route to his berth. His current condition would be all too short if he merely went to bed. It was his intent to savor the delicious emotional numbness for as long as possible. He certainly had no other pressing social commitments, not like that social butterfly Roz, who, if he read his watch correctly, was currently flitting among the social elite.

After another half hour of walking, Vonn stopped to lean against a bulkhead. With all of the plodding he had done, the effect of the bourbons had been short-lived. To his dire misfortune, he felt his head beginning to clear. With a sigh, he stuffed his hands into his jumpsuit pockets and turned back in the direction of the berths.

Three men, standing shoulder to shoulder, blocked his way.

He smiled. "Excuse me."

They stood fast.

"Salvor trash," one said.

Vonn squinted at them. The man in the middle, the biggest of the three, had spoken. "What did you say?"

"Salvor trash." The man enunciated every letter.

Vonn shook his head. "You got it wrong. Mercenary trash, yes. I'd be a hopeless salvor." He took another step toward them, but they held their ground.

"You go out and get stuck in the middle of nowhere," the man in the middle said. "You get rescued, and they give you a private berth and drinking money."

Vonn unclipped the card from his breast pocket and held it out to them. "Take this," he told them, "and go get drunk on it. Try it. Really." He waved the card in their faces. One of them knocked it to the floor.

"Some people have to shell out all they got for a lousy ticket in steerage. Then trash like you comes along, and without a cent they give you the royal treatment. With the money they made offa us."

"You've got to be kidding," the mercenary told them. "I didn't ask for any of this—"

The middle one wriggled his right arm. A long, cylindrical object slid down into his hand.

"And now we're going to show you what it's like. We're going to deprive you."

Vonn braced himself. "Amateurs," he spat, and launched a spinning kick to his rear. True to his suspicions, his foot planted squarely in the chest of a well-muscled woman with a club. Ribs snapped under the impact of his foot, and she grunted as she hit the floor.

His foot touched down, and he turned back to the three in time to see their advance. He took a confident step forward and threw his right fist at the big man in the middle. His target blocked it easily, wielding the cylinder with both hands. Vonn came in with his left fist, crushed the man's nose, and kicked him back into the remaining two, who staggered under the weight of their leader.

Vonn glanced back at the woman. She had abandoned the club and was retreating. He turned back, and a fist connected with his temple. His back hit the wall, and he blinked tears from his eyes, trying to shake the blow off.

When his senses returned, the two lackeys had him by each arm and the leader was groping the floor, looking for his cylinder. Fat fingers closed around the object, and the man with the broken nose leapt to his feet with stunning agility.

Keeping a grim look on his face, Vonn let his knees buckle, and he began to slide to the floor.

"Oh, no," one of the lackeys grunted. They shifted their grip, locking their arms through his and putting their inside shoulders against him, forcing him back up.

Vonn set his feet flat against the floor and kicked with all his might. He shot up in the air, tucked his legs, and clamped his hands on their wrists. In midspin, a crack told him the shoulder of the one on his right had been compromised. Pointing his feet at the floor, he touched down and shook the man from his right.

With two hands, the leader swung the cylinder. Vonn stepped back, yanking the man on his left into the path of the attack. The cylinder connected, and Vonn's left arm was freed.

"All right, fat boy," Vonn taunted, making a come-and-get-me gesture with his fingers. "Let's see how brave you are."

The cylinder clattered to the floor. The leader turned and ran.

Vonn grabbed the weapon and was instantly airborne. He landed high on the leader's back and had the cylinder across his neck before they hit the floor. The bloodied face tried to look back in panic.

The mercenary tightened the bar across the leader's neck. "Back where I come from, we call this 'doing the chicken.' Do you know why?"

The leader's head shook.

" 'Cause you can't get air in your lungs or blood to your brain, so you start flopping around like some frigging decapitated bird. You want to try it?"

The head shook again.

"Give me one reason why I shouldn't do it, pal. Why shouldn't I prove that I'm typical salvor trash?"

"Because it's clear that you're not."

The voice came from behind. Vonn jumped back and turned, bringing the cylinder to bear. The fat man on the floor wheezed.

"Bachman!" Vonn exclaimed.

"I'd appreciate your sparing Brutus. He's simple but well meaning, and good help is so hard to find."

"This guy works for you?"

"All of them did. And now, I'm afraid, they're going to be costing me some in medical bills."

"Why?"

"I had to be sure you weren't, as they put it, salvor trash. Frankly, sir, I'm impressed with your prowess."

Vonn cleared his throat and blew saliva and blood onto Brutus's back. "Hell, if I'd been sober, I would've killed them."

"How are you with small arms?"

"This incident would've lasted exactly ten seconds."

Bachman smiled. "Excellent. Consider yourself hired."

"For what?"

The thin man walked to the woman and picked her up in his arms. "If you'll help me get everyone back to their berths, I'll tell you."

"They can do it themselves," Vonn growled. "Medical assistance isn't in my contract."

4

"What in the name of the Fifth Region are you trying to pull?"

The door to the Polondo Suite hissed shut, and Duke slammed into the opposite wall. May stepped over to pick him off the floor, Roz at his heels, trying to calm him down.

"You didn't just make a scene. No. Scandal is a more appropriate word."

He lifted Duke from the floor and banged him into the wall.

"After I promised Maggie that there wouldn't be any trouble. I gave her my word, Duke!" He banged him again for emphasis. "I know that rocket jock was insufferable, but did you have to grab him like that? And what you said to Maggie—"

Roz tried to step between them. "We all know what he said, May. You're not making things any better."

Slowly Duke's head raised. The eye that was not swollen opened, and a weak smile came over his features. "May," he said happily. "What are you doing here?"

"*Maggot!*" He shifted to throttle the young commodities broker, but Roz forced herself between them.

"He's drunk, May."

"And a good thing, too." Duke continued his smile. "My arm's still broken." He took his right hand in his left and lifted it for their inspection.

May released his hold and paced the hall, spitting every oath he could think of.

"When you're done—" Roz started, but May was too wrapped up in vilifying Duke's name. She raised her voice. *"When you're done—"*

May stopped and looked at her.

Roz gave him a stern look. "We need to assess the damage that's been created by this little incident."

"Right," May said. He had spoken too loudly, so Roz told him to lower his voice. After two more attempts he reached a civil tone and began his list. "To start with, we're on *everybody's* shit list—"

"The phials, May."

"They're safe, Roz. Nobody's going to find them—"

"Duke," she stressed.

May paled. "He might talk."

"Worse yet, someone might start poking around his psychological profile and find out that he's got the chemical essence of another person inside his body."

"Are you serious?" May asked. "You think that little outburst was caused by . . ." He orbited a finger around his ear.

"Think about it. That wasn't Duke we saw in there."

"But he'd had a few—"

"Since when does Duke drink Aiaagan gin, May? And while you're chewing on that, when was the last time you heard him use the word 'fuck'?"

May sighed. "Duke didn't even swear until he started hanging around me."

"Eric Dickson," she said. "His personality is emerging. It's got to be."

May folded his arms tightly and looked up at the ceiling. "That's not how that stuff was supposed to work," he said. "Duke was just supposed to get Dickson's knowledge, not the whole damned personality."

Roz shrugged. "You told me yourself that the Essence had never been tested."

"Maybe drinking did it," May said quickly. "Lowered Duke's inhibitions, and that allowed Dickson to take over. All we have to do is keep him from drinking."

"Not good enough." Roz took him by the arm and led him down the hall. "We've got to isolate him, James. If he's in a weakened state, heaven knows what'll happen inside his head.''

May looked at the crumpled form on the floor. "Let's get him out of here."

They ran to Duke and picked him up. He screamed when May tried to pull him up by the right hand and cursed a blue streak at them.

"See what I mean?" Roz said.

They looped his arms around their necks and started down the hall. Behind them, they heard the door to the Polondo Suite open, and a clatter of heavy footfalls. They kept moving, desperate to secure their ill friend.

"Stop," a voice filled with authority ordered.

May's legs froze. "Maggie."

Boots on metal clattered behind them until the merchant was staring into his ex-wife's face. She was flanked by two grim-looking security guards, and her protruding lower lip quivered.

"*It,*" she threatened, "is about to happen. And if *It* does happen, you can guess the course your future will take."

May shifted. Duke was growing heavy. "It's all right—"

"It's not all right," Margaret O'Hearn said. "You assured me that nothing was going to happen."

"He was goaded into taking a drink," May explained. "There were witnesses. And when it hit his system, well—"

"That's a lie," O'Hearn said coolly. "His profile showed no predisposition toward alcohol-induced sociopathic behavior. Now unless that man is someone he's not—"

"Oh, no," May cried. "He's exactly who he is. I swear—"

"Then you've got—"

There was a chime, and the elevator door opened. The air filled with the scent of ammonia.

Duke's eyes popped open.

Ensign Revel Tesla stepped into the hall and snapped a salute at O'Hearn. "Ma'am. The Arcolian delegation."

The ammonia changed to a floral scent. May felt Duke's muscles tense.

"Son of a—"

"Easy," Roz told Duke. "You'll be fine."

"Move," May hissed.

"Captain May," O'Hearn said. "I'm not done with you."

May pointed frantically at the limp figure on his shoulder. The air in the hall became overwhelming, changing from lilac to smoke to stagnant water in a fraction of a second. From the open elevator came the clatter of chitin on metal and an odd shuffle as a hulking figure moved into the hall.

Crrrr-ack!

It stopped for a moment, and a crackle behind it said, "Indeed, redbutler, we do this to study, to study—"

Duke's left arm knotted around May's throat and pulled the merchant captain's head down into the wall. Roz screamed as Duke shouldered her back, knocking her clear.

"You murdering, traitorous—"

"Take him," O'Hearn snapped.

The guards moved in on Duke, blocking the path between him and the Arcolians, who had spilled into the hall, cocking their heads with curiosity.

Under her breath, O'Hearn told Tesla, "Get them out of here."

There was a grunt, and the commander turned in time to see the first guard roll to the ground. The second pulled something from a sheath at his side, and Duke hit him low, spinning both of them around and back toward the crowded hallway.

"Filthy xeno bastards," Duke shouted. "You got her, didn't you? That's why she's late. *She's not coming back!*"

Tesla was back with the delegation then, apologizing, mumbling something about ancient human customs, and hurrying them toward the Polondo Suite. The door hissed open, and music leaked into the hall.

Scents were changing faster than any of them could register: rotten fruit, wet sand, exotic aerosol scents, molds . . .

The second guard buckled under Duke's left fist. The guard kicked his legs and hit the wall, carrying his attacker with him. A bare hand reached out, touched a leather pouch on the guard's hip, then grabbed for it.

O'Hearn shouted. *"Tesla!"*

The ensign was struggling to get laceylane into the suite; people were streaming into the hall, staring at the xenos and the struggle in the hall.

"Back, folks!" the commander ordered. She started toward the crowd, waving her arms. "Everything's under control . . ."

May shook his head and found himself on his hands and knees. He looked up and saw Duke wrapped around a security guard, fingers unsnapping the flap of a holster.

"Maggie," he said, struggling to his feet.

Duke slammed the guard against the wall; the fingers of his left hand touched something cold. They wrapped around it and pulled.

A gaudily dressed woman stepped out of the Polondo Suite, took one look down the hall, and screamed, *"Gun!"*

The crowd scattered, bowling misterbob and leighbrand over onto their backs, leaving them struggling like upended turtles. O'Hearn looked back and saw Duke struggling to hold a guard up like a shield while balancing a sidearm in his left hand.

"I saw what you did," he gasped. "You mangled her like all the others . . ."

"The xenos," O'Hearn shouted.

"Run—"

"Duck—"

"Got a gun—"

Arms outstretched, May started a wobbling run at Duke. *"The xenos . . ."*

"Get down, Commander!" Revel Tesla shouted, and he hit her running.

A hulking red figure wrapped in purple staggered in front

of the barrel's path. Duke pulled the trigger as it turned to face him. His nose filled with the satisfying smell of cordite.

There was a burst of black. Purple fabric tore, and the figure staggered back. Screams. Ammonia.

Crrrrrrrrr—

He fired again.

The second shot patterned just below the first. His arm was beginning to tire.

—aaaaaaaaaaaaaack!

Once more.

There was another smear of black, and a sudden spurt of thick, yellow liquid sprayed walls and floor and passengers.

Duke's finger trembled on the trigger for an instant.

"You son of a *bitch*!" With every last erg of strength, James May launched himself at William Wesley Arbor, fully intending to murder him on contact. He connected with the younger man's lower back in a crunch of bone and tissue and plastic, and as the tangle of merchant and broker and guard tumbled to the floor, there was one last explosion to remind everyone in the hall of how truly mortal they all were.

5

When it was all over—whatever the hell it was—they took him to a place he affectionately called the Vicarage.

They checked the cast on his arm—something he did not remember from before—and searched every bit of him that could be searched. They dunked him in a vat of too-cold water and dressed him in a too-big coversuit.

Then he was taken to his cell by a wide, muscled bitch of a matron, who locked him up in a room with a lo-grav toilet, a hard bench, and a zipbed. He sprawled on the floor, fingered his cast, and laughed hysterically.

"And what's so funny with you?" the matron bitch growled.

He did not even look at her. He just laughed.

"You'll think funny," she said. *"You're in here for keeps for murdering Derrald Deakes."*

He liked the matron bitch, and gave her the two-fingered salute. *"That's what's so funny,"* he told her. *"That skinny-assed little pimp is too dead to enjoy my predicament."*

6

"What do you know about the Arcolians?"

Vonn did not answer the question. He was sitting with a handful of other mercenaries in Bachman's suite, hands folded over a stomach that had been soured by an overdose of Leuten's Alcohol Neutralizer.

"They're like giant lobsters," said the man who had established himself earlier as the group smartass.

"Almost correct," Bachman said. "On the evolutionary scale, they're closer to the tribe of crustaceans known as *Astacurs*, the crayfish. In and around the territories of Arcolus their physical appearance maintains the semblance."

"Like I said," the smartass said. Some of the others laughed appreciatively.

"Have any of you seen the ones on board this ship?"

"I got a glimpse of one during the stink last night," a tough-looking woman offered.

"And what did they look like?"

"Not a fish, that's for sure." That brought more laughter. "They looked like big, puffy hunchbacks, deep red in color."

"She's lying," yet another said. "I got into Ground Occupation Forces on Bettendorf a few years ago when a handful of them passed through, and that's *not* what they looked like. They were big, sluggish crawlers—"

"No," the woman insisted. "These things walked upright and had big, swollen heads—"

"You lying bastard," the veteran grumbled.

"Both of you are right," Bachman explained. "The crawlers described by Mr. Haggis are the standard, or A-forms, of Arcolian being. They are characterized by their horizontal plane as opposed to our own vertical plane, their highly tactile manipulative organs located just below the mouth on the front of their head, their modified open circulatory system—"

"And the fact that they're cruel sons of bitches," Haggis said.

Bachman ignored the remark. "Since the forging of the Arcolian Accord, we have discovered that these beings seem to be like ants in that they have different physical types to do different jobs, which accounts for the discrepancies. Some have speculated that they may have some kind of psychic link—like a hive mind—since they view and value life much differently than we do. In fact, they behave toward their own in a manner that we would consider inhumane."

"Like I said," Haggis repeated.

"If we had, say, a member of the Elite Fighter Wing with us, and that person had been so lucky as to take part in the capture of an Arcolian pilot, they would give us yet another different description of the creature—a greenish, amorphous blob with tendrils that resembled electrical leads and serve to wire the creature into its fighter craft systems. These, of course, are the notorious B-forms that you've heard so much about.

"We know that the Arcolian physiology can have one of six different forms. They run the gamut from the 'giant lobsters' that Mr. Haggis described to a creature that can fly a craft without the inherent clumsiness of the parent race or one that can walk upright, in a vertical plane.

"The E-form Arcolians—the ones Ms. Steubing saw on board this ship—are the ones we are the most concerned with. They appeared just prior to the end of the war, and it was with the E-forms that our emissaries negotiated the terms of the accord. Besides the vertical plane, the E-forms have a most interesting circulatory system, which our scientists have dubbed a Shunting complex. They have specialized organs that permit them to hear from five to twelve thousand hertz, and another that can form what we would call speech, yet they maintain their ability to communicate with the other Arcolian forms via a very sophisticated olfactory code.''

"I'm lost," Haggis said.

"They communicate with pheromones," Bachman said.

"By sense of smell," Steubing translated.

"Fantastic," Haggis said dourly. "What about the man on the street?"

Bachman looked at him. "I'm sorry?"

Vonn unfolded his arms and sat up in his chair. "What my brother means is, what does this have to do with all of us? You've told us that the Arcolians we're going to be seeing are no beauty queens. Big deal. Who's fronting the disruption?"

The skinny man paced a tight circle around the mercenaries. "Disruption?"

"You heard me," Vonn said. "It's pretty clear to me that you've hired us to upset the terms of the Arcolian Accord. A lot of people, after all, are pissed off over being at peace with the xenos."

"Hear, hear," Haggis said.

"The way I see this," Vonn continued, "your financier must be an arms manufacturer, grubstake broker, or systems designer that lost a big pot of money when peace broke out, and he wants us to pull the plug on it."

Bachman laughed. "Would it surprise any of you to hear that I don't care whether the Accord stands or falls?"

"No," Steubing said. "People like us can always find work, war or peace."

"Peace." Haggis snorted.

"Peace," Bachman said, waving his arms with a theatrical flair, "has made our job easier by putting the Arcolians within our grasp."

"All right." Vonn's tone was one of disgust. He eased back in his chair. "Pretend that we're all stupid and spell it out for us."

"Pheromonal communications. The name of the ticket is pheromonal communications. Used by thousands of members of the known plant and animal kingdoms, yet almost neglected by the species at the top rung of the ladder.''

"Except for the Arcolians," Steubing said.

Bachman pointed and smiled. "Except for the Arcolians, who seem to have elevated it into an art that we couldn't have dreamed possible. The organs they carry can generate scents to express ideas and emotions our best writers have had trouble expressing. One reason they seemed so fearful during the war was because these scents were so powerful and changed so decisively and at such a quick rate that it induced fear and confusion among our personnel. Even though we generally ignore the sense of smell, it can be very influential, and a lot of our fighting forces became emotional basket cases.''

"We were basket cases," Haggis said, "because they were nailing our people to the bulkheads with spikes.''

Bachman ignored the remark. "Naturally, if you're going to communicate this way, you've got to have a highly sensitive receptor. The Arcolian olfactory system is one of the most sophisticated we've seen yet. From the scents I give off just by standing and speaking, they can tell my emotional state, my health, if I'm telling the truth or lying.

"When we entered into negotiations with the E-forms, there was so much worry about the Arcolians communicating between themselves that we resurrected a nearly extinct breed of dog—the bloodhound—and trained them to react in certain ways to various aspects of Arcolian communication. We used them to prevent the Arcolian negotiators from communicating among themselves so we could negotiate on equal footing. This is where we get that quaint expression 'bring in the dogs.'

"In the ensuing years, many people have realized the potential value in being able to fully detect and interpret the Arcolian pheromonal code. Alas, there have been many attempts at both creating artificial intelligences or modifying the human form to do so, all of them sad failures.

"Perhaps more important, if we can learn to interpret, we can learn to synthesize the pheromones they use. Whoever makes that breakthrough will not only garner the undying gratitude of the galaxy's xenolinguists, but they will also be staring a veritable fortune in the face. As I said earlier, ladies and gentlemen, some of these pheromones have rather marked influential effects on the species Homo sapiens.''

The corners of Vonn's lips turned up. "All right," he said. "You're saying that our job is not directly related to whether or not the Accord stays in effect."

"Correct."

"And I can probably figure who's footing the bill for this little excursion if I gave it some thought. But Mr. Bachman, what exactly is the nature of our mission?"

"In simplest terms," Bachman said, pulling himself up to his full height, "you are going to assist me in kidnapping the xenos and transporting them to a place where they can be . . . examined."

"Roving mother of the universe," Steubing said with a whistle. "We've hit the jackpot."

7

Being alone in his ex-wife's office made James May nervous. In the darkness it was intimidating: the massive surface of the administrative desk, cluttered with stacks of simfiles and z-notes; the commander's chair with its high headrest, looming above it like the dark shape of an alien creature; the way the sounds of his breathing and footfalls resounded in the cavernous structure and then vanished into the thick carpet.

May wandered around the desk and looked at the plaques that were magneted to the walls. Her graduation notice from the academy. She had been at the top of her class. The certificate that listed her as Status Important at the time she had mustered out.

Beyond that were plaques that he had never seen. Maggie had gone back to the academy after the divorce and entered the paramilitary program. She had come out in the top ten of her class. From there, she had gone to command school. There she had been in the top five. After that had been the long, hard drive: the Certification for Commercial Vehicle Command.

From there, no one had placed higher than she.

James May sighed and wandered about the office. "I hope I haven't ruined it for you, Maggie."

He found an overstuffed chair and slumped into it, hands burrowing deep into his pockets. He rubbed the soles of his feet across the carpet, feeling the hairs on the back of his neck rise from the sensation. He closed his eyes and tried to let the rushing silence of the big room swallow him up.

And then, after what seemed like several weeks, there was a squeal.

He sat up straight in the chair. He had been dozing. The opening door had awakened him, and a figure stood in the hatchway, silhouetted by the dim light from the reception area.

"Maggie?" he said groggily, struggling to his feet.

"James?" she said, stepping into the office. The door closed behind her, cutting off the new source of light.

"Just a minute." He started toward the desk, hands out, groping. His shin smacked into something hard, and he staggered back, cursing.

"What are you doing?" Margaret O'Hearn asked.

"I thought I'd be a gentleman and bring up the lights." He looked around the room. He was finding it harder to see after having been momentarily blinded by the outside lights.

"That won't be necessary," she said firmly.

"I thought—"

"You thought nothing. Stay where you are."

He heard her moving. The room's strange acoustics made it impossible to track her.

"You rang?" he asked innocuously.

"You know damned well why you're here, James."

May heard her bump into the command chair and find her way into it.

"I want to know about Duke."

"What's there to know? You got his retinal prints. You probably know more about him than I do."

Her chair hummed. May groped his way back to his seat.

"You're sure you don't want the lights?"

"Positive," O'Hearn snapped. "I want to know who this man *really* is, James. No more fooling. And I want to know where this William Wesley Arbor identity came from, and how he was able to get around the retinal print confirmation. And I want the answers *now*, or you're going to lose the *Angel's Luck*."

He sat down too fast and his back cried out in pain. Wincing and rubbing, he answered his ex-wife. "I swear on the ship, Maggie, I've told you everything I know about Duke. He's a commodities broker from Tetros—"

"Wrong," she said suddenly. "That's wrong. The basic profile on Arbor or Duke or whatever he's calling himself this time around shows that he is no danger to anyone but himself, that he's a balanced individual with no basic phobic tendencies. What we saw outside the Polondo Suite was a classic Psych 13, a xenophobic reaction that could have come out of any behavioral textbook."

There was an electronic chirp from her desk as she activated one of the simfiles.

"Something else interesting, James. Before they locked him up, they ran another Basic Profile just to make sure there wouldn't be any other surprises. You know what they found?"

May was silent.

"That's right. Nothing. He was William Wesley Arbor of the Tetros system. While there were levels of relative guilt, they seemed to be attached to something other than the incident in the hallway. Feelings toward the assault on the Arcolians are nonexistent, James. No remorse. No satisfaction. Not even amusement. What we're seeing here is a complete and utter amnesiac state surrounding what has happened.

"I'm sure you realize the implications of that, don't you?

If we find out this man is a brainwipe, things are going to go badly for you.''

"He's not a brainwipe," May said quietly.

The shadows shifted as Margaret O'Hearn stood at her desk.

"I'm talking *conspiracy*, James, and I don't dare think otherwise. There are a lot of people out there who would like to see the Arcolian Accord fail, many of whom have vast personal fortunes resting on that ultimate outcome. It would mean nothing—and I do mean nothing—for them to bribe some down-and-outer to waste his engines in deep space near the known intersect of a route to Council 5 and plant someone on that ship, someone who is very much the picture of a loser, but who was really a skilled assassin with a wipe wired into his brain. The only problem, James, is that whether or not you knew it, whether or not you were on their payroll, they're going to cut off your head and mount it on a pike because you were directly involved. You were the owner of the damn stellar vehicle!''

"Maggie—"

"I'm not through."

He watched her shadow as her hands rose and fell from her face.

"That hurts me, James, because you're my ex-husband. How is that going to look on my record? It's not like I haven't had enough problems . . ." She trailed off and fell into her seat.

May rose and quietly crossed to her. He knelt and raised a finger to her cheek. It came away moist.

"Maggie—"

"Don't start with that tenderheartedness," she growled. "You never could understand that about me, could you? Whenever I do this, you figure I'm in anguish or my heart is broken or I'm hurting like some damn big-eyed mammal. This happens when I'm *mad*—"

He took her by the shoulders and repeated her name.

"I've put up with this, you know it? I've hidden it, made

excuses, tried to find other outlets because I knew it would keep me from sitting in this office. I *knew* it. But I made it here, James May, and I'm determined that *nothing* is going to take me away from this. Understand?''

"Nothing," he said, wiping tears from her eyes.

She suddenly went cold. Her back became stiff and straight. "That includes you, mister. I swear by my commission that I'll see you in jail or exiled to Sol before you mess up my life again."

He backed away. "I know. I wouldn't have you any other way."

"I let you get away with that half-baked salvor story because I didn't want to know what you were up to," she said. "But all of that's changed now. It's you or me." She took a moment to dab at her eyes and clear her nose. After a deep breath, she made a threat in a low, resonant voice. "You'd better come clean, James."

A chill ran down his spine. "I wanted to tell you, Maggie, and I would have—"

"Spill it," she barked.

"I've got to have your promise of silence, Maggie."

It was the wrong thing to say. She seemed to grow in her seat, shoulders widening, voice dropping, and teeth flashing white in the darkness.

"I promise *nothing*. Where favors from me are concerned, you're through. You don't have a leg to stand on, James May, and I'm going to get to the bottom of this business with or without your cooperation."

He sat on the carpet and crossed his legs. With a hesitant bite on his lip, he started to speak. As usual, he started with details that bore little or no relevance to the initial story other than to set the tone: He focused his ex-wife's attention on his lugging computer components to Edas 11, a planet that he found was known for its silicon deserts.

When she realized that the story was going nowhere, she interrupted and made him move forward in time. His skill in negotiating deals she knew of, as well as the tendency he had of making the worst of a good situation. All he needed to say was that he had taken a few bad breaks. Her imagination was more than capable of filling in the blanks.

So May skipped ahead to his planetfall on Tetros 9 with a cargo of agricultural machinery, and the serendipitous Angel's Luck that fell upon him in selling it. For once he had money, lots of it, and it was to prove his downfall. His co-pilot—surely Maggie remembered Dexter? Of course she remembered him, and she had never trusted the low-life bastard—had absconded with money owed him and left May stuck in a situation of such desperate debt that he would do anything to get out of it.

O'Hearn looked at him. Anything? She knew of things that May could not be paid to do. Stealing the ship back from the debtor she could believe because of the story behind it, something about a criminal organization that Ryuichi Hiro was mixed up in and how they had tried to use that organization's code of honor to buy forgiveness. But when May mentioned the mercenaries, one of whom was deeply involved with the same criminal network as Hiro, her sensibilities were offended.

"You paid Hiro off once," she said in disbelief, "but he upped the ante. So you decided to *rob* him so you could pay off the whole amount?"

May gave a shrug. "Beautiful, isn't it? Robbing Peter to pay Peter."

Hiro had come into possession of a product that was quite valuable to the original owners—so valuable in fact that a large reward had been posted for the product's return. So May and a handful of other brave men and women had landed on Hiro's home world and physically taken the product. Most of them were killed in the ensuing chase across the galaxy, and in the final moments the engines of the *Angel's Luck* had been overloaded until they were nothing less than a hydrogen bomb and jettisoned them into the face of the dreadnought chasing them.

"The *Roko Marie*," James May said. "The wreckage of which now litters the old Garland–Jubilo route."

In the darkness, Margaret O'Hearn raised her hand to massage the bridge of her nose. "You mean to tell me that you deliberately destroyed your engines in order to keep possession of what you had stolen?"

May shifted uncomfortably. "It wasn't exactly me, Maggie. I wanted to self-destruct the ship, us with it."

She gave him an incredulous look.

"It seemed the honorable thing to do," he said.

"So who is the real hero of this story if it wasn't you?"

He drew breath. "Duke."

Quite naturally, she did not believe him. The fact that Duke was from a backward agrarian world was hard enough to believe under the circumstances that at the moment had the young man sitting in the brig of the *Hergest Ridge*.

"Let me get this straight," she said. "Duke is a professional assassin, a pilot, and a nuclear drive logistics expert all rolled into the guise of a mediocre commodities broker from a Class C world? I don't know what's more incredible, James—that story or the fact that you expect me to believe it."

"He's not an assassin," May said. "And he's certainly not an expert in anything that I know of. All I've ever known him to be is a commodities broker, with the exception of one time . . ."

The key, May told her, was in what had been rescued from the clutches of the *Yueh-sheng*, the syndicate for which Ryu-ichi Hiro worked. What they had were the Essence Phials, two hundred of the greatest minds in recent history, their brains processed after death in an attempt to extract the precious knowledge that had been biochemically stored in them. Sometime during the raid to save them, Duke had gotten hold of one, and later on it had been injected into him by a guard who had mistaken it for some kind of psychoneutralizing drug.

"There's the explanation," O'Hearn said. "He's a Psych 21. He was having delusions . . ."

"That's what I'd think, too, were I in your position. But that's not the end of the story."

May told her about it in explicit detail. There was heat. There was fear. The *Yueh-sheng* was on their tail, and while the *Roko Marie* had sustained damage, it would still capture the small merchant ship in a matter of moments. In a flash of passionate idealism, they all decided to destroy the *Angel's Luck*, the phials and themselves included. May bent to the task while Duke disappeared to calm a panic-stricken Winters.

But when Duke returned, there was a gleam in his eye. May would never forget those next few moments. With less than three standard months of practical shipboard experience, the young commodities broker sat in the pilot's chair, expertly overloaded the engines, and then ordered Vonn to jettison them into the face of the oncoming dreadnought.

O'Hearn stared at May, arms crossed. "I suppose you're going to tell me that your friend was given the knowledge of some famous hot pilot."

"Not just any famous hot pilot," he said. "Eric Dickson. 'Reckless' Eric Dickson."

Her face went blank.

"I looked him up in the ship's library—"

"I *know* who he is," she snarled, turning away from May.

"The fact that he sold the laboratory rights on his brain to the Essence Corporation is a matter of public record. Only in his case, they didn't want his mind so much as his name. They figured if a big hero like that signed, they'd have no problem in getting a handful of peckish scientists to follow suit."

"Oh, damn," Margaret O'Hearn said.

"Only knowledge was to be taken from the brain, but apparently some personality was mixed in with it. It didn't occur to me that Dickson was responsible for the shooting until I started thinking back on the whole incident—the bit with the Aiaagan gin, what Duke said just before he fired the gun—he was talking about what had happened to some woman.''

He walked to Margaret O'Hearn's chair and, with a finger to her chin, turned her head to face him. Her eyes shone in the pale light.

''Leigh Brand,'' May said. ''He was talking about his lover, Leigh Brand. Her fighter was captured on one of the Arcolian frontier worlds.''

''Dammit.'' She said the word hard and fast, biting off the end.

He grabbed her shoulders. ''Maggie, it's the truth! What you saw was a xenophobic reaction, but it didn't come from Duke. It came from—''

Her hands turned and knotted around his forearms. ''I'm not cursing you, James,'' she said softly. ''I believe you. I believe you, but there's nothing in the universe that I can do about it.''

8

Duke sat on the bench, knees pulled up to his chest, arms wrapped around his legs. It was the middle of the night, shiptime, and except for the matron and a drunk who had been found wandering the lower decks, the place was empty. From his vantage point, he could see nothing but variegated shades of black and gray and hear the drunk's long snores from down the hall.

He shifted, and his ears filled with the sound of his own motion. The past twenty-four hours had been truly confusing. His last recollection was of being in the Polondo Suite, anxiously awaiting the arrival of the Arcolian delegation. He had gotten a beer and was in the process of lifting the glass to his lips when—

No, he remembered with a smile. It had not been beer. It had been gin, Aiaagan gin, and he had actually been swallowing a shot of it when things had become hazy and dark.

He looked back on taking the drink with a certain amount of pride. He had never been able to bring himself to smell the stuff on Aiaaga. On the other hand, no obnoxious drunk had been goading him, either. That was something he admired about himself; his contempt was often strong enough to over-ride even his own physical urges. Otherwise, he never would have been able to choke down that foul stuff that people supposedly drank for pleasure.

He wondered if his actions had had the effect he had in-tended. But it was beginning to look as if he would never know. Things had grown warm and blurry and had been interrupted by a dream of being in a sweaty little combat-zone jail on some outpost world. Wakening to find himself in the luxury craft's brig had rattled him far less than he would have expected. His dream of the Vicarage seemed to have prepared him for it.

What he was not prepared for was the brace of physicians who came to see him. They irradiated him with strange light, poked electrical contacts into every available orifice, and asked questions composed entirely of non sequiturs such as "answer the following, true or false: How big is the color red?" They drew blood, forced foul liquids through his mouth and nose, and came at him with even more questions. "Yes or no?—Choose a, b, or c."

They were done with him in time for his dinner. The meal was sumptuous looking and delicious smelling, but after gag-ging up what had the feel of grease and the taste of tar all afternoon, he had no appetite. He ate just enough to keep his strength up and turned the rest away.

Next the drunk was brought in. Duke was curled into a ball as the matron, an electric baton in her hand, herded the new prisoner past Duke's cell and down the hall. Duke thought it amusing when the matron referred to the man as lucky, but after a few moments he realized that that was the man's name.

Lucky livened things somewhat by making various de-mands. First he wanted to speak with a solicitor. Then he

wanted to be given a detox injection so he would not get sick.
The matron explained that they did not have any of that kind
of detox, and they sure were not going to hand out Leuten's
to every drunk that wandered through. Lucky then complained that his restraining collar was too tight. "Tough,"
the matron said. In a drunken show of bravado, Lucky tried
to step out of his cell, but the collar lit up and jolted him with
enough electricity to prevent another such display.

After Lucky recovered, he kept Duke entertained with a
monologue about the unjust persecution of the innocent.
Eventually the diatribe slowed to nothing, and the cellblock
was again quiet. Snores came from the direction of Lucky's
cell, and Duke unrolled across the bench and decided that
there was nothing worth staying awake for. He closed his
eyes and started to think of alarming answers to the doctor's
pointless test questions. If they were going to hold him for
no apparent reason, he might as well give them an interesting
psychological profile to play with.

A clatter at the end of the cellblock startled Duke and told
him that he had dozed off. He sat up, momentarily disoriented, and watched as shadows fell down the length of the
hall.

Another Lucky, Duke thought, and started to recline again.
But familiar voices came with the clatter. He stepped up to
the edge of the cell door, being careful not to step into his
collar's activation field. Two figures were being shepherded
in by the matron.

"Duke!"

"Roz!" he said with relief. "Winters."

They walked up to the door and stepped through. Winters
grabbed Duke in a bear hug and lifted him from the ground.
"Mr. Duke," he said. "I'm glad you're okay."

Duke coughed and caught his breath. "Glad you could
come, big guy. How's everything?"

"Okay." Winters reached into a satchel and brought out
an optical reader. "We figured you'd be bored, so we brought
you something to do."

Duke took the device. "Thanks." He smiled.

Roz held out a small box with a small silver disc inside. "Reading material," she said thinly.

He took it and looked at the title. *A Flyer's Life—The High and Wild Times of "Reckless" Eric Dickson.* The blood drained from Duke's head, and he sat hard on the bench.

"I don't think I like this," he said to Roz. "What's going on?"

"You really don't remember what happened?" she asked.

Duke shook his head. "Nobody's bothered to tell me." He handed the reader and disc to Winters and asked him to set it up. Smiling, Winters sprawled on the floor with the device and started to tinker.

"How much," Roz said, "do you remember about saving the *Angel's Luck*?"

"I was there," he said bitterly.

"What about the way you saved the ship? The procedure you used to overload and jettison the engines."

"Vonn did the jettison."

"The overload, then. What do you remember?"

He closed his eyes and tried to recall the noise, the panic, the way the bridge had filled with the smell of raw fear. "I had dreams leading up to the event. Looking back, it seems like they were almost prescient. And yet . . ."

"What about your actions?"

"Like having a word on the tip of your tongue and not being able to get it. Knowing it's there, but not being able to reach it. Only it was frightening, Roz, because in this case I couldn't say for sure that it was there; I'd never studied what I'd done. But it came nonetheless."

"Could you do it again?"

"I don't know. It's all hidden by shadow now. Perhaps under the same circumstances—"

"Fear," Roz said. "Stress. Strange environment. Maybe a few drinks under your belt?"

"I knew the *Angel's Luck*, Roz, and I hadn't been drinking. Not unless—'' He turned for a moment and listened to Lucky snoring in his cell. ''What are you trying to tell me?''

''Duke, you assaulted one of the Arcolians. You took a sidearm from a guard and shot it.''

He fell until his back hit the wall and his hand clapped over his mouth. His eyes filled with tears.

''The Arcolian will live, Duke. Something to do with the bullets in the gun.''

Winters looked up from the reader. ''Mutiny pills,'' he said confidently. ''They've got a hollow metal jacket and inside it is smaller bullets packed in a heavy stuff like oil. They put them in guns on ships because they won't go through the walls. They just go splat.'' He licked two fingers and struck his palm for emphasis.

''The shots you fired didn't penetrate,'' Roz continued, ''but the impact cracked the Arcolian's shell. There was some loss of . . . fluid. It could have been bad because of the way their circulatory system is set up, but they were able to seal it up. They're treating it now with some kind of lime paste—''

''Wait a minute.'' Duke rose from the bed and started to pace the cell. ''Are they sure it was me?''

''I saw you do it,'' Roz said firmly. ''May saw you do it. So did Commander O'Hearn, that ensign of hers, some guards, half a dozen passengers, and two other members of the Arcolian delegation.''

Duke looked out his cell door. He wondered if throwing himself through with enough force would result in a fatal jolt. ''Do you believe me when I say I didn't do it?''

''I believe that you have no recollection of what happened.''

''Dammit, Roz—''

''What's the absolute last thing you remember happening last night?''

He closed his eyes again. ''Aiaagan gin.''

''Is it possible that the gin suppressed your personality to the point where someone else's could come out?''

Duke looked down at Winters, who was running the pages of the biography through the reader. "I see what you're getting at," he said. "It's possible, I suppose. The Essence Product was set up to transfer accumulated knowledge—"

"What did Eric Dickson know about the Arcolians, Duke? Have you given that any thought? To him they were the enemy. His life was devoted to fighting them."

Winters stopped scanning. "You shot a really good pattern, Mr. Duke." He put his thumbs and forefingers together to indicate an oval shape some fifteen centimeters across.

Duke looked at Roz helplessly. "I don't even know what he's talking about. I've never fired a gun in my life."

"But Dickson has."

He turned away from her. She went to him and laid a hand between his shoulders.

"Where's May?" he asked.

"Meeting with the commander. He wanted to come, but under the circumstances, he thought it best not to."

"Thanks, May," he said under his breath. "Thanks a lot."

"I think you should read that biography," Roz told him, "in spite of what you think about the man. You may find some answers. You may even save your own life."

Duke gave her a look of disbelief.

"You assaulted an ambassador with a deadly weapon," she explained. "Not good when the ambassador is human. Worse when the ambassador is Arcolian and most everyone wants to see the peace kept. You might be a hero to a twisted minority, but you're in the hands of the majority." She walked to the cell door. "Come on, Winters."

The big man slowly pulled up to his feet. "I got it fixed for you." He smiled. "I left it at the best part. The pictures."

"Thanks." Duke returned to the bench and curled into a ball.

Roz and Winters walked out and turned down the hall. Duke sighed and looked at the reader's screen. A craggy-featured man with jet-black hair and a too-big nose was leaning with one arm up against the exhaust vent of a single-man zero-atmosphere fighter. Letters stood out from the three-dimensional picture: *Dickson with his most famous fighter, the* Lovely Leigh. *The "Double L," as he called it, was the one in which he led the relief column to Bering's Gate.*

He uncurled and picked up the reader, striking the AD-VANCE button with his index finger. Another holo material-ized, showing a roomful of seated pilots, their helmets on the desks in front of them.

The briefing before the raid on Jasmine 1, where the Ar-colian C-form hatchery was discovered. Dickson is in the third row, second from back. Other notables include Thomas Fortunado (first row front), Leigh Brand (l. of Dickson) and "Laughing Larry" Prieboy (fifth row, third from front).

Staring at Leigh Brand, Duke found he was getting angry because the jockey suit she wore did nothing for her figure and her face was partially obscured by the person in front of her. He punched ADVANCE. Dickson sat in a familiar-looking bar with a bottle of Aiaagan gin raised high in the air. On his lap sat a small woman with hair trimmed into a pilot's cut, cold, hard eyes, and an incongruous smile on her face. She was wearing a duty shirt and fatigues, and Duke recog-nized that her shape was feminine yet well muscled. She had almost beaten him, he remembered, at arm wrestling.

Dickson and Leigh Brand, the caption said, *before the initial sortie to Bering's Gate.*

Duke's throat went rock hard and his lower lip thrust out. Something tickled his cheek, and he brought up his finger to investigate. It came away with a film of liquid on it.

"Dammit," he growled, and shut the reader off. He stuck it under the bench and curled up once again, closing his eyes and moving his mind ahead, trying to pierce the darkness. The shapes and phosphors faded into pure blackness. Search-ing, he tried to open the recesses of his mind.

"Eric," he whispered.

Images flashed and danced across the black curtain he had drawn.

"Are you there?"

Nothing. He cursed. Where was the power of observation that Tetrans were supposed to have? Where was the luck that Anders—poor, dead Anders—had staked his life on? He saw a terrible, bitter irony in his current situation. There he was, William Wesley Arbor, the master of observation, and he could not even look into his own mind.

"Dammit, Eric."

"Yes?"

Duke's eyes flew open. His hands clamped over his chest to feel his heart hammering wildly. He sat up and looked around the cell. There was nothing there. He looked out the door. Nothing still, not in the hall, not in the other cells—

"Lucky," he said in a hesitant whisper. He held his breath and waited. "Lucky?"

There was a loud rasping from down the hall. It was a snore he would recognize anywhere, one that could not be faked.

Duke sighed and leaned back, shaking his head. Asleep and dreaming, he thought. He had to be asleep and dreaming.

He started to lean back, and the light shifted. He rose up again. He felt as if a shadow was growing, not in front of his eyes but behind them. His eyelids felt heavy. He called the matron's name. The feeling passed.

It's the lack of food, or those obscene tests, Duke convinced himself. They've unnerved me. He started to ease down again.

The shadow moved through his mind, slowly, haltingly. Duke's eyelids fluttered shut, and his head started to slump. Catching himself, he snapped his head back up.

The feeling faded.

Duke tried to call the matron, but his voice cracked. His eyes felt gluey, and the light in the cell seemed to dim.

The feeling inched forward again. Duke slid his feet off the bench and stood straight up. His mouth fell open, and he looked down at himself, dropping his gaze from his shoulders to his torso, waist, legs, toes—

He had no conscious memory of jumping up. It was as if he had been jerked to his feet by some unseen force. Trembling, he went back to the bench and sat, waiting for it to happen again.

Nothing.

He bit his lip.

Nothing was happening. His mind felt strangely clear, and he was almost too aware of the detail in the room. He had the eerie feeling that he was not controlling his eyes, that they were independently darting about the room as if seeing it for the first time. Gradually he realized that the shadowy feeling was spreading back into his skull, and his eyes felt thick with it. He became dizzy, recoiled, and lay down on the bench. The feeling filled him, rolling down his spine to the base of his feet.

Don't just sit there. Do something.

Me or it?

Do I have to tell you, boy? Better you than it—

Duke gasped. Someone was talking to him. He had the distinct sensation of someone leaning over his shoulder and pointing out the serious flaws in what he was doing. He looked down to see what he was doing and saw the main board of the *Angel's Luck*. He reached out a hand.

No, not that one. You'll blow the fucker up. The one next *to that . . .*

"May?"

He blinked again. His body felt swollen, bloated with that feeling, and he fought to keep his breath.

"Eric!"

There was a sudden rush that welled up from deep in his bowels, taking the breath from his lungs and flooding it into his brain; the top of his skull corkscrewed off, and the sensation gushed straight up, splattering the ceiling.

Duke's hands knotted, and he opened his eyes. The feeling was gone.

9

He looked sullenly at the bottle before him. It was empty. The glass before him was almost that way. He took a swallow. It tasted bad, worse than he had ever remembered it. Funny, he thought. Usually by the end of the bottle you don't care what it tastes like. Wonder if those little maggots at Supply Q have been watering this stuff down.

Whatever the case, it was something to think about, something to look into. Something to kill the time and take his mind off of the inevitable truth.

He picked up the tumbler and looked into it. Why, he thought, did I have to be so damned good? Why do I have to put up this false front of reckless valor and bravado? Sure as hell the media eats it up, but—

He paused and looked out the window of the officer's club. Outside, the twin suns were making the heat rise from the vast tarmac. It was getting late. The sortie should be coming in before the tarmac got too sticky.

Pain brought a tremor to his right arm. He looked at it blankly. As much gin as he had consumed, there should be no pain, not even from the broken arm.

But the arm was not broken. There was no cast on it, yet the ache was familiar. He had no recollection of a broken arm. Sure as hell, he had split open his head on four occasions, the most infamous of which was on a frontier outpost where it took thirty-three staples to hold the skin over his gleaming skull. His flyer at the time, the Trigger Mortis, *had gone down hard and fast.*

His arm throbbed. He managed to get the glass to his lips and tilt it back. The gin hit his throat, and nothing happened. Typical. Things were going wrong everywhere. This magic stuff was magic no more. General Biej, the sour old bitch, was at the end of her menstrual cycle and she had never liked him anyway—and the sortie due in was late. It had never, ever, been that late before. Something had happened. Something bad, just as he had seen happen to the others.

He looked outside the window again. Shadows flickered across the tarmac, dark arrow shapes that shivered until flickering, silver vehicles started to land.

The glass slammed down, and he hurried out the door. A rushing sound filled his ears as the engines wound down, and he looked into the sky as a small cluster of arrowheads approached. He ran across the landing field, feet sticking in the slowly melting asphalt, until he reached the first fighter down. Smoke was pouring from one of the exhaust vents, and the frame was battered and covered with black smudges.

"Ay," he called to the man scrambling from the control cradle. "Who you with?"

"Ninth Vacc Battalion," the man said. "Squad group six, The Hammerheads." He pulled off his interface helmet and drop-kicked it across the field.

He felt compelled to say something about the abuse of equipment but stifled the urge as he looked to the sky. "You on reconnaissance?"

The flyer stopped ripping off his support suit long enough to nod. "Bering's Gate." He wadded up his suit and unceremoniously stuffed it into the cradle.

"This is your wing, then?"

"No," the flyer snapped, flashing his teeth. "This is the whole fucking sortie!" He jammed his foot into an exposed control panel. "They had something, looked like oil from a distance, hanging around the gate's event horizon. We closed and found it was particles of sand and marbles, nothing bigger than two centimeters. When we hit that . . . shit!"

"The others?"

"Crippled up, mostly. Didn't lose that many in the debris, but we couldn't run. And they had this net, some kind of slender, silvery thing, maybe magnetic, liquiform, hardened in vacc, shot from cannons on their ships. Son-of-bitching xenos!"

"Captured?"

The flyer put his fists on his hips. "Unless our people popped their own tops."

His legs jumped beneath him, scrambling as the battered remnants began to land. One after another they opened, the flyers bailing out at high speed, screaming, crying, cursing, all reporting the same thing.

Captured. Captured. Captured. They wouldn't fire on us, they wouldn't shoot, some kind of nets or glue or magnets in cannons, battered the hell out of us with junk and then reeled us in.

And she was late.

She was nowhere to be seen.

And he had seen what had happened to the others. He had led the sortie to the Cloud of Magellan, *thought to be derelict. But the crew was on the ship, all of them, and they had been disemboweled, their empty carcasses mounted on the bulkheads with metal spikes through their skulls, a warning to all who found them.*

In the blistering midday heat, a metallic voice rolled across the landing field, ordering all available flyers into an emergency scramble.

Numb, he ignored it. He went from one returning craft to another, and she was not there.

"Murdering bastards," he said.

Then came the sirens.

10

"Leigh!"

The room was flooded with light. The casted arm ached miserably, and his clothing was drenched with sweat. Duke realized he was flinching from the loudness in his ears.

"Come on, dammit!" It was the voice of the matron, carrying loud and clear over a harsh, staccato buzzer. Duke ran to the door, then hesitated.

The matron was carrying Lucky over one shoulder, half-dragging him from his cell. She looked up at Duke.

"The door's off," she said, grunting.

He cautiously stepped out. The collar on his neck did nothing. He ran to the matron and took half of her burden under his left shoulder. They started toward the main door.

"Thanks," she said. "I'm pulling a solo tonight."

"What's with the noise?"

"Scare you?"

He nodded.

"Lifepod drill," she told him. "Galactic Trade Commission rules."

"Is that all?" Duke sighed in relief.

"What were you expecting, son?"

"I don't know," he admitted. "Monsters, I think."

11

People were flooding down the hall of the *Hergest Ridge*. Roz stayed to one side, back against the wall, and made her way against the flow of people. She was bumped and battered and given dirty looks, but in spite of it all made steady progress toward the core of the ship.

At last she came to a familiar door and thumbed its buzzer. Nothing happened. She put her ear to the door and tried to listen, but between the intermittent alarm and the noises of the people around her, it was useless. With an open hand, she slapped on the door and shouted.

"Winters! Winters, are you in there?"

Again she tried to listen. Nothing. She leaned on the access button, but it was locked out. Whether it had been done from the inside or outside, she could not tell. Bashing the door with her fists, she called his name again.

From down the hall, motioning to herd passengers, came someone in a ship's uniform. Roz raised her arm and waved until she caught his eye, then signaled him over. With a stern look on his face, he cut across the line of drilling passengers and shook his head reprovingly.

"Why aren't you helping these people to the—" His gaze came up from her borrowed jumpsuit and looked her in the eye. "Oh," he said in recognition. "How can I help you?"

"Peter." She smiled. "I'm trying to find one of our party. You remember Winters?"

"The big guy, right? He's probably on the drill with the others." He took her by the crook of the arm. "You need to come, too."

"You don't understand," Roz said. "Winters is mentally retarded. I'm afraid this alarm may have caused him to panic."

Chiba nodded. "You think he's in there?"

"Locked in."

He pounded on the door.

"I've tried that. The only way to know for sure is to go in."

Chiba pulled a slim plastic card from his breast pocket. "Master key." He smiled, slipping it into the lock. After a moment, the door slid open.

Roz stepped inside the berth and found Winters cowering in a corner. "It's all right," she said, taking him by the shoulders. "Come on out."

He shook his head vehemently. "Mr. Duke's going to blow up the ship again."

Chiba eased in next to Roz. "Everything's fine," he said. "It's just a lifepod drill. We have to make sure everybody knows where to go."

Winters studied Chiba. "Are you telling the truth?"

"It's the rules," Chiba said. "One drill for every standard week of travel time."

The big man's eyes narrowed. "How do I know we're not being chased by the *Yueh-sheng* again?"

"Winters." Roz gasped. "Shame on you."

"It's all right," Peter Chiba said. He inched toward Winters and crouched. "You're worried about me, right?"

"Mr. Li was an Ori, too," Winters said bluntly. "And he got killed."

"So you think if I'm with the *Yueh-sheng*, then I'd be trying to kill you."

Winters nodded emphatically.

"Then," Chiba said, "why wouldn't I have killed you on the *Angel's Luck*? I could have done that, told my boss there were no survivors, and taken my salvor's percentage on your ship and its cargo. As it stands, I'm stuck with my regular salary and a small rescuer's bonus."

Winters shrugged.

"Well, then. What more is there to be scared of?"

"The noise?" It came out in a whimper.

"It scares me, too," Chiba confided. "So if you come with me, we can be scared together."

A smile broke on the big, sullen face. "I forgot about that," he said. "Bear always told me if you had two scared people in the same place, it made them both very brave."

Chiba stood and held his hand down. "Let's go, then."

Winters grasped the hand and pulled to his feet. "C'mon, Roz," he said confidently. "We're going to the lifepods."

Roz gave Chiba a warm smile. "Thank you."

He put his hand on her back and ushered her out of the berth. His touch felt warm and reassuring.

12

There was pandemonium in the Arcolians' suite. At the first sound of the buzzer the air had become heavy with a confused tangle of scents, and the aliens' behavior had become wildly erratic. redbutler, immobilized on its back in one of the adjoining rooms, began a long, unbroken croak and rocked back and forth, legs agitating. killerjoe spun around the room in tight circles, knocking over anything in the way. leighbrand found a corner and shrank down. laceylane was beating the door with its arms, and misterbob was roaming the suite at random, bumping into walls, backing off, and starting in a new direction like some child's toy.

"Indeed," misterbob would say on impact. "Indeed, indeed, indeed . . ."

In the middle of it all was Revel Tesla, who was running from one Arcolian to the other, trying to calm them down.

"There's nothing wrong—" he said to killerjoe, just before the circling Arcolian bowled him over.

"It's a lifepod drill," he told misterbob. "But you don't have to go anywhere. In an emergency, this suite—"

misterbob struck a wall. "Indeed. Indeed. Indeed."

"It's all right," Tesla shouted at the pounding laceylane. "The door's sealed for the drill. It'll be over in . . ." That tack was getting him nowhere. He reached up and grabbed laceylane's arm with both hands to stop it from striking the door. The best he could do was slow things down. He gasped for breath. The Arcolians seemed to have settled on a uniform odor, a heavy, oily scent that made Tesla think of corrosive materials. He shivered, thinking of his one experience in a transgear bay.

Of course. That had to be it. With their chitinous bodies, corrosive materials would be one of the things they would universally fear. The creatures were clearly frightened by the situation.

Another wave of sound and scent swept over him. The buzzer was numbing his ears, and his stomach was becoming sick. He stopped to lean against a chair, breathing deeply, closing his eyes, making himself aware of everything in the room. He concentrated on the smell, tightening his throat to keep from vomiting.

The odor thickened, threatening to overpower him, and then ceased for a moment. There was a pattern to it, a distinct rhythm.

The buzzer. The scent was keeping perfect time with the sound of the buzzer.

Tesla moved quickly across the suite, trying to stay out of the paths of the frightened Arcolians. He went to a holo that was magneted above the suite's decorative hearth, grabbed the top of the frame, and pulled. Servos vibrated and it pivoted down from the wall, revealing an Emergency Standby controller in the holo's underside and a screen where it had covered the wall. The words DRILL—THIS IS ONLY A DRILL flashed in amber.

Tesla activated the board and ordered OVERRIDE.

DRILL, the system insisted. THIS IS ONLY A DRILL.

He keyed another switch. "Priority Three Condition," he told it. "Emergency override."

UNABLE TO READ ORDER.

The buzzer, Tesla thought. He typed the order on the console.

UNABLE TO CARRY OUT ORDER.

He fed it, PRIORITY TWO CONDITION—EMERGENCY OVERRIDE.

UNABLE TO CARRY OUT ORDER—PRIORITY 1A MODE AMBASSADORIAL PRIVILEGE—PROTECTIVE FUNCTION—CANNOT COMPLY WITH ORDER.

"You're scaring the hell out of them!" Tesla shouted.

SYNTAX ERROR UNABLE TO READ ORDER.

Cursing bitterly, he keyed in PRIORITY ZERO EMERGENCY—SYSTEM KILL.

The screen went dark. Tesla was about to cheer when the display filled with random letters and the buzzer returned. One by one, the scramble of letters turned into a message.

UNABLE TO COMPLY—SYS KILL LOCKOUT—PROTECTIVE FUNCTION—LOOP—UNABLE TO COMPLY—SYS KILL LOCKOUT—PROTECTIVE FUNCTION—LOOP—UNABLE TO COMPLY—

Tesla was down to one option. He knelt to one side of the controller and opened an access panel. On the other side was a small door covered with the seal of the UTE Fleet's head office. After shredding the seal with his fingernails, he opened the door and jerked out the controller's logic component.

The terminal went dead and the buzzer stopped. The frantic motions of the Arcolians began to slow as if some internal battery was drained of its last bit of energy. The corrosive scent left the air, replaced by something humid and green.

From its room, redbutler croaked and then stopped.

Tesla could hear the buzzer sounding from other parts of the ship, but the sound was faint, and the Arcolians began to recover. He began to wonder when he heard "indeed," but realized that it came from laceylane, astonished by the fact that it had been trying to break down the door.

"How foolish I smell," it told Tesla. "Trying to batter when I could have used the switch."

He wiped the sweat from his forehead. "It wouldn't have worked. The door seals to form an airlock with the outer passageway. In a real emergency, this entire suite is ejected as an escape pod." He let the logic component dangle from his finger. "Complete with small engines and a nav system."

misterbob clattered over. "Apologies, reveltesla. This behavior of ours is not . . . typical."

The ensign sat heavily in one of the chairs and laid the component aside. "Not to worry. It scared the hell out of me, too."

"Ah, no. Ah, no." That was killerjoe, lumbering toward the others. "Perhaps we had a fearscent manifestation, but it was not entirely the fear. It was more a *chitinous* reaction."

misterbob's head nodded. "Not quite proper, killerjoe. Sapient A-forms hold no knowledge of chitinous reactions." It pivoted. "Assist, laceylane."

"Intermittent vibrations of certain wavelength cause resonances within chitin. Resonances cause involuntary behaviors in chitinframes."

"Reflexes?" Tesla asked.

The room filled with scent as the Arcolians discussed his response.

"Erratic," laceylane said. "Involuntary erratic."

"Like convulsions."

More flowing scents.

"Indeed," misterbob said.

"Convulsions of nerve bundles coupled with fear from chitinous reaction," laceylane elaborated.

"So I was correct when I smelled your fear, then."

The three Arcolians froze, then slowly rotated their heads to look at the ensign.

"You detected fearscent?" killerjoe asked.

"Yes," he said apprehensively. "It was heavy, unpleasant . . ." His hands circled the air, looking for words to describe it. He remembered the transgear bay. "Corrosive," he said decisively.

There came what could only be described as the Arcolian equivalent of a gasp.

"Indeed." misterbob sighed.

"Very good," killerjoe croaked. "Very good."

"Fascinating," laceylane said, pacing. "Unconscious manifestations correctly convey emergent meaning to Sapient A-forms."

"Corrosive," killerjoe echoed. "Abstractive fearscent correctly interpreted."

"Indeed. The potential for pheromonal interactions with Sapients transcends mere emotive manipulation."

The air in the room began to change as the three Arcolians huddled to discuss the new idea, occasionally clicking their arms together. Tesla detected a postthunderstorm freshness, a rich and yeasty aroma, and then a bracing draft of something that reminded him of citric acid.

He could not help but smiling. He had the distinct impression that the Arcolians were very, very pleased.

13

The buzzer had stopped. A hundred people had gathered around a central evacuation hatch and were milling happily, discussing all manner of things. Once the crowd had been given a moment to calm down, Peter Chiba keyed into the local public address system.

"Ladies and gentlemen," he said. "I'd like to thank you for your cooperation. This is one of the smoothest lifepod drills I've had the pleasure of working." He paused to smile at Winters and Roz. "Potentially hazardous situations were dealt with in the proper manner, and everything ran smoothly. In a true evacuation, we would have gone through this airlock to a life-support pod, taken a seat assignment, and proceeded in an orderly manner."

There was laughter.

"Between systems, the pod would deliver a high-priority emergency signal until pickup, and is capable of sustaining its passengers for twenty-one days, which is more than enough time for rescue."

Winters and Roz exchanged nervous glances.

"Within an orbital system, an alert beacon would be activated that would ensure pickup in a matter of hours."

"What about pirates?" someone asked.

"We're too close in to the Civilized Core to worry about pirates," Chiba said confidently. "The worst you're going to find in this part of the galaxy is privateers, and they're much easier to deal with. Most will see that you are returned to safety, and some will go out of their way to do so. You may wish to pay tribute to them, and some may require it. You won't have your furs or your jewels, but you'll at least be alive."

The crowd's reaction was mixed.

"Are there any more questions?"

"When is the next one?" someone asked.

"There are no further drills scheduled between now and the time we reach Council 5." Chiba put his finger to his ear, listening to a message from the bridge. "If there are no further questions, this group has been given the green light on the exercise. After you congratulate yourselves on your conduct, you're dismissed."

Slowly the people in the hall began to go their separate ways, punctuating their exit with the nervous laughter of having completed an undesirable task. Winters started to leave, but Roz insisted that he stay behind to thank Peter Chiba.

The salvor stayed busy until well after the hall had emptied, relaying information to the bridge through a small handset and reading feedback on its small screen. When he had the results of the drill, he disconnected the handset from the airlock's control console and holstered it on his belt.

"Not bad," he told Winters and Roz. "An eighty-seven percent success rate."

"That doesn't sound that great."

"It would have been better, but there was some sort of component failure in one of the Ambassadorial Suites, which accounted for ten percent of the error. The other three was due to people dragging their feet or going to the wrong escape pod—there's always someone."

They fell into step and started down the hall, chatting about nothing important. After a while, Winters thanked Chiba profusely for his help during the drill. Chiba treated him well, shaking his hand, talking to him as if he had been just another errant adult, and answering his questions as simply as possible.

Winters was all talked out by the time they reached his berth. He shook Chiba's hand, pecked Roz on the cheek, and then painstakingly punched in the code to open his berth. The door sealed shut on the big man, and he smiled as it did, grinning like a child with a new friend.

"I want to thank you for being so nice to him," Roz said when they were walking again.

"It's no problem," Chiba said. "I deal a lot with—don't take this wrong—that age group."

"No offense taken. I think it's important for him to have that kind of reinforcement."

"You're talking like I'm something special. I'm not."

"But you're normal," she said. "You have to understand that Winters is coming from a mercenary background. All of the acceptance he's ever gotten is from men who admire his capacity for violence."

"His childlike capacity for it."

"Exactly. It comes naturally to him, and it's been exploited. To him, toughness is the norm, which is why he didn't want to come out of the room. The alarm made him a little scared, but he didn't want to show that side to total strangers. He was afraid of rejection. What you showed him is that it's all right to be scared, and that there are ways of dealing with fears other than striking out at them."

"You sound like his—" Chiba caught himself. "Sister."

"Thank you," she said. "I'm glad you were the one who came along, Peter. Winters was impressed with you from the beginning."

He stuck his hands in his pockets. "You mean when I came onto your ship?"

"Exactly. You and your partner came in without weapons. He figured you were extremely brave to do something like that."

"Well," he said, pleased with himself. "Wait until Zack hears about this."

Roz stopped at a door, finger hovering over the lock. "Well," she said, "here's where I get off. Thanks again for your help."

Chiba stretched uncomfortably and checked the chronometer on his wrist. "Listen," he said, not quite looking at her. "I'm going to be off this watch in a few minutes. If you'd like to tag along, maybe we could go somewhere after I get checked in, maybe have a friendly drink?"

She cocked her head.

"Of course, if you're attached to one of those guys on the merchant ship—maybe I'm out of line here . . ."

"No," she said quickly. "You're not. I'd love to go with you, Peter Chiba, and if you try to back out, I'll be very disappointed."

"All right, then." He smiled. With a slight bow, he extended his arm. "After you."

All Roz Cain could think was: how nice. How nice that he asked instead of assumed. How nice that he thought of me first. How nice that he's polite. How nice that he doesn't kill for a living.

14

Vonn sat in a chair in his berth, staring at the holo that took up one wall, assembling the parts that Bachman had given him until they resembled a blunt canister with a snubbed barrel on one end and a handle on the other. He continued adding parts: a round grip that could be attached just behind either side of the barrel for right- or left-handers, a trigger assembly, and a clip that slid up inside the bottom of the body.

He felt uncomfortable with the weapon. Not only had Bachman armed everyone with standard bullets that could puncture and ricochet, but the weapons to fire them were highly unreliable, their popularity stemming from the fact that they could be broken down into innocuous-looking parts like pens, lighters, and flashlights. Vonn thought of the shipboard inspectors with a certain amount of disdain. Any seasoned mercenary would know enough not to allow merchandise from Xegg Manufacturing on board. Of course, Bachman had managed to get the ammunition on, as well. He struck Vonn as being resourceful and opportunistic.

According to plan, the fireworks would begin when the *Ridge* geared down into the Council system. Bachman had it on good authority that a blockade was being organized by anti-Accord factions in the hopes of keeping the Arcolian delegation off number five. When the commander realized that, her immediate duty would be to her passengers and the delegation itself, and she would begin negotiating with the blockade leader. It was such a good diversion that Bachman was not about to ignore the circumstances.

While all that was going on, Vonn, Haggis, and Steubing would assemble near a lower airlock, breach it to give the impression that the liner was being boarded, and begin shooting their way toward the main drive system. Vonn had immediately protested, saying that the diversion would not fool anyone. Real pirates would not be found in that part of the galaxy, let alone near a flotilla large enough to blockade a planet. Should they be crazy enough to approach a luxury liner the size of the *Ridge*, they certainly would not shoot their way on board—with standard bullets, no less.

Bachman stared the mercenary down. "Yours is not to debate the logic of this plan," he said. "Your job is to threaten the continued functioning of this ship. By heading toward the main drive and inflicting as many casualties as possible, you will be doing exactly that. As a result, the commander will be forced to compromise the guard around the Arcolians, which will make them inferior to our numbers and firepower.''

Once the diversion was well under way, Bachman's group would go into action. Wearing filtration masks so the Arcolians' pheromones would not affect them, they would shoot their way into the suite, force their way in, and convert the suite to an escape pod. After pressure-sealing the Arcolian delegation into one of the smaller rooms to prevent pheromonal influence, Bachman would jettison the suite and be intercepted by a member of the blockade who was on their payroll.

''What about us?'' Vonn had asked.

''You must reach Drive Logistics,'' Bachman had said icily. ''Your lives depend on it. You are to sabotage the main controller so the *Hergest Ridge* cannot move—we certainly don't want them to follow us. Then you can evacuate in one of the escape pods. You will be picked up by people on my payroll.''

Or blasted all to hell and gone, Vonn thought. Sure. I've heard this scam before. ''What about the other passengers and the crew of the *Ridge*?''

''If they're between you and the engine room, kill them. If not, they can be left to fend for themselves.''

Vonn sighed and polished the Xegg gun with the edge of his sleeve. He had not liked the sound of that, either. It was one thing for a ship the size of the *Hergest Ridge* to stare down a handful of smaller ships, but cripple the engines and not only would the electromagnetic shielding and weapons be out, but the maneuver and life-support systems would be seriously compromised, as well. With a friendly blockade, the ship could sit safely with passengers and crew rotting until one side gave in. If there was any aggression on the part of the blockade, the smaller ships could pick the liner apart before anyone realized what was happening.

There had been a time when that would not have bothered him. There had even been a time when the prospect of such a job would have amused, even delighted, him. But he had been through so much of late. He had been close to death before, but it had never seemed real until stealing the phials and escaping from the *Yueh-sheng*. And while he had held death in his arms, there was something about holding Anders in the halls of the *Angel's Luck*, the body growing slowly cold after vomiting blood, that had overwhelmed his emotions. It haunted him even now, as he sat with closed eyes in the quiet of his berth.

With a shiver he opened his eyes, trying to avoid the grisly images. It did no good. When his lids fell again, the scene faded back into view. If there was only some way he could change it, alter it so he could live with it.

Let's give it a try, he told himself. All I've got to lose is the memory of a brother.

Vonn closed his eyes and let the scene rise again.

"I don't feel so good," Anders said. His back hit the wall, and he started to slide to the floor. There was blood.

Vonn's mouth opened in a scream. Someone, Winters, had pushed him to the ground. Then Winters was stepping over Bear, and Bear no longer had a face.

"Anders. *Anders!*—" He reached a hand to his brother-in-arms and stopped. That was it. This was where the revision had to come. Under no circumstances was he to let Anders die in his arms. Squeezing his eyes shut, he pushed against his memory, trying to keep his feet rooted to the spot. The scene began to look strangely surreal. Winters and May were moving in slow motion, as if they were slogging through water. After a moment, they stopped.

Did it, he thought. I did it I did it—

"What a rotten brother you turned out to be."

"What the hell?" Vonn looked around at the frozen scene. He thought it had been Anders's voice, but Anders was not speaking.

"Pick me up," the voice said.

Vonn startled.

"Do it, Vonn. There's no way you can do this, no way you can alter the past. Besides, I've got something I need to tell you."

"You can tell me now," Vonn said.

"Vonn, you bastard, you pick me up right now."

Vonn started to move, slowly, sluggishly. The scene came back to life, and Anders's face lit with a dying fire.

"Vonn. Promise me something. Don't go under. All right?"

Vonn was still reaching, mind still trying to formulate an answer. Blood gushed from Anders's lips, and he closed his eyes.

Winters was still screaming, still jerking grenades from his belt and tossing them at the well-dead guard. May threw himself at the big man and knocked him into the wall, telling him to stop.

Vonn reached for Anders and pulled him up. "Don't, brother. Don't—"

The dead mercenary's eyes popped open. "Don't 'brother' me, you bastard."

Vonn felt his grip on Anders's shoulders grow weak. "But it wasn't my fault," he bawled.

Anders looked down at the holes in his chest. "These? Hell, that's all part of the game." He paused to cough and to wipe clotting blood from his lips. "It happens."

"If you're not mad then why—"

"I'm not mad about dying, Vonn. I'm mad about you selling out your friends. In fact, I'm *pissed*."

"No!" Vonn cried. "Me? Never! What do you think I am, a member of the *Yueh-sheng* auxiliary?"

"No," Anders said grimly. "But you're no brother of mine. No brother-in-arms would dare take up another job before the one he's on is finished."

"What are you talking about?"

Anders smiled. Blood was congealing in the cracks between his teeth. "I'm talking about the Essence Phials."

"That's through with!" Vonn protested. "You missed that part. We beat the *Yueh-sheng* fair and square—"

"What about getting them to Council 5? Wasn't that part of the deal? You're running out on the contract."

"Like hell I am." Vonn released his grip on Anders and pushed him away. "We're headed there now. Commander O'Hearn is May's ex-wife, so she's tight with us. We don't even have to screw with covering our tracks by way of the Jubilo system, because everyone thinks we're dead."

Anders let go of his weapon. It clattered to the floor. "Have you forgotten about the blockade? What happens if you leave this ship crippled and those foam-at-the-mouth xenophobes get on board? By the time the law gets here it'll be every man for himself, and there'll be such an investigation—"

"Don't give me that." Vonn tagged Anders in the chest. It made a strangely hollow thump. "May's a smooth operator. He can handle himself. He can—"

Anders raised a bloody finger. "Just a minute." He looked away, cocked his head, and nodded as if listening to something.

"Anders?"

Anders looked at Vonn. "Li wants me to tell you something. He says, 'What about Duke?' "

"Duke can handle—"

"Duke is a commodities broker." Anders glared. "Damn what you might think about his Tetran luck, he doesn't belong in any of this. And what about Winters? What about your dear Roz?"

"Roz," Vonn said with a sniff, "is out of the picture."

"They all are. You've sold them all out."

"Anders, you don't under—"

"And worst of all, *brother*—" His lip curled up at the last word. "You've sold yourself. You really think that Bachman will have someone pick up your escape pod once you eject from the engine room? You're talking about a man who set up his own people to take a beating just so he could prove that you're worthy of being on his side. Those people were certainly on his regular payroll. How do you think he's going to treat temporary help?''

''It's not going to make any difference. I'm sure that May's cut me out of the Essence deal.''

Anders shook his head. As he did, the skin of his neck tightened and cracked. ''Did he really say that, or did you just get on a mad and think it? You screwed up, Vonn.''

''How?'' Vonn demanded.

''You forgot our code of honor.''

Vonn's hands tightened into fists, but before he could bring them to bear, Anders stretched back and started to lie down. ''No,'' Vonn said quickly. ''Don't.''

Anders stopped and stared into his eyes.

''I'm really confused. You've always been the one who talked sense to me. Can't you do that now?''

Anders shook his head. ''I can't. I'm not really Anders, you see.'' He started to cough.

''Don't play games with me, brother.''

Anders kept coughing, a deep, rasping hack that sent jolts through his entire body. Blood leaked from the holes in his chest and the skin of his face began to peel. The cough turned into a gag. Anders cleared his throat, put his hand to his mouth, and pushed something into his palm with his tongue.

''Are you all right?''

''No,'' Anders said bluntly. ''I'm dead.'' He took Vonn's hand and pressed something cold into his palm. ''Here's something for you to think about.''

Vonn closed his fingers around the object and looked down at his hand. When he looked back at Anders, the mercenary was slumped on the floor, eyes closed. He slowly lifted his fingers, sticky with blood, to study the object that Anders had coughed up. It was covered with blood and tissue and phlegm. Mushroom shaped, it was chipped and pitted and stressed from heat.

A lead slug.

His mouth dropped open and he recoiled in horror, head shaking, room spinning, gasping for air—

A short cry from his own throat made him realize where he was. Breathing hard, he looked at the Xegg gun that had fallen to his feet. The air in the berth seemed stale and humid. Vonn stood to activate the climate control, and something heavy rolled across the palm of his hand.

His throat closed.

He opened his fingers and looked down. He was holding one of the loads for the weapon. Powder combustion, lead slug, metal jacket, the way they had been made for centuries. Fully capable of puncturing bulkheads, making wild ricochets . . .

. . . and killing.

He dropped the round onto his bed and sat heavily in his chair. Nervous laughter spilled from his lips.

Battle fatigue. Is that what it was? Was that what it felt like?

No. Never. He had never had that problem. He had heard some real horror stories from others, true, but he had laughed them off as figments of alcohol-soaked imaginations.

Somehow, it didn't seem as funny to be experiencing one of those stories. Especially since he was stone sober.

15

Duke rubbed his eyes. He had been reading about Eric Dickson for several hours already and the glare from the screen was giving him a headache. Still, he could not help but be fascinated with the flyer's life. As foreign as the concept of enlisting to fight a war was to the young commodities broker, there were elements in Dickson's biography that had an eerie, familiar ring to them.

One week before combat assignments were given out to those who would be leaving the Narofeld Training Station, the Arcolians launched an assault sortie against P-3-A, a manned recording station in an asteroid belt that down-loaded information directly to Narofeld. The sortie was jumped and repelled by two squadrons of green cadet fly-ers, but not before the Arcolians had damaged P-3-A's analytical recording system. This blind-sided the Narofeld system, and the only way to restore it to full defensive capabilities was to effect immediate repairs.

Word reached the Narofeld Training Station late on a weekend evening. Twenty-four of Top Flight's members were off base on liberty. The twenty-fifth, Eric Dickson, was on the field, performing a maintenance on his Vacc Fighter that was ordered by Derrald Deakes, the top po-sition cadet who was resentful of Dickson's reckless but much-admired style of piloting. At the time the message requesting components for the P-3-A system came in, Dickson had come to the Aerodome's Nerve System in search of spare parts.

According to record, Dickson was under no obligation to volunteer for the mission. As an unassigned fighter with no prior record, he was still considered a cadet. But when he stepped forward from the group of murmuring pilots and requested the duty, none of the others objected to letting the young upstart go. Most of them had seen Dick-son fly. Those who had not had heard of his style. With the possibility that Arcolian shift fighters were still within the asteroid's sphere of influence, it would be dangerous, but nothing the young flyer would not be able to handle.

As fate had it, the mission went off without a hitch. Piloting an old Jaluka 26 cargo heist, Dickson had the parts to P-3-A in a matter of hours. None of the dreaded shift fighters appeared, and he was back at Narofeld before Deakes's leave had ended.

Duke looked up. He had been hearing voices from down the hall, and he had just noticed a faint scrabbling sound across the hull of the ship. For a moment he was back on Tetros, listening to the sound of rodents exploring the concrete floors of the family abattoir. But the current sound had a resonance to it, a rich sound that told him it could not be one of the easily frightened slaughterhouse voles.

It sounded bigger. Much bigger.

He instructed the scanner to save his place, shut it down, and laid it on the bench. With slow, deliberate movement, he eased to the door. A shadow was growing in the hallway, big and hulking, without a head. He stared at the floor, fascinated.

"Mr. Arbor?"

Duke startled and jumped back, hand to his chest. He looked up to see the matron.

"Are you all right?"

"You scared me." He laughed nervously and then looked back at the floor. The shadow was still there, but it was not coming from the matron.

"You've got a visitor," she told him, "but you can refuse if you want. As a matter of fact, if you'll trust my judgment, I think you'd rather not, but under the circumstances I have to ask."

"Who is it?"

The shadow continued to grow until it filled the hall. Duke looked up to see a small hunched figure, brick-red, wrapped in purple, shuffling his way.

"Oh." He smiled. "Oh, my. Yes. By all means." He bit his lip and stared at the Arcolian. "Are you certain?" he asked, looking directly at it.

The head moved up and down. "Yes." It was a cracking sound. "I am certain."

The matron shrugged. "Go right in, Ambassador. I'll be right here if you need me."

"Indeed," it said. "You must call me misterbob, matron-maam. I am in no danger from this one. I smell no fear from him, no malevolence. You must go about your duties."

"I have orders," she protested.

"Indeed. Then I must claim Ambassadorial Privilege. I must speak with this Sapient in private."

"I'll be watching on the monitors," she insisted, then vanished down the hall.

Duke could not help but smile at the large creature as it hobbled into the cell. "Welcome," he said in a loud voice. "Do you need a place to sit?"

The head shook. "No, williamarbor. E-forms have chairs built in." The Arcolian found a suitable place in the cell, shifted forward, and shrank a dozen centimeters.

"It's nice to see you, Ambassador, although I regret the circumstances—"

misterbob waved a hand. "You need not to shout, william-arbor. E-form capacity for hearing is well adequate to hear you. Indeed, also, you must call me misterbob. We have labored hard to take names comfortable to Sapient A-forms. We have studied many coded transmissions from your worlds in order to find these."

"misterbob," Duke said. "Mister Bob? The old holo series? *It's Mister Bob!*"

"Indeed." The Arcolian seemed pleased. Duke could smell what felt like salt air at the beach. "You are familiar, then?"

"A little," Duke said. "I've only seen it in rebroadcast. I don't think it's at all appropriate for you, though. The hero of *It's Mister Bob!* was a real—"

"It matters little," misterbob interrupted. "You find the name comfortable?"

"Yes," Duke nodded. "Very."

"My assistant is called laceylane."

"laceylane. Lacey Lane? The singer?"

"Indeed, indeed. One of our group fears the Sapient A-forms. He is called redbutler."

"redbutler," Duke echoed. He could not exactly place that one, unless it was the mispronunciation of a character's name on an old series called *The Tara Chronicles.*

"killerjoe."

Duke laughed. "You're kidding. One of your group took the name Killer Joe?"

"We inferred from your broadcasts that he is a man of importance."

"He's an actor," Duke explained. "Well, sort of. He's a professional zero-grav wrestler."

"Not the most least of our group is leighbrand."

Duke's mouth fell open, and he choked.

"This name is familiar to you?"

He fought to swallow but could not, and words would not come out of his mouth. He nodded.

"You scent of strong emotive reaction."

Duke sighed. He finally forced out. "Leigh Brand. That is very moving, Ambassador."

"Indeed. And you must call me misterbob, williamarbor."

Duke closed his eyes and was finally able to swallow. When the sadness had passed, he looked up at the Arcolian. "Then you must call me Duke."

"That is so simple," misterbob said. "I wish to speak to you with respect."

Duke considered that for a moment, then broke into a wry smile. "All right, then. How about Mr. Duke?"

"Indeed. misterduke." The scent of pleasure was there again, and Duke found that he could understand it. There was a definite thrill in being able to communicate with an alien sentient being.

Duke shifted in his seat. "As I said before, misterbob, I'm terribly sorry about the reason you had to come here. What I did, it was inexcusable, but—"

misterbob's hand came up again, and Duke paused. He thought for a moment and was amazed. It was not just the spoken language that they were learning. They were picking up every nuance of it, even the body language.

"I scent no guilt, misterduke. What I do scent is pain, confusion, grief."

Well, bring in the dogs, Duke thought. "Ambassador—"

"misterbob. Please."

"misterbob, forgive my lack of guilt. I—"

"Forgive?" misterbob pondered that. "laceylane is not here to explain this."

"Excuse," Duke said. "Overlook. Forget."

"Indeed. I understand now."

"I have no guilt," Duke continued, "because I have no memory of the event. I have only the word of others who insist that I was the one who shot—" He paused. "Which of you was it?"

"redbutler."

"redbutler. Well, I only have the word of others who saw me do it. Because of that, I do feel grief and confusion. I am accused of this, but I don't remember it, and while the tests show that I am not capable of such an act, I seem to have done it."

"Speculation among us suggests that redbutler's phobias may have triggered responses in williamarbor," misterbob said. "Pheromonal action on his part may have had subliminal effects on Sapient A-form williamarbor."

"I can follow that," Duke said. "In other words, you think we scared the hell out of each other."

"This hell part I do not understand, misterduke."

"Forget it," Duke said. "It's a pheromonal inference used frequently among Sapient A-forms."

"Indeed," misterbob purred. "Much like 'fucking son of bitch-bastard.' "

Duke bit his lip to keep from laughing. "Indeed," he slurred.

"It is forgiven. And now, williamarbor, we must have you forgiven of your actions on redbutler. You scent of the truth when you speak of this event. It may be redbutler who was as much at fault as you, so you must forgive us this."

"I wish it was as easy as that," Duke told him, "but it's not. By doing what I did, I broke the laws of my people, and I have to pay whatever penalty they assign."

misterbob rocked back and forth on his built-in chair. "This is a most curious behavior among the Sapient A-forms. Such a respect for The Life in others that form-shifting experiments are forbidden and alteration of form by others is punished. Indeed, this is hard for me to scent."

Duke sat on his bunk, studying the ambassador. "I don't . . . I'm not scenting you, misterbob."

"On Arcolus," misterbob began, "we put no value on The Life within us. Our chitin-forms exhaust, and we must pass through to . . . perhaps you would call it a Z-form. The task we have is to live and be useful. We colonize, we adapt. We are directed to become symbiotic with the places we find, and to that end we shift our own forms. It is what we do, williamarbor. It is our joy. No Arcolian would think to refuse assistance with shifting. If the shift is of no use, they pass on to Z-form. If the shift is of use, they will serve us well."

Duke took a deep breath. "So when you go to other planets, instead of changing the planet so you can live on it, you change yourselves."

"Indeed," misterbob said. "One reason for the war between our Sapient forms."

"How do you do this?" Duke asked. "I mean, do you use surgery? Ah, what I mean is, do you open the chitin and shift the inside? Do you have extra parts that can be exchanged? I do not scent how you can do this."

There was a grating sound that set Duke's teeth on edge. With the pleasurescent that was in the air, it could only be taken for a laugh. "No, misterduke. Form-shift is a simple matter. We determine which form would best function on the found lands. Then we rewrite the spiral codes for new forms and alter the roe before they become hatchlings."

"Spiral code." Duke's face burned with the realization. "Genetic engineering!"

misterbob's frame heaved in a shrug. "I cannot scent this 'genetic engineering.' "

"Never mind," Duke said. "How long have you been doing this, misterbob?"

"I do not do this, williamarbor. I am an ambassadorial E-form."

"Y-your people," Duke stammered. "Your race. How long have they had this ability?"

"For much of our history. We have many forms, but the Sapient A-forms are only interested in what they call our A-forms, B-forms, C-forms, D-forms, E-forms, and F-forms."

"But there's more?"

"You would number them in the hundreds, misterduke."

"Have you told any of my people about this? They'd love to hear about it."

The air grew strangely heavy. misterbob's throat gave off a dissonant rattle.

"This is kept to ourselves, williamarbor. I scent your excitement. This is not good. Forgive my mention of this. We understand this is a break in the chitin for the Sapient A-forms."

"You don't . . . you don't scent me, misterbob. We've been trying for centuries—"

The rattle came again. "We assimilated much about the Sapient A-forms during the war," misterbob explained. "We sought peace over the found lands, but our A-forms were unable to communicate with the Sapient A-forms. Pheromonal messages only served to agitate the Sapients, while the Sapients' frequency modulation went unheeded by Arcolians. Thus, misterduke, we sought to create the E-forms exclusively to communicate with your forms. This necessitated that we study the Sapient A-form spiral code."

An image came to Duke: a derelict ship, airlocks blown, hard vacuum inside and out. Along the bulkheads of the lower decks was the crew. A single, shining metal spike had been driven through each forehead to attach the body to the wall. Skin had been removed from the bottom of the rib cage to the top of the pelvis, and all of the internal organs were gone. There was no blood, no brain, no sign of a struggle.

"The mutilations," he said, astonished.

"Understand, williamarbor, that it was necessary for us to have evidence of your spiral code. No harm was meant. The Sapient A-forms fought against us with no scent of fear.

The Sapient A-forms were keen to capture Arcolians, seemed fascinated by our chitinous forms. We wrongly scented that you were doing the same, looking to make peace. We wrongly scented that it would be equitable for us to take matter containing the spiral code from the Sapient A-forms and let them pass on to the Z-form.''

''Instead,'' Duke said, shocked, ''the war was prolonged.''

''Indeed.'' misterbob's epithet was almost a sigh. ''At last we ended it by allowing you to capture E-forms, which learned to communicate. A fascinating time, williamarbor.''

''But useless,'' the Tetran sighed. ''No war is ever good, misterbob.''

''What strange creatures you Sapient A-forms are. You claim to have no use for the war between us that ended, yet you fought it so well. Can you explain this behavior?''

''No.'' Duke gave a bitter laugh. ''No more than I could explain why I attacked redbutler.''

''Indeed.'' misterbob began to nod. ''Again our attitude toward The Life separates us. You have done nothing to redbutler, unless to perhaps reinforce his fear of your forms. I feel that no harm has been done, yet you insist on penalty.''

Duke shrugged.

''A most fascinating situation. Most fascinating. When you cracked redbutler's chitin, I noted a most distinct fearscent. Yet you scent delight when communicating with me. Do you fear me?''

''No,'' Duke said. ''Why should I?''

''You do not fear me as a butcher of your kind?''

''That was the memory of another.''

''Most fascinating. Most fascinating. Indulge me, misterduke. I wish to communicate with you.''

''Sure,'' Duke said, relaxing and sitting back. ''What do you want to know?''

''Close your eyes, misterduke. It is part of the process.''

Duke closed his eyes. ''All right.''

"You must cease modulated communication. It distracts from pheromonal essences."

Duke took a deep breath. The smell shifted to that of a pine forest and then to greasy tar. He marveled at the way the fragrances changed so utterly, without mixing.

"What does this evoke?" misterbob asked.

"Roses," Duke said.

The Arcolian shifted. "And this?"

It was hard to identify. "Sawdust?" he asked.

"And this?"

"Home." It was drying manure in the fields.

"And now I clear your sensory apparatus."

Duke inhaled. He smelled—nothing. Not the room, not his skin, not the clammy atmosphere of the cell. He was receiving nothing. "Amazing," he said. "It's—"

Suddenly the smell was overpowering. It was sharp and choked him, making him cough. He bolted up, eyes watering. "What the hell's that?"

"Communicate it with me," misterbob said.

"Heavy cleaner," Duke said, coughing. "Ammonia."

"Indeed. And what does it evoke?"

"It makes me sick. I used to have to work with the stuff at home, cleaning the killing slabs at the abattoir. That was one season I'll never—" He stared at the Arcolian, stunned. "—forget."

"Indeed. A most interesting behavior in the Sapient A-forms. Pheromonal stimuli serves not to communicate but to bring forth memory. Your memory of home, misterduke, is a most interesting development. Close your eyes for one more."

He did so. There was nothing, and then something he recognized immediately. "The hit," he said.

"Most interesting!" the Arcolian exclaimed.

Duke's eyes popped open, and he was overcome by a wave of dizziness. "What did I just say?" he asked in panic.

"Something I could not scent. Would you elaborate on what this evoked?"

Duke sighed with relief. The Arcolian had not caught it. Even if it had, it might not catch the connection. "It smells like guns," he said. "It's the smell after you've fired a gun."

misterbob wavered for a moment. "You scent of the truth, williamarbor. Your memory is most pure. I value the communication we have had." The creature leaned back, lifted up, and began to move toward the door.

Duke hopped off of the bench. "Wait," he called. "Where are you going? I don't understand. I cannot scent this."

"williamarbor," it said. "You have been given two scents from the event with redbutler. What you described as ammonia is the scent of our life fluids. The other, the cordite, you correctly identified, but you put no context on them together. Your memories are pure, your scent reveals. As the Sapient A-forms say, I believe you. I saw you there and scented you, although your pheromones strike me now as different. I can only conclude that you are innocent, misterduke. I must do what I can that you do not face penalty." It inched out the door.

"misterbob—"

"We will continue this mutual study at a later time. Indeed. I must communicate with my others."

The Arcolian ambled down the hall, its scrabbling sound diminishing until it was out of the jail complex. Duke watched it leave with disbelief, then slowly relaxed as his sense of smell returned to normal. When misterbob came back, he promised, he would tell him of Eric Dickson and Leigh Brand. Perhaps the Arcolian could even intoxicate him with the scent of Aiaagan gin, and it would evoke the memory that he did not have and did not want.

16

He woke up disoriented.

The place was dark, seemed cold, and smelled funny.

He hopped off of the bench, started for the hall, and ran into a wall. Looking around the room, he saw a zipbed, a lo-grav toilet and sink. There was no door, just an opening in the wall. He headed straight for it, but as he neared, his neck began to tingle. Putting his hand to his throat, he felt the collar.

"Jail," he said. "I'm in a damn jail."

There was rustling from down the hall and a discontented voice. "Not again."

"Who's that?" he barked.

"Who else?" it grunted. "Lucky."

He stepped away from the door, and the collar stopped tingling. "What am I doing in here?"

An annoyed sigh. "What else, pal? You broke the law."

"What did I do?"

"Ease up, pal. It's late."

"I mean it!" he shouted. "What did I do?"

"Last I heard, you killed someone. Nice going, pal. I bet you do the dangle."

He turned away from the door and looked around again, eyes accustomed to the darkness. He felt so alone, so helpless. If only he could find something to help ease the nagging sense of loss he felt.

Under the bench he found an optical scanner. He sat on the floor and pulled it into his lap. It was a model he had never seen before, yet he was very familiar with the way in which it operated. It was disconcerting, yet that was the way things had been of late.

He switched it on. The screen flickered to life. *A Flyer's Life—The High and Wild Times of "Reckless" Eric Dickson.* Odd, he thought. Why would I be reading this? The machine asked if he wanted the last page he had read. Cautiously he pecked YES.

The screen filled with letters.

But the gears of justice were not free to turn on Narofeld. They were inexorably tangled in the red tape of military procedure and slowed by the machinations of the war effort. Eventually, the High Tribunal received the official autopsy report on Derrald Deakes. He had received a severe blow to the throat and suffered a crushed larynx and windpipe. Swelling had set in, and he had suffocated to death while lying in the hopelessly outdated Narofeld Station Hospital.

"Deakes," he said, astonished. Deakes had been killed and—

Had he done it?

He leaned against the wall and rubbed his eyes. It was there, he knew. If there was not so much fog . . .

There were drinks, one right after the other. The officers' club at Narofeld. Pilots, real pilots, were buying him one round after another and clapping him on the back. The run to P-3-A, they told him, had been done in record time, and none too soon. The station had picked up a second, bigger wave of the Arcolian shift ships, but the spaceborne squadron of green cadets had reassembled in time to head them off before they got near the secondary asteroid belt. It was all a bit much for him, but a small part of his brain was gloating. He could handle it.

More beer. It was flowing freely. He raised his mug to toast someone, maybe it was Colonel Mogadore, when a loud voice cut the happy din.

"There you are!"

He turned to see Derrald Deakes, eyes bloodshot from a hangover and not enough sleep, stalking through the doorway.

"Hello, Derrald!" he announced happily. "I thought you'd be sleeping it off!" He tipped his mug in salute. "Come join us!"

"You little bastard!" Deakes said. "When I give an order, I expect it to be carried out before anything else!"

"Don't be such a hardcase, Deakes," one of the real pilots said.

"Instead you went off to the asteroids like some half-cocked space rigger!" Deakes grabbed him by the lapels and

pulled him off of the stool. "What do you have to say for yourself?"

His broken arm that had never been broken ached. *"Nothing,"* he said quietly. *"Combat assignments come out tomorrow, and we'll be rid of each other at last."*

"No." Deakes grinned. *"Not you. I'm busting you out of Top Flight. I'm purging your records. You're going to have to start out all over again, with nothing."*

He set his glass down. *"You wouldn't. You wouldn't dare."*

Deakes smiled. *"Watch me,"* he said. *"I'm going to Colonel Mogadore."* He turned and stalked toward the door. *"Insubordinate bastard."*

His face was burning. He rushed toward Deakes and shouted his name. Deakes spun, arm coming up in a right cross. He sidestepped the blow and plunged his right fist deep into Deakes's solar plexus. He hooked a foot behind Deakes's ankle, kicked it out of the way, and sent him to the floor. Then he cleared his throat and hacked a glob of spit onto the leader's face.

"There. Go to Mogadore now that you have good reason."

The memory made him reel. After that, he remembered, he had walked out of the club without a word. And now here he was, waking up in jail, accused of murder, with Deakes stone dead.

A crushed windpipe? Were they sure? He had no memory of hitting Deakes in the throat. A fist to the chest, a kick to the ankle, and a little saliva. There was no way he could have killed Deakes, not unless—

He cleared his throat. "Lucky?"

"What the hell do you want now?"

"I'm innocent."

"My mother's grave you are. I heard what everyone's saying."

"Well, they're wrong."

"Feh," Lucky grunted. "Go suck transgear lube."

He sat heavily on the bunk and shut down the scanner,

fingers drumming across its surface. If everyone said he was guilty, then he was the only one capable of proving himself innocent. And sure as hell, he could not do that sitting inside a jail cell.

His eyes closed, but he did not sleep. He had much planning to do.

17

Bleary-eyed, Vonn plodded through the decks of the *Hergest Ridge*. He had not had much sleep. Every time he closed his eyes Anders was waiting for him, bloody, chest punctured, eyes sunken. Then there was the laugh. It began deep and quickly pitched upward into a high screech. The quality of it reminded Vonn more of Alan Jents than of Loren Anders. The sound of it was enough to drive him out of sleep in a panic. Before he woke he would always take one last look at his comrade. Anders would smile that toothy, blood-caked smile of his, as if he had done what he had set out to do.

And Vonn would find himself sitting up in bed, clutching the sheets with white knuckles.

After two such nights, he decided to find someone and talk out his problems. He threw on fresh clothes and went directly to Duke's berth.

There was no answer. Vonn checked his watch. It was late for breakfast. Perhaps Duke was at the library. He had spent a lot of the time waiting for rescue with data from the *Angel's Luck* files, trying to learn more about the ship's operations. He went there, but Duke was nowhere to be found. Vonn grunted with disgust and decided to go in search of food instead.

On the way to the cafeteria he saw May, who was wearing a dress uniform and seemed to be in a great hurry.

"May," he called. "Wait up."

The merchant stopped. "Vonn. You look like hell."

"Feel like it, too. Got a minute?"

May shook his head. "Sorry. No time. Don't worry, though. The stuff is safe."

"I need to talk to you, May."

"I can't," May said urgently. "I've got an important meeting with shipboard security."

"Tell me where to find Duke, then. He can help me."

May's eyes narrowed. "Don't you know?"

"What?"

"Obviously not. Duke can't help you, Vonn. He can't even help himself. He's in the brig."

"The brig!"

"He assaulted one of the Arcolians. I don't know if it's because of the Essence product or not. I'm trying to save his skin without tipping too much of our hand."

Vonn tossed his hands in the air. "This is great. This is really great."

"If you want to be a help, go and see him. Roz and Winters have been visiting him, and you should, too. I haven't had the chance because I've been so busy trying make sure they treat him humanely in that brig of theirs."

"I'll do that," Vonn said decisively.

May fished a card from his pocket and handed it to the mercenary. "Here's his ID card so you can access his berth. You might see if he needs anything from there, toiletries, reading material—"

"A lase welder baked into a soyabran muffin."

"Don't get cute," May glared. "I'm trying to paint him as suffering from chronic Deep Space Stress Syndrome. If it doesn't work, well . . ."

"You'll get him out of it," Vonn said confidently. "I'll tell him that. Better get to your appointment."

"Tell Duke I'll see him soon," May said as they parted.

Vonn made a steady pace, heading for the bank of lifts that would take him up to the detention level. His stomach rumbled loudly, protesting his recent fast.

"You were right," he told Anders under his breath. "They

still need me. I turn my back for a couple of days and everyone gets in a jam.''

A cold voice resonated in his head. *Told you.*

He reached the row of lifts, rang for one, and waited, foot nervously tapping the floor.

"Hurry up, dammit."

He heard someone call his name. Turning, he saw Haggis heading his way. Vonn swore bitterly.

"Where do you think you're going?" Haggis asked.

"Infirmary," Vonn mumbled. "Got a sick aunt."

"Right," Haggis said, grabbing his shoulder. "Funny as hell." He started to drag Vonn away from the lifts.

Vonn pulled loose. "What do you think you're doing?"

"We've got to meet with Bachman. You've already got him hopping for not showing up yesterday." Haggis wrinkled his nose and regarded Vonn's slovenly appearance. "What's wrong with you, brother? You on a drunk?"

"Been sick," Vonn said. "Contagious, too."

Haggis shoved Vonn in a tight circle and pinned one arm up between his shoulders. "Funny. Come with me." He guided Vonn through the hall at a brisk pace. "You're going to screw things up if you're not careful. Can you act sober long enough to sit through the meeting?"

Why fight it? Vonn thought. "Yeah, yeah. Sure, sure."

Haggis patted him on the back with his free hand. "Good boy."

They went deep into the ship, then up to Bachman's suite. He was speaking when they arrived, and he waited indignantly while Haggis and Vonn found places to sit.

"Glad you could join us, Mr. Vonn," he said sourly. "If you've decided to be a permanent part of our little group, then we'll continue with the briefing."

Vonn gave him a sheepish nod.

As it turned out, they covered no new ground. There was a discussion of the assault on one of the Arcolians, which Bachman thought was a mixed blessing. On one hand, he was outraged at the thought that anyone would try to kill one of the creatures that he intended to make money on. On the other, shipboard security had been tight during the entire trip. They had been expecting anti-Arcolian sentiment to manifest itself in some way, and now that it had, they were free to relax. By relaxing, Bachman's hirelings would find their job of moving about the ship that much easier.

After the discussion, there was a review of the action they would take when the blockade was officially discovered. Again, no new ground was covered. It was the same type of memory drill—men and women sitting in front of the leader reciting their jobs and what they would do in an emergency— that Vonn had endured since the beginning of his career. Bachman called on him first to make an example of him, but he recited his part flawlessly. The only criticism offered was "Speak up next time, boy!"

Vonn headed straight for the door when the briefing was over, but Bachman stepped in his way. He knitted his eyebrows and glared at the rumpled mercenary.

"I don't like your attitude."

Vonn looked down at the floor. "Your shoes are scuffed," he said.

"I mean it. You need to watch your step."

"And your fly is open."

Bachman grabbed the front of Vonn's jumpsuit. "I don't appreciate your not showing yesterday."

"There's gravy on your shirt."

"In fact," Bachman said, voice slowly rising out of its coarse whisper, "I've half a mind to cut you out of this little operation. You know what that means, don't you?"

"Your teeth need flossing," Vonn told him.

"You want to tell me what your problem is?"

Vonn smiled. "I've got the Jeremacis Jump." A pained look crossed his features and he looked around the suite. "Where's the head?"

Bachman released him and took a step back. "Why didn't you tell me?"

"You didn't ask." He pointed at Haggis. "And he didn't believe me."

Haggis stepped forward to grab Vonn but thought better of it and kept his distance. "You going to be over it by the time we get to the Council system?"

"The question," Vonn said, pointing at Bachman, "is 'will he?' "

"Get out of here," Bachman snapped. "And don't come back until you're well."

Vonn started out the door, turned back, and smiled. "No. I won't be back until *you're* well."

Smiling, he left the suite and headed for the outer decks, stomach protesting loudly. His hand fell into his pocket and clutched the card May had given him. He needed to see Duke and find out how the kid was doing, but if he did not get something to eat, he really would be sick. With a sigh, he determined that Duke certainly was not going anywhere, and that a meal was next on the list of priorities.

He detoured, took the lift down to one of the restaurant rows, and wandered from shopfront to shopfront, checking out the menus on display. After a few minutes of searching, he found himself looking through the window of a place that specialized in Senegalian cuisine. It was exactly what he wanted: bland, hot, and plentiful. He glanced around to see what seating was available, then froze.

Roz was sitting at one of the tables, laughing and bringing a glass to her lips. Vonn smiled and started toward the door. Halfway through, he stopped. There was a man at the table with her. Not just any man, but that salvor, the Ori who had found them.

Vonn backed quickly out of the door and sat on one of the benches, fuming. How dare he? he thought, grinding his teeth. Never mind that—how dare *she*? Wants some space, eh? Breathing room? Looks more like she just wanted to ditch me for some *Yueh-sheng* gangster.

It was all too much. The memory of Anders would not let him sleep, his stomach would not let him eat, Roz would not let him get physical, and Bachman would not let him do anything else. It was a grave; he was down inside digging, and it kept getting deeper and deeper, with no way out. Things were piling up hard and fast, and no one solution would take care of it all.

First things first. Perhaps he should eat.

Vonn bolted up from the bench, walked a dozen meters, and ordered a hot, greasy sandwich from a fast-food outlet. He wolfed it down and chased it with a couple of false beers, wiped his mouth on his sleeve, and headed for his berth. The haze was clearing from his mind. His stomach, appeased, was allowing his brain to concentrate on more pressing matters.

Problem one, he thought. Nightmares of Anders.

Solution? Guilt. Obviously it was the way his subconscious was dealing with repressed feelings of guilt over something else.

What?

Duke, for one. Simple enough. Visit him. Soon.

What else?

Obvious. Bachman and his plan to kidnap the Arcolian delegation. He should never have gotten involved with it. It was too much too soon after the rescue of the Essence Phials. As Anders had said, that job was not over.

That was problem two. How to get out of Bachman's plot with ass intact.

The answer to that question was more complicated. Not only did he have to kiss Bachman off, but he also had to deal with the prospect of retaliation. On top of that, Vonn's absence would not stop the kidnapping attempt. People were going to die unless a way could be found to cripple the movement.

Last of all, there was Roz. Perhaps he should let her go. That thought made his face burn. Battlefield romance or not, he had made an investment in her, and he was not about to forget it. If only there was some way of discouraging the salvor's attentions.

There was so much to think about, so much to do. If only there was a way to take care of it all, to end all of his problems with one master stroke. Obviously he could stick the Xegg gun in his mouth and pull the trigger, but what good would that do in the long run? Roz would still be lost to him, and Bachman would still pillage the ship.

There had to be something he could do to discourage the salvor's attentions and get Bachman in trouble at the same time . . .

He stopped dead in his tracks, smiling.

Yes. That was it. That was exactly it.

18

May drummed his fingers on the tabletop and tried to remain calm. He would sooner volunteer to work maintenance on the luxury ship's transgear system than formally address a crowd of people. Unfortunately, physical maintenance of the *Ridge* would not get Duke out of the brig nor reduce the charges that the UTE Fleet currently held against him.

May hurriedly went over his notes, taking deep breaths. The ship's security personnel and medical consultants were sitting at a table not three meters from him and were going through stacks of simfiles and medical printouts. A low hum drifted from their table as they discussed the fruits of their labors and reviewed their strategies.

Shifting uncomfortably, May looked at his hand-stylused notes, which took up all of a single slate. It made him wish that Vonn or Roz had been able to come for moral support. But Roz was nowhere to be found—she was probably off with that Chiba fellow. He deliberately had not asked Vonn for fear that the hot-headed mercenary would inadvertently spill the facts about the Essence Phials.

His lips turned up in a bittersweet smile when he realized who would be perfect for addressing the council with limited preparation and nothing to go on but a handful of fabrications. Unfortunately, that very person was the one May was there to represent.

Commander Margaret O'Hearn appeared from a side door wearing a Formal Court uniform. Tesla, who was acting as bailiff, called the room to attention as she walked to the desk and took her seat. He called the meeting to order and then stood at Parade Rest to the side of O'Hearn's platform. The commander read the date, the standard ship time, and the intersect route they were traveling. Then she rang the ship's bell and the hearing was officially underway.

"We are assembled to discuss the matter of William Wesley Arbor, also known as 'Duke,' and the charges pressed against him by the various organizations and law networks represented on this ship. May I have the agenda, please."

Tesla broke from his stance, politely handed her a simfile, then resumed his watch. O'Hearn keyed it on and cleared her throat.

"Item one. UTE Fleet versus William Wesley Arbor. Who is the authorized representative of the UTE Fleet at this hearing?"

A balding man with a thin nose stood. "I am, Commander."

"The hearing recognizes Pearson from Legal Logistics," Tesla announced.

"Commander," Pearson said. "Due to the circumstances surrounding Mr. Arbor's presence on this ship, we will not be bringing forth charges of Falsification of Records or Attempted Flight. Because the weapon he used belonged to ship security, he cannot be pursued for Weapons Possession or Weapons Smuggling. The charges he faces on his home world are nonextraditable, and therefore we will not be concerned with those."

Pearson took a moment to glance at a simfile of his own. "What we are to concern ourselves with is Assault and Theft in the matter of relieving our guard of his weapon, Prohibited Discharge of Weapon, Assault with Intent to Kill, and Breach of Mannered Protocol in the matter of firing on the Arcolian;

Endangerment of Contracting Patrons because a crowd was present during the event; and general charges of Failure to Heed Warning and Resisting Restraint.''

May jumped to his feet. ''I object. These last two charges are puffs. Duke—ah, Mr. Arbor was knocked unconscious during our struggle and therefore was in no condition to heed or resist.''

The commander gave him a stern frown. ''Captain May,'' she said, ''this is not the time to voice protest. You will be given ample time during your recognition.''

''Sorry.'' Red-faced, he plopped into his chair. ''Forgot.''

O'Hearn announced item two on the agenda, the charges brought against Duke by ''The People,'' which was an all-encompassing word for Galactic Law. The charges were read by a dark, somber man who enunciated them so skillfully that for a moment May forgot who the perpetrator was and imagined a person that oozed pure, liquid evil. He snapped out of the daydream when he realized the seriousness of the charges: Endangerment of Innocents on a Public or Charter Transport Vehicle, Assault on Persons of Governmental or Ambassadorial Status, Conspiracy of Incitement to War, and Attempt of Incitement to War.

May grunted when the last two were read, and his palm slapped the tabletop.

O'Hearn glared at him again. ''Captain May, is there a problem?''

Of course there was a problem. Again, the last two charges were puffs, thrown in to make things sound more dire than they were—if that was possible. He chewed his lower lip and shook his head.

''Please remain within protocol,'' O'Hearn advised.

Item three was by far the worst, not for the seriousness of the charges but for the sheer number of them. They were delivered by Query, a man from Passenger Relations who was lawyer pro tem for the fourteen guests who had been in the hall when Duke had opened fire on redbutler. Most had pressed only the basic charge of Endangerment, but some had been quite creative in puffing, which brought the number of charges up to fifty-six. May became slack-jawed as they were read. The list was quite numbing, and he could only imagine what Duke would have to say about the situation.

"Item four," O'Hearn said. "The First Ambassadorial Delegation of Arcolus 6 versus William Wesley Arbor. Who is the delegation's authorized representative?"

A pale, bony man stood, stretching out a thin hand that looked as if it belonged on an Arcolian. "I am, Commander O'Hearn."

"This hearing recognizes Ketterling from Galactic Directive," Tesla announced.

May held his breath.

"Commander O'Hearn, ladies and gentlemen in attendance, the Arcolian delegation wants it to be known that they wish to press no charges against Mr. William Wesley Arbor."

The hearing room filled with murmurs.

"Furthermore," Ketterling continued, "they want it to be known that they wish all charges on the agenda against William Wesley Arbor to be dropped—"

There was sudden uproar. Query stood and loudly proclaimed that the request was most irregular, that Mr. Ketterling had not announced it to other members of the agenda, and sought a continuance so the ramifications could be discussed. O'Hearn shouted for him to follow protocol, and it was only when Tesla stepped up and aimed a Comealong at Query's chest that he quieted and returned to his seat.

May's face flushed and his heart leapt. It was all he could to keep from jumping up and embracing Ketterling. He continued to drum his fingers on the tabletop and kept his seat, and when his ex-wife looked at him, he gave her a look that made her notice that he was following protocol. With a shrug, she rang for order. The room fell silent.

"We will allow Mr. Ketterling to finish his statement."

Ketterling gave her a gracious nod. "The Arcolian delegation wants it to be known that they wish all charges on the agenda against William Wesley Arbor to be dropped and that he be released from incarceration.''

Protests rose again, but O'Hearn was quick to give an extended ring for silence.

"This declaration," Ketterling concluded, "has been verified by *all* members of the Arcolian delegation, *including* the one called 'redbutler,' who was assaulted by Mr. Arbor.''

"This is impossible!" Query shouted. "They can't just—"

Ketterling raised his hands. "They also wish it known that, although they don't want to use it, they will fall back on Ambassadorial Privilege to enforce this—"

Query was on his feet. "Coercion has no place at this hearing!" he shouted. "What about the rights of the passengers? They're entitled to their percentage of justice, and certainly they're—"

At a nod from O'Hearn, Tesla pointed the Comealong at Query's chest and pulled the trigger. Query snapped back as if being pulled by some invisible leash, knocking his chair over in the process. His limbs went rigid, and the muscles in his neck went rock hard.

"Exit," Tesla commanded.

Query began a seizing, stiff-legged walk around the prosecution's table to the door. It was clear from the look on his face that he was fighting it, and the gait made May think of a marionette trying to resist the commands of its puppeteer.

Query's face went crimson. "You," he forced through clenched teeth, "haven't . . . heard . . . the . . . last . . . of—"

"Silence," Tesla said.

The words vanished in a cross between a grunt and a choke. The ensign kept his aim on the lawyer until they were through the door and it closed behind them. In relative silence, the people in the hearing room turned toward the commander to hear what she had to say.

"I will have order in this hearing," she admonished. "And

I will enforce protocol. I am not above having my ensign repeat the treatment you just saw in order to maintain the discipline that this council demands." She looked out at the faces of those present, and all save May and the Arcolian representative looked like rebuked children. "Mr. Ketterling, have you finished your opening statement?"

"Yes, ma'am," he said with a slight bow.

"Very well. I respect the Arcolians and their intentions, and I am highly impressed by their ability to forgive a transgression." She looked out at the others and gave them another cold stare. "Certainly, many of us in this room could learn something from that." She paused for effect. "However, I also respect legal protocol, and if you as their representative will indulge me, as a courtesy to the remainder of the prosecution bench, I wish to complete the agenda."

Ketterling gave another gracious bow. "I have no objection, Commander."

O'Hearn gave him a polite nod. "Item five. The Medical Section of the *Hergest Ridge* wished to make a statement about this subject. Who is the authorized representative of the Medical Section?"

A woman stood and flagged the attention of the returning Tesla, who announced her as Dr. Rollins. She quickly glanced at a slate and then stepped forward.

"The others on the agenda, including Mr. Ketterling, have been briefed on what I am about to say.

"The matter of William Wesley Arbor and his assault on the Arcolian ambassador redbutler has proven to be a frustrating experience for those of us in Medical whose job it has been to diagnose the pathological behavior that caused it. From extensive interviews with witnesses, we believed that what caused the assault was the violent manifestation of a xenophobic reaction."

May leaned back in his seat. Yeah, yeah, yeah, he thought. I've been hearing this for days now.

"What made this even more fascinating was the fact that Mr. Arbor's psychological profile showed virtually no tendencies toward xenophobia. Rather, his profile showed him as being open, willing, and enthusiastic about contact with nonhuman sentients. This was confirmed when Ambassador misterbob visited misterduke—excuse me, Mr. Arbor—in his cell. Mr. Arbor was highly receptive to the Arcolian's visit.

"This gave our department a number of things to think about. Mr. Arbor had been drinking before the incident, so we thought that may have been a factor. But in an interview, Mr. Arbor told us that there was no history of dipsomania in his family, nor does his blood or genetic predispositional chemistry indicate that he is or ever has been prone to alcohol-induced changes of personality."

May felt his stomach turn. Written on his slate as a possible excuse for Duke's behavior was: *strange when drunk—lied about pilot status to get on ship*. It was not true, of course, but the security council did not know that. Only he could no longer use that explanation. He quietly thumbed a key on the slate, and the words vanished without a trace.

"Likewise," Rollins was saying, "there seemed to be no predisposition toward multiple personality disorders or sociopathic behavior, and he admits no history of it in his family. We ran a battery of psychological and chemical tests in order to force a manifestation of one of these behaviors, but none surfaced. All of them came back well within limits of the Balanced Personality Curve."

"What you're saying," Commander O'Hearn said, "is that William Wesley Arbor appears sane."

"Not *appears* sane, Commander. *Is* sane. We ran every test we could short of getting him blind drunk, and they all came back with more than acceptable results."

"Acceptable," Pearson said, rising, "to everyone except those who were involved in the assault."

O'Hearn slapped the desk. "Protocol," she ordered. Pearson sat. "Dr. Rollins, what about the possibility that Mr. Arbor could have scammed the testing? Is it likely that he's been through this before and knew how to respond in order to sway the BPC into the acceptable range?"

"The testing compensates for that," Rollins explained. "Even someone who knows how the testing system works and deliberately tries to influence the balance will be capable of getting only a borderline rating. As I've said, Mr. Arbor was well within acceptable parameters.

"The only thing we could think of was that there was another factor at work, something that we haven't been able to discern through the normal regimen of testing. It is therefore the opinion of the Medical Section that William Wesley Arbor be held for further evaluation in spite of the request of the Arcolians."

May shivered. He did not like the prospect of them running any more tests on Duke. What if Dickson showed up at an inopportune time and gave them a radically different test result? Worse yet, what if Duke broke under the strain of testing and told everything he knew about their recent activities? His fingertips rattled nervously on the table.

"Item six on the agenda. Do we have someone authorized to speak on behalf of William Wesley Arbor?"

May rose and smoothed out the lines of his uniform. "I am, Commander."

"The hearing recognizes James Theodore May, merchant captain of the vessel *Angel's Luck*," Tesla said.

May cleared his throat. He reached down and erased all of what he had written on the stylus. "This is difficult for me," he told O'Hearn. "Perhaps only the commander could appreciate how difficult it is to testify on behalf of one's own crew. And perhaps only the commander can appreciate the position that I find myself in."

He paused to see what kind of reaction he got from his ex-wife. The opening statement was all that had remained of his erased defense, and it was aimed more at Maggie, the former wife and confidant, who knew about the phials, than at Margaret O'Hearn, commander of the *Hergest Ridge*, who would coldly and with great calculation dispense a ruling that would serve the interests of all involved—including the reputation of her employer. But if there was an emotional charge in

May's words, he could not see it register on O'Hearn's face. He cleared his throat again and continued.

"Indeed, I find myself without a defense under these circumstances. I myself had suspected that Duke—William Arbor, as you know him—was suffering from a malady common to those spending their first year off-world called Deep Space Stress Syndrome, or DS3. Unfortunately, the good doctor here has the results of tests which show that my colleague is not even suffering from *that*.

"She has proven that Duke is sane, that he was completely responsible for what he has done, yet she has failed to show motive. In spite of the wishes of the Arcolian delegation, she wishes to restrict the movements of my colleague in order to perform further—" He let his lip curl into a sneer. "—*experiments* that will hopefully show beyond the shadow of a doubt that Duke is guilty of his act. Ladies and gentlemen, I witnessed this act. I can assure you that I saw Mr. Arbor assault the Arcolian redbutler. What I object to is the fact that this doctor and her cronies wish to use him as a field test for methods of psychological extraction which would surely leave him in a less than sound state.

"It is wrong for this to happen. We live in a time when criminal behavior must be cataloged and typed for the good of our future. I can appreciate that. And I can appreciate that this type of research has enabled us to prevent many types of deviant behavior that has plagued us in centuries past. But I cannot condone pure research being done on an otherwise sane and penitent person just for the sake of categorizing his crime for the files.

"We are living in a wonderful time, ladies and gentlemen. We are living in a time when we discover that our species is not alone in this galaxy. We are living in a time when an unfortunate war with other sentients has ended and given us the prospect of centuries of cultural and technological exchange. You and I in this very room, through circumstance, have gathered here to make a decision that will drastically affect the future of those centuries to come. Are we going to heed the first lesson we have learned from the wise creatures known as the Arcolians, or are we going to spit on it and go about our ways, damn the consequences?''

May gave a nod to Commander O'Hearn and then sat, congratulating himself on his impromptu defense and praying hard that his ex would buy it.

"I do have some questions I'd like to ask before coming out with a decision,'' O'Hearn said. ''The first is directed at Captain May. You said that Mr. Arbor now feels penitent for his deeds. Is this true?''

The merchant squirmed in his seat. He had not been able to see Duke to find out. He drew breath, mind racing to come up with a big lie, when salvation came from a most unlikely source.

"If I may interrupt,'' Dr. Rollins said, ''I believe I can shed a little more light on this situation.''

"Captain May?'' O'Hearn asked.

"Certainly.'' He nodded, happy to have the extra time to think.

Rollins stood, taking a simfile with her. ''According to our tests, William Wesley Arbor does have full emotional faculties.''

That's it, May thought. I'm saved. She's going to bail me out.

"However,'' she continued, ''our interviews show that he has no remorse whatsoever regarding this incident.''

May cringed. She's going to bury us! I shouldn't have let her talk . . .

"This is one of the anomalies we want to investigate,'' Rollins continued. ''Mr. Arbor's lack of remorse over the assault seems to be based in the fact that he has absolutely no recollection of the event. When we checked this through various tests, we were forced to evaluate him as having a clean memory. That is, he truly believes that he has no recollection of firing on the Arcolian. Under the circumstances, he may have no memory of it, although we haven't yet been able to determine whether or not it has been suppressed by his subconscious. One reason we ask for detention of this subject is so we can see if we can get this memory to surface."

The color drained from May's face. Sure, she might get the memory of it to surface, along with heaven knows what else Eric Dickson had knowledge of.

O'Hearn considered what Rollins had said. After a moment of thought, she looked down at the prosecution's table. "Mr. Ketterling, when you communicated with the Arcolians regarding their feelings toward Mr. Arbor, are you certain that there was no misunderstanding? Do they realize that they wish to free a criminal who has offended their race?"

Ketterling stood, nodding. "Yes, Commander O'Hearn. Ambassador misterbob's exact words were, 'Indeed, this williamarbor must pay no penalty. He has not done wrong to us in any manner. You must see that he is forgotten by your laws.' The only note I would make here is that I believe the ambassador meant that Mr. Arbor should be 'forgiven' by our laws."

"And what was their rationale behind this, Mr. Ketterling?"

"You must remember that Arcolians look at their own, individual lives quite differently than we do. The war records are rife with examples of unthinking sacrifice, especially among the C- and D-forms—"

"I know of that," O'Hearn interrupted. "What I'd like to know is, did the Arcolians give any reason for their decision other than the fact that Mr. Arbor did nothing that was taboo to their culture?"

"They are convinced—but convinced isn't the word for it. They independently came to the conclusion that William Wesley Arbor did not assault redbutler. No details on this were offered other than misterbob's insistence that, and again these are the ambassador's words, 'williamarbor smelled of the truth.'

"Off the record, ma'am, I did get the impression that misterbob felt that redbutler was somehow responsible for the assault's taking place. The ambassador didn't exactly say as much, but once you start watching and listening to them, you can almost read subtext in their conversations like you can with . . ." He trailed off and thought for a moment to collect his thoughts. "I don't know what's more embarrassing, Commander. The fact that I didn't think Arcolians could be *that* intelligent, or the fact that they're so damned fast at picking up what we consider our unique traits."

O'Hearn showed a wistful smile. "Mr. Ketterling, your xenocentric attitude I can understand and appreciate. What I don't understand is their unyielding support of Mr. Arbor. Correct me if I'm wrong, but two of them witnessed the assault, and misterbob was one of them. Didn't they see Duke, didn't they hear the shots? Didn't they *smell* what happened?"

"I'm convinced that this decision was not a rash one," Ketterling explained. "Arcolians are notorious for not giving credence to visual and aural stimuli, which their culture refers to as 'the false senses.' Perhaps they received some olfactory stimuli that convinced them of Mr. Arbor's innocence."

The commander sighed. "Dr. Rollins, is it possible that a person could so completely convince himself of an alternate version of the truth that even subtle vestiges of it could be erased from the mind?"

The doctor looked grim. "There is no precedent for the complete and utter repression we're seeing here. The regimen of tests we put him through would have shown *something*."

O'Hearn smiled wryly. "I don't suppose that he'd be the first G-form Arcolian."

There was nervous laughter.

"I'm going to my chamber to consider this situation and all of the ramifications involved. All persons present will be notified of my findings, whether I reach a decision or decree that another hearing is in order. In the meantime, this hearing is dismissed." She rang the bell. Ensign Tesla opened the door, and the participants began to file out.

"Captain May," O'Hearn said. "I'd like to speak with you for a moment. If you would come with me, please."

May followed her through a short hall, flanked by Ensign Tesla. The trio stepped into a small room furnished with a desk and executive chair, disc library, and a pair of lo-grav chairs.

"If you will excuse us, Ensign," O'Hearn said. "Make sure nobody enters the hallway and give the room a Confidential Seal."

Tesla saluted curtly and vanished out the door. O'Hearn waited until a light on the desk winked green, then gave a deep sigh, shoulders slumping.

"Nobody will hear us," she told May, slumping into one of the lo-grav chairs. "Not even if this place is bugged, which is unlikely."

May perched on the edge of her desk. "What do you want, Maggie?"

She put her hand to her forehead. "You've really got me over a barrel, you know that, James? I don't know what I'm supposed to do."

He studied her. She was pale and beginning to shake. "Talk to me."

"How much of the Essence Product would account for the result of Medical Section's tests?"

"I don't know," May said. "I don't know a thing about the way the stuff assimilates into the brain. I suppose it could . . ."

"How are the doctor's tests going to affect this stuff? Will it be better, worse, or no change?"

"I don't know."

"Are there any tests that would detect this stuff? Is it going to show up on a Protein Shift Stain?"

"It's organic; it's human." May shook his head. "I don't know."

"Dammit, James, this man is your friend and you don't know anything about what's going on with him?"

"Maggie," he barked. "In case it hadn't occurred to you, with one early and miserable exception, the Essence Corporation hasn't even had the chance to test this stuff. Duke is the first person to ever go through this new process, which makes him a walking test case."

"I owe," she said. "I am duty bound to the UTE Fleet to see that things run smoothly, and should any problems arise, I'm to see that justice is served. I'm also bound to their New Discovery code, which binds me to allow research on Duke because they think that he's got something special. I'm bound to you—"

"No, you're not," May interrupted. "You haven't been for years. I'm an insignificant part of this, so I'll not hear any more of that kind of talk."

O'Hearn sighed. "I'm still bound to you through Duke's rights as a citizen, and I'm bound to the Arcolians through their Ambassadorial Privilege. If I uphold it, the entire legal department is going to be on my throat, and they hold rank, James. Which ideal do I snub? The will of the company or the wishes of the first delegation from Arcolus?" Her hands knotted into fists. "I knew it wouldn't be easy when I swore the oath, but I never expected something quite like this. Two decisions, both of them wrong."

"Who says you have to make a decision?" May asked.

She stared at him, eyes like daggers. "What?"

"We're going to arrive at the Council system in a matter of days. All you have to do is stall and let the professional arbiters on number five make the decision. By that time Vonn and I will have had time to get the phials off of the *Angel's Luck* and turn them in to Essence for the reward. It'll make a sensational news story, and once selected bits of it hit the media, it'll corroborate what I've told you about Duke and Eric Dickson."

"That's wonderful," O'Hearn said, rising from the chair. "That's just great. For you."

"For you, too, Maggie."

"That's where you're wrong. I am a commander. My job is to lead, organize, and discipline, but most of all my job is to make decisions. I don't suppose you remember the lectures at the academy about the Command Decision, do you?"

"That was never my forte," he said weakly. He sighed and squared his shoulders resolutely. "Why don't you talk to someone whose forte *is* command? You've got a sterling example right here on the ship."

"And who would that be?" she asked.

"Admiral Studebaker." May smiled.

O'Hearn shook her head slowly. "A nice thought, but impractical. First of all, this has to be my decision—"

"You're not asking him to make a decision. You're asking him for advice."

"And second of all, I'm not sure what his advice would be worth. The Admiral is 133 years old and has a revoked rejuv card. His free advice would be worth exactly—"

"A Terran dollar," May nodded.

"Besides, you've got to consider that it's not just Duke's fate hanging on this. It's not being in the good graces of the company's legal branch and the Medical Section, and it's not over whether I make war or peace with the Arcolians. It's about my job, and my ability to carry it out.

"The UTE Fleet doesn't want some spineless bit of tissue that is incapable of making a decision, they need someone who can put their foot down and stand by their decision, right or wrong. Or in my case, wrong or wrong."

"Surely they'll take that into consideration—"

"You never understood." It came out loud, almost a shout. "Never, ever. I've *got* to make this decision, for the good of absolutely everyone. If I don't they're going to see it as a sign of weakness, and I've fought against that too hard to have it happen now. I was older than the average pilot who went into Command School, I had all that down time as a merchant, I had a temper, and yes, I cry when I get mad. I overcame it, I'm here now, but I'm scared as hell that it's not going to last. I feel like they're watching me, James, and one slip is all it will take before they jerk my chain and I'm dispatching tugs.''

She fell onto him, sobbing. He wrapped his arms around her.

"Easy," he said. "There's a way to handle this, and we'll find it." Her body quivered against his. May flushed and the breath left his lungs.

"I know what it is." Her words were muffled against his shoulder. "You've got to understand. I need to do it this way."

May eased her around the desk and sat in the executive chair, pulling her onto his lap.

"I'm going to the Arcolians to find out what they know about Duke." She sniffed. "And then the three of us are going to see him."

May's stomach turned. "Three of us?"

"You and misterbob and I. I've got to see how the Arcolians were convinced."

The merchant's skin erupted in gooseflesh. "Of course."

"Thank you." She sat up, wiping her eyes and sniffing. "I know it wasn't easy for you to sit here and listen to me like that. It was never easy for you, was it, James?"

He shrugged. She was beginning to grow heavy on his lap. "It wasn't that bad," he mumbled.

"Still, thank you." Her hand found the back of May's head, and he was looking straight into her eyes. His heart rattled nervously in his chest.

"I'm glad I could help," he said, shifting and realizing that he was pinned in the chair. "Now that we've got things settled—"

He tried to avoid her glance but could not. He saw the look and knew what was coming, and thought quickly about being graceful about it: *Look, Maggie, you and I haven't seen each other in a while and we're both under a hell of a lot of stress, so we don't want to do anything foolish. Besides, I've got to get with Vonn and Roz and set up something to keep Duke from spilling his guts before the appointed hour . . .*

"I need to get to the *Angel's Luck*," he said. "Transgear needs—"

Her lips touched his. They were every bit as soft as he remembered.

19

They kissed.

They kissed again.

They kissed one more time, and when he thought it would not end, her hands came up, caught him by the shoulders, and pushed him away.

"I'm sorry. I thought—"

"And you were right." Roz took a nervous step back. "I did want it, Peter, although now I'm not so sure."

Chiba stepped back, hands held up defensively. "Maybe I'm being too forward—"

"You're not." Roz sighed. "It's not that at all. You just have to understand what I'm going through."

"DS3," he said.

"Not really. I come from an outpost station, remember. It's all the changes I've been through in the last month— losing my home and all of my friends, nearly getting killed, spending an awful lot of time with a man I knew nothing about."

"You're still in love with Vonn."

"I can't say that I am, Peter. If I am, I'm not sure that I want to be. And if I'm not, I'm not sure what direction I want to go from there. Don't you see? It's not that I haven't enjoyed the things we've done over the past few days—it's just that, whatever happens, I don't want you to get hurt."

Chiba nodded. "I understand that."

"Does that discourage you?"

"Not at all. I've been through worse things in my life. Besides, I can always hope that you'll—" He cut himself off.

She cocked her head and gave him a suspicious look. "You hope I'll what?"

"You'll take it wrong."

"Try me."

He shrugged. "I can always hope that you'll come to your senses. About me, that is. I'm not trying to be egotistical, but I have it on good authority that I'm a nice guy around the right person."

"You're trying to tell me that I'm a right person?"

"One of the rightest I've found in a long time, Roz. For that, I can respect your desire to have some time to yourself." He gave her a platonic kiss on the cheek. Her hand came up to touch the spot.

"You're not making things any easier."

"That's my nature. Here's something else for you to ponder while you're thinking. When the *Hergest Ridge* reaches Council 5, my salvage contract with the UTE Fleet is finished. I've got a good record so I can sign with them again or I can use my reputation to go into business for myself. Either way, I can make a decent living."

"Peter Chiba, are you asking what I think you're asking?"

"Not exactly. To be honest, I haven't known you long enough. But I want you to know that if you're prone to hanging around the Council system, well, I can, too."

Roz gave him a sweet, sad smile. "You know I can't promise you anything beyond the fact that I'll think about it."

"That's all I ask," he said. "That you consider me."

She kissed him on the cheek, then turned and vanished into her berth. Chiba lingered outside the door for a moment, then turned and started down the hall. It had gone as well as he could have expected. All he had to do now was wait.

He stepped into the lift, and it deposited him near the transgear bay. Following the hall, he found his way to the hangar where the *Jamming Jenny* was docked. He stopped outside the hangar, pulled the *Jenny*'s maintenance log from a file, and started to leaf through it.

The lift groaned, and two people stepped off. Chiba continued his study of the tug's maintenance. It looked as if Zack had put in a request to check the CHRIS's personality calibration, the third since bringing in the *Angel's Luck*. Chiba smiled, thinking about how the night had gone with Roz, and authorized the work to be done. Zack would be deliriously happy when he got the go-ahead.

"Got the time?"

Chiba turned. It was a woman in a shortcut top and clingpants. Her hair was cut short, and she was muscular, looking every bit as if she had come down to put in a night in the bay. He checked his chronometer and gave her shiptime. When he started to turn away, her hand fell on his shoulder.

"What about sack?"

"Zack?" He turned to face her again and inhaled a warm, yeastlike smell. She had obviously had more than a few before coming down.

"Sack," she tried to enunciate. "As in sack time."

Chiba shook his head and laughed. "If you're going on duty," he said, "you should reconsider. The foreman won't even let you into the bay like that."

The woman frowned. "What's wrong with me?"

"You're intoxicated." He took the woman's shoulders and turned her around. "Take my advice. You're better off calling in sick from your berth than showing to post drunk." He gave her a slight push toward the lift.

"You don't like me?" she whined.

"I get the feeling we're talking about two different things," Chiba said, shrugging.

A man appeared and demanded to know what was going on. The woman wailed and fell into his arms. "He doesn't like me."

"We've had a misunderstanding," Chiba explained. "I thought she came down here to report for duty, and she must have mistaken me for you . . ."

"For you?" The man laughed in Chiba's direction, and the salvor stepped back. The newcomer was equally as intoxicated as the woman. "That's a laugh."

"So it is," Chiba said. He started for the lift, leaving them to their reunion.

"He didn't want sack time," the woman told her friend.

"Is that true?" the man shouted after Chiba.

The salvor rolled his eyes. "Yeah," he shouted back turning. "She asked, but I told her 'no.' "

"What the hell for?"

Chiba shrugged. "Figured she was taken. Anyway, it all worked out. You showed up to get her home before—"

The man pulled away from the woman and stalked down the hall. "What's wrong with you, salvor? You insulting me?"

Chiba stopped, not liking the turn the situation was taking. "No. Of course not—"

"You don't like my choice in sack mates?"

"Hey." Chiba held up his hands defensively. "I didn't say that."

"You'd sack her, then?"

Chiba dropped his hands and stood his ground. There was a loaded question if ever he had heard one. "I've already got a sack mate."

The man stopped and nodded cynically. "Yeah. You're sacking some passenger. Transgear personnel not good enough for you."

"I never said—"

"You son of a bitch."

The man telegraphed his swing, giving Chiba time enough to sidestep. His assailant twisted into the bulkhead.

"The both of you had better get back to your berths before Security comes along," Chiba said. "I'd hate to see something bad happen to you."

"I'll bet." Panting, the man stepped away from the wall. "Salvor trash."

He came at Chiba with a wild swing. Again Chiba sidestepped, but that time he turned, lashed one foot out, and kicked the man's feet out from under him, causing him to flip in the light gravity.

"Somebody needs to teach you a lesson." The woman

was bounding toward him at full speed. "For fraternizing with the passengers."

Where the hell had they gotten that idea? Chiba watched her approach and ducked a series of swings aimed at his head. When it became apparent that she was not about to back off, he threw out his fist to impact with the side of her jaw. It had no effect other than making her stop for a moment to shake off the blow.

"You bastard," she said.

Chiba shrugged. "So much for sexual protocol." His next fist broke her nose.

That was the mistake. The alcohol that slowed her down also kept her from feeling too much pain. She jumped him, bowling them both down the hall toward the lift. Chiba tried to wiggle out of her grip but could not do that and duck her impaired punches at the same time. Instead, he rolled with her and kept jerking his head from side to side, the woman's knuckles making an impressive series of clangs on the demi-metal floor.

Just as he got a grip on the woman's shortcut and was preparing to toss her off, her partner joined in. Striking hard, the three of them rolled farther down the hall, bumped against the lift door, and grunted as one. Chiba was sending out kicks and punches in all directions, most of which connected with his assailants.

The problem was that he was outgunned. Even in their intoxicated state, the two of them managed to match Chiba blow for blow. He felt his nose crack when it was pushed sideways, and one eye began to swell shut. Something connected with his upper chest, and he felt a strange series of pops from his rib cage. His fist connected with someone's mouth, a tooth gouged a knuckle, and his hand twisted sideways, ligaments tearing. There was a blow to the side of the same arm near the elbow, and fiery spines of numbness shot all the way to the tips of his fingers. His testicles were driven upward by someone's knee, and an elbow found one of his kidneys. His own attacks began to slow, and he started to succumb to the pummeling he was receiving. Through it all, the same strange thought kept running through his mind: *What the hell did I say?*

One eye was swollen shut. He closed the other and waited for the yellow fireworks of imminent unconsciousness to appear. His breath was falling short in his lungs and his head was starting to swim when he heard the lift door open. The corners of his mouth turned up in spite of the fact that they were swollen and bleeding.

"What in the hell is going on here?"

The voice sounded vaguely familiar to the battered salvor. More important, it made the attack stop.

"What are you two doing to that poor man?" The tone was not so much one of shock as pleased indignance.

"We thought—" The woman's voice faltered. There had been a whistling sound when she had made the *th* sound; it told Chiba whose tooth he had broken. "We *th*ought we'd help you out."

"Salvor trash," the man's voice explained. "You were so down, we figured—" He momentarily trailed off. "What was it we thought?"

"What *the* hell," the woman whistled. "Maybe we could get *th*is guy off of your back *s*o you could get your—"

"Get off him!" shouted the familiar voice. "Get off!" There was a scuffling, and Chiba felt the weight being pulled from off of his body. "That was a really stupid thing to do. What if you'd been caught?"

"We didn't *th*ink—"

"No. Of course. You never think. You always leave that to me, don't you?"

The anger and assertiveness of the new voice made Chiba's mind race. It was so close, right there in the recent past—

More scuffling. The man and woman were being pulled down the corridor. The voice continued its tirade. "Look at you. You've both taken a real beating. You'd better be back in shape by the time we reach the blockade or somebody's going to cut off a piece of your ass and feed it—"

The tirade was cut off by the closing of the lift door. The machinery hummed as Chiba slid down and put his cheek to the cold deck.

Voice. Who was that voice? So familiar he could reach out and touch—

Blockade.

What was that? Something had been said about a blockade. In the Council system? Never . . .

His good eye popped open, giving him a skewed view of the deck.

"Arcolians," he said through bruised lips. Chiba lifted up on his arms and inched forward. "The Arcolians. Oh, no. Oh, *no* . . ."

He crawled toward the transgear bay. He got two meters before his flailed ribs made it impossible for him to breathe, the air in his lungs cut short, and he passed out.

20

May opened one eye and rotated his head toward the ceiling. The numbers projected there seemed blurry, but he could still tell that it was just after 0300. He started to roll over, but the pounding came again, long and insistent, against the hatch of his berth.

He eased out of bed and checked the image screen. Outside his door stood two men in uniform.

"What do you want?" His voice was low and hoarse. He wondered what it sounded like on the other side of the speaker.

"Ship security," one of the uniforms said. "Commander O'Hearn sent us to pick you up."

He grabbed a rumpled jumpsuit from the floor and stepped into it. "Did she say what for?"

"She merely indicated that she wanted your presence in the infirmary."

Infirmary? A lump formed in May's throat. "Is she all right?"

"The commander is fine, Captain May. She wants you there because of a situation."

He fastened the jumpsuit and opened the hatch, stepping out into the hall.

The trip to the infirmary was fast. The guards had pass-cards and overrides for the lifts and keyed them into express mode, and when they were on foot they walked a brisk double-time. May barely had the chance to speculate on who had been hospitalized before he got there.

The guards flanked him and led him to a third, who took charge of the merchant and dismissed the others. With a nod, he signaled for May to follow.

"What's the problem?" May asked.

"Commander O'Hearn would like you to make a diagnosis."

May shrugged. "I'm a merchant, not a doctor."

They turned a corner and walked onto a ward lined with various healing beds, from the zero-gee zips to the standard folding recliners. Maggie and another woman were standing next to a hanging suspension cot, speaking to a patient. O'Hearn looked haggard and worn—about like May felt.

"Commander?" he asked politely. "You requested my presence?"

His ex-wife's face looked grim. "What do you know about this, James?" Her head tilted toward the cot's occupant. Canvas supports were under his neck, upper back, buttocks, and thighs, and were wired to the ceiling through a network of shifting pulleys. An abused face looked back at him.

"Chiba!" he said in surprise.

The other woman shushed him.

May took another look. The salvor was covered with bandages, bruises, and small lacerations. One arm was held straight out and was encased in a Warm, likewise his left shin and both ankles. "What the hell happened to you?" he asked in a concerned whisper.

"We thought you might be able to provide the answer to that," O'Hearn told him.

He whirled on her. *"Me!"*

The doctor hissed again for silence.

"Have you lost it, Maggie? This guy saved my life. What makes you think I'd—"

"Not you," she said. "One of your people."

"Who? Winters? No way. Duke? I think he's got an alibi—"

"Listen," O'Hearn told him, and she nodded again at Chiba.

"I got beat up"—he grunted—"by a couple of people looking for a fight. They were dressed like transgear crew, but they had to be passengers. They were drunk—"

"This doesn't sound like anyone I know," May protested.

"Let him finish," O'Hearn said.

"Like I said," Chiba continued. "They were looking for a fight. Called me 'salvor trash.' 'cused me of sacking a passenger."

"That would do it." May scratched his chin. "Were you?"

"Seeing, yes. Sacking, no."

"Same difference to a transgear—"

"They weren't crew," O'Hearn stressed.

"I still don't see what this has to do with me," May protested.

"Been seeing Roz," Chiba said. "About a week."

May's chin dropped. "One of them was Vonn?"

"No," the salvor said. "Would've recognized. Wasn't one of the two. But there was a third, stopped the fight, familiar voice."

"Him?"

"Could be. Tip was, the two said they were helping him, doing a favor. He was mad about it. It all fell together. Roz cools on him, she sees me. Vonn mentions his state to them, they get drunk, decide to give their brother a hand."

May's eyes narrowed. *"Brother—"*

"We nabbed them," O'Hearn said. "Right here, coming in to get bandaged up. Like Specialist Chiba said, they were drunk and hadn't exercised good judgment. We ran their retinal prints through the bank and got an interesting list of their last few ports of call. They've got to be mercenaries.''

May gave an exasperated shrug. ''Fine. Terrific. Big deal.'' He turned to Chiba. ''I'm sorry you got beaten up over Roz, but at least Vonn kept you from getting killed. You see what I'm saying? They acted on their own—''

''There's more.''

May turned to his ex.

''Specialist Chiba heard something else right before they left. He heard the word *blockade*.''

''Spoken by Vonn?''

''Yes.''

May rubbed his eyes. ''Maggie, I swear I don't know—''

O'Hearn grabbed his elbow and pulled him away. ''Then you had better find out, James. I don't give a righteous damn what you do with your life, but the moment it affects this ship, my passengers, and especially the Arcolians, it becomes my business.''

May fought for breath. He was beginning to feel lightheaded. ''No. Of course. The Arcolians—''

''What do you know about it, May?''

He took a step away from her. ''Nothing. I swear.''

''Where did you get Vonn?''

''It was—'' He took a deep breath and lowered his voice. ''It was coincidence, Maggie, you've got to believe me. Bring in the dogs if you don't—''

''Keep your xenist remarks to yourself, Captain.''

''I'm sorry,'' May said, ''but you've got to trust me. There's no way, no way in hell that Vonn could have set us up to be on this ship, not with the way we met him.''

''Are you willing to acknowledge that he's become involved with some type of anti-Arcolian faction since boarding this ship?''

May's face flushed hot. ''Why don't you ask him yourself?'' he snapped.

''I'd sure like to,'' O'Hearn snapped, ''but he seems to have disappeared.'' She paused a moment to wait for her ex-husband's thoughts to slow, then said, "And yes, we've checked the *Angel's Luck*. In fact, we've staked it out."

"Come on, Maggie—"

"Commander." She looked sternly over his shoulder at the milling shipboard personnel.

"Commander," he said bitterly. "There are only so many places on this ship that somebody can hide."

"Tell me about it. We seemed to be really good at finding them, weren't we?"

At any other time that statement would have brought a blush and a smile, but May realized how she had meant it. It was a point well taken. "I'll see if I can find him." He sighed. "And I'll find out what's going on if I have to—"

"That's not your place. You'll bring him to me, Captain May. Understand?"

He nodded. "What about Duke?"

"The decision on that is pending. You'll understand that I'm more concerned with this situation."

He nodded.

"About this blockade business—"

"I won't say a word," May said, anticipating her order. "It might just be a rumor. No sense in getting too riled until we find Vonn and learn more about the situation."

"It's not that easy on a ship this size," O'Hearn told him. "I can't dismiss it, yet I can't treat it as the truth. I've got to put shipboard intelligence to work interrogating the prisoners."

"Are you open for suggestions?" May asked.

"Serious ones."

"Don't mess with interrogation. There are too many legal aspects that will let the prisoners keep their mouths shut until we reach the Council system. Instead, have that wonderful Medical Section of yours give them the same treatment they've given Duke."

"That'll make trouble, James."

"There'll be more trouble if we don't find out the truth

about the blockade. If it isn't a rumor, then it may already be too late.''

O'Hearn stared off over May's shoulder. ''It'll be tricky. There'll be mountains of paperwork, and if something goes wrong, it's my rank that'll get brought up before a corporate hearing.''

May smiled. ''I'll testify on your behalf.''

O'Hearn looked at his face. He was giving her the look she had relied upon so often in the past: firm, loving, supportive.

''It'll take some time,'' she said. ''I'd better get started on it.''

21

Around and around and around.

Duke walked the perimeter of the cell in slow circles. His jaw hung open and his eyes were dark and sunken, his face a blank. Occasionally he stumbled into the wall or tripped over his own foot. Always, he caught himself and then kept moving, tight circles, never stopping.

It was better than sleeping, he told himself.

But then, some inner part replied, who is to say what is sleep and what is not? Maybe this is sleep. Maybe this is death . . .

''Waking nightmare.'' At one point many hours earlier, the sound of his own voice had comforted him. He tried to convince himself that it still did. ''Over soon. Waking nightmare. Over soon.''

He stopped for a moment, breathing hard, and leaned against the wall. Then he went to the zipbed and wiped beads of sweat from his face to the linen.

Distinct memories with no basis in reality plagued him. The persistent sensation of flight. Brawls that began and ended with no reason. A chronic ache across the back of the head from a fractured skull, sustained in an accident that he could not put his finger on. The way the holos he had found of Leigh Brand caused tears to well up in his eyes. It had reached the point where the memories came whenever he reached for the optical scanner. He had entirely given up on trying to read the volume that had been provided.

Most curious was the way the cell felt. There was the dim recollection of a cell somewhere, and he thought that most certainly he deserved it—yet the cell was wrong from the way he remembered it. The one he remembered was old-fashioned, with metal doors. That much he knew for certain. But the rest of his memory was faulty. He had left there, it seemed, two different ways. One version said that he walked out, was released. Another had him being choked by an angry merchant captain, and when the guard came in to break things up, they bolted.

Duke's arm ached. There were multiple memories of it being broken. One option said it had never been broken. Yet it was enclosed in a cast.

The only thing that all of the fragments seemed to have in common were the last few days of time, the increasingly feverish sleeps, the haze he had dubbed a waking nightmare. In and out had been the matron or the matron-bitch, depending on which memory was in charge. Both versions showed her as nice, tolerant, and understanding. They blurred her name and her race.

The focal point had been Lucky. It had been almost as if the memories had all converged into one single entity since being confined, and the chronically drunken passenger had been the glue that was holding things together. They had had many fine conversations with Lucky, and in spite of their ragged and rambling content, it had been a comfort to be able to look into the past and see a single sequence of moments where everything converged.

But Lucky had been dry-cured by the Medical Section, the same ones who had interrogated him, the ones who stopped in front of his cell to stare longingly, as if being deprived of a great treasure.

All that was left were the down-and-outers. A man and a

woman had been brought in, hurt and complaining bitterly about their citizenship being infringed upon. Like Lucky both were drunk, but they had sobered much too quickly and ignored Duke, preferring to talk between themselves about a mysterious entity named Bachman who would soon come to set them free.

Duke turned away from the bunk and looked down at the scanner. Then he closed his eyes and watched the darkness. The confusing memories were still. Quickly he sat and turned on the scanner, programming it to skip the holographic section and move right to where he had been forced to quit reading. With a last glance around the cell, he keyed into the page.

. . . the High Tribunal received the official autopsy report on Derrald Deakes. He had received a severe blow to the throat and suffered a crushed larynx and windpipe . . .

Duke gasped. "No. That's not right. That's—"

The feeling welled up behind his eyes, making them heavy. "What do you think you're doing?"

Duke blinked, fighting to stay alert.

"Haven't I told you to leave that alone? I can't—"

"Listen to me," Duke said. "There's something wrong here." His finger tapped the scanner screen. "You shouldn't be here."

The feeling thinned slightly. "That's where you're wrong. I put Deakes out clean, and you can bet your pair that they're going to make me do the dangle for it."

"Will you shut up!" Duke shouted. It worked. The feeling receded enough for him to keep his eyes open. He looked around the empty cell. "You didn't kill Deakes. I think I can prove it."

It moved toward Duke. "Can you, now?"

Duke nodded. "You had come back to Narofeld after running the parts out to P-3-A, and you were drinking with the commissioned pilots. Deakes came in and was going to wipe your record—''

''Oh,'' the feeling taunted. ''We've been looking at the investigation records, have we? Turned into a famous litigator of lost causes?''

''Stow it,'' Duke barked. ''You've got to hear me out. Your life is at stake—''

''Big fuckin' deal.'' It welled up inside until Duke almost choked.

''They're going to hang you,'' Duke said, breathing slowly to ease the tightness in his chest. ''They'll probably do it before we get to the Council system if you don't fight it. They'll just bring the grav up to two gees and drop you down one of the wells.''

''It doesn't scare me,'' the feeling said bluntly.

''You're not afraid to die?''

''I've been there.'' If the darkness could smile, it did then. Duke could hear the smile in its tone of voice. ''It's not all it's cracked up to be.''

''I care,'' Duke said coldly. ''Although I don't know what that would mean to you.''

The feeling rushed into Duke's arms, which suddenly folded impatiently. ''Don't give me that look,'' it said indignantly. ''I hate it when ground crew looks like they're going to cry.''

''I was there,'' Duke insisted. ''At the officer's club on Narofeld station. When Deakes grabbed us, we punched him in the gut and then tripped him. He hit the floor, and we spit on him.''

''Yeah.'' The shapeless inner voice was smiling in pride. ''I did that.''

Duke glared. ''The autopsy on Deakes showed that his throat had been crushed.'' The feeling began to lighten up. ''Dammit, will you listen to me?''

It threatened to overwhelm.

''We've been framed.''

It snorted. ''Really, now.''

"Really. We walked out of the bar leaving Deakes gasping for breath. We didn't hit him again. We were done, we were—"

"Satisfied." They said the word together.

"Somebody else had to have done it. Somebody hit Deakes in the throat, crushed his trachea and larynx. I'd lay odds that it happened in the infirmary. There were too many witnesses in the officers' club."

The feeling shifted uncomfortably. "You're a pushy little bastard, aren't you?"

"You might not care, but I'm not going to let them hang me."

"I told you, it's not as bad as—"

"Witnesses," Duke demanded. "We need people who saw you hit Deakes in the bar. Who was there that night?"

The inner voice sniffed.

"You can't expect me to remember everything," Duke barked.

"Prieboy. Larry Prieboy was there."

"That's good. Who else?"

"Thomas Fortunado." The shadow pointed with an arm. "We called him 'Misfortunado Farmbuyer' because he always used to crater his ships on landing and we just knew—"

"Who else?"

"MacKenna, Hastings, Silverton, O'Donnell—"

"Where can we reach them?"

The feeling laughed bitterly. "MacKenna, Hastings, and O'Donnell are in the common grave on Bering's Gate, along with about a thousand others. Silverton went Psych 13 and blew a blood vessel in her brain."

"What about Prieboy?" Duke said loudly. "I read about him."

"Prieboy's a fucking comet," the feeling said grimly. "His flyer blew a gasket during the cleanup of the Onaria system. He's in a long orbit now, visits the main planet once every couple of hundred years."

"Fortunado."

The thing laughed. "There's a *real* funny story about how he bought it, and believe it or not, it wasn't in a crash—"

Duke's eyes fell to the floor. "I knew that. I knew about every one of them. Isn't it funny how I'd forgotten until you mentioned that?"

"About as funny as how you came to break your arm. What was it, twice in a row? This is just as confusing to me as it is to you."

"Isn't there anybody else?" Duke implored. "Anyone that you can think of that was there?"

"Deakes."

"Besides him, Eric. Isn't there anyone else—"

"This was a long time ago. Even if it wasn't, I wouldn't be able to get help. I was the last one left alive out of all of them." The shadow sighed. "Out of every single stinking last one of the pilots at Narofeld station, it was me and Misfortunado who were left at the end of it all. The two of us that everyone thought would be the most likely *not* to survive."

"All dead," Duke lamented.

"It's really not so bad as all of that—"

"Stop saying that!"

The feeling jumped into Duke's chest, and the broker felt his heart begin to race. Quickly he thumbed a switch on the scanner, and a holo appeared on the screen. The caption read, *Dickson's favorite picture of Leigh Brand. He kept a copy magneted to his flyer's console.* There was a choked gasp, and when Duke caught his breath, the feeling was gone. He closed his eyes and took a deep breath, then stretched out on the bunk and closed his eyes.

The prospect of sleep no longer bothered him. He had worn himself thin trying to avoid it and had spent so much emotion over the last few moments that weariness appealed to him at last. The world around him began to spin, and he became strangely numb, feeling as if he were tumbling backward, head over heels.

And then he was lying on something soft. There was perfume in his brain, but it did not belong to his mother or to one of his aunt-mothers or to either of his forsaken fiancées. The place was barely familiar, and it occurred to him that perhaps the comfort he felt was not from zero gee, but from a mattress filled with ticking. Feather ticking. He thought, I should be having a serious allergic reaction. That's why Dad sent me to work at the abattoir. Couldn't handle being around the poultry plant . . .

Something moist brushed and pulled at his lips. He opened his eyes and looked up, and hair fell into his face. It tickled his nose, and he squinted. The hair vanished and another kiss came. When he looked again he saw familiar cold eyes.

"Leigh," he said quickly.

"Quiet, my darling," she said.

"You're in the wrong memory." He started to rise, but she grabbed his shoulders and pushed him down. Duke struggled but could not move. She was clearly stronger than he.

"I don't care. Kiss me."

"Wait a minute—" His protest was smothered by her lips. He brought his hands up to push her away, but she caught them and wrestled them back down to the feather-filled mattress. Squirming to get away, he could feel her warmth against him. Neither of them were clothed.

Leigh broke the kiss and lowered her head, letting her short crop of hair again tickle his face. Duke closed his eyes against it and tried to sort through the scrambled phosphors of memory.

"Wait a minute!" he shouted, rolling his head to one side. "This isn't a memory—"

She eased up but kept him pinned, still so close he could feel her breath on his face.

"What do you mean, lover?"

Duke gritted his teeth, trying to fight the physical reaction she was giving him. "I mean," he hissed, "that this never happened to me—"

"I know that—"

"And it never happened to Eric—"

Leigh Brand took his lips in her teeth and pulled. "You think he never thought about this?" She wiggled against him.

"I *know* he never thought about this. He didn't have to. This isn't a memory." He took a deep breath and closed his eyes hard. "It doesn't have that lucid quality. And it's not a fantasy, because it's too detailed."

"You're saying this isn't detailed?" She started to move and loosed her grip. Duke bent at the waist, and Leigh Brand yelped, shifting sideways. He grabbed her by the wrists and pushed, throwing her sideways and half-pinning her to the bed.

"Oh, yes." She smiled. "I like it."

Duke looked around the room, and the breath caught in his throat. The walls were spattered and caked with dried blood. "This is some kind of construct!" he growled, tightening his grip, trying to hurt her. "You weren't here at all. It was someone else. This was after you were killed."

Leigh Brand's expression froze solid. "You little bastard, I'll use you to wipe up the floor—"

"You're weak!" Duke shouted. "I remember you as weak. You're no match for me. I'm stronger than you. I remember you as weak—"

"Shut up." It came out in a feline growl.

"This is a construct," Duke said quickly. "This room is a memory, something that Eric saw. You're here because it's convenient—"

A voice boomed from beyond the cheap door. "What in the name of the Fifth Region is going on here?"

Leigh Brand went pale. "It's him. He's going to be mad."

Duke smiled. "No. Don't you see it? That's not what was really said, not according to Law Enforcement records. He's taken that from *my* past—"

Leigh rolled out of his grip and fell naked to the floor. She reached under the bed and produced a cutlass. The forged steel glimmered in the light of the single bulb above the bed. "You're supposed to take this," she urged. "You're supposed to tell me not to be scared, that you'll take care of everything."

Duke sat up and regarded her. "I'm not moving from this spot."

There was a commotion from the outside hall. "Where's the young Arbor? Where is he? I'm going to teach him that my daughter isn't another one of his hot commodities—"

"See?" Duke laughed. "That's exactly what Mr. Landon said. He's the father of one of my betrothed—"

"Take this," Leigh Brand urged.

With an ursine shout, the door to the cheap room burst open.

"Hello, Mr. Lan—" The smile dropped from Duke's face when he saw who was standing in the door. "Wait a minute," he yelled. "This isn't the way it happened to me!"

"Exactly." Eric Dickson smiled. He raised a shotgun level with Duke's chest and fired both barrels.

Duke jerked tight with the impact, spun out of the bed, and landed on the tile floor of the ship's brig. The coldness of it shocked him, and he swore loudly. It was dark, and there was laughter.

"You *bastard*," Duke hissed.

The feeling eased into a comfortable section of Duke's brain; not intrusive but definitely present. "Had to teach you a lesson for desecrating the memory of my woman."

Duke clenched his fists. "You put her there."

Laughter. "What are you going to do about it? Kill me?"

"I'm getting really sick of this, Dickson—"

"Now, now," the feeling said, and Duke could imagine it wagging a finger. "Surely you can indulge me in a little fun and games. How else was I going to wake you except by one of those maddening nocturnal jolts?"

Duke's eyes narrowed. "That's not you speaking."

"No, of course not. I stole it from someone in your recent past. I don't remember who—"

"What do you want with me?"

The feeling began to ooze through Duke's head, almost as

if it were restlessly pacing. Duke pushed in on his temples in order to stop it.

"I thought you might be interested in what you missed while you were trying to preserve your integrity against the passions of my lovely Leigh," the thing said. "Really, Duke, you should have surrendered. She would have given you the wet dream of your whole life, one you'd be proud to tell your—"

"Get on with it!" Duke shouted.

A voice rose from down the hall. "Stow it, kid! We're trying to get some sleep!"

"Pissed, aren't they?" the feeling said. "They've got every right to be. They got set up by one of their own people. Of course, if they find out what *your* relationship is to that particular person . . ."

"Get on with it," Duke said in a low whisper.

"It seems that your friend Vonn—is Maurice *really* his first name? No wonder he's such a homicidal—"

"Dickson—"

"All right," it sighed. "It seems Vonn has thrown in with the lovebirds down the hall—only they're jailbirds now—"

"The point."

"The point is, this so-called friend of yours seems to have gotten involved in a plot against this ship, something about a blockade when the Council system is reached. Anyway, they're really upset about it, and so is their boss, some person named Bachman. He's not really pleased with Vonn, either."

Duke sat on the bench. "Why should I believe you?" He felt his shoulders shrug of their own accord.

"You don't have to. However, you should be aware that while you slept, I took a few liberties with—"

Duke could feel heat rising in his face. "You," he said. "You're the waking nightmare. No wonder I can't get any rest. No wonder my sleep burns—"

"Watch your blood pressure," the feeling said smugly. "It's bad for us."

"You—"

"Keep it down in there," one of the other prisoners cried.

"We're going to cause a scene," the feeling said. "Let me do something else. Close your eyes, please. This is really quite amusing."

"Dickson—"

"Please. Cooperate. You'll understand in a moment."

Duke closed his eyes.

He was lying down on the bunk. He had been staying back, hiding, until he heard the click of the optical scanner shutting itself off. He opened his eyes. To his amazement, he saw the ceiling of the cell. His co-tenant was nowhere to be found.

He began to explore and found out why he had such persistent memories of breaking an arm that had never been broken. His right arm was encased in some high-tech kind of healing cast that had only been conjecture the last time he could remember. The rest of the body was somewhat battered, but besides being pathetically weak, it was otherwise in good shape.

Much to his surprise, he could make it work. He sat up. Then he stood. Then he went to what looked like an improved lo-grav toilet and tried to empty his bladder, but nothing was there. He had a vague memory of having already done it. Whatever the situation was, it was certainly interesting.

He had started to pace, thinking about what type of isometric exercises he could use to build up his current muscle tone, when the main door opened down the hall. He quickly went back to the bench and sat. A tall, lanky figure—looked as if he had been raised in lo gravs—ambled down the hall. Quietly he rose from the bench and slipped to the door, craning his head to see what was going on. The visitor was meeting with a collared man and woman in what looked like a dayroom.

"That's Bachman," Dickson told Duke.

Duke nodded.

Bachman placed a metaplast box on the table and stood looking at the couple, hands on hips. "Mr. Haggis. Ms.

Steubing. I don't know what to make of this. I am very, very, disappointed.''

They mumbled apologies. They were drunk, they said, and Vonn had seemed so depressed about things. They had only wanted to help.

"Help," Bachman echoed.

"With his woman," Haggis said. "Lost her to a salvor. He was very unhappy, and we figured it might interfere with the job."

"Did he dwell on it?" Bachman asked coolly.

"No," Steubing said. "But he did talk about it a lot."

"While you were drinking?"

They nodded.

Bachman's hands turned circles in front of them. "And you were just all sitting around in the bar, having a good time, buying each other drinks."

"Oh," Haggis volunteered. "Vonn was buying."

"Oh, he was, was he?"

Steubing nodded. "He had money he was going to spend on his girl, and he was, like, 'What the hell do I do with it now? Might as well spend it with my friends.' "

"I see," Bachman said.

Dickson laughed. "How do you like that? He set them up, and they fell into it like they were pulled with a hook through their nose."

"We haven't messed you up, have we, Bachman?" Haggis asked anxiously.

Bachman held a finger to his lips.

"Told you," Dickson said.

"Quiet," Duke complained.

"Quiet yourself," one of them said from their cell.

"I mean," Haggis continued, "that we're still go for when the ship hits the blockade?"

"Of course," Bachman said.

"We haven't got Vonn into trouble, have we?" Steubing asked. "I mean, we'd hate to work without him. He really *seems to know his way around things like this. I wouldn't want to try and take the ship without him.''*

"Take the—"

Duke's fist suddenly plunged into his own stomach and the words cut off.

"Watch this," Dickson urged.

"Rest assured," Bachman told them, "that everything will run according to plan. I've already spoken to ship security about your release, and they've agreed to let me speak on your behalf at the hearing tomorrow afternoon.''

The couple thought that wonderful.

"In the meantime—" He pulled the lid from the box and produced a slender bottle and three glasses. "They permitted me to bring you some celebratory cheer since you will be missing the festivities I'm holding later this evening.'' He eased the cork from the bottle and filled the lo-grav goblets. "I trust that you two have a corroborating story to tell the commander tomorrow.''

"We're working on it," Haggis nodded.

"If need be, we may have to sell out Mr. Vonn.''

Steubing started to protest, but Bachman raised a finger.

"I realize he is important to your team, but I can replace him. However, I will make every attempt not to do that. Allow me to listen to the prosecution's testimony and let me judge the tenor of the proceedings. Then follow my lead when you're allowed to speak. I expect everything will go well, but we must be prepared for the worst.''

"Of course.'' Steubing raised her glass in a toast. Haggis followed suit.

"Drink up, dreamers.'' Bachman smiled. He drained his glass.

"Some friend." Dickson sneered.

"What happened next?" Duke asked.

"The usual stuff between friends. The big shot even offered me a toast, but I told him it'd make me sick. You've got a funny voice, Duke."

"Why are you remembering this for me?"

"Because you've got to learn that you're the only person who can do any good for you. You don't trust anyone, not even one of those bastards with that 'brothers-in-arms' code. Isn't worth the simfile it's saved to."

"Is that right," Duke said cynically.

"The truest thing you'll ever learn from me."

"What about Leigh Brand, then? Did you trust her, Eric?" His words reverberated through the cell.

Down the hall, Steubing shouted, "If you don't shut up, I'm going to pull your lungs out."

"Eric?" he whispered.

Nothing.

"Eric?" Duke leaned back and sighed. The feeling was gone. Where are they now that I need them? Duke thought. Where's May? Busy with the commander, I suppose. Roz? Winters? And I can't trust Vonn anymore, not as a friend, not as a partner, not as a brother. This trouble with Deakes comes up and everybody bails out. Sounds like Eric was right.

Duke closed his eyes and tried to pull the feeling of Dickson back. When that failed he tried to find Leigh Brand with the moist lips and soft hair in that cheap, dirty room with the ticking-filled mattress. They were nowhere to be found in recent memory.

He shivered. The room was cold. He could never remember ever having felt so utterly alone.

22

Waking in Duke's berth had a disorienting effect. Generally speaking, Vonn liked to sleep perpendicular to the angle of thrust because it gave a rocking sensation that lulled him into an easy sleep. He had arranged his own berth to facilitate that.

Unfortunately, he had not thought of that before crashing out in Duke's bed, and he woke feeling light-headed. Had he wanted to look in the mirror, he was sure he would look pale and worn. That was what he got for sleeping with his feet toward the engine compartment; the thrust drained the blood from his brain.

There was nothing he could do about the situation. He felt bloated and sick, and it would be days before he felt right again. If only he had taken another five minutes to rearrange things.

But that had been the last thing on his mind the previous night. His situation had gone sour fast, and it was going to take every bit of his quick wit to keep him alive until they arrived at Council 5.

It had started off with drinks, or rather, a lack of them. Vonn had been craving alcohol, and while he ordinarily would have disciplined himself, his resistance had been down. He had felt bad that Peter Chiba had gotten a worse working over than he had expected at the hands of his two teammates, and the incident had not made things any better with Roz. There had not even been opportunity to talk to her. She had left her berth for the infirmary to be at Chiba's side as soon as she had heard the news.

After that he had tried to go and see Duke, but found that the brig was not a safe place for him. His two teammates had been incarcerated, and their legal counsel was in speaking to them. On top of that, the brig's matron, a dour-looking woman who looked as if she was torn between wanting to murder or make love to him, frowned when he gave his name, and without a further word, she disappeared into another room.

Vonn's stomach made a pre-danger plunge and he walked out of the waiting room, hurrying to put distance between himself and the brig by heading in the direction of his berth. If ship security was going to be looking for him, it would be better if he could move some of his incriminating personal effects back to the *Angel's Luck*. More important, he would feel better if he could get his pistol from his locker on the merchant ship instead of being stuck with the unassembled bits and pieces of the Xegg gun.

He arrived on the deck where he was berthed, turned the corner to his hall, and froze. Three security uniforms were crowded around his door. One of them pulled out a card and slotted it into the lock. The door opened, and two of them stepped inside. The third turned to guard the hall, and Vonn jumped back around the corner and flattened himself against the wall, heart pounding wildly. Down the hall, the door to a lift opened. He headed straight for it.

On the lift, his lower jaw started to tremble, a warning that the rest of him was going to follow suit unless he could get his nerves in check. He closed his eyes, took deep breaths, and pictured himself cut loose in deep space, peacefully drifting, but it did no good. Things were coming at him too hard and too fast for conventional means of stress release to help.

He told the lift to stop at the next commercial floor and stepped off when it did. His course took him straight to the first place that advertised liquor, an expensive-looking grill called The Accord, whose atmosphere was patterned after the room where the treaty with the Arcolians had been forged. The place made Vonn tremble all the more. There was just no getting away from it all.

The barman was right there when Vonn sat, and the mercenary ordered three straight shots of bourbon, holding his card out with two fingers. The barman took it, plugged it into the register, and keyed the order in, studying the printout on the screen. After a moment, he lined up three lo-grav shot glasses and filled the order. Vonn downed them quickly, one after the other, then exhaled and slumped back on the stool. He twitched his finger at the barman and pointed at the register, which still held the card.

"Yes, sir. Another round?"

"I'd like my—" Vonn dropped his hand. "I'm sorry?"

The barman turned his hand to indicate the three empty glasses. "Would you like three more shots?"

The mercenary blinked in disbelief. He looked at the machine that held the card. It was supposed to tell the barman that there was a three-drink limit—unless it told him something else . . .

Vonn sighed loudly. "Yes," he said quickly, mind racing. "Uh, Aiaagan gin please. A *bottle* of Aiaagan gin."

The barman did not blink an eye. "Very good, sir." He turned and keyed the order in, and a shelf opened on an empty compartment. He looked bewildered, then returned to Vonn. "I'm sorry, but that item is not in our regular stock. If you'll excuse me for a moment—"

"Of course." Vonn slouched and crossed his arms, trying to give off an aura of infinite patience. He watched while the barman wandered back to access the storage room, not missing a beat of his calm façade. When he was out of sight, Vonn walked out.

On the lift down, he ran his hands through his hair. He was dead. With ship security on his tail, the computer had swallowed his card. It should have been a blessing—the ID would have marked him and enabled ship's personnel to track his movements within the ship. But without it, he could not get food or drink or a place to sleep. With a sigh, the mercenary closed his eyes. It would not even be safe for him to try hiding in the *Angel's Luck*. He leaned his head against the wall and stuffed his hands in his pockets.

His left hand touched something cold.

Vonn pulled it out. It was the card May had given him to access Duke's berth. Turning it over, Vonn saw that it was Duke's ID. He closed his fingers around it and laughed.

The lift deposited him right where he requested. He went to the nearest intersection, looked down it, and saw that the door to his berth was still open and that one of the guards was busy reprogramming the lock. Trying to lay a trap for him, no doubt.

Vonn had turned the opposite way, walked down the corridor a dozen meters, and carded his way into Duke's berth. He had noticed vaguely that the bunk was not oriented the way he preferred, but with the events of the last few days colliding with the bourbon he had just taken, he had no trouble getting to sleep once his clothes were off and he was zipped into the covers.

After the initial disorientation upon waking, he began to feel good in spite of his psychosomatic hangover. He checked the odds and ends that filled his pockets to make sure that they still added up to one complete Xegg gun, redistributed them, and dressed.

The next few hours were uneventful. He moved and acted as a legitimate passenger, making sure not to get into a situation where someone would check the holo on Duke's ID with the person carrying it. He breakfasted in a nice but inexpensive restaurant where the waiters did not even look at the card when it was handed to them. Eating slowly, he outlined what he should be doing until the ship reached the Council system, only a matter of hours away.

He left the restaurant and wandered until midmorning, at which time he headed for Bachman's suite. The meeting was to be the conspiracy's last before the *Hergest Ridge* shifted into real space, and it was Vonn's hope that the arrest of two of Bachman's people had disrupted things enough to call the whole thing off. His nagging, practical side told him that a person of Bachman's caliber would make a go of the plan despite bad luck. Vonn patted himself to check himself on his inventory of Xegg gun pieces. It might take something more to discourage Bachman's plans.

He arrived at the suite with moments to spare. The room was buzzing with talk, all of it speculation on the future of the mission. Vonn took a seat in the second row, pulled the Portalight from his belt, unscrewed the cap, and spilled the batteries into his lap, looking around nervously.

Before long Bachman walked in. He cast his gaze around the room and, with a nod, began.

"No doubt," he said darkly, "some of you have heard of the unfortunate situation that has arisen involving members of the diversionary team."

There were murmurs of consensus. Someone in the back asked what had happened. Vonn took the writing stylus from his breast pocket and, working by touch, reassembled it into a long hollow tube.

"An unfortunate incident occurred near the transgear bays." He gave Vonn an icy look. "Apparently, after our last meeting, the diversionary team took it upon themselves to have a few drinks. Two of the members became rather intoxicated and gave a salvor a rather severe beating."

"Salvor trash," someone hissed.

Vonn inserted the tube into the hollow center of the Portalight's body. Then he popped the top off of each battery and removed the three brass cylinders that had been stored in each. He turned the Portalight over and inserted them into a hollow chamber.

"He may have deserved it," Bachman said, "but the point remains that there has been an act of irresponsibility on the part of our people."

Vonn's hands trembled. He pulled a magnetic utility spanner from inside his boot and snapped it into a gap on one side of the Portalight. It became a handle.

"In fact, certain members of this project have demonstrated a rather marked contempt for proper job procedure . . ."

Vonn probed a breast pocket with his fingers. Nothing was there. A shiver crept up his spine. The last component was missing.

"It makes me wonder about the integrity of the mission, which, I assure you, will go off as planned . . ."

Smoke stung Vonn's eyes. He turned to the mercenary sitting next to him. "Say," he whispered, "you wouldn't have another one of those cheroots, would you?"

The man grunted and slipped him a twisted stick of dried leaf. Vonn wet the end and stuck it in his mouth.

". . . in spite," Bachman was saying, "of some of the members of this organization who have proven to be less than competent."

"I need a light," Vonn whispered.

The man grunted. "You'd better listen up, brother. That's

you he's talking about." He pressed something cold into Vonn's hand. Turning it over, Vonn saw that it bore the crossed lightning bolt insignia of the Xegg company.

"I have just spoken with shipboard security on behalf of our brothers who were incarcerated as a result of this. Unfortunately, because of the nature of their crime and the fact that there is a delegation of Arcolians on board, I was not able to win their freedom in time for our move." The room filled with discussion. Bachman called for order. "We will proceed with the mission," he said, "without the diversionary force. And without you, Mr. Vonn."

Vonn brought the lighter to his lips and fired the end of the cheroot. Then he cleared his throat. "Fine. I've no intent to give blood for my working percentage."

Bachman interlocked his fingers and cracked his knuckles. "What do you mean by that, son?"

Eyes on his boss, Vonn blew smoke and worked the lighter in his fingers. He fumbled its housing into the base of the Portalight just in front of the spanner-handle. "I mean that my partners are better off where they are. You had the three of us set up as a sacrifice."

"You'd better have a damned good explanation—"

"I do." He pushed the lighter's body flush into the Portalight. A stub emerged from the end of the lighter. "You had no intention of sending a ship to link up with us once we ejected from the ship, did you? We would have drifted out between planets until we died. Maybe if we were lucky the Orbital Police would find us, and even if we spilled our guts to them, it wouldn't hurt you, would it?"

"This is totally unfounded, Mr. Vonn. You know the rules as well as I. You have to maintain integrity and morale among your men. Had I done that, I would have violated all conventions—"

"Stuff the conventions," Vonn snapped. His fingers worked a circular piece of metal from the lighter's firing mechanism and began to screw it onto the stub. "You're standing to make a hell of a lot of money on this, aren't you?

I mean, this is your enterprise, isn't it? You have no backers. I'll bet your name isn't even Bachman."

"You *bastard*," Bachman growled. "You did it on purpose, didn't you? You got them drunk and set them up to beat up that salvor—"

"I saved their lives, didn't I?" Vonn worked his hands over the weapon. It felt complete. He put his index finger through the ring of the metal and spun the spanner-handle into his palm.

"We're going anyway," Bachman said. "Without the diversion and without you." He waved at a familiar broadshouldered man who was standing by the door, then pointed at Vonn. "Brutus. Grab that son of a bitch and kill him."

The man took three steps before Vonn raised the Xegg gun up and fired. The shot caught the man in the center of the chest and knocked him back into the wall amid an explosion of blood and viscera.

The one who had given Vonn the cheroot rose and started to grab the assembled gun. Vonn brought the weapon up and slammed its body into the man's forehead, then kicked and leapt over the people in front of him.

"Get him! *Get him!*"

There was an explosion, then a cracking from the wall behind Vonn. He looked back to see a large splatter of dark, oily liquid clotted with bits of round metal shot. Sweeping the weapon across the room, he bore it down on the woman who had shot at him, and fired. A standard bullet caught her in the abdomen and knocked her down hard.

Two more rushed him from each side. He fired at the one on his right, but the range was too close; the round whistled off the bulkhead and felled someone else. The others converged on him in a tangle of limbs. Staggering back, Vonn sprayed the room with fire.

"No!" Bachman shouted. "No more shots! We can't afford to lose any more—"

"Yes, we can." Vonn smiled. "You."

Bachman's hand crossed his torso to his belt as his frame came into Vonn's line of sight.

"I was right, wasn't I?" Vonn shouted.

Bachman looked up in alarm as the trigger was pulled.

The weapon exploded in Vonn's hand with an impossibly loud report. Pain that burned to numbness flared to Vonn's shoulder, and he screamed in agony, falling back into the wall.

A woman started toward him. Vonn grabbed his wounded hand and brought it up in a wild swing, uppercutting her and splattering her face with fresh blood. She stumbled back into the others, and Vonn turned, slapped a switch with an elbow, and staggered out the door.

He turned down the hall and tried to run. It took too much thought, too much concentration with his arm on fire. One foot in front of the other, left, right, left, right, in the name of the Fifth Region get me out of here—

A black spider appeared on the wall ahead of him, legs oozing down to the floor at the speed of freezing transgear fluid. The sound rolled in behind it in a leisurely sort of way, a sharp crack followed by a loud *snik!* Vonn turned right at the next intersection, and another spider jumped onto the wall just ahead of him. His stagger took him in a slow, looping circle. Looking back, he could see that a series of dark, red blotches was following him on the floor. He weaved back and forth to elude them. His eyes stung and tried to close, his feet would not carry him straight, and ahead was a blank wall.

Vonn plunged numbly toward it, unable to break his forward momentum. Another mutiny spider appeared. And then the wall in front of him parted into a dark maw. A woman emerged from it, took one look at him, and screamed. She ducked out of his way, and he jumped past her. A wall appeared in front of him. He hit it and turned. The wall was closing up behind him then, putting metal between him and the screaming woman and the advancing figures who were sending the spiders. Slowly he sat.

"What floor please?"

He looked up. He was alone in a tiny compartment.

"What floor please?"

Vonn grunted.

"Shall I open the door for you?"

"No," he said quickly. "Down. Take me down."

"Which floor, sir?"

"Go till I tell you to stop."

The room lurched and Vonn's stomach jumped. He shook sweat out of his eyes and looked down at his hand. It was convulsing with a life of its own. His thumb and index finger were missing. The fingers that remained were black and charred, and a piece of metal was stuck deep into his palm. The back of the hand was bloody from the same piece of metal, which protruded from it. He could feel nothing from the elbow down. As he dropped his death-grip on the wrist, blood began to squirt from where the fingers had been.

Vonn ground his teeth. Combat set, combat set, he told himself. Time to save your ass, old boy . . .

Suddenly he groaned. The hell with it. This was the big one. Checkout time. Forlornly he looked around the elevator.

"Anders? Where are you, brother?"

The only noise was the hum of the servos.

"Don't hide on me," Vonn said bitterly. "This is the part where you come to pick me up, right?"

Still no response.

"The hell with it." He leaned his head back and closed his eyes. "I'll come and find you."

The small room filled with a voice. "Your attention please . . ."

Vonn startled. It was not Anders, nor was it the usual elevator voice.

". . . your attention please. The UTE Fleet liner *Hergest Ridge* will be downshifting into the Council system in one hour. All passengers and nonessential crew should go to their berths or places of waiting as per GTC ruling two zero seven stroke five one nine three, subsection 'c.' To repeat, this liner will be making downshift to real space in the vicinity of the Council system within sixty minutes . . ."

The cabin started to spin around Vonn. "Oh, no," he said, panic filling his voice. "Not yet, old pal. You're going to have to wait. I've got one more thing to do."

With his left hand, Vonn unbuckled his belt and pulled it off. Fumbling the switch, he brought up the torque, looped it over his wounded arm, then flipped the switch. It tightened, then stopped. He nudged the torque up more until the bleeding stopped.

He drew a deep breath. "Don't lose it, brother. Don't lose it."

The elevator continued to hum around him. His face grew slick with sweat, and he was feeling light-headed.

"Can't die," he breathed. "Can't die yet."

Nausea hollowed him out from his throat to his bowels.

"Don't lose it. Don't lose—" He ran out of breath.

"Don't lose . . . don't lose . . ."

Yellow phosphors flared at the center of his vision and spread outward. Vonn bit his lip, but the pain did not stop the blindness.

Don't . . . don't . . .

He gulped for air.

. . . don't—

. . . don't—

His head bobbed forward.

—n't . . .

23

Dorienne Junnell had to say it twice to be heard over the insistent ringing of the alarm. "All preparations have been made, Commander. The ship is at ninety-eight percent readiness for the shift into real space."

"Very well," Commander Margaret O'Hearn said. "Cut the intership alert and get ready to place us in system."

Junnell acknowledged. O'Hearn turned to Tesla. "Are you ready with the scanners?"

He nodded. "We've tweaked the Vasac to its maximum tolerant radius. If there's anything between us and number five, we're going to know it with time to spare."

O'Hearn checked the chronometer on her wrist. "Damn it," she whispered. "Where's May?"

"Begging your pardon, ma'am?" Tesla said.

"Nothing," she said quickly. "Junnell. Status of relative position."

"We'll be within optimal system positioning in one minute."

Another minute for him to show up with information from security. Another minute spent waiting on him. That was the story of her life with James May.

O'Hearn sighed. "Very good, Mr. Junnell. If your confidence is high you may take us in at will."

"Yes, ma'am." Junnell smiled.

O'Hearn eased down in the command seat and studied the tactical display. "Let's see who's waiting for us."

_____ THREE _____

"We've got to show these bastards that we're not afraid to die."

May was running down the hall when the wave hit. It started with the sensation that he was not covering as much ground as he thought he should and then worsened to the point where it felt as if the air around him was a heavy, thick liquid that was slowly suffocating him. By the time the throbbing reached his ears, his brain at last made the connection.

They were making the shift into real space.

He wanted to swear, but he could not bring himself to heap insults on his ex-wife's name. She had more than her share of problems at the moment, and the shift down was certainly going to compound them.

Of course she had not known, not officially, about the blockade—but couldn't she have waited another sixty seconds?

He was interrupted by the shudder, which started as a slow-motion series of pulses rippling through him and then gradually increased in speed until it was a quick rattle. The sensation cut off, and May leaned against the wall to brace himself.

It was over. They were in the Council system.

The merchant found his bearings and began to run again, faster. The guard at the bridge door saw him coming and politely stepped out of the way, allowing the doors to open.

"Maggie," he said, stumbling onto the bridge. He caught his breath and looked around. A dozen puzzled faces looked back at him. "Commander O'Hearn," he amended. "I thought you were going to wait."

"You were late," she said, looking at her chronometer.

May shook his head. "You downshifted early. It doesn't matter now. It's too late for—"

"Commander," Tesla interrupted. "I've got shadows showing on the scanners."

"Report," O'Hearn snapped.

"Small, varying sizes, about a half-dozen of them. Zero speed, between—" He stopped for a moment to check the board. "Between us and Council 5."

"The blockade," O'Hearn said. "It's real."

"You'd better believe it's real," May said. "Security reports that the blockade was mentioned repeatedly by the two passengers who assaulted Peter Chiba."

O'Hearn spun on him angrily. "Why didn't you tell me that, Captain?"

"Why didn't you wait to downshift?" he snapped back. "You should've known that this information was confidential net traffic, and the net is down because—"

She nodded, stung. "I am well aware of downshift procedure," she said. "My apologies—"

"Confirmation of two shadows as small vehicles," Tesla said. "Merchant size or smaller. Three more shadows showing on screen—"

"Continue monitoring, Ensign. Mr. Junnell, bring our speed down and keep us distanced from their sphere of influence. You've got command while the captain and I go to interrogate the prisoners."

"Begging your pardon, Commander, but that won't do any good. The two prisoners are dead."

"*What?*"

The bridge went silent, save for the noise of the operating systems.

"The brig log shows that they were visited by their legal counsel last night, a man who identified himself as Bachman. He gave them drinks that apparently contained a degenerative neuromuscular toxin—"

"Mr. Junnell," O'Hearn shouted. "Excuse us!" She grabbed May's shoulder and pushed him toward the door. They hurried down the hall where she palmed into a small lift. As May caught up, he could see that her face was streaked with tears.

"Close," the commander choked out. The door slid shut.

"Maggie, don't—"

"Dammit, James, *why wasn't I told*?"

"Security was waiting for autopsy results and—"

"They should have notified me! I'll have their ranks for this, I swear it." She pulled a cloth from her pocket and dabbed her eyes. When her composure returned, she spoke resolutely. "I want this Bachman. I want him picked up and interrogated, whatever it takes, I want complete intelligence on this blockade."

"That's not going to be immediately possible," May said.

"This is my ship, May," O'Hearn hissed. "The sooner you get used to that idea the better, because I'm sick and tired of being contradicted by a—a *merchant*!"

May grabbed her shoulders. "Maggie, security has already tried to pick up Bachman. There is no Bachman listed on the passenger manifest, and there are no lawyers on board who fit the description. They're running a video record through the manifest files to find out who this guy really is."

O'Hearn took a deep breath and nodded. "All right. They're following procedure. Why did things have to get so balled up—"

"There's more," May said grimly.

She looked at him hard.

"Security reports that there's been gunfire on one of the inner decks near the ambassadorial suites. A female passenger was found dead by one of the lifts, and there were mutiny-pill splatters on the walls. Security found blood in one of the lifts and followed its path back to a suite registered to a freelance investor. They found more dead—"

Her hands knotted on May's lapels. "Is there any end to this?"

May shook her. "Maggie—"

"I want them, James. I want them to answer to me—"

"*Maggie—*"

"This is my ship, my command, they can't do this—"

He shook her hard. *"Maggie, you're still in control!"*

Tears streaked her face as she shook her head.

"Oh, yes you are, *yes you are*! You put up with the academy and the active duty grind, and you put up with me, and you put up with all kinds of grief to get here." May tightened his grip for emphasis. "I'm going to be madder than hell if you lose it now. Dammit, Maggie, this ship cost me a divorce—"

Her eyes went wide and she stared at him.

"It's got to be worth something. I refuse to believe that you gave me up for nothing."

She nodded. "Yes. Of course." She gestured at the lift door and what was beyond that, the corridor and the bridge. "They need me."

May took the cloth from the commander's hand and wiped her face. "What are you going to do, Maggie? Tell me what you're going to do."

"What have we got?" she asked thinly. "Tell me, James."

"Double confirmation of an anti-Arcolian blockade around Council 5. Shootings on an inner deck. Possible fugitives loose."

She nodded. "Secure quarters," she said numbly. "Seal up all nonessentials."

"Good. Good." He folded the cloth and stuffed it into her breast pocket. "What else?"

"Screen the blockade. We'll need intelligence, numbers, specifics." Her voice was growing strong. "And I'll need to make a command decision on action to be taken depending on what data we get."

"Excellent." He straightened out the lines of her uniform.

"The Arcolians," she said, "will need additional guards. The inner deck shootings may be unrelated, but they may be the result of anti-Arcolian sentiment. A general one-level add-on should do it."

May kissed her on the cheek and released her shoulders. "Yes," he said. "You're ready, Commander." He gave her a formal salute.

She wavered for a moment. "Thank you . . . Captain."

"Open," he told the car. The door obeyed, and he followed O'Hearn out, staying a step behind her. The monitor stepped aside, and Margaret O'Hearn became a presence the instant she stepped through the bridge door.

"Ensign Tesla," she said loudly. "Status report on the blockading vehicles."

"Total on the screen of forty-nine," he told her. "Only thirteen of those have been confirmed through Vasac-to-Vasac as actual vehicles. Of these, two are merchant size, and the remainder are between pursuit and pleasure craft–size."

"It looks as if some may fall into the Vacc Fighter class. Any communications?"

"None, Commander," Junnell said. "Although there's still a great deal of distance between us—"

"They're waiting to make a positive identification, which won't be long because of our size. Keep the general beam open and sound a ship-wide General Quarters."

"Yes, ma'am." Junnell bent over her console, and an alarm sounded.

"Twenty-one confirmed," Tesla said.

O'Hearn nodded. "Captain May. Opinion?"

The merchant captain shrugged. "My only opinion is the

obvious. The choices are to run it or back off and head for another system.''

"Your opinion, Captain."

May straightened out of his slouch. "Were I in a ship this size, without benefit of passengers or an ambassadorial delegation—''

"You would run it."

"Of course."

O'Hearn bounded through the bridge and sat. "Mr. Junnell, key in a beam to the Council 5 Port Authority. When you've an opening, I'll give you the message to send. Ensign Tesla—''

"Twenty-nine confirmed, Commander. The largest vehicle confirmed is an Empire-class Tanker.''

"They're going for mass, not efficiency. That would never catch us.''

"But hell to run into," May advised.

"At this point, a tug would be hell to run into," O'Hearn told him.

May bit his lip.

"Ensign Tesla, put a security scramble on all intership communications. Any highly sensitive communications will nonetheless be made by courier. Captain May, would you be so good as to call security and on my authorization double the guard on the Arcolian delegation?''

May bowed. "At your service—''

Revel Tesla squeaked.

O'Hearn turned and cocked her head. "Ensign, did you have something to say?''

"Indeed," Tesla said. "I didn't think anything of it because things were going by routine—''

"Ensign—" O'Hearn warned.

"misterbob had plans to visit William Arbor in the brig today. He had me set one up for postshift—''

"How soon?''

Tesla swallowed. "Commencing immediately.''

"General Quarters has been sounded," Junnell advised.

"Explain that to an Arcolian," O'Hearn said. "May—"
He started for the door. "On the way."

"Freeze!" May did so as O'Hearn rose from her chair.
"Mr. Junnell, when you get an opening to Council 5, advise
them of our situation and request a relief squadron. You are
not—I repeat, *not*—to say anything about the ambassadorial
delegation on this ship."

"Yes, ma'am."

"I'm going with you," O'Hearn told May. "I only hope
it's not too late."

2

In time—and it was not long—Eric Dickson returned. It
had been his idea to take the optical scanner apart and use it
as a weapon. Duke countered with the fact that the laser
inside would be nothing but low-grade and useless for much
of anything but perhaps etching graffiti onto the walls. Eric
countered, saying that perhaps they could use it to temporarily blind someone. Duke did not like the idea. He was
opposed to hurting people, and that still would not solve the
problem of getting out of the cell.

That led to Eric's masterstroke—they could access the laser in the scanner and use it to knock out the sensors on the
collars they wore. From there, escape would merely be a
matter of timing.

The next problem that presented itself was that they had
no tool with which to open the scanner's case. It was Duke
who solved that one. He went to the zipbed, grabbed the
tongue of the zipper that ran across it, and with a few deft
twists broke it off. That gave them a flat surface to use as a
screwdriver and a D-shaped opening that might serve as a
small ratchet.

Once they got the outer shell off the reader, Duke was lost.
It was up to Eric, whose memory came in fits and starts, to
find the laser's circuit and isolate it from the inner workings

of the scanner. Once that was done, power was channeled from other parts into the beam's power supply. With some delicate trial and error, they were able to tweak the laser to its maximum available output.

Eric positioned the cannibalized scanner in Duke's lap and aimed it in the general direction of the collar's minibrain. After raising two blisters on Duke's neck, they decided to try using the mirror to make the aim. Eric wanted to aim *into* the mirror and reflect the beam back out, but Duke prevailed and merely used the reflection to direct where it would go. Within minutes, the minibrain gave off a spark and raised a third blister on Duke's neck.

The next order of business was to test what had been done. Duke inched cautiously toward the door, waiting to see if the warning tingles came. Eric took over and pumped the legs, boosting them through the door with no apparent ill effect. They had access to the entire cellblock. Their only remaining obstacle was getting through the main doors.

"Tell you what," Eric said. "Let's call for that matron-bitch and we'll threaten to fry her brains out with that toy of ours."

Duke could feel Eric's disdain for what he was about to say but went ahead nonetheless. "You know I don't like that idea, and yes, I have a better one." He had learned to read the feeling's expressions by its intensity. "There's just one catch—"

"I don't trust you," Eric said. "I don't. I can't—"

"Knock it off," Duke said. "You can't be around for this one. You'll lose it."

"How do you know?"

Duke closed his eyes. It was there, something dim trying to break through the clouds. An arm, a hand, holding something heavy and metallic, pointing . . . "I can feel it."

"I'll bet," the pilot scoffed.

Duke kept his eyes closed. "How's Leigh?" he said aloud. He called up the construct, the seedy room, the lips, the hair, the flesh-to-flesh—

The sensation in Duke's head was like that of something bursting, a rush of wind leaving an empty room.

"Eric?" he asked, opening his eyes.

He felt quite alone.

"All right," he said. "All I have to do now is wait."

The waiting part took longer than Duke thought. The morning meal came, followed by the discovery that the two most recent tenants of the brig were extremely dead. The Medical Section swamped the place, questioning Duke—who could legitimately say that he had no memory of anyone visiting—and even going so far as to take a sample of his blood. In the excitement, lunch was all but forgotten until midafternoon, and Duke had to keep himself entertained with thoughts of Leigh Brand to keep Dickson's shadow at bay.

Lunch, when it finally came, was cut short when the matron came back for the tray. She told Duke that they were preparing to downshift into the Council system and that he should get into his zipbed until the all-clear came. He secured himself as recommended, trembling in wait for the shift's numbing effects.

As he waited, a calm washed over him. Don't sweat it, he told himself. It's nothing. You've been through this before, on the *Angel's Luck*, remember?

He peered out the hole in the bag at the room.

"Eric? Was that you?"

Nothing.

Duke closed his eyes and relaxed. There was a shudder, and the downshift was over before he knew it.

The matron gave him the all-clear, and he climbed out of the bed, checking the altered optical scanner once it was safe to do so. He placed it on the shelf, the case loosely propped on it so at a glance it would look normal, then sat on the bench to wait.

"Duke. Hey, Duke."

The feeling was back, pressing in on his mind.

"Nice job you did with the downshift. Couldn't have done

it better myself. Of course, you were lying in a zipbed and not trying to pilot a—"

Down the hall a door opened and a scrabbling sound began to rise.

Duke turned to the shadow. "Get out of here," he hissed urgently.

"That's rude of you, son. Should I take you back to the room Fortunado was killed in and teach you another lesson?"

The corners of Duke's lips turned up. "Yes," he said. "Do that. I'd like to see Leigh again."

The *pop!* inside his skull was almost audible to him that time; he swayed under the impact. He filled his lungs with air and dropped his head down between his knees, waiting for the vertigo to pass.

Another sound filled his ears. It stopped, and then—

"williamarbor? Do you hibernate?"

With a gasp, Duke sat up. "misterbob," he said. "No. I'm, uh, fine." He gave a nervous smile, hoping the Arcolian would be able to interpret it. "I've been waiting for you."

misterbob shuffled into the cell and eased into its sitting position. "Your physical status has changed since our last communication," it croaked matter-of-factly. "I scent changes in you, not for the best, misterduke. Indeed, your levels of internal fluid tension are causing problems throughout your physiological structure."

"Blood pressure," Duke corrected. "That's what you're scenting." He took another breath, wishing that he could stop sweating. If he kept it up, the Arcolian would find out . . .

He went cold.

"You know," he said to misterbob.

The Arcolian's head bobbed. "You are under a great stress, misterduke. I sense traces of malevolence that your being is repressing. You are honorable for that, williamarbor. Can you explain your reasons for this?"

Duke took another deep breath, then lifted his eyes to

the ceiling. "There's no hiding anything from you guys, is there?"

misterbob's throat rattled as it considered his words. "If I am making you feel uncomfortable, you may bring in your dogs."

Duke laughed. "No," he said. "That won't be necessary. I will give you the truth. If you scent other than the truth, you tell me, misterbob, and I will make it correct."

misterbob's throat rattled again, and it brought one hand up to stroke its chitinous chin. The gesture took the Tetran aback.

"Indeed," it said. "In return, of course, I will be truthful with you, williamarbor. It is bad fortune that you will have no way to scent this. Therefore, you will have to—" Its throat started to rattle.

"Trust you," Duke said.

"Indeed."

"I trust you, misterbob, more than anyone on this ship. I trust you because . . ." He faltered and looked around the room. His eyes were clouding.

misterbob cocked his head.

"Dammit," Duke breathed. "I trust you because you're not another Sapient A-form."

A long hiss came from misterbob's torso, forming words in a way that Duke had never heard before. "MMMMMosssssssst Interessssssstinggggggggg."

Duke broke out in gooseflesh. "All right. I am accused of assaulting redbutler, correct? Everyone—every one of the Sapient A-forms, that is—who was there thinks that I was the one who did it. But you don't think so, misterbob. You get the scent that tells you I am being truthful. But it's un—it's bad fortune that you are the one who can scent me because I am still subject to the Sapient A-form laws."

"Indeed," the Arcolian clicked.

"Yet you were there," Duke continued, "and you are convinced that I am innocent. Is it possible, misterbob, that another Sapient A-form with a strong resemblance to me committed the assault? One who resembled me so much that it confused the sight of the other A-forms?''

"Yes, misterduke. It would explain the anomaly of their insistence on your guilt which contradicts my proof of your innocence.''

"Let me make one more assertion," Duke said. "Would it be possible—would you believe, misterbob, the possibility of *another* A-form inhabiting my body, taking control of it long enough to perform the assault?''

The Arcolian's head cocked. "Most interesting if accurate, williamarbor. It is your contention that you are a varied form of Sapient—shall we call it a B-form?''

"Let's call it an A/B form, misterbob. Two separate A-forms, one body. One controlling most of the time, but the other surfacing under unusual circumstances.''

The hissing came again. "Yessssss.''

"Let's take that one step farther now. What if I told you that I *was* an A/B form Sapient, misterbob. That because of circumstance or accident, I have become an alternating personality. What would you say to that?''

"I would say this is most irregular. Perhaps williamarbor is confused.''

"So is misterduke." Duke put his hands to his head. "Indeed, misterbob. I know this all fits together somehow, but I can't explain it, not entirely, without endangering the lives of my friends.''

"Your scent is concern," misterbob said. "This obsession in your species for The Life—''

"Am I still telling the truth?''

"Yesssss.''

"Then you understand that this all has to tie together. If there was a way I could explain it—" He looked up and studied the Arcolian for a moment. Suddenly he flushed, his face coloring with frustration.

"Scentchange," misterbob advised. "Something new. You have been prevented from reaching a goal. There is a slight anger to you, misterduke—''

"Scentchange," Duke said. "Of course. That's it. If he can use my body, he'll use it *his* way, differently from myself. He'll use my voice differently and walk differently." He beamed at the Arcolian. "That's it, misterbob!"

"Again scentchange," the Arcolian advised. "Openness. Clarity."

"Understanding," Duke said softly. "I understand now how to explain it to you. Besides my own scent of the truth, misterbob, is it possible that the Sapient A-form who assaulted redbutler had a different scent than I did? Is that why you had no fear of coming in to see me, because I did not scent of the A-form who assaulted your colleague?"

The creature's head bobbed. "Most intriguing, williamarbor. Please to explain how you came by this new scent."

"I can't," Duke said. "I wish I could tell you, misterbob, but it's too early. Look—scent, I mean. You have been the only one to be convinced of my innocence of the charges against me. *Something* must have given false signals to the other Sapient A-forms that the Arcolian E-forms observed. *That* was the difference, Ambassador. I *have* become a Sapient A/B form, and the other existing form is the one guilty of the crime."

"Then by your own laws, this other A-form must be sacrificed."

"Yes," Duke said. He stopped to wipe sweat from his forehead. "It's a hell of a situation, isn't it?"

"There is that hell element again. I do not comprehend it."

"Doesn't matter." Duke shook his head. "It's just ironic to me—the Sapient A-forms aren't willing to sacrifice The Life for the sake of manipulating the Spiral Code. The Life is very precious to us, and we spend most of our time trying to preserve it in ourselves and the ones close to us. Except for those who deviate from our social norms."

"Indeed," misterbob purred. It had given up trying to understand and was now merely observing.

The Tetran laughed bitterly. "Because of the situation I

am in, I will be sacrificed so the A-form who is guilty will be punished."

"It is important that you sacrifice the guilty A-form?"

"To them it is, misterbob. What they don't realize is by sacrificing one, they sacrifice both of us." Duke stopped and leaned against the wall. He bent at the waist and took deep breaths.

"You scent of confusion, williamarbor. It is time for you to rest."

"I can't rest. I've got to clear this up."

misterbob stood. "Indeed. Then we must go straight to margarethearn and explain this. We must explain this to everyone who was present and seeks to sacrifice you."

"No," Duke said. "Not yet."

"misterduke, I hate to be so impolite as to interrupt—"

"Excuse me," Duke said, holding up a hand. "But if the word gets out to the people right now that I have become an A/B form, there are those who will still try to sacrifice me. Please don't ask me to explain why, not unless you understand the concept of the word *gangster*."

The Arcolian nodded gravely. "Indeed," it said. "elliottness."

"Whatever that means," Duke said. "All you have to do is scent me, misterbob. Do I scent of truth?"

The ambassador was silent.

"Well?" It came in a shout.

"williamarbor," misterbob explained. "You should know that your truthscent has been supplanted by beliefscent."

"And what the hell does that mean? That I'm lying?"

"Indeed, no. It means that you believe in something which you believe to be true. It is—how to describe it in one of your falsesense concepts? I believe you call it a shade of truth."

Exasperated, Duke looked around the cell. He was never going to get out of there if—

"misterduke, your scents change much too quickly. You are ill, perhaps. If you were to lie down—"

"Wait a minute," Duke said. "I've got to get out of here."

"Yes," misterbob said. "And I will assist you in any way I can. Indeed, you have rejected my offer to go to margare-thearn—"

"Do you mean that?" Duke asked. He picked up the mod-ified optical scanner. "Will you really do anything to help me get out of here? Especially if I ask you to do it right now?"

"For what reason?" the Arcolian asked cautiously.

"I believe that a friend of mine is about to make a serious mistake. If information I have gotten from the B-form I carry scents of the truth, then my friend has somehow gotten mixed up with an anti-Arcolian faction. He may harm your race, and I wish to prevent this from happening. He is my friend, and I don't want to see him sacrificed for making a mistake, and you are my friend, and I don't want to see you hurt."

"You flatter me too much, misterduke."

Duke pulled cover from the optical scanner and clicked on the power. The beam struck the wall and blistered the paint. "Afterward, I will cooperate with you completely as far as going to the commander or telling the other Sapient A-forms. But first I have to help my friends, and to do that I must get out of this cell. I will not harm you. Am I scenting the truth?" He shut the beam down.

"Most interesting," misterbob said.

"I will not be able to get out unless the other Sapient A-forms believe that I intend to harm you. I must behave like I will harm you so that I can escape and stop the anti-Arcolian faction."

"Indeed. I must see how this thing you call escape works." The Arcolian shuffled to its feet and raised an arm at the door. "Do we go?"

"Yes." Duke nodded politely. "You must go first, Am-bassador."

"Indeed." misterbob made its chuckling sound. "Indeed, indeed."

They went down the hall to the door, and misterbob rang

the other side with a bony finger. As the door slid open, its chest came alive with the scent from the A-form in charge. There was that spike of apprehension along with slight nervousness and distinct unease that she did well to mask. misterbob watched her face carefully, fascinated by the disappearance of the smile as Duke stepped into view.

The matron's scent changed quickly to one of alarm, and she stepped back.

"He's not supposed to be out, Ambassador."

"Indeed," misterbob said, glad that the matron could not read liescent. "It seems he is giving me no choice in this matter."

"Get back," Duke growled, "or I cook the xeno's brains." He wielded the laser and let it sting the matron's arm for emphasis.

The matron stepped back, hand groping across a desktop as she did. misterbob scented and knew what was coming. She smelled of duty, and her hand was going for the piece of bent metal near the monitors. The Arcolian flexed its chest and put out a close sphere of scentkill.

Duke shook his head. "What's that?"

Flexing its chest again, it shot scent directly at the matron, pushing a quick series of alarms at her; ammonia, transgear lube, old blood, decay, burning sulfur.

Duke saw what the matron was doing. "Hey," he barked. "Watch that—"

What caught her was the scent most A-forms described as tigerscat. It hit her just as her hand touched the handle of the weapon, and the reaction bordered on the electric. Her hand snapped away from it as if she had been shocked. Indeed, noted misterbob.

"Knock it on the floor," Duke ordered.

The matron's hand batted the weapon as if it were a bad thing. It clattered to the floor.

"Kick it over here."

Her foot hit it, and it spun between Duke and the Arcolian. Keeping the laser trained on misterbob, Duke squatted, grabbed the gun, and stuffed it in a front pocket of his brig-suit.

"Now get my clothes," Duke ordered.

The matron did not budge.

misterbob eased off on the tigerscat and hit her with another odor that resembled pine rosin.

She smiled. "Right away."

"No funny stuff."

"No," she said dreamily. "Of course not." She disappeared into another room.

Duke snuffled. misterbob turned to him and directed a larger dose of scentkill his way.

"This is working," Duke said with a laugh.

"A most fascinating behavior," misterbob replied.

Duke sat down behind a computer terminal. "I might have to have her access code." He drummed his fingers on the glass screen of the terminal. "I need to find—" His eyes locked on the screen. "Here it is!" He stared at an entry at the bottom of the screen.

INMATE # 99048. VONN, MAURICE. STATUS: CUSTODY. SPECNOTE: SUBJECT WOUNDED, CURRENTLY IN LEVEL 12 GA INFIRMARY. MEDSEC TO ADVISE WHEN CONDITION ALLOWS HARD INCARCERATION.

"I've found him," he said happily. "This is going to be easier than I—"

The door from the hall hissed open, and with a shout of outrage, Margaret O'Hearn stepped through.

"misterbob! Are you all—"

Duke threw an arm around the Arcolian's head and brought the cannibalized scanner to bear. "Freeze," he barked.

"Duke," said May, who was a beat behind her. "Don't do it."

"Don't give me that," Duke answered. "Ever since I've hooked up with you, you've been telling me the importance of how only you can look after yourself. That's exactly what I'm doing. I'm taking the initiative."

"Sure you are," Margaret O'Hearn said. "But if you have information, you've got to share it with ship security. You've got to give the system a chance."

"Don't patronize me," Duke said loudly. "The system is exactly why I'm here."

"James," O'Hearn said under her breath. "You've got to do something."

May nodded. "Duke," he said. "Trust me."

"Why should I? You didn't come to see me, May, not when I needed you. Why should I listen to you now?"

misterbob's chest pulsated. It sensed that Duke was beginning to hurt inside; his internal fluid tension was going dangerously high. The commander was mostly a scent of frustration with rising levels of rage. If things got out of hand, she would be capable of doing great harm. Caught in the middle was the one called May. He was scenting so hard and fast that misterbob was scarcely able to believe that such could come from a Sapient A-form. Anger, compassion, duty, love, guilt, pity—it was as if the whole gamut of human emotions were instantly running through him. This was going to be tricky, misterbob thought. Much harder than handling the matron. There needed to be one sharp pheromonal message that could deal with both of them safely, but the barrage of scents being received made it impossible to focus.

"Because I got you off of Tetros," May said. "Because I treated you like my own son and taught you how to run my ship even though you had no qualifications. Because we've been through too much together and we've built a friendship that should be worth something, Duke. In the name of that friendship, I ask you to hear me out." He took a step toward Duke.

"To hell with friendship." Duke swung the laser out and flicked the switch. The beam caused a flare against the shoulder of May's uniform, and the merchant jumped back, yelping.

"May!" O'Hearn shouted. She stepped to his side and knelt.

misterbob scented her at once: compassion, concern. Yes, of course, indeed, that was it. The Arcolian flexed its chest and bombarded the pair with every tender message it could think of until it was receiving quantity for quantity what it was giving out.

"James. Oh, James . . ."

O'Hearn began to sob and fell into May's open arms. They melted into an impenetrable embrace.

"What happened to *them*?"

The matron was standing at the door, Duke's civilian clothes under her arm.

"I understand they had once undergone a ritual spiritual bonding," misterbob explained. "I merely restored this." It directed scent at the matron, and she yawned.

"How nice." She yawned again.

"You should hibernate," misterbob suggested.

The matron nodded. "And I know just the place to do it." Yawning, she retreated in the direction of the cellblock.

Duke stowed the laser and hurriedly changed clothes. "Forgive me if I leave you behind," he said. "Time is of the utmost importance."

"I regret not being able to observe," misterbob answered, "but I scent your urgency and respect it."

"I can't thank you enough for your help, Mr. Ambassador."

"Indeed. You are to call me misterbob."

"Indeed." Duke wrapped his hand around two of the Arcolian's fingers and shook them. "I call you friend." He pulled the gun from the discarded brigsuit and bounded out the door.

misterbob shifted back to sit and watched O'Hearn and May. They were still sobbing, touching, and calling each other by name.

"Such fascinating creatures," the Arcolian noted.

3

His head hurt. Badly. He had the sensation that he was almost floating. His right arm was numb from the elbow down, but the ends of his fingers throbbed. His chest was covered with a myriad of absorption patches, and a Direct Osmosis Fluid Induction Unit was strapped to his neck, a line leading away from it to a pressure bag of clear fluid.

When he looked around, he saw no one.

The first words out of Vonn's lips were "What time is it?"

There was no reply.

"Come on. Anybody. What time is it?"

He tried to sit up. The move was successful, but it made him woozy.

"How about it. Somebody got the time?"

"Funny thing," said a voice from a few beds down. "The usual question is 'Where am I?' "

"That I can tell," Vonn said. "It's not like I'm an idiot." Moving both hands down to brace himself, Vonn was alarmed at the bandage he found around his right hand. The sensation of the exploding Xegg gun came back to him and made his stomach wrench. "I've had better days," he said.

"I know the feeling," the figure in the other bed said. "But in your case, I'd say it was poetic justice."

Vonn turned and squinted in the direction of the voice. There was a figure swathed in bandages and patches, suspended from the ceiling by a series of pulleys and wires.

"Chiba? Peter Chiba?"

The figure nodded. "And that makes you the biggest ingrate I've ever met. Some thanks I get for saving your life."

Vonn shook his head. It made him feel worse. "Not me, pal. I didn't lay a finger on you."

"Then how did you know I was beaten up? Unless, of course, you were the sponsor of that little incident."

"You're lucky I stopped them when I did," Vonn grumbled. "It could have been a lot worse—"

"It *was* a lot worse," Chiba snapped. "I had to go through

downshift like this. I hope I never have to live through something that bad again.''

"Downshift.'' Vonn cursed under his breath. "Oh, no. I've got to get out of here—'' He stood and the blood drained from his head. The strength left his legs, and he flopped back down on his cot.

Chiba laughed. "Excuse me, but I'm enjoying this.''

"Yeah.'' Vonn held his head in his hands, taking deep breaths. "Excuse me for not enjoying this more. It's been a long time since I've been in a friendly rivalry over the attention of a woman.''

"Friendly rivalry?'' Chiba swayed on his supports. Had he been in a conventional bed, he would have been up and at Vonn's throat. "It ceased being friendly the minute you set those two goons on me.''

"All right. You have my most formal and penitent apology, Mr. Chiba. I thought I was losing Roz, and I'm afraid that I took it rather badly.''

"Losing?'' Chiba laughed. "You've lost her, pal. You lost her long before Zack and I pulled you out of that stinking tin box of a merchant ship.''

"It's not my ship,'' Vonn said, straightening up. "Insulting it won't hurt me.''

"You're missing the point. If you'd hadn't treated Roz like some piece of meat from the very beginning, things certainly wouldn't have come to this.''

Once more, Vonn put his feet to the floor and stood. "No. You're missing the point, pal. You might have Roz and vice versa, but none of our lives is going to be worth a pile of very small Njit droppings unless I can walk out of here.'' He became pale, wavered, then sat hard. "Son of a bitch.''

"You're going to need some rest before you try to save the galaxy,'' Chiba said.

Vonn shook his head. His eyes were growing heavy. Somewhere, a door hissed open.

"Mr. Vonn. Mr. *Vonn*—''

An attendant in a powder-blue uniform was on him, her

hands on Vonn's shoulders, gently pushing him down onto the bed.

"Mr. Vonn, you shouldn't be trying to get up. You've suffered a severe trauma and lost a lot of blood. You need to let the fluid replacement regimen take effect before you try any serious movement."

The mercenary's head swam as he tried to think of an excuse. "Where's the head?" he asked.

"One moment," the attendant said. "I'll be right back to take care of you."

Chiba laughed as she walked away. "I'm going to enjoy this, too. You know what you're in for?"

"Go to hell," Vonn said weakly. "I've had my share of neocaths, and I'm not going to . . . to . . ."

His head flopped back on the cushion and he fell into a profound, thick blackness. His extremities felt heavy and swollen, and bright phosphors of color danced across his field of view. The air in the room started to thicken, and he watched in horror as a mote of falling dust slowed to a halt. When he looked over, he saw that Peter Chiba had frozen in mid-grin.

"Not again," Vonn said. "I'm sober, dammit. I don't need any of this."

"That's a matter of opinion."

Vonn turned to see Anders, white as a sheet, waiting patiently. The last of his remaining blood had drained out through his mouth and chest and dried hard on his face and clothes.

"You look like hell."

"Your fault. The least you could've done was plug me up before you left."

Vonn tried to move. He could not. "I had things to do."

Anders nodded. The skin over the muscles of his neck splintered and flaked off. "And a hell of a lot of good it did you. You're worse off now than you were before. Should have listened to me."

"I did," Vonn barked. "How do you think I got here?"

The dead mercenary smiled. The skin over his face crackled. "You always let yourself go off at half-cock, brother. You should've stuck it out with May. Now you're in a bind. Might as well pack it in and come with me."

"Beat it," Vonn replied.

"Seriously. You were carrying Duke's ID card, and the computer flagged it because he's in the brig. It obviously didn't take long for them to figure out who you really are. Now you're going to have to come clean, and that'll only make things worse because you're wanted, too—for every charge in the known universe." Again Anders shook his head. "Come with me, Vonn. Get it over with."

"No," Vonn said. "Where were you when I needed you?"

"What. You mean the elevator? I was getting ready for the big influx of people we'll get when Bachman and his crew go to work. We're expecting—"

"Not funny," Vonn said. "I'm leaving. I've still got things to do."

"If that's what you want, brother—"

"Stop calling me that, Anders. You're dead."

"So are you." Anders smiled. "By the way, Jents has a message for you. He says—"

"Suck on it," Vonn said. He fought against the thickness he felt until the suspended mote of dust began to fall once more. The image bent and tilted, then snapped into focus. He was still in the infirmary. On the table beside him, a neocatheter kit had been left by an attendant not wishing to disturb his rest.

He turned to look at Chiba. The salvor was asleep, and a tall figure had wandered into the ward, slowly studying each empty bed. Vonn blinked to pull things into focus and watched. The figure stopped and studied Peter Chiba for a long time. It stepped over to the screen and studied the salvor's vital signs, nodding slowly.

"Yes. Of course. It had to be you."

It reached into the front of its trousers and removed a pistol, bringing it into a left-handed aim.

"Duke?" Vonn asked. "What the hell do you think you're doing?"

Startled, the Tetran looked at him. Their eyes locked, and then Duke smiled with unpleasant recognition.

"Maurice Vonn. I'm here to see you."

Why don't I like that tone in his voice? Vonn thought. Smiling, he sat up and waved his right arm. "We're twins now. I blew half of my frigging hand off. What are you doing with that gun?"

Duke's eyes narrowed suspiciously. "How did you do it?"

"Call it a transgear accident. Would you mind telling me what—"

"Funny that I find you in the infirmary, Vonn." He paced toward the mercenary with deliberate steps. "Of course, it should be obvious that you would be here. Clearly you should be involved in something like this."

"If you're talking about the blockade," Vonn said, "it was an accident. And I did my best to put a monkey wrench into it—"

"I'm not talking about that, although I find that it doesn't at all surprise me."

"Yeah, well the galaxy is full of little surprises. Listen Duke, you've got to help me get out of here. There's going to be trouble—"

"Oh, yes," Duke's head bobbed. "There's going to be trouble. Lots of trouble." His thumb pulled back the hammer of the pistol.

"What the hell's wrong with you, Duke? Are you crazy—" Vonn's eyes widened as he stared. "Oh, no. *You.*"

"Yes," Duke said. "Of course. It had to be you." He leveled the barrel of the weapon at Vonn's face. "You killed Deakes." He moved in on the mercenary. "Now it all fits in with what William showed me."

"William?" Vonn asked.

"William Arbor. If I hadn't been in the brig with him, I never would have seen this couple there, talking to some guy about a conspiracy, and they mentioned your name.

"No sense in denying it," Duke continued. "Deakes couldn't stand the way I worked, and you wanted me out of the way because I learned too much about this anti-Arcolian blockade of yours. Deakes moved first and tried to strip me out of my Pilot's Certs, but he didn't count on me putting him in the hospital. Then you and your friends saw a way to get us both out of the way, so you had yourself put here." He paced around the bed, manically waving the weapon. "It was an easy matter for you to get up out of bed, walk over to where Deakes was, and crush his throat."

"It must be nice," Vonn said bitterly, "to have everything make sense in a twisted sort of way."

Duke closed the distance. "Then you tried to cover your tracks by killing the two in the brig. The only problem with your plan—"

"Haggis and Steubing? They're dead?" Straining hard, Vonn forced himself to stand.

"—was that O'Hearn didn't execute me fast enough." Duke poked the weapon under Vonn's chin. "So I'm going to execute you first." His finger nudged the trigger.

"What's happening in here?" The attendant's voice was loud and outraged. Duke turned his head toward her, the pistol swayed and discharged, and black ooze splattered against one of the bulkheads. Peter Chiba started awake, cursing and causing his bed to sway violently. The attendant ran for the corner as Vonn batted the weapon out of Duke's hand and tried to crook his right arm around the commodities broker's throat.

From the corner of one eye, Vonn saw the attendant racing toward them with a small canister in her hand. With a curse, he pushed Duke into her, filled his lungs with air, and dove over his bed in the direction the pistol had gone. There was a loud clatter as medical supplies spilled across the floor, and Vonn burned in a half-dozen places from where the patches and inductors were pulled from his body. There was an explosive hiss as he grabbed the gun, and clouds of blue gas billowed into the air.

Vonn stumbled to his feet and feinted around the struggle between Duke and the attendant. Ultimately the Restcure overcame them and both slumped to the floor.

"I don't know what you do, Vonn," Peter Chiba said, grinning like a fool, "but I do know that nobody else does it that way." His eyes rolled to the back of his head, and he succumbed to the gas.

Lungs aching for air, Vonn began making his way out of the ward. At the nurses' station he bumped into a magnetic cart, and the sight of its load of ampules inspired him. He rifled the row of lockers until he found a nursing vest that almost fit him. He stuffed a pressure injector into one of the pockets and filled the others with as many ampules as they would carry.

After a pause to put a mutiny pill into the infirmary's communications console, he was off down the hall, running and then walking and then stumbling, finally crawling to a lift and banging on the door with the butt of the gun until the vibrations caused it to open. He rolled in, croaked "Up," and then started to sort through the ampules, putting the ones he thought would help him into the injector and shooting them into his thigh.

4

Tesla was the one who made the discovery, and the news was not good.

"Mr. Junnell," he said. "Would you step over here for a moment, please?"

Junnell rose from the command chair and went to Tesla's side. "Yes, Ensign?"

He pointed to the tactical display he had brought up on his screen. "Forty-eight of the ships in the blockade force have formed a spherical pattern between us and Council 5."

"That's normal for an operation such as this," Junnell explained. "It takes too much time to run around, and if you try to cut straight through, you're surrounded."

"The forty-ninth ship." Tesla struck a key, and an oblong shape highlighted on the screen. "This is the Empire-class tanker. It's shadowing us, ma'am, matching us movement for movement on an intersect course."

Junnell straightened and looked at the main viewscreen. "If they don't stop us one way, they're going to do it another. Clever of them."

"Are they thinking of ramming us, ma'am?"

The first officer sighed and clasped her hands behind her back. "I don't know, Ensign. Are they? Perhaps that's what they want us to think. They don't make the Empire series any more. They're something of a rarity. On the other hand, they're a highly expendable rarity. Off the record, Ensign Tesla, I wish Commander O'Hearn was here. She's from the old line of the academy, and they trained them right back then."

"For the record, ma'am?"

"For the record." Junnell sighed. "For the record we continue the slow-in and keep trying to contact Council 5. Any word from the commander yet?"

"No word from the brig at all," Tesla said. Color flashed on his board. "Stand by. Incoming on direct beam."

"Let's hear it," Junnell said.

There was the crackle of subspace interference, then a male voice filled the speakers.

"This is Tristan Swain, the acting commander of the Blockade Fleet. You will cease your transmissions to Council Port Authority as we have been jamming them since your downshift. You must also cease your slow-in approach of system planet number five, or we will prevent it by any means possible. Our request is that you divert course back to the shift point and leave the Council system immediately."

"Give me a beam back in," Junnell said.

"You've got it," Tesla replied.

"Citizen Swain," Junnell said, "this is the *Hergest Ridge* of the UTE Fleet, a corporate entity ship engaging in routine transport of cargo and passengers. What is the meaning of this illegal attempt to deny us of enterprise?''

"It's *Commander* Swain" came the reply.

"I'll bet," Junnell said under her breath. Tesla smiled.

"This fleet was formed specifically for the purpose of dealing with your ship. The Arcolians are murderers and infidels. We object to the Accord, which was signed against our wishes, we object to the diplomatic relations that this Accord has called for, and we most specifically object to their presence on our world."

"Sore winners," Tesla whispered.

"Arcolians?" Junnell asked, trying to sound shocked. "Citizen, are you *certain—*"

"Listen," Swain replied. "You and I don't have to put on a façade. I'm not going to lie about what'll happen if you continue your senseless xenophile attempt to bring those creatures in." There was a pause. *"Hergest Ridge*, please zoom your direct view onto sphere center. You'll find a moving vehicle with a blue beacon pattern. Please observe it carefully."

Junnell nodded at Tesla, who brought the image up on the board. The system located and closed in on the blue beacon until everyone on the bridge could see that it was a merchant ship, one about the size of the *Angel's Luck*. It broke from its position in the sphere and headed directly toward the *Ridge* until it filled the screen. Tesla nudged the zoom back.

The merchant ship continued forward, then turned perpendicular and started across the screen. From all sides of the sphere broke small single-pilot vehicles. They converged on the merchant like a swarm of hornets, running and strafing, peeling off from the attack and coming in again in a tightly coordinated attack.

Tesla stood. "Vacc Fighters," he said, astonished. "They've had them refitted."

"They're serious about this," Junnell said. "That's in direct violation of the Accord."

The merchant blossomed into a burst of shrapnel.

Swain's voice returned. "You see what we're capable of doing in just a few short moments to a merchant ship," he said. "It shouldn't take us much longer to do the same to you. You have fifteen minutes to alter your course back to the shift point before we take aggressive action."

"He's bluffing," Junnell said quietly. "There's no way a fleet with so many small ships could do that to a ship this size. They might beat the hell out of us, but they won't destroy us."

"What about our shadow?" Tesla asked.

"That could be what they're counting on. The problem is, if they've gone this far, it seems foolish of them to leave so much hanging on an obsolete ship."

"Fifteen minutes. That doesn't give us much time."

"For the record, then," Dorienne Junnell said. "Ring for a state of emergency and summon the commander to the bridge."

5

May was looking at Maggie, her lips swollen from kisses, when the warbling of the Emergency Stations alert hit his ears. His hands, which were running through her hair, stopped short.

"Something wrong?" she asked softly.

May looked to his left. "What's that noise?"

"It's nothing."

May looked to his right.

Maggie reached up, took his chin in her hand, and turned his head to face her. "It's nothing, really. It's just an alarm they ring to get the crew to their stations."

"Are you certain?" May asked.

Maggie nodded. "They only use it during an emergency when they need me on the bridge."

"Well." May grinned. "As long as it's nothing serious." He brushed her hair back, looked into her eyes, and started another kiss. His hands came up to cradle her head, and her arms slid around his shoulders.

Suddenly he felt the muscles in her neck tense.

"James, you were right." She tried to struggle out of his grip, but he held her fast. "It's General Quarters. I'm needed on the bridge."

May looked dreamy. A broad smile covered his face, and his eyes were half closed. Then it snapped. His back straightened, his eyes became alert, and his mouth opened wide. "General Quarters? Yes!" He jumped to his feet and offered an arm to his ex-wife. She grabbed it and pulled herself up.

A hunched figure in the corner of the room raised up and shuffled their way.

"Indeed, this has been a most fascinating observance of the interactions between Sapients."

The commander gasped in surprise. "Ambassador—misterbob. Uh—"

"misterbob," May said suspiciously. "You've been here this whole time?" He nervously cleared his throat.

misterbob's head nodded. "You must forgive me. I see that I have intruded. I scent that you both suffer from emotional discomfort. I believe I have created what you call embarrassment."

O'Hearn straightened the crumpled lines of her uniform. "We've got to get to the bridge."

"Wait a minute," May demanded. "You mean that Mag—the commander and I were merely one of your pheromonal *experiments*?"

"No, jamesohjames. I merely inflicted you to facilitate other things."

May started to ask what those things were, but he noted that the ambassador's chest organ was fluctuating, and the question suddenly dropped from his mind. Instead, he took the commander by the arm and led her to the door.

"I apologize," he said. "This shouldn't have happened to us. The ambassador, in his misguided wisdom, somehow made us—"

"Permit an interruption," misterbob croaked, shuffling toward them. "I would be pleased if you do not think of me as a manipulator such as were the first E-forms. I would not inflict such emotional discomfort on one I respect so as margarethearn. Merely instead I caused to surface what was already there."

O'Hearn looked at May. "Then what we're feeling now—"

"Is the hangover," May finished.

The fingers on misterbob's hands clicked against each other with delight. "Indeed, indeed. It is such a pleasure to communicate with such an intelligent species."

May opened the door for his ex-wife and began to usher her out of the brig. "They need you on the bridge. I'll see that the ambassador gets back to his suite."

"That will not be necessary, thank you," misterbob said. "You should remain with your spiritual-bond partner."

"I should escort you," May said unwillingly. "The ship is in an emergency state. You should be protected."

The Arcolian pulled itself up to full height. "After what I have put you through, jamesohjames, is it not possible that I am capable of self-protection?"

May looked at O'Hearn.

"The ambassador has a point," she said. "I may need your help, and I want your support."

"All right." May studied the Arcolian from the corner of his eye, then brought up an accusing finger to point at the chest organ. "I agree with no undue influence from *that*."

misterbob's fingertips clattered. "Indeed. You must go now."

May kissed O'Hearn's cheek and ushered her out the door. "We'll run by the infirmary and see if they can give us something for this."

O'Hearn stopped. "No, James. This isn't the sort of thing they can give you an ampule for."

"I don't want a cure, either." May looked deep into his

ex-wife's eyes. Before they could again fall completely, he looked away. "The bridge," he said, and led her away.

6

The warbling hit Vonn's ears, too, and his eyes popped wide open. His bowels were cramping hard, he had goose-flesh, and a mild tremor covered his body. His arm no longer burned, and he felt round-eyed alert, a feeling he had not had in years.

He looked down at the empty ampules that littered the floor.

"What have I done to myself?" he asked, noting that his voice sounded thin and brittle.

Vonn had no problem standing. As he dusted himself off, it occurred to him how ridiculous he must look: raw patches on his arms and chest, a too-small nursing vest, and an open-backed hospital gown. He was hardly combat ready.

The car lurched.

"Emergency override," its voice told him. "This car is responding to an emergency override."

Security, Vonn thought. The perfect time to get an appropriate uniform. He picked through the ampules still in his pockets, loaded one into the injector, then went down to the floor in a sprawl.

In a moment, the car lurched shut and the door opened. Heavy boots sounded on the floor, bringing someone closer.

There was a groan. "Not this." Hands grabbed Vonn by the vest. "C'mon, you—"

Vonn raised the injector up and fired the ampule into the guard's hip. The guard cursed and fell to the floor.

"Close," Vonn said. The door obeyed. "Wait." He bent down, pulled off the guard's protective vest, and laid it aside. "Sorry, pal, but I need this stuff worse than you do." Thumbing the zipper button, the uniform shirt split down the middle. Vonn took one side with his left hand, started to pull, then froze.

"No," he said, stepping back, shaking his head. "No. Not this . . ."

The guard was a woman. A very short woman.

7

"Wake up!"

Duke heard the voice but did not see its source. He could see a hand swinging toward his face. He never felt the impact, but his head snapped to one side from it.

A familiar thickness crept through him as he opened his eyes and studied where he was. He was on the floor of the infirmary, tangled around the inert frame of a female attendant. He gently extricated himself from the situation and stood, thumping the cast on his arm to check its integrity and knocking the dust from his clothes.

There was a dull ache behind his eyes. Duke recognized it as a Restcure hangover, but another part of him questioned that, not having any recollection of a product or device by that name. He crawled to the lo-grav sink and turned the water on too fast. It splattered off the basin and sprayed high in the air. Bending at the knees, Duke put his face over the torrent of cold water and let it sting him. When he was done his thoughts seemed clearer.

Peter Chiba was still lying in his cot, unconscious. Vonn was nowhere to be seen. There were dim memories of the mercenary getting away and taking the pistol with him. Sluggishly Duke rose from the floor, stopping just long enough to pry the small Restcure container from the unconscious attendant's hand.

He was starting a slow plod toward the door when he realized that there was sound in his ears, loud and incessant. Exactly what it was eluded him. By rights it should have been a General Quarters alert, but here on Narofeld they had no need for such a thing.

Unless . . .

Unless the Arcolians had struck. Unless something had

again happened to the lookout station and they were headed insystem under some kind of cover. Was it too late to get to the fighters? Was it all he could do to man one of the cannons and hope for the best? Duke fell against the wall, eyes clenched shut, and tried to sort things out. He had no recollection of such a raid on Narofeld, had no warm confidence that it would turn out all right. He ached for the memory— any memory—of what had happened.

They had been disemboweled and—

With a shriek Duke bolted out of the infirmary, plowing through the crowds of people who were trying to get to their drill positions. Every new floor and every turn of the corner only added to his confusion. Somewhere, *somewhere* there should have been something that would identify where he was on the Narofeld base. The place he was in was big and intimidating. There were few buildings on the grounds that were that big, and thus far he had not been able to identify which one it was.

He continued his trip downward, avoiding the lifts, trying to find staircases, but settling for ladders and gravity wells. Things would be all right, he knew, if he could only reach the ground floor and get to one of the particle cannons.

Gravity wells?

The oddness of it all struck him as he was tumbling down one of them, shaping his body into a basic catfall that he had learned during basic—*May could never teach me how to do it but somehow the DI at the station could . . .*

Gravity wells on Narofeld? There were none. They had had to go into orbit, to a platform, to have access to one. Duke searched the memories that were there. The only time he had ever used a gravity well while at Narofeld was on a platform, in orbit.

Duke finished the twist and hit bottom, bending his knees and letting the impact carry him forward out of the well. He stumbled onto a wide hallway, something that looked very used, very industrial. None of it made sense.

He grabbed the first person who appeared and demanded

to know the directions to the ground floor. The person laughed and said something about having too much to drink, then told Duke to get to his berth.

Berth. More spaceborne jargon. He continued to stumble down the hall until another sound, a familiar whine, assailed him. Looking about as if he were coming home, he turned the corner and came to face a large access door in front of which presided a guard. He knew what lay beyond that door from the vibrations in the soles of his feet.

"Transgear bay," he whispered.

The guard cocked his head at him. "What? You say something, son?"

Duke pointed. "This is a transgear bay."

"If you're not on shift," the guard told him, "then you'd better get to your berth."

"Berth," Duke echoed. "This is a platform."

The guard gave a knowing smile. "Ship," he said. "This is your first year, isn't it? A touch of the old DS3?"

"Never," Duke said. "Never had it." After a moment to reflect, he said. "I've got to man one of the particle cannons. That's my job."

The guard shook his head. "General Quarters. If you're not on shift—"

"But the Arcolians are coming," Duke said urgently.

"Hell, son." The guard smiled. "The Arcolians are here. We're taking them to Council 5—"

"No!" Duke screamed. *—disemboweled and nailed to the walls of the ship with large metal spikes. He could see it just as if—*

The guard advanced. "There's no reason to get upset about it, son. The Arcolians aren't going to hurt—"

"Traitor," Duke snapped. He brought the can of Restcure up and vented the blue gas into the guard's face. The guard fell back, and Duke stepped out of the way of the dissipating cloud. "You'd feed us to them. Fucking xenophile."

When the blue cloud could no longer be seen, Duke pocketed the Restcure and searched the guard's belongings, turning up a master key card. He plugged it into the access box and the door opened. A warm, oily breeze pushed against his face. The vibration of the machinery enveloped him. He started forward, and with his third step he crossed the line into the bay and an alarm sounded.

"Security breach," a mechanical voice said. "Security breach. Security breach."

Duke ran deep into the bay, making his way through the maze of turbines and field-effect generators, past arrays of monitoring equipment and controllers. The vibrations became fiercer, and the thrumming was so intense that he could barely hear the intrusion alarm and the nagging mechanical voice.

He turned another corner and stopped dead. Directly in front of him was the systems distributor, a huge thing that looked more organic than mechanical. It pulsated and throbbed, and Duke realized that that was what was making the noise, the vibrations.

The finger Eric had lost to a transgear all those decades before throbbed.

Feeds the Harmonic Processing System, he remembered. *Keeps things dampered and lubricated and cooled with that all-in-one fluid—*

"Heart," Duke said. "The Heart." His lips turned up.

He started toward the distributor, and the vibrations, the noise, and the heat became intense. When he came within five meters he was suddenly struck blind and sent spinning across the fluid-slick floor.

That's not how they're protected, he recalled. *There was some kind of myoelectric charge—*

Picking himself off the floor, Duke's tongue probed his mouth and found that two of his bottom molars were loose. Yes, he blinked. That was it—

The blindness came again, and he staggered back into a wall that protected one of the transturbines. He shook it off that time, faster, recognizing what was happening. Between himself and the systems distributor was a man—a *big* man.

Duke blinked at him. The side of his face tingled with something warm and wet, and his eyes burned. "Sullivan?"

The figure stopped, feet shoulder length apart. His shoulders were broader than Duke, broader than any of his memories of Sullivan, yet he was easily ten centimeters shorter than the battered broker. His neck was thick, his face hard, and fingers were absent from each hand. In his hand was a rod that gleamed in the dim light of the transgear bay. When he smiled, Duke saw that his opponent had no teeth but two solid bars of bronze.

Okay, I won't try an uppercut, he thought.

The man's jaw trembled, and the metal teeth clicked together. The sound was loud.

"This has to happen at least once every trip," the man told Duke. "Someone has to see the systems distributor for himself. Someone has to make a big statement about what we do with these things. They want to let it free, or they want to put it out of its misery."

Duke flexed his tongue in his mouth. It was numb.

"I'm here to tell you something, friend. You can't eat it. It *ain't* alive. It sure as hell might look it, but it's vat grown, organic metal and plastics. Stretch fiber. Makes its own electric."

Duke remembered having learned that somewhere, although he could not place the circumstances.

"And I'll tell you something else. The only way to *it* is through *me*." The transgear puller raised the rod with one hand and spun it effortlessly. "And from standing here, I can put this right through your skull. Got that?"

Duke nodded.

Let me take him, Duke. I can do it. I can leave this guy in the dirt.

All right, but don't hurt him.

Dammit, Duke, he's going to get hurt.

Don't kill him, I mean. I know how you think. I won't cooperate if I think you're going to kill him.

All right. Have it your way. You're such a fucking loser, Duke.

Duke looked down for a moment, then raised one finger and put it high on the bridge of his nose. "Put it here," he said. "Right between my eyes."

The puller spun the rod into throwing position and cocked his arm.

You're not making things any easier on me, Duke.

The arm started forward in a pitch, and Duke sidestepped. The puller corrected for the throw, and as the rod left his hand, Duke shifted again. The rod clanged harmlessly into the transturbine wall. With Eric Dickson's reflexes, Duke spun and caught the bar before it could hit the floor. "Nice try." That was Dickson's touch. Duke was too scared to say anything.

Eric twirled the bar with Duke's left hand. "Now come and get it back."

You promised you wouldn't kill him.

The puller's muscles tensed. Duke saw it through his eyes, amazed with recognition. He had never before understood the concept of telegraphing a move, yet there it was.

The puller was heading for him fast, launching himself with a kick and flying fast in the diminished gravity. Dickson spun the bar with a flourish—*your reflexes need work, Duke*—stepped to the side, and slammed the bar hard into the attacker's stomach. The puller landed with a grunt, rolled across the deck, and hit the wall.

"That was great!" Duke exclaimed. "I never could have done that in a million years!" He threw the rod to the side.

The puller rolled onto his stomach and looked at Duke through narrow eyes. "You trying to be funny?"

We've got trouble, Duke. That should have put him out, but you didn't have enough upper body strength. Did you have to throw that rod away?

"What are you talking about?" Duke asked, alarmed.

"I mean," the puller said, rising, "that you've just had your one lucky shot."

It's your move, Duke.

My move? I'm no fighter!

You were the one who didn't want to kill this guy.

I can't even bruise this guy, Eric.

What do you want me to do about it?

Buy some time.

The xenos are about to grab us for their lunch and you want to kill time. This had better be good.

It will be.

The puller was up and moving again, covering the distance between himself and Duke in a pair of deft hops. His fist came hard at Duke, who ducked out of its way. He tried another. Duke dodged again. The blow missed by centimeters, and Duke could hear the rush of air it had displaced. A third blow rushed by, and Duke felt its wind on his face.

"Hold still"—the puller grunted—"and show me what you're made of."

Duke spun away from a fourth strike and reached into his coat. His hand emerged with the can of Restcure, and he turned to face the puller, can at the ready. The puller went into a spinning leap. His foot darted out and caught the edge of the can, knocking it into a high arc through the transgear bay.

Duke's face fell. "Oh, damn—"

Dickson jolted Duke's muscles and pulled them to the side as the second kick whizzed by.

The puller came out of his spin and planted both feet on the floor. He was not surprised to see that Duke was still standing, but then his gaze went above Duke's head. "Son of a *bitch*—"

Now, Duke—while he's trying to distract us!

Duke started to leap into an assault, but when the result flashed in memory—nose broken, bone shards driven up and into the brain—he tightened his muscles and held to the spot.

Duke, you've just thrown it all—

"The cannister," the transgear puller said.

In spite of Dickson's roaring objections, Duke turned.

Dickson hunched his shoulders and tightened his neck muscles, waiting for the blow to come, but it never did. Through Duke's eyes he watched as the Restcure cannister tumbled down into the systems distributor's protective field. He felt Duke start to panic.

"No, no, *no*—" Duke's voice squeaked shut and then returned in a lower tone. "You said that stuff was harmless—"

The cannister caught fire as it passed through the field, and a massive blue spark lifted from the surface of the Heart and lashed out at the intruding object.

Jents sighed and handed the cannister to Duke. "It's only Restcure, but it's under a lot of pressure. There'd be shrapnel if it ruptured."

There was a muffled roar, and the cannister vanished into tongues of multicolored fire. Billows of the blue gas spread from the Heart in great plumes. Duke nudged Dickson and they stepped back, bumping into the puller.

"I hope to the Fifth Region," the stocky man said. "I hope to the Fifth Region—"

The Restcure dissipated. As it did, they could see several gouges in the fabric of the distributor. Black fluid shot out from the rips, and the air grew heavier with the scent. It covered the fence and the rails and the floor, and burning droplets landed on their face and clothes.

"Evacuate," the puller said.

"Repair," his intended victim said. The same thought was strong on both the minds of Duke and Dickson. "We've got to—" He took a step, but the puller grabbed him around the waist.

"We'll never get to it, not the way the fluid's coating this part of the bay. The pressure's going to tear that thing apart, and when it does—"

"A sudden, unchecked drop in transgear fluid pressure can result in intense, catastrophic damage to the drive systems and hull integrity of a ship," Duke recited in a cold, mechanical voice.

"Move—" the puller began.

He was interrupted by a shrill tearing. Duke shuddered as Dickson was seized by paroxysms of fear and then vanished. What he was hearing was familiar to him, much too familiar—he had heard it a hundred thousand times during summer season at the abattoir, the sound of raw meat being ripped from the bone by the factory's mech arms. As he watched, the escaping fluid shredded the synthetic muscle until it was gushing.

The two turned and ran, with Duke letting the puller lead the way. The bay was beginning to flood with the pungent fluid, and it made their going slow. They took turns slipping, falling, and helping one another to their feet. A siren had begun to call, and in quick glances around the bay, Duke could see crew members deserting their positions.

They turned the corner and saw the door that Duke had breached. It was standing open, and black fluid was spilling into the hall. With a nod of determination they picked up their pace, a step at a time, one foot carefully sunk into the fluid until it had a precarious hold on the now-slick deck.

Three meters from the door a metallic rending deafened them, followed by a cold blast of air and a sudden pitch in the angle of the ship. The puller stumbled into the emergency railing and broke his fall. Duke's feet went backward; he hit the floor and slid headfirst into the nearest wall.

The next thing he remembered was a burning sensation. He was covered with the slick black stuff from head to toe; it was leaking into his shoes and had coated the inside of his mouth. There was a tug on the back of his collar, and suddenly he was kicking, trying to get his footing on the coated floor.

The transgear puller was holding him up with one hand. Duke brought up his right arm in a mock salute and what remained of his cast melted away, dissolved by the escaping solvent.

"Leave me!" Duke shouted. "Get out of here!"

"No way!" The puller shook his head. "I'm gonna get

you out of here so you can pay for all of this." He muscled the stunned broker toward the door.

"Have it your way!" Duke put his hand out to the wall and tried to steady himself.

The intensity of the siren increased and then was drowned out by the cries of compromised organic metal. As they stepped through the door there was the shrill sound of a whirlwind, a flash of light, and a wave of heat. Then there was the noise, and a giant hammer made of compressed air and vaporized transgear fluid and twisted shards of metal smashed them down.

8

Junnell nervously paced the bridge. "Ensign Tesla, how much time is left on the blockade leader's threat?"

Tesla checked his tactical display. "In theory, we're coming up on the ten-minute mark—"

"In theory?" Junnell interrupted. "What is that supposed to mean?"

The ensign warily studied his board. "I've been keeping a close eye on the trajectory of that tanker," he explained. "And there's been a slight but discernible shift in its course. It's no longer running parallel. It's coming in to meet us. It'll be within striking range in . . . ten minutes."

Junnell swore. "Where is Commander O'Hearn? Did you ring General Quarters?"

"Yes, ma'am. Most sections are ready-secure—"

"I take it the bridge is not one of them," Junnell snapped. "Send out a unit of security people to find her. Start with the brig."

"Thank you, but that won't be necessary." Margaret O'Hearn stepped through the opening hatchway and onto the bridge, flanked by the merchant captain. "The reason for General Quarters, Mr. Junnell?"

Tesla keyed up a replay of the first officer's conversation with Citizen Swain. O'Hearn watched intently as the renovated Vacc Fighters jumped and destroyed the aging merchant ship. She could only shake her head.

"This Swain character has put his neck out on the line for this. Small wonder with the serious amounts of money that must be supporting it." O'Hearn walked to the command chair and seated herself. "That's going to be their problem. I anticipate that Tristan Swain is going to be brainwiped as a result of this, but not before he spills every last name behind this blockade."

"We're going through, then?" Tesla asked anxiously.

"Captain May," O'Hearn said. "Your opinion?"

May cleared his throat. "A handful of armed Vacc Fighters is certainly no match for a ship this size. Certainly we've got them outgunned. The biggest threat is that tanker they've got shadowing us. That could delay us long enough for the Vacc Ships to get in some really good licks."

"Your recommendation?"

"Were it just me," May said, "I'd take them. But you've got other considerations, Commander. Once the Vacc Fighters score a hit on this ship, we're going to have a lifepod alarm on our hands. Pods will be ejecting into the middle of a battlefield. That'll cripple our targeting systems. We won't be able to fire, but the Vacc Fighters will, and you can bet they won't be aiming at the pods. They'll have us by the throat."

"Well thought out," O'Hearn said.

"In the final analysis . . ." May turned and looked the commander right in the eye. "It's a good thing that the Arcolian ambassador is such an understanding creature."

She smiled at him. "Indeed." Turning back to the tactical display, she sat straight in the chair and spoke in a firm voice. "Mr. Junnell, have navigation give us a slow, wide turn in the direction of shift point. I don't want to give Citizen Swain the impression that we're in a hurry."

"Yes, ma'am." Junnell hurried to her board. In his seat, Tesla cocked his head at a light display and punched a series of keys.

"Lieutenant Orbison."

"Yes, ma'am."

"You will allow Captain May to operate the weapons board. Take the standby position."

The young lieutenant vacated his seat and busied himself at another console. May slowly approached the defensive systems board.

"Think you can handle it, Captain?"

"It's been awhile." May smiled.

"Just like in our academy days, Captain. Our best defense is a strong offense. If you see anything that looks like a sucker punch coming our way, you have free initiative to do to it what you did to the *Roko Marie*."

May saluted before he took the seat. "Yes, ma'am."

"We're beginning the turn, Commander," Junnell advised. "Grade-six arc."

"Excellent," O'Hearn said. "Notify me when we're three minutes from shift point. I have a little message I'd like to give Citizen Swain before we leave."

"Yes, ma'am."

"Ensign Tesla. Notify the transgear network to prepare for a shift into short space. Calculate destination to the Keibus system. We're going to deliver the Arcolians to the doorstep of the board of regents."

Tesla started hard at his board, punching in orders and mumbling.

"Ensign Tesla—"

"Ma'am—" He looked up at O'Hearn, face urgent. "I'm showing a stations red in the starboard transgear bay."

"Then they're on short staff from the General Quarters call. Give them my orders and a stern reminder of protocol."

"But, Commander," Tesla said quickly, "they were on full staff from General Quarters. There's an intruder—"

May spun his seat around. "Duke!" he shouted. "He's loose! That Arcolian son of a bitch made us *forget*—"

O'Hearn's fist came down on the arm of her chair.

"Tesla," she shouted. "Pull the three units of security from the *Angel's Luck* and send them down there *now*!"

Tesla turned back to his console, hand reaching. Then he snapped back in his chair. It felt exactly as if the deck had turned to liquid and a large wave were passing through the bridge. The ensign was pulled up in his seat, then tumbled backward over the top, hitting the floor and skewing sideways into a wall. He looked up to see Junnell flying past him in slow motion. His arm shot out and caught her around the waist, and he pulled her to his side.

May was thrown sideways against his seat harness, and the pivot mechanism locked into its emergency position. He shook off the stun and energized the plasma turrets. O'Hearn had felt the first wave coming and had slung her arms through the battle harness on the command chair. The backsling pitched her forward, but her grip on the unfastened harness held her in place.

"*Situation!*" she shouted.

"Turrets ready!" May snapped.

Junnell unwrapped from Tesla's grip and jumped to her station, buckling into her seat with one hand.

"No targets," May said, frustrated. "There are no ranging targets in the area."

"We weren't hit," Junnell said quickly. "It was from inside."

"Status," O'Hearn demanded.

Junnell looked up from her console. "There's been an explosion in the starboard transgear bay. Damage appears to be considerable—"

The light in the bridge vanished. In a wink, it came back up, bathing everything in red.

"Ma'am," Tesla said, crawling into his seat. "Damage appears to be more than considerable. The entire starboard shift system has been incapacitated, and there is the possibility of hairline structural damage to—"

His voice was cut short by a buzzer that startled everyone

in the bridge. The pattern was familiar: one second on, one second off.

"This is not a drill," advised a calm voice. *"This is not a drill. Proceed to your lifepod stations immediately."*

"The blockade," Junnell said.

"The passengers," Tesla said.

"Duke," May said.

"The Arcolians," Commander Margaret O'Hearn said.

9

Against her sense of better judgement, Roz headed straight for the infirmary. Winters seemed to be having no problem dealing with the lifepod alert and even went so far as to insist on tagging along in case Roz needed help. So, together they went through the crowded halls as the other passengers obediently queued to their respective evacuation pods.

When they got to the infirmary they were turned away cold. There had been security problems, which were complicating the normally lenient Alert procedure. She could rest assured, she was told, that the best of care would be given her friend Mr. Chiba and that he would be safe. It sounded suspiciously as if Chiba would be going into a stasis chamber for the duration, but there was nothing she could do about it. In spite of the risks, it would be the safest place for him.

"Come on," Roz said to Winters. "We need to get to our pod."

The trip back took considerably less time. While the buzzer still annoyed them, the halls were beginning to empty as the pods were sealed into a state of readiness. Most of the people they saw in the halls were security personnel who advised them to get moving, to get to their pod quickly lest they be sealed out—and in the event of activation, left behind.

As they took the lift back down to their level, Roz noticed that Winters was becoming distant. His hands went into the pockets of his jumpsuit, his feet shuffled, and he looked around the four corners of the ceiling nervously.

"What's wrong?" she asked. "Is it the alarm?"

Winters shook his head. "I feel like there's something bad coming."

"Nothing bad is going to happen to us. The pods are perfectly safe."

"It's not that." Winters gave a hopeless shrug. "It's like I forgot something really important and there's going to be trouble 'cause I didn't remember."

"It'll be fine."

The lift stopped, the door hissed open, and the two of them stepped out. They turned a corner and, in a moment, were passing their cabins.

"I hope we're not too late," Roz said, trying to urge Winters to move faster.

"*Oh, no!*" He stopped dead in the hall. "We have to go back, Miss Roz! We just *have* to!"

"Winters—" She pointed down the hall. Their pod was less than fifteen meters away. The door was still open, and a member of the crew was leaning out of it, waving and shouting for them to hurry.

The mercenary reached down with two massive hands and grabbed Roz's shoulders. "We have to guard the *stuff*, Miss Roz," he said in a coarse whisper. "You know, the *stuff* we ain't s'posed to talk about."

Roz put her hands on the big man's forearms and tried to break free. "Winters, we can't—" She looked up at him. *"The phials . . ."*

Winters broke his grip and put one finger to her lips. "Shhhh."

Roz shook her head quickly. "Oh, but surely May—Duke—Vonn—" She gave an emphatic sigh. "You're right. It's got to be us." Taking one of Winters's arms with both hands, she turned him around and steered him back in the direction of the lifts. Shouts of protest reached their ears just as they turned the corner, prompting Roz to place one hand between Winters's shoulder blades and push.

When they came to the lift, Winters stopped and rang to open the door. "You don't have to push me, Miss Roz," he said. "I get it now. We gotta move fast."

"Yeah," she sighed, looking around nervously.

There was a chime and the lift door opened. Roz screamed.

A figure staggered out of the lift. It was tattered and bloody and was wearing a strange amalgam of clothing—the bottom half of a security uniform jumpsuit with the sides of the legs split out and strips of cloth holding them up like crude suspenders; the top half of a suit of body armor that was at least two sizes too small; and beneath all of that, something that looked to be the color and shape of a hospital gown.

Winters's reaction was immediate. He started to laugh. "You look pretty bad, Mr. Vonn."

Vonn pitched sideways and hit the wall. He leaned against it and cocked his head at them. "This is nothing. You should see how I feel."

Roz took a hesitant step forward. "Vonn? What happened?"

"I don't have time to explain." He shook his head, shivered, and looked at Winters. "I need your help, brother. We've got some unfinished business to take care of."

"The *stuff*!" Winters cried triumphantly.

Roz put her hand on Vonn's shoulder. "You're in no shape to do that."

"Oh, yes, I am." He pulled away from the wall and stood straight. "I've shot enough amps of stuff into me that my body's going to be on autopilot for a week. All I need is an hour."

Smiling, Winters reached past Vonn and rang for the door.

"I need you to do something," Vonn said to Roz. "I need you to go to the *Angel's Luck* and get on board. Just sit there. If anyone you don't know tries to board the ship assume that they're trying to find where May has the phials hidden and kill them."

She nodded uncertainly. "I was afraid it would come to this."

Vonn retreated into the lift. "One of us will come and give the all clear."

"Are you sure you can handle this?" Roz asked.

"Yeah," Vonn sighed. "Once the rush hits, I'll be fine." He waved at Winters, who joined him in the car. "Later," he said as the doors closed.

There was a lurch, and the two mercenaries were on their way into the depths of the ship.

"How come you're letting Roz rescue the *stuff*?" Winters asked.

"We've got business up there," Vonn said, pointing.

"But I thought you said—"

"There's some men on this ship who are going to hurt, maybe kill, civilians unless we stop them. They might even start another war with the Arcolians. We've got to stop them."

Winters nodded solemnly. "What do we stop them with?"

"This." Vonn laughed bitterly and held up his pistol. "I've got ten mutiny pills to go with this. They've got Xegg guns and standard ammo that'll punch holes in the bulkheads and body armor, so our mutiny pills won't hurt them. And we're outnumbered."

Winters thought about it. "It'll be dangerous."

Vonn's head lolled back and he closed his eyes. "Where oh where is your precious Angel's Luck now that we need it?"

"*Mine?*" Winters asked.

Vonn shrugged. "I was talking to Anders."

Confused, Winters glanced around the small car.

"Forget it." Vonn sighed.

Winters shivered. "But Mr. Vonn, are you okay?"

"Don't worry about it, big guy," Vonn explained. "I was joking. I always talk like this when I'm about to die."

The car came to a stop. Winters's face was stoic. Vonn reached over and punched the HOLD button.

"There's something I want to tell you, Winters. When Anders brought you and Bear into that dingy bar on Cypress 13, I thought he'd lost his mind. I didn't think you'd be worth the time of day. May's the one who talked me into giving you a chance.

"I guess what I'm trying to say is that I was wrong in doubting your abilities. You're a hell of a good hand. It's been a real pleasure to work with you, and you're welcome on my fire team any time." He grabbed Winters's big hand and shook it. "I mean that."

"Thanks." Winters smiled. "Don't look so sad, Mr. Vonn. It won't be that bad."

The car door opened and they walked out. Vonn held the pistol out at arm's length, trying to aim with his left hand.

"Dammit," he said. "This isn't going to work. How are you with a pistol?"

"I'm okay," Winters said noncommittally.

Vonn handed his weapon over to the big man. "Here. I can't even cock the damned thing."

Winters chambered a round.

"Remember, the people we're after will have body armor on. If you want to make a kill, you're going to have to aim for the head."

"Okay."

"There's one other thing I need to tell you, Winters. And if you hear this and think it's too scary, you don't have to help me. Okay?"

Winters grunted.

"We're going to help the Arcolians."

The big man grunted again.

"Does that scare you?"

"I'll think about that," Winters whispered, "when we finish this part." He stopped at an intersection and sniffed the air suspiciously.

"What—" Vonn began.

Winters waved his hand in Vonn's face to silence him. "Someone's down. Smell it?"

Vonn shook his head.

"Blood and guns. Can't you tell it with your nose?"

Vonn closed his eyes and inhaled. With a little imagination, he could almost detect the lingering scent of nitrates and a sharp, organic wetness. He opened his eyes and looked at Winters. "You're sure?"

The big man pointed to the left. "That way. I'll cover you." He flattened himself against the wall, pistol at the ready, and went around the corner, keeping one hand in Vonn's view. After a moment, he slapped the wall twice and Vonn went around.

The guard was lying dead in the hall in the middle of a slick of his own blood. Vonn crouched down next to him and studied the body. The guard's body armor had three slick punctures that a man could put a finger through. Vonn swore that the look on the guard's face was one of surprise.

He pried the Rapid Fire from the guard's hands and checked it. Unfired, it carried a full clip of ammunition. Vonn cradled the end of the barrel in the crook of his right arm and gripped the stock and trigger with his left. It looked unwieldy and felt uncomfortable, but there was no doubt that he could bring the weapon to bear if need be.

"Winters," he whispered. "You want this body armor?"

Winters started to look at him, but something caught his eye. Vonn turned to see one of Bachman's crew rounding another corner down the hall. Surprised, the man brought up his Xegg gunn. Vonn rolled, trying to get an aim out of the Rapid Fire, but could not do it. He looked up at Winters, desperate. "Duck!" he shouted.

But Winters did not duck. In slow motion, he stepped away from the wall as the first shots from the Xegg scarred the place where he had been and ricocheted down the hall. He bent at the knees, brought the pistol into an aim, and steadied it with his other hand.

Vonn turned back to the assailant as Winters's shot filled the hall. The shot caught the attacker just below the right eye. The mutiny pill detonated his head.

"You said you weren't that good with a pistol," Vonn said, rising with the guard's weapon cradled in his arms.

Winters shrugged.

"Do you want the body armor or not?"

The big man shook his head. "Not if they don't have mutiny pills."

"It does seem rather pointless."

They advanced on the fresh body, Vonn practicing a crude aim on the inert figure. Winters knelt for a moment and picked up the Xegg gun.

"Should I take this?"

Vonn studied it for a moment. His right hand throbbed.

"Vonn—"

"No," the smaller man said quickly. "No. We're not going to sink to their level."

Winters removed the trigger assembly and stuffed it in one pocket. The remainder of the weapon hit the floor. "Good," he commented.

"The man we're after calls himself Bachman," Vonn explained. "He wants to kidnap the Arcolian delegation for money. He doesn't care how he does it or how many of our friends get hurt. We've got to find a way to stop him."

"What about the *stuff*, Mr. Vonn?"

"I hope we live to see it through."

Winters turned the body over and pulled a small packet off the front of its belt. "Maybe then we should use this." He proudly held the object up with two fingers. It was a MiniComm. Smiling, Vonn took it and thumbed the switch, listening to the erratic conversations and comments coming from the speaker.

"Terrific," Vonn smiled. "Now we can find out where Bachman's people are, avoid them—"

Winters scowled and took the device from him. "We use it like this," he said, matter-of-factly. After a quick glance around the hall, he keyed another button. "I need some backup at the liftport," he shouted uncertainly. "Security's about swamped me!"

He let up on the key and listened to the orders. "Now," he said, pushing Vonn toward a maintenance door. "Let's wait in there."

Using the dead guard's master key, they squeezed themselves into the closet. Once inside, they exchanged weapons, and when a commotion could be heard in the hall, Winters called for silence.

"When I tell you," he said, "open the door."

The big man closed his eyes and listened to the voices as they drew closer. When they peaked, he began a slow count. He reached three, began the count over, and on reaching three a second time, he nodded at Vonn.

Vonn hit the switch. Winters stepped out and sprayed the hall with fire. Splatters of dark fluid marred the walls. Others struck the relief party, dissipating against their vests or incapacitating any flesh that had been left exposed. After fifteen seconds, Winters released the trigger. Ten meters down the hall from him, four men lay dead.

He cocked his head at Vonn. "It really ain't fair to do that," he said apologetically.

"I'd like to shake the hand of the man that trained you."

"It was a woman."

"Figures." Vonn bent over the body of the guard and relieved it of one last clip of ammunition. "Down this hall and to the right. The Ambassadorial Suite is about twenty-five meters from the intersection. It's a straight shot down the hall. They'll have guards at the door. *Their* guards."

"How many?"

"Three. Maybe four. Five if Bachman's still trying to gain access to the suite."

Winters sighed. "We could charge them. One of us might make it to the door."

"No good," Vonn said, shaking his head. "I need you around, big guy. Besides, Bachman's too slippery. I want you backing me up."

Winters finished reloading the Rapid Fire. "Let's see."

The pair walked toward the intersection, listening to the

MiniComm as they went. There was nothing to be heard, so Vonn clicked it off and stuffed it in a pocket. "Strange to be hearing that," he whispered. "They're not checking on the status of the ones we lured away. I don't hear reports from Bachman, either. Maybe they're already inside—"

Nearing the intersection, they could hear a frantic pounding. Vonn signaled for Winters to stop and listen. After a moment, the story became clear. Two people were beating on a hollow section of wall, calling out Bachman's name and cursing bitterly.

Vonn's heart jumped. "He's done it." He gulped, trying to hold his voice to a whisper. "The son of a bitch has done it. He's double-crossed the last of his men."

"I don't—"

Vonn clapped his hand over Winters's mouth. "That explains the lack of radio traffic. I don't hear Bachman on the freq, so he must be in. We don't hear guards because they're trying to get into the Ambassadorial Suite. Only their leader's not about to let them in. Listen to what they're calling him."

Winters listened to the torrents of profanity coming their way from down the hall. He smiled. "So what are we going to do?"

Vonn handed the pistol butt-first to Winters. "They're brothers," he said. "I'm going to give them a chance."

Winters laid a hand on Vonn's shoulder.

"If something happens to me, big guy—"

"No—"

Vonn grabbed Winters's chin with his thumb and forefinger and shook his head. "Finish them. Like you did the others in the hall. Got that? Then find May. May will take care of you better than I have, maybe even better than Bear."

Winters nodded, eyes filling with tears.

Filling his lungs with air, Vonn stepped out into the intersection, hands away from his body. Bodies of *Hergest Ridge* security guards littered the floor, and among them were two of Bachman's hired mercenaries. The two survivors of the raiding party had their backs to him and were concentrating on the door. One had pried open an access hatch and was trying to hot-wire it. Another was pounding and swearing. Neither of them had a weapon at hand.

He kept going, fighting the urge to rush that the ampules wanted to give him, until he was halfway down the hall. Then he stopped, observed the efforts of the two men, and cleared his throat.

"You've been screwed," he said.

The pounding man stopped. He and his partner turned.

"*You*—"

"I'm unarmed," Vonn said quickly. "I've come to strike a deal."

"Bachman wants you dead."

"Bachman wants *you* dead, too. Ever think of that? Why else would he seal you out of the only place that could save your skins right now?"

The mercenary that had been trying to hot-wire the door took a step forward. "You filthy—"

"Don't go for a weapon," Vonn urged. "I'm your only shot at coming out of this situation alive."

"Like hell," the other said.

"Remember Haggis?" Vonn asked. "Remember Steubing? Remember what a nice couple they made? They're both dead."

"That's part of the job—"

"Bachman killed them both while they were in the brig. He had no intent of picking us up after we'd ejected from the ship. Why do you think he was so hot to have me killed?"

The trapped mercenaries exchanged glances.

"Don't pretend to be so surprised. He put a contract out on me, just like he signed your death warrants when he sealed you out of that room. Face it, brothers, he used you up. He got what he needed out of you, and now you've been discarded."

"Why should we listen to you?"

"Because I'm out here with you. I'm making the best offer you're going to see in a situation like this. Of course, if you still believe in that son of a bitch you call a sponsor, go right ahead and kill me. You'll still be trying to open that door when ship security overruns you.''

They exchanged glances again.

"Of course, they probably won't kill you. They'll just flood the hall with Restcure so they can make an example out of you. This is a *luxury* ship, boys, so you're looking at High Piracy right off the bat. Then there's Murder of Law Enforcement Personnel, Possession of Restricted Weaponry, Attempted Kidnapping, Attempted Assassination, Attempted Incitement to War, High Treason—''

"Enough!" shouted the one who had been pounding. "What are you offering?"

"Your freedom. You're brothers, so that's the very least I can do for you.''

"And in exchange?"

"You walk away from here," Vonn said. "You leave your weapons, walk out clean, make up some big damned lie, and report late to your lifepod. What you give me in return is Bachman. I was the first one wronged in this situation, and I deserve the first crack at him.''

The pounding mercenary shrugged and started to walk toward Vonn. He had gone less than three meters before the other began to follow.

"No other strings, brothers," Vonn said, smiling. "Live a long life, drink a long drink.''

"Thanks." They nodded as they passed.

Vonn shouted instructions to Winters to let the two men pass. When they disappeared around the corner, he ran to assess what had been done in an attempt to breach the door. In two minutes, Winters appeared at his side.

"They're gone, Vonn. I made sure.''

"Thanks." Vonn closed the access hatch to the door's electronics. "Bachman's isolated the circuits, so hot-wiring it isn't going to work." He plucked two Xegg guns from the floor and handed them to Winters, then led him ten meters from the door and stopped. "Wait here. Keep your aim on the door."

"But Mr. Vonn—"

"Trust me." He pulled the MiniComm from his pocket and turned it on. "All right," he announced. "Enough playing around. This is Maurice Vonn speaking. Remember me, Bachman? I'm the thorn in your side."

He let up on the key and waited for a reply. None came. He keyed the mike again.

"I haven't just taken this MiniComm from one of your people," he said sternly. "I'm standing outside the door. To prove it, I'm going to do something that may startle you."

Vonn raised his pistol and fired. A black spider appeared on the off-white surface of the door. He stuffed the weapon under his body armor.

"That was a mutiny pill. The next shots fired into the door will be your special issue of bullets fired from those nasty little guns you had smuggled onto this ship.

"Of course, you realize what that will do to the integrity of the door. And once I get the outside door open, I should have more than enough bullets left to make a few nice holes through the inner door. I'll even bet that I can do it before you can get the suite to eject from the ship, which you certainly would have done by now if you only knew how to do it.

"Needless to say, a door full of holes won't hold in your air supply. You and the Arcolian delegation will find that, after a short while, you're going to have some difficulty in breathing. If you ask me, it's a sorry end to such a beautiful plot."

He let up on the key and waited. After a moment, a voice crackled.

"What do you want?"

Vonn smiled.

"Dammit, what do you want?"

"The first thing I want is in. Then my partner and I will discuss the terms of being cut in for a piece of the action."

The first door opened.

"Both doors at once," Vonn advised.

The inner door slowly lifted. Bachman's voice carried from inside. "I bid you entrance."

Vonn handed the MiniComm to Winters. "Not quite. My partner will remain outside to ensure that the negotiations go smoothly."

"All right," the impatient voice said. "But hurry."

"If I don't call you in ten minutes," Vonn whispered, "breach both doors as quickly as possible. If you can get inside without getting hurt—"

"Kill Bachman," Winters said.

With a nod, Vonn walked through the doors. He was in the main room of the suite and was quick to notice that most of the furniture had been moved out of the way or removed altogether. From what he understood, the Arcolian E-forms had little use for chairs and couches, and what remained in the room was for the comfort of their hosts. The doors to the private rooms were sealed, and the only creature in sight was Bachman. The filter mask dangled loosely from his neck, and he was standing in front of a control console that was built into the wall.

"Having problems?" Vonn asked.

"The logic controller is missing," Bachman said bitterly. "Without it, I can't get a hard lock on the doors. Without the hard lock, we can't eject. I can't override it."

Vonn glanced around the room. He spotted the missing component lying sideways on a low table near one of the remaining couches. He quickly looked back at Bachman.

"Apparently someone took it out for repairs," Bachman continued. "Without it we're at a dead stop. There will be no deal, Mr. Vonn."

Vonn walked away from the open doors in an arc, away from where the component lay. "Oh, yes. There'll still be a deal."

"Are you out of your mind? Any time now the security people will be here. They'll kill us both."

Vonn shook his head. "Not me."

"What makes you think so?"

"Because I've got two brothers who will come forward and testify on my behalf. They owe me, you see. They'd owe you if you hadn't betrayed them."

"What are you talking about?"

"It's obvious that you've not worked with many mercenaries, Bachman. They've got an unwritten rule. No matter what side you're on, you take care of your men. You treat them with dignity, with respect, and you keep up your contracts to them. In return, you get their very best, right up to the point of death.

"You didn't do that, not with any of us. You went around like some megalomaniacal villain in an adventure vid, disposing of us at your whim. You betrayed the trust, and in return you'll get *nothing* from us. The two men who will testify on my behalf? They're your men, the ones you left outside that door—" He pointed for emphasis. "So when Security comes, I think it's safe to say that you're going to dangle. And you're going to do it alone. Unless—"

"Unless what?" Bachman spat.

"Unless you walk out of here with me. Unless you make reparations to your surviving people and compensate the families of those killed. Unless you completely humble yourself, we're going to let you die cold and alone."

Bachman turned away, head bowed, and faced the console.

"Come on," Vonn said. "You've lost—"

There was a hiss from behind. Vonn whirled to see the doors to the suite closing. He spun back toward Bachman, sinking his left hand under his body armor.

"Don't." Bachman was drawing down on him with a Xegg gun. "Your eyes betrayed you, Mr. Vonn. I know where the logic component is. I owe you nothing but this—" He shook the weapon for effect.

Vonn smiled and moved his arms away from his body.

"*That?* You want me to be afraid of *that*? Only if I was firing it."

Bachman pulled back the bolt.

"As long as you're learning about the mercenary business, let me teach you something about Xegg guns. No brother in their right mind would carry one as a combat weapon. They're notoriously unreliable. They're only well known because they can be smuggled easily, but then only if you've got customs people who don't know their ass from a transgear lube point. They're usually used by cheap, sleazy hotshots or terrorists. Which are you?"

Bachman shook his head. "Which are *you*, Mr. Vonn?"

"You should also know that what happened to me was no fluke. With Xegg weapons the odds are against you," Vonn smiled, "even if the other guy is unarmed. Four in ten malfunction. You did know that coming into this, didn't you?"

"Quiet," Bachman barked.

"None of your people appear to have gotten a bad one except me," Vonn said calmly, "which means there's at *least* one more bad one waiting to surface. I wouldn't put money on the odds of that one working properly."

"That's it—"

"Fine." Vonn lifted his wounded arm so that Bachman could see the blood-blackened bandages. His too-small body armor left a large gap running down the center of his chest. "Do it. Take your best shot at me. You've got a forty percent chance of becoming a cripple like me."

The barrel of the weapon trembled.

"What are you waiting for? If you're as hardcore as you want us to think, those are pretty good odds. You've got a sixty percent chance of killing me outright."

"Damn it," Bachman cried. "Damn it, damn it, *dammit*—" He let the gun fall.

Vonn slowly lowered his arms. He reached under his body armor, brought out the pistol, and cocked it.

Bachman's eyes flickered to the Xegg gun, deep in the

thick carpet of the Ambassadorial Suite. "You bastard," he said. "I should have let Brutus kill you."

"Yes," Vonn said. "You should have."

He was aiming with his left hand, so it took four shots to kill Bachman.

10

"Three minutes to go on Swain's deadline," Tesla said. "Lifepod alert indicates an eighty-nine percent readiness."

"The starboard transgear bay appears to have been completely destroyed," Junnell reported. "We can make the shift, but it'll tear the ship apart."

May made adjustments on his board. "Reports of gunfire near the Arcolian delegation's suite. I've dispatched extra security units to the area. Energy to the plasmas is up to full, but I haven't energized them yet. I didn't want to tip our hand."

"Understood," O'Hearn said. "We can't run and we can't go around them. What's the alternative?"

"Not surrender," Tesla said.

"Certainly not. We can't guarantee the safety of the Arcolians that way."

"Our only alternative," May said, "is to stand and fight."

"Not with the passengers in the lifepods," O'Hearn said. "I'm not going to dump them into a—"

A voice crackled on the internal communications line. "Hello?" it asked.

"Who is this?" Junnell demanded. "State your position."

"I need to talk to the commander right away. It's about the Arcolians."

"Make it fast," O'Hearn said.

"My name is Maurice Vonn, and I'm in the Arcolians' suite—"

"You *bastard*—" May said, turning in his chair.

"You've got to call off your guards," Vonn said urgently.

"Everything is okay in here. Winters and I have neutralized the kidnappers."

"Kidnappers?" O'Hearn said, outraged.

"It's a long story, but the Arcolians are safe with me. Tell them, misterbob."

"Indeed," a new voice croaked. "mauricevonn scents of the truth. margarethearn, you must do what you can to promote the safety of your fellow Sapients on this ship."

"How do I know," O'Hearn asked, "that the ambassador is not under duress?"

"That is something," the Arcolian answered, "that you and jamesohjames should be somewhat familiar with."

"He's got a point," May said, blushing.

"I've got a problem here," Vonn said. "I've tried plugging the logic controller into the emergency standby console, but when I do the system goes crazy. If something happens, I won't be able to eject the suite—"

"The component is defective," Tesla said suddenly. "I found that out during the last drill. But in calming the Arcolians down afterward, I seem to have—" He looked down at the floor. "Forgotten."

"That's it!" O'Hearn said loudly.

"Commander?" May asked, looking at her in disbelief.

"Tesla, eighty-nine percent readiness is as good as we'll get. Give the order to ready the lifeboats for ejection. We're going to run *through* the blockade."

"Ma'am?" Junnell said.

"I don't care how cold-blooded Swain thinks he is. When the pods start firing off the ship, he's got to bow to galactic law and begin rescue operations. While his ships are scattering to do that, we're going to run the Arcolians straight through to Council 5."

"The Arcolians—" Tesla said.

"Will be deep inside the ship, protected by layer upon layer of the hull. The ships in the blockade will be looking for the Ambassadorial Suite to eject, and that'll add to their scramble to pick up the pods."

"And the tanker?" Junnell asked.

"If the tanker doesn't join the rescue operations and won't yield to us, we'll make them move," O'Hearn said confidently. "Mr. Junnell, swing us around into a direct confrontational vector with the tanker."

"All lifepods give the all clear, ma'am," Tesla barked.

"Give the order to begin ejection, Ensign. Mr. Junnell, when we're in confrontational position, you have the initiative to bring us up to maximum subshift speed."

"Yes, ma'am."

"Captain May, how much do you trust Vonn to keep the Arcolians safe in their suite until we arrive at Council 5?"

May let his hand slip down his board to the communications switch. He discreetly palmed open a channel to the suite. "How much do I trust Vonn to keep the Arcolians safe? He's working for me, isn't he? And he's found the initiative to uncover and spoil a kidnapping plot that we knew nothing about."

"Answer the question," O'Hearn said.

"I'd trust him with my life on this," May said. "If he screws up he knows he won't get paid, and he also knows that if he ruins things, I'll pull his spine out through his throat." He cut the switch.

"Very well," O'Hearn said. "Notify him that he's to sit tight. Emphasize that he is *not* to replace the logic controller. He is to stand guard over the delegation and make sure they are secured in their sleeping quarters. We may have high-gee or impact situations. We don't want them being jostled around."

"Yes, ma'am," May nodded.

"And, Captain," O'Hearn continued. "Dump the full energy charge into the weapons system, limber them, and activate the targeting computers. It's time to show that we mean business."

May snapped a salute and turned to the task.

Commander Margaret O'Hearn settled back into her chair

and studied the tactical display. "We've got to show these bastards that we're not afraid to die."

11

Vonn shivered and cut the connection to the bridge. "All right," he said, voice cracking. "You heard the commander—" He looked uncertainly at the hulking figure before him. "Uh, sir. I guess it's time for you to strap in."

"Nnnnn," misterbob croaked. "Strap in. I do not scent this concept."

"Uh—" Vonn broke out in gooseflesh, and his throat was beginning to harden into a solid lump. "Well, that means you should be secure in your, ah, seat? We may be making some rough maneuvers, and we don't want you to get—" His eye wandered up and down the chitinous red frame, and he felt his gorge start to rise. Swallowing hard, he continued. "Smashed," he said unceremoniously.

"Indeed," misterbob replied. "margarethearn's concern for our safe arrival we have scented before. We shall all honor her request."

"Great." Vonn pulled at the collar of his hospital gown. It was soaked with sweat. The suite seemed to be getting smaller.

"I must indulge you before belt-in," misterbob said. "I was most interested to hear jamesohjames make remarks about alteration of errant personality. My species has what seems a similar procedure in order to rectify the illness of errant cerebrocortex electronic patterns. Is this removal of the Sapient spine a common procedure?"

"Oh, yeah," Vonn said, starting to shake. "In fact, mine is already gone."

"Most fascinating," misterbob chanted. "Most fascinating creatures." It shuffled across the suite to its cabin.

"We'll come and check on you, misterbob!" Winters shouted happily.

Vonn stood solid and took a series of long, deep breaths.

The shaking was slowing and color was coming back into his face. "Well," he said as his sweat began to cool, "we'd better do as ordered. Let's secure what's loose and bring up the command chairs."

"Right." Whistling a happy tune, Winters picked up Bachman's body and stuffed it in a storage bin, then began policing loose items on the floor: Bachman's ammo belt and battle kit, weapons, and spent shell cases. Vonn stabbed orders into the console, and two plush chairs with maneuver webbing rose from the floor and locked into place before the console.

Vonn took one of the seats and began to fasten himself into the webbing. Before long, Winters joined him, a broad smile on his lips.

"What the hell's wrong with you?" Vonn growled.

Winters looked at him, confused. "Me?" he asked, looking hurt.

Vonn pointed at himself with his thumb. "I've got an impeccably solid Psych rating. I can stand up under situations that would make most normal people blow a fuse. My Xenophobe Potential rating is so low they don't even list it on my profile."

Winters smiled.

"So when *It's Mister Bob!* comes out of his cabin to greet us, I go into this hyper overload, this fear that I've never felt before in my life. And you sit there with a Psych 13 rating, you shouldn't even be on the same ship with them, and you're talking to that thing like it's your long-lost brother. I just don't get it."

"I guess I'm just not scared of him," Winters said plainly.

"Why? What do you have that I don't?"

Winters shrugged. "misterbob reminds me of something I used to eat on Fagin 2."

"Well." Vonn sighed and tightened the webbing until it bit into his skin. "To each his own."

12

It started as a bass thump, so low that one felt it before one's brain realized that it was a sound. It rose quickly in pitch and became rubbery-sounding as it did, squeaking and echoing back on itself, reverberating into a quick clapping sound and then suddenly cutting off. It was almost a comic sound.

The noise was distinctive to anyone who had heard it before. And Roz Cain, having come from a deep-space outpost, knew exactly what that sound meant.

The lifepods were ejecting.

She stopped and the breath caught short in her lungs. When she was a young girl, her worst nightmares had run almost exactly like this. She was out, alone in a strange part of the station, when all of a sudden the pods started popping. And there she was, left behind, with no knowledge of where to find refuge. Those who would worry about her had already been evacuated and were incapable of doing anything but spinning in their pods and waiting for the inevitable rescue.

The nightmares had kept her straight. When her friends went out for a night on the town, she had stayed in, a secure distance from her designated lifepod.

But it had finally happened. She had picked up a strange man and had been carried away across the galaxy, had left him behind for another who was too hurt to help her, and was quite alone in the middle of an emergency.

Trying to keep a grip on her fraying sanity, she ran down the hall, trying to remember the words that had been given to her, magic words with a most delicious double meaning.

"Angel's Luck," she whispered. "Angel's Luck, Angel's Luck. *Angel's Luck.*"

She made her way down lifts and across halls, trying to remember where the merchant ship was supposed to be. It had been anchored to the outside of the *Hergest Ridge*, she knew. May had said something about repairs and holes through the hull and security precautions because of the Arcolians. All she had to do, she knew, was keep going until she found herself in familiar territory. Then she would be safe.

As she approached the outer decks of the ship, the halls became wider and larger. She trembled from the spaciousness of it. This was it. It felt right. She was getting close.

Roz came to a sealed door. On it, letters informed her that on the other side were repair bays, the transgear systems, and outer hull access ports. Trembling, she palmed the switch.

The door rose. She screamed.

Ten meters from where she stood the hall was blocked with a tangled criss-cross of debris. Girders from below had pierced the walls, severing power lines, connecting cables and duct systems. Flakes of metal had been peeled from the walls and tossed around like strips of foil. A black, foul-smelling fluid gushed upward from a ruptured line to coat the ceiling, and in the low gravity it pooled, flowed, and rained down to the floor. The severed ducts and vents blew air into the hallway, turning it into a wind tunnel.

Stunned, Roz took uncertain steps toward the wreckage. Wind tossed her hair and coated her face with droplets of the warm fluid.

"No," she said. "No, no, no—"

She started to draw breath but cut short because of the smell in the air—fluid and cooling molten metal, burnt plastics and something utterly indescribable. It was too much like being chased, like what the *Angel's Luck* had been like after—

"*Angel's Luck*," she said with resolve. "*Angel's Luck.*"

Roz made her hands into fists and let her fingernails dig into her palms. She moved forward.

The first obstacle was a large fissure in the floor. Whatever had done the damage had caused a crack in the floor that had grown into a three-meter gap between her and the pile of debris. Looking down into it, she could see more ducts and vents and the deck below. She thought about going down, but there was more debris, and that black stuff was everywhere. Fighting to keep her breathing in check, she looked across the chasm and tried to reason things out.

She was in good shape. It had not been that long since school and the Upper Level Zero-Gee Gymnastics. She could jump, but three meters? One slip and she would end up quite a mess . . .

The deck pitched sideways under her feet and she went down—hard, she thought, but she landed with very little impact. Of course, the gravity. It was light there.

Roz looked back at the gap. It had grown wider, four meters at the least. A fissure was opening up on the opposite wall, and hairline cracks were beginning to coat the ceiling. Another lurch like that and she would be cut off.

Shaking, she climbed to her feet, walked back to the door, then turned. She ran, trying to pick up speed, finding it difficult between the gravity and the slick floor. At the edge of the crack she leapt with all her might, screaming.

The walls shuddered and buckled.

Roz was pushed upward, and the blasts of air from below buoyed her higher. She stretched her arms out, stretched out her fingers—it was coming back to her, the exhilarating sensation of flight . . .

She hit the deck on the other side belly first, bounded back up into the air and hit again, then slid to the edge of the debris on the black-slick floor. Nervous laughter erupted from her throat, and she looked back at the breach in the floor. The last shift had opened the gap, and twisted beams and floor plating had pushed up from the level below, cutting off her path back to the door. The wall had split wide, and ceiling fissures had opened. Components were falling down into the hall from above. The wind had increased, and she squinted against it.

"No turning back now, girl. Remember it. Say it. Angel's Luck. *Angel's Luck.*"

She squeezed up to her hands and knees, studied the debris in front of her, then reached out tentatively and started to climb. Black fluid was coating her hands, and the metal and plastic made the going slow. Her shoes became coated with the stuff, but she left them on. Slipping and falling against the metal as she was, she needed the protection they offered her feet. Already the soles were torn and gouged, and she had to stop at one point to pick out a sliver of metal that was pricking the ball of her foot.

When she was halfway up the side of the field, she could see an opening that would get her through to the other side. It seemed impossibly far, but when she looked back, she saw that behind her, things had gotten much worse. Damage from the surrounding decks was pushing in, and the wall was neatly folding back, boxing her in. The damage pushing up from the floor was about to merge with the mountain she was climbing. She could see it inching toward her.

"No," she whispered, blindly reaching. "Wait. Wait. Give me a chance to get out."

The debris below her groaned.

"No, no, no, in the name of the Fifth Region—"

The mountain began to grow beneath her. Screaming, Roz grabbed above her and pulled, her legs sliding up and out of the way of a jagged girder that emerged from the jumble. She scrambled up through. The legs and knees of her jumpsuit snagged and shredded. Shards of metal slashed her arms and hands.

The floor heaved once more and her footing gave way. She started to slide back down the jagged heap, but her hands flailed and caught something cool and slick. Gripping it for all her worth, Roz climbed, pulling herself hand over hand, to a more secure point higher up.

When she was perched on a flat plate of wall, she paused to assess the situation. All that remained was to crawl over the top of the twisted wreckage, which was still a good two meters from the ceiling. She studied the path carefully, deciding which way to cross and where her footing would be. Her only risk would be the fact that she might be trapped and then crushed as the debris mounted.

All right then, she told herself. Time to cross. That's it. Just start across, carefully. Don't be in any hurry.

Roz brought her arms up to hug herself. "Coward," she said. Perhaps there was another way out. She turned on her tilting platform, trying to see down to the damaged level below. Again she touched something cool and slick, the object she had pulled herself up with. Her eyes dropped to examine it. It was smeared with transgear fluid and bent. It got narrow, then widened suddenly, and hooked—

It was an arm. A large, muscular, battered arm with multicolored tattoos, a broad flat palm, a thumb, and two and a half fingers.

Shrieking, Roz scooted back on the piece of bulkhead. It began to tilt. She flung herself toward the top of the mountain as her perch clanged to the floor. Her landing was bad—she sprawled flat out among snags of wiring and shredded duct work and blown plates of ceiling tile.

Panting wildly, she stretched out her arms and tried to pull herself forward. She was slick enough that she started to move rather easily, and then she stopped suddenly, unable to go any farther. Clenching her teeth, she pulled harder and tried to kick with her leg.

Her leg. Only her right leg was cooperating. She closed her eyes and concentrated. Her left leg was numb.

She shifted to look, but before she could the sensation hit. It started deep in the flesh of her upper leg and radiated outward. The toes and sole of her foot burned and her calf knotted and cramped. Roz cried out and buckled toward her leg.

The initial wave passed and she tried to roll onto her left side. She could not go that way. She tried to roll onto her right. It hurt too much. Drawing a deep breath and clenching her teeth, Roz tightened her muscles and, with grim determination, lifted up.

There was a pulling sensation from her leg and a wet suck.

Roz flopped onto her back and looked down. Blood was flowing from a jagged puncture in the center of her upper leg. Where she had been seconds before, a jagged shard of metal protruded up from the tangle, glistening with fresh red.

Cries slipped from Roz's throat as she pushed back onto her belly and began flailing across the debris, hands tearing at metal that tore back, her right leg kicking and pushing wildly to compensate for the dead weight she carried. She did not realize she had made the crossing and was on the way down until she was facing downhill, her forward momentum coming easier.

Taking a moment to subdue her panic, she made a quick assessment of the situation. She was on the far end of the debris, and in front of her was the rest of the hall, a clear shot to where the *Angel's Luck* would be docked. All that remained was for her to get out of the rubble and past the last obstacle, a body that had fallen, crumpled, in the hall, partially covered with refuse.

She stopped and turned, going feetfirst, trying to keep the weight on her right leg, new spines of pain from her left reminding her to be careful. As she descended she eyed the body nervously, watching for any sign of movement.

Wait a minute, she thought as she neared the end of her task. That person is awfully slight for a transgear puller. He's got all of his fingers and that face—

"Duke," she grunted, making a frenzied scramble off of the pile of ruined metal. "Duke."

Roz fell as soon as she tried to stand. She ended up crawling the remaining distance, trembling and hoping that her strength held up until she reached him. Tossing off the garbage that covered him, she saw that he had been coated with a thin gray film that resembled ash. Ignoring that, she grabbed his shoulders and shook.

"C'mon, Duke," she said, sobbing. "C'mon, Duke. Live. Duke, I need you—"

Duke's head bounced lifelessly.

"Duke!" she shouted. Her eyes were burning, and she was beginning to lose control over her trembling. She slapped

him across the face, and her hand came away smeared with gray.

Duke's face twitched, a wince of pain.

"Come on," she said, and slapped him again.

A more definite wince, and then he grunted.

"Duke!" She backhanded him, and his eyes slowly pulled open, blinking and rolling in disbelief.

"Roz?" His expression sounded hurt.

"Get up," she ordered, tugging at his lapels. "You've got to get me to the *Angel's Luck*."

Duke propped his arms under his back and sat up. "Did we make it?" he asked. "Did we get away from the *Yueh-sheng*?"

"I'll fill you in later," she said, nodding. "You've got to get us both to the ship—" Her words cut off and she doubled over, clutching at her punctured leg.

"You're hurt," Duke said, rising to his feet.

"Damn," she grunted through clenched teeth. Then she bit her lip and looked up at him apologetically.

Duke reached down and pulled Roz up, wrapping one of her arms around his neck. He looked at her and blinked his eyes.

"We're on the *Hergest Ridge*, right?"

"Yeah," she said thinly.

"Why is it I don't remember much of this trip?"

She shook her head. "Can we go?"

"You know the way?"

"Start by going straight—" Her teeth clenched to fight off a wave of nausea.

"Right." He put his arm around her waist, and they started to walk. She closed her eyes and briefly dreamed. First Vonn was carrying her, and then it was Peter Chiba. Then Duke was unceremoniously dragging her through the halls of the *Hergest Ridge*.

When she opened her eyes again, they were on the *Angel's Luck*. She closed them again, and they stayed that way for a long time.

13

The ploy was working. They could see it on the tactical display. Dozens of small blips radiated from the graphic of the luxury ship, moving out and away from the Council in-system. The incoming ships, those that belonged to the blockade, began to scatter, chasing the errant pods. It was better than anyone could have hoped for, but not a soul on the bridge of the *Hergest Ridge* would admit it.

"Engaged on confrontational vector with the tanker," Dorienne Junnell said.

"What's our positional status with regard to Council 5?" O'Hearn asked.

"Direct line in to orbital influence, ma'am."

"Very good. Lock the course in. Bring up the impact proximeter, override the collision avoidance mechanism, then engage maximum preshift speed. Let's see what kind of stuff these people are made of."

"Yes, ma'am." Junnell turned and repeated the order. A jolt ran through the ship.

"What was that?" O'Hearn snapped.

"A sympathetic harmonic vibration," Tesla said. "It was caused by our change in the drive feed."

"That's not supposed to happen on this size ship," May said.

"It would depend on the degree of damage to the super-structure," O'Hearn replied.

"Twenty-five percent speed," Junnell advised.

"Acknowledged. Captain May, what are you showing on the defensive perimeter?"

"Vasac-to-Vasac shows the same as tactical," he said. "Most of the blockade ships are following the letter of the law and are scattering to retrieve the pods."

"Most?" O'Hearn questioned.

"I'm showing a handful of ships, maybe a dozen, that don't seem to be responding. Vasac shows they're smaller—"

"Incoming!" Tesla shouted. "I'm showing tracers of plasma energy inbound—"

"Calm it," O'Hearn said. "These'll be warning hosts."

"Formation," May said. "The scattered ships have aligned into the trident formation. They're on approach. I've got our weapons at the ready—"

"Don't fire on them until one of their shots impact," O'Hearn advised.

"Maggie—" May hesitated. "Commander, I can take them out now and we'll be done with it."

"Policy," O'Hearn said. "So far they're just a few misguided but well-meaning souls. Until they show us differently, we're to treat them as such." A burst of static rose on the subspace frequency as the incoming fire detonated harmlessly. "See?"

"With all due respect, Commander, Vasac shows these ships in the class size of the single-man fighters. If they get too close to us, they can rake us apart—"

"Captain, a ship this size can take a lot more damage than a merchant ship. With the passengers safely off and the Arcolians deep in, they can rake all they want and we'll still make it to Council 5."

"I was just thinking of your ship, Commander."

O'Hearn sighed resignedly. "It's their policy," she said. "It's their ship."

"Thirty-five percent power," Junnell said. "And a communication request from Tristan Swain, acting commander of the blockade."

"Tell Citizen Swain," O'Hearn said icily, "that I'll speak with him."

There was an electronic pop. "To whom do I have the pleasure of speaking?" Swain's voice sounded annoyed.

"Commander Margaret O'Hearn of the United Terran Empire Fleet and ranking officer of the *Hergest Ridge*. Speak your piece, Citizen."

"You have no doubt tracked our warning shots," Swain

growled. "My question concerns your sanity. To eject your passengers and attempt to run this blockade—"

"Excuse me," O'Hearn interrupted, "but firing on an evacuating ship during an emergency operation is a capital offense. Who is sane and who is not, Citizen?"

"And what of bringing in the xenos?" Swain hissed. "You are doing nothing but profiteering, cashing in on a tragic war that cost the lives of millions of our brothers and sisters—"

"The Arcolians suffered similar losses. All the more reason that you should allow us to keep the peace."

"Isolate them and that will keep the peace. I for one will not stand idly by while those fellow humans who have no real recollection of the war revel in the glorification of our enemies. I'm talking about our pride as a species, Commander. Do you have any desire to see these beasts deified? Do you want your children to bring home synfoam Arcolian toys and have their images graven onto bed linens and lograv goblets and school lunch trays?"

"Better for my children to do that than become cannon fodder," O'Hearn said calmly. "Which is how you would call their fate. Come clean with me, Citizen. How much money have you invested in PlasmaLaseCorp's target-imaging system, or some other defense net? Who are the real profiteers out here today?"

"We will not allow the Arcolians to pass," Swain ordered.

"You will not hinder the passage of a damaged vehicle," O'Hearn countered, "unless you'd like another charge to be added to your already growing list."

"You will surrender the Arcolians."

"They're not on the ship."

"Commander," May said. "The trident formation is turning. Looks like it's going to make an attack pass."

"You will allow us to make an inspection of your ship to verify this," Swain said.

"You will engage in rescue operations and pick them up

yourself. Your insistence on this trivial arguing is only adding to the list of charges you are going to face—''

''Not compared to the charges you and your crew will face when my siblings rise up and expose you. You're traitors to your species! You'll feel our wrath, our rope on your neck, you'll feel—''

''Cut it off,'' O'Hearn snapped.

Junnell complied.

''That son of a bitch is history.''

''Trident closing,'' May said. ''Speed increasing. They're closing in a rather sloppy angle of initial attack.''

''Mr. Junnell,'' O'Hearn said. ''Current rate of speed?''

''Forty-two percent.''

''Notify all stations to batten down for gravity boost. Sub-shift engines should prepare for a hot boost as soon as those fighters make their initial pass. Captain, are the armaments ready?''

''Yes, ma'am.''

''Recorded as my order, don't fire until I authorize return fire. Then you can give them hell.''

''Yes, ma'am.''

''As for the damage to this ship,'' O'Hearn said in a general announcement to all of those on the bridge. ''The UTE Fleet is footing the bill for all repairs under policy procedure. Is that clear?''

There was a unanimous murmur of acknowledgment.

''All right, then. Snap to. Stations alert. We're going in.''

14

Roz was lying on the medicouch, strapped down, passed out. Duke felt her forehead, then her pulse, then finished cutting away the leg of her jumpsuit and putting contact compresses on her wound. When he felt certain that there was nothing more he could do for her, he dimmed the lights and started to leave the room, pausing to turn back to the medications locker.

A memory peeked out.

He crossed over to the locker and used the manual override to open it, expecting to see rows of small bottles filled with a thick amber fluid.

The locker was empty.

He staggered backward, stomach plunging.

"No. Not again. I don't want to go through that—"

He turned to the door. The feeling rose into his brain, shooting straight up from the bottom of his gut.

"Come out here," it said. "I want to tell you something."

With slow steps, Duke started toward the door. "You mean I never went through any of this? It's all been a dream. Is that what you want to tell me?"

"Your words. Not mine."

"I know how it's going to turn out, but I don't want to go through it. It was bad enough as a dream."

Duke found himself involuntarily lifting an arm and making a sweeping gesture toward the empty locker. "There's a way out of this. Let me show you." He began to take slow, jerky steps toward the outer hall. Duke relaxed, and his legs carried him as if they instinctively knew the way.

Then the smell reached his nose. It was strong and sweet and closed his throat. His stomach twisted into a hard knot, and his steps halted.

"Come on," it urged. "Come on. Come see what you're promoting, Duke."

Duke hesitated. *It had been a hot summer, and the cooling system had failed in one wing of the abattoir, and over a thousand sides of beef had slowly gone sour* . . .

The feeling boiled up. "Come out here *right fucking now, Duke.*"

He reached up and slapped himself hard in the face. Then he punched a control pad, and the door sealed him in Medical. A loud *"No!"* howled in his brain. "Don't, Duke! Don't!"

Duke scrambled across the room and dove under a medicouch that had been set into the wall. He squirmed into the corner headfirst and huddled.

"I won't go out!" he shouted. "I won't! It's Leigh Brand, you bastard! *Leigh Brand!*"

The feeling sucked out of him so fast and hard that it left him trembling. He stayed where he was, and after a few moments, he gave in to a creeping deep sleep.

15

"Acknowledged." Vonn pulled his headset off and looked at Winters. "This is it, old buddy," he said. "You're strapped in, I'm strapped in, and the xe—the Arcolians are strapped in. One way or another, we're going to end up on Council 5."

He reached out, and Winters grabbed his thumb. They shook hard.

"See you on the other side," Winters said confidently.

Vonn sighed and managed a smile. "You got it, brother."

16

In stasis, Peter Chiba slept without dreams.

17

"Fifty percent power, Commander."

"Noted."

"They're fanning," May said. "The individual formations have tightened, and they've shifted into position for a rotary strafing run. The weapons are limber, I can—"

"You'll hold your fire, Captain. We haven't established that Swain is capable of giving such an order to his pilots."

May shifted in his seat. "I suppose they're closing so they can spit on us."

"That's *quite* enough. Ensign Tesla, let me know the moment they fire on us. We'll have a few seconds for hot boost before—''

"They've done it!'' Tesla cried, voice cracking. "They're pivoting around the circumference of the ship—''

May leaned over the console and stabbed a line of keys. A low *hum* went through the bridge, and the lighting flickered and dimmed. On the tactical display, a series of red slashes radiated outward from the *Hergest Ridge*.

"Dammit, James!'' O'Hearn shouted. "I hadn't given the order—''

"Like they're flying by as a Trident to scare us? You can't let them—''

A low, metallic pounding silenced them.

"Their shots are connecting,'' Tesla said. "We're being strafed in a spiral pattern beginning amidships—''

"A stern warning,'' O'Hearn said.

"But they're still firing on us,'' May added.

From the display came a soft *chirp*. One of the rear ships from the trident formation disappeared.

"Got one!'' Tesla shouted.

"We can see that, Ensign,'' Junnell said flatly.

The pummeling on the ship grew louder.

Chirp.

"I let them get too close,'' May said. "They're going to come back to haunt us.''

"Hot boost ready for your order, ma'am,'' Junnell advised.

"Wait for it,'' O'Hearn said. "We'll see how the captain's initial fire does.''

Chirp. Chirp.

"That's a third of them,'' Tesla said. "That should put the fear into them—''

"Not if they're running by the book,'' O'Hearn replied. "Vacc Fighters are trained to expect that kind of initial attrition.''

"If they're following the book,'' May said, "they'll do a hard turn before they get out of our aft blind spot.''

"Then—"

"Then they'll come back and pick us apart."

Tesla swallowed hard.

"We'll make it to Council before they can do that," O'Hearn told the ensign.

"What about the tanker?"

"We can outmaneuver them if we get close enough. Let's see if we can make them move first. Mr. Junnell, what's our current power level?"

"Fifty-nine percent of shift threshold," she advised.

A loud *bang* startled them. It was followed by the sounds of smaller impacts and metallic scrapings and rattlings.

"The debris field," May advised. "From the destroyed fighters."

"We're in position. Prepare for hot boost."

"On your order, ma'am," Junnell said.

"They're swinging out," Tesla said, eyes glued to the display.

There was another *chirp*. May shouted "Yes!" and shook his fists. "Sloppy, Swain. Really sloppy."

"Seven remaining in formation. The lead ship is turning, ma'am. The others are—"

"*Now*, Mr. Junnell! Give us that hot boost!"

"On your orders—"

Before Junnell could finish, a screech deafened them and they were thrown back into their seats. The rattling of debris on the outer hull quickened and stopped, and the tactical display showed that the luxury liner was pulling away from the re-forming attack ships.

"Target them!" O'Hearn shouted. "Get them off our tail, James!"

"With pleasure." The merchant brought up an image on his screen, checked the position of the turning Vacc Fighters, and punched in the orders for the aft defenses to locate and fire. Four green crosshairs appeared on his screen, scanned the tactical area, and began to close in on the nearest ships. The first one found its mark, flickered to red to indicate it had locked on, and gave May an audible request for the firing order. He punched all four keys at once.

Nothing happened. The crosshairs remained red, flickering, lettering below each one advising him TARGET ACQUIRED. He hit the keys again, one after another.

"Take them, Captain," O'Hearn said urgently.

"Something's wrong," he said. "The guns aren't responding—"

The bridge rumbled, and warning alarms began to sound. May's board lit up in amber and red, and his screen winked out.

"Overload!" he yelped, and tried recircuiting to conserve energy. He unlimbered and shut down the forward and starboard weapons, but it was no use. The alarms were sounding all over the bridge, and the entire crew was scrambling to prevent a shutdown.

"Junnell!" O'Hearn barked. "Situation!"

"We're losing power to inboard systems. Everything's failing—"

"It's the damage to the starboard side," Tesla said. "Damage to the superstructure is spreading, and there's been a breach to the starboard power plant. We're creating a demand that the other two plants can't handle."

"Put priority to engine drive and maneuver systems," the commander ordered.

Junnell put the orders into her board. They could hear the beginnings of distant thunder.

"They're firing," Tesla said. "They're homing in on the aft drive suspension."

"Trying to keep us from running," O'Hearn said. "May, get those guns up and take them out before they get too close."

"I'm trying," he complained. His hand trembled as he reached out to cut the power back. He made a fist to stop the tremors, but the feeling had spread down his arm and across his back and shoulders. He drew a quick breath. By the time he pushed it back out, his entire body was quivering.

"Seventy-five percent power," Junnell said.

"Maggie," May said. "We've got a problem." He could hear something: a nervous rattle. A quick glance around the bridge told him that others were noticing it, too. "We're hitting the ship's resonant frequency."

"Impossible," she said. "We're supposed to have maneuverable speed up to two hundred percent of shift threshold speed."

"When we're not damaged." The rattling was getting louder, and he had to raise his voice to speak. The vibrations were becoming visible across the bridge. "Maggie, we're not going to make it—"

"Eighty percent," Junnell said loudly. The tremors were coming hard and fast, and the crew was beginning to feel the pressure as they were thrown against the webbing of their seats.

"Cut back nonessentials and bring up the gravity. Let the Arcolians know what's coming so they'll be prepared."

Tesla's reply was lost in the din.

May turned back to the board and restored power to his screen. He brought up the emergency maintenance lists, looking for sources of power he could divert to the guns. One listing caught his eye: CARGO ATTACHMENT. His jaw dropped. "Of course," he whispered.

"Ma'am," Junnell said. "This development is going to make our game of chicken with Swain's tanker rather difficult. We're going to need the speed to outrun it and keep targeting distance to the Vacc Fighters, but our maneuverability is going to be seriously compromised."

May brought up the report on the cargo attachment and studied the glowing letters for a moment. MAGLOCK ATTACHMENT STARBOARD SIDE: SALVAGED MATERIALS 129,418 COMMERCIAL TONS STRESS FACTOR PLUSMINUS 5.72%.

"Captain May, can you divert enough power to the forward guns for Devastational Fire?"

May started. While he had been reading the data the stress

level had climbed to 7.03. "Ma'am," he said nervously. "I can, but I'll have to shut down the aft guns completely—"

"Do it," O'Hearn snapped. "Junnell, put a request to speak with Citizen Swain."

"Ma'am."

Grinding his teeth against the shaking, May unlimbered the aft defensive systems and brought up the forward guns. The pounding from the Vacc Fighters was increasing, and at one point Tesla reported that they had closed range and again were strafing the *Hergest Ridge*.

"Don't worry about it" was O'Hearn's reply. "The debris will take care of them."

Debris? May thought. Surely she wasn't going to—

"Eighty-five percent power," Junnell shouted. "We're starting to stress badly, Commander."

"Push it," she urged.

May looked at the stress reading. Under normal conditions, the *Hergest Ridge* had the power capacity to lug a half-dozen ships the size of the *Angel's Luck*. But with a power plant out on the starboard side, keeping the merchant ship clamped to the side with a failing superstructure was beginning to take its toll.

"I've got Citizen Swain for you, Commander."

"Very good, Mr. Junnell. How long until we reach the point of no return with that tanker?"

"Hard to say, ma'am. With the damage we've taken and the low resonant frequency—"

"Do your best, Mr. Junnell. And do put Citizen Swain on."

Numbness was creeping into May's extremities from the pounding, and the noise was making his head throb. With thick fingers, he began to key in orders.

MAGLOCK DISENGAGE READY.

"Ah. Commander." Swain's voice was covered with static from the Vacc Fighter's fire. "How good of you to call. I trust you have decided to listen to reason?"

"I was going to ask the same of you," O'Hearn said.

May shook his head. The vibrations were getting bad. Junnell had gotten the *Ridge* up to eighty-eight percent power, and the plants were working hard to get it beyond that. May brought up another program and armed the thrust bolts that would throw the *Angel's Luck* clear of the luxury ship on ejection.

"You have no room to talk," Swain was saying. "Your ship has sustained severe damage, it doesn't take a fool to see that. My ships report—"

"Your *fighters*," O'Hearn said. "Your illegal fighters."

"—that there is external damage to your starboard side. Even a transgear puller could figure out—"

"The reason I called," the commander interrupted, "is to tell you that you have five minutes to get that tanker out of our way."

"What?" Swain sounded indignant.

May drew a deep breath. The stress rating was up to 10.7 percent. If relieved of that, the *Hergest Ridge* would make speed. What would their pursuers or those on the tanker do at that point? Was that his ex-wife's intent—to confuse them into making a wrong move, into shifting to short space, leaving the *Ridge* free to make orbit around Council 5? Whatever her intent, the move he had to make was clear. He flipped up a protective cap and tripped a toggle switch.

CARGO EJECTION ARMED.

"We have been seriously damaged," O'Hearn explained to Swain. "We're nearing one hundred percent shift velocity and our maneuvering systems are crippled. If that tanker is not out of our way, we are going to go *through* it."

There was a long pause. The frequency crackled with subspace interference. "Commander," Swain finally said. "Certainly you're not serious about—"

"Our starboard transgear bay is out," O'Hearn interrupted. "If you can get your fighters to quit attacking and confirm this, you'll see that I am quite serious."

"In the name of the Fifth Region, Commander. We'll all be killed—"

O'Hearn nodded. "He's on the tanker. We'll have to soften him up a bit, eh, James?" She looked at her ex-husband and saw his hand opening the cap to a detonator switch. She would have been out of her seat, but the webbing held her down. *"What in the hell do you think you're doing, Captain?"*

May's hand hesitated over the switch. "We've got to jettison the *Angel's Luck*, Maggie. It's the only way we're going to make speed." He was screaming, trying to make himself heard above the vibrations. "It'll buy you that extra power and maybe even more time against the fighters. They'll break off to investigate."

O'Hearn pointed an accusing finger. "You'll do no such thing to my ship."

"I bought out your share!" May screamed. "You always pulled that on me but you're not going to do it now—"

O'Hearn turned to Junnell and made a slashing motion across her throat. Junnell nodded.

"The *Angel's Luck* is mine," May continued. "It was part of the divorce settlement."

"I invested a lot in that ship, James May, and mine or not, I'm not going to see you waste it—"

"I'll recover it afterward—"

"The fighters will pick it apart."

"Tough," May said. He flipped the switch.

STRESS RATING 11.21%.

"Dammit!" he cried. He flipped the switch again.

STRESS RATING 11.37%.

"Open log," O'Hearn said.

"Done," Junnell replied.

"Backdate entry to the point at which we diverted to investigate the debris field on the old Garland–Jubilo route. Make note that the derelict ship was recovered by and for use of personnel of the United Terran Empire Fleet for whatever profit can be motivated from such materials."

Junnell encoded the entry and managed a satisfied smile. "Done, ma'am."

"And now, Captain May," O'Hearn said decisively, "if you will show some inclination toward following orders, Mr. Junnell will restore control of the relevant parts of your board and we can get on with the business of delivering the Arcolian delegation to Council 5."

May tipped his hand to her in salute.

"Mr. Junnell, take care of the captain's board. Citizen Swain, are you still there?"

"Commander, I ask you to consider the gravity of the situation. This is not something lightly dealt with."

"I realize that," she said. "And you had to make a similar decision before organizing this blockade. Unfortunately, one of us was wrong and is going to have to pay for his mistake."

"You don't intend to run this blockade, Commander."

"I do, citizen," O'Hearn said sternly. "And if need be, I'll run right through that tanker of yours unless you're out of my way. You now have two minutes to accomplish that."

"Commander! In the name of the Fifth Region—"

"Yes, Citizen," she said, cutting him off. "In the name of the Fifth Region."

"Forward armaments ready," May said.

"Damage report," Tesla said. "Things are holding, but at our current rate and with these vibrations, nobody is willing to guess how long it's going to last."

"It only has to last long enough to get us through that tanker."

"You're serious, then," Junnell said.

"I am."

Junnell nodded. "If we reach the point of no return, we'll have about thirty seconds before impact."

"Noted. May and Tesla, I want you to follow these instructions explicitly."

"Ma'am," they noted.

"May, I want you to rake the side of that tanker and raise some blisters. Tesla, once he's done that, I want you to run spectrography to see if it's leaking anything. I want to know if the tanker's hold is empty or full. Commence this imme- diately.''

"Gladly," May said. He fed the orders to his board. On the tactical display, the *Hergest Ridge* threw out a hail of red streaks at the intruding tanker.

"Ma'am," Junnell said. "I can temporarily divert some power from life support to limber the aft guns in the event the Vacc Fighters continue their pursuit."

"They won't follow us through the tanker," O'Hearn said. "Not unless they're crazy. There'll be too much debris."

It looked to O'Hearn as if her first officer had paled. "Not from us, I hope."

O'Hearn sighed. "I hope so, too."

With hesitating fingers, James May brought the forward guns to bear. They raked the tanker a savage blow from the exhaust nozzles across the port side, stopping just short of the command compartment. Tesla swept the area with the spectrograph.

"What am I looking for?" the ensign asked. "Anything special? I'm on a broad area sweep, but what should I keep in mind?"

"Anything," O'Hearn said. "Anything that could be in the tanker's hold."

"High-density metals are a favorite," Junnell said.

"Sand is even better," May said. "Cheaper. Very dense. And heaven help ship travel in the spill area."

"There's nothing," Tesla said. "The only thing of note is that the tanker seems to be listing from the damage we've put on it."

"Listing," May repeated.

"That's the word," O'Hearn said quickly. "They're empty. May, target the tanker amidships and hit it with ev- erything we've got. I want a half-kilometer-wide band of damage in the middle of that tanker."

May squinted at his screen. The motion was making it hard to be precise, but he locked in rake paths and set the plasma guns to work on them, one after the other, in a repeating pattern.

"Junnell. How long until we're committed?"

"A minute at the most."

"Give Swain one last message. Tell him to get the hell out of there. *Now.*"

"Oxidation!" Tesla shouted. "I'm showing oxidation!"

"What are they carrying?" May asked.

"Nothing," O'Hearn said. "It can't be loaded—"

"The superstructure," Tesla blurted. "It's melting under our fire."

"Pour it on," O'Hearn told May. "Mr. Junnell, I want this ship to go straight for the section of ship that the captain is targeting. That's where our hole is going to be."

"Affirmative," Junnell said. "Citizen Swain has been given your message. He wishes to speak with you."

"Citizen," O'Hearn said. "Your hour is at hand."

"We're trying to get out of your way!" Swain shouted. "Your fire has severed our control lines, crippled our power plant—"

"Everyone has an excuse," she growled. "Cut the line, Junnell. We'll have no further communications with the tanker."

"Wait—" Swain's voice choked before it was cut off.

"As far as I'm concerned, we're committed," the commander said. "Captain, lock the armaments into an automatic firing pattern and prepare to be secured. All other hands ready for grav secure."

Over the racket came a sudden roar, and the bridge pitched sideways. A new line of alarms sounded, and flame sprouted from one of the control consoles.

"Damage report!" O'Hearn screamed.

"It's not internal," Tesla returned. "One of the fighters bore in and impacted us on the port side."

Another blow came, this one from the top of the ship. They were thrown hard against their webbing.

"Pattern locked," May said.

"Another collision," Tesla said. "This time—"

"Ignore it," O'Hearn said. "They're making their last effort to stop us. Mr. Junnell, bring us up to maximum secure gees."

"But, Commander, the impacts—" Tesla was silenced as a third Vacc Fighter obliterated itself against the side of the *Hergest Ridge*.

"Gravity coming," Junnell said. "Twenty seconds until full effect."

They all began to sink into their seats, and the webbing tightened around them. The air became thick.

"See if you can cut some of those alarms!"

Junnell bent to the task, and the shrillness left the din in the bridge. She let a circuit board drop to the floor and eased into her seat.

"That's the best I can do, Commander."

"Fine. Until further notice, nothing said in this room is a matter of record. Understood?"

May looked at her and smiled. "For the record," he said, "you became a hell of a commander, Maggie."

"I can't say that it's been worth it," Margaret O'Hearn replied. "I've missed you—"

There was a last deafening shriek, and the *Hergest Ridge* impacted against the molten side of the tanker. The trembling gave way to a violent jolt that pushed the secured crew into their webbing in spite of the gravity. New alarms screamed to life and then fell silent as the circuits that contained them blew. Through it all, the *Ridge*'s engines fired unfailingly as the liner ripped through the softened flesh of the opposing ship. The grating of metal on metal chilled them into gooseflesh and set their teeth on edge. Compromised computer stations and screens whose antennae had been shorn off the liner's side went dark.

And then it was silent.

They lay in their seats, staring at the ceiling, waiting for more.

It never came.

Then there was a new sound, the whine of the engines as they labored to take the ship back up to shift threshold.

"We're through," May said. He strained to sit up in his seat but could not. "That's it, Maggie. We're through!"

"We're back on record," she said sternly. "Mr. Junnell, gravity back down to trip standard. Ensign Tesla, as soon as you're able I want you to check on the Arcolians."

"Yes, ma'am."

May's ears popped, and he shook his head. The gravity in the room was dropping, and the sensation made him feel as if he were in free fall. He loosened his webbing and sat up to check his display.

"Tactical, Captain?"

May stabbed at keys, trying to figure out what circuits were still available to him.

"There's not much to work with," he said. He paused to squint at a distorted display. "There's debris. A lot of debris."

"Are we still being pursued?"

"Commander," Junnell said. "We were slowed by the impact, but we have enough crew remaining to bring us back up to threshold."

"Stand by," O'Hearn said. "Well, Captain?"

"I've got two major pieces of debris. I'm assuming that those are pieces of the tanker. They're spinning away from what would have been the impact point."

"The *fighters*," O'Hearn stressed. "Any sign of them?"

May thumped the screen with his fist. The image straightened long enough for him to make a quick study of it. "If they're out there," he said, "they've split off from their pursuit or are traveling in a debris pattern."

"Junnell. Speed."

"Forty-eight percent of threshold, ma'am."

O'Hearn closed her eyes and nodded. "Very good. Notify engineering that we'll hold at fifty percent." She turned to the others. "We're going in slow and easy. After all, we're not in any rush, are we?"

18

With Tesla's orders still ringing in his ears, Vonn pulled himself from his chair and did a slow shuffle to an inner compartment door. His head throbbed, his wounded hand burned, his joints ached, and he blamed all of it on the combat maneuvers. He could handle different worlds and their different gravities, but something about quick changes in gravitic pressure made him suffer. He tried to put it behind him as he stood at the door to the sleeping quarters, trying to summon the nerve to go inside.

"What's wrong?" Winters asked, rising from his seat and stretching.

"I'm sore from all of this screwing around they did with the ship. It's been a hell of a trip, I'll tell you."

Winters flexed his hands together and bones cracked. "I've had worse rides."

The corners of Vonn's lips turned up. "Tell you what, big guy. Since you get along so well with the ambassador and his entourage, why don't you go in and make sure they're all right?"

"Me?" The big man wriggled with excitement. "Sure." He strolled over to Vonn and poised his hand above the switch. The smile dropped from his features. "Vonn? What if—what if something's wrong with them? What if they're hurt?"

Vonn's stomach churned. "They're not going to be hurt," he insisted. "They've got that big, thick armor on them. Now go check on them."

Winters tugged at Vonn's shoulders. "But, Vonn, what if they're—they're—"

"Dead?"

Winters nodded.

Vonn ground his teeth. "Then we'll boil some water and have a big feast."

Winters's eyes bugged out.

"No!" Vonn shouted. "No, Winters, I'm kidding. That

was bad of me to make a joke like that. Now go check on
. . . them.''

"Right." Winters hit the switch. As the door raised, a
rush of odor hit them. It was heavy and stung their eyes and
reminded them both of burnt matches.

"Go on," Vonn urged. "They're waiting on the bridge.
Hell, people are going to be waiting all over Council 5 for
the word.''

Winters eased into the dark room, sniffing and looking at
the large, egg-shaped pods lined along the walls. The scent
made his eyes water.

"misterbob?" he asked meekly.

There was a rustling from one of the pods. Winters froze,
then took a step back. "misterbob?"

"No need," came a croak. "No need for fearscent. We
are all what you call intact.''

"But are you okay?" Winters asked earnestly.

"Yes." It sounded almost like a sigh. "We are what you
would call 'okay.' Your scent of concern is on a primal level
and is most touching.''

"I don't understand," Winters said.

"Ah," misterbob replied. "You must be the one called
bigguy. You have no complex scents, which is most interesting.''

"Vonn calls me big guy," Winters said bluntly, "but I
don't remember him talking about any of that other stuff.''

"The fault is mine." A chitinous hand appeared and misterbob rose up from the pod, turning and easing out. "This
late part of the journey, what you call the blockade run. It
was a most interesting experience.''

"This is nothing," Winters said. "You should've been on
the *Angel's Luck* when me and Duke kicked the *Yueh-sheng*'s
ass.''

misterbob blinked at the big man. "Indeed. Something to
consider. bigguy, do I scent a certain exhilaration from you?"

Winters cocked his head at the Arcolian. "You do what?"

The creature's head bobbed up and down. "I sense that

you feel excitement. You feel good because of the danger you have faced. Is this so, bigguy?"

"Oh, yeah," Winters said. "There's nothing like coming out of a tight spot like that—"

"Am I to understand," misterbob asked, "that this is common among your people?"

"Oh, yeah," Winters boasted. "Most of us love a good scare."

"And you and misterduke experienced this exhilaration upon your angelsluck?"

"Mr. Duke's ship," Winters explained.

"Indeed," the Arcolian thrummed. "Such curious creatures. I must experience this kickass some time."

"Then you should come with me and Vonn and Duke. We do this stuff all the time."

"Indeed, I may have to do that. I should confer with the others. Such an exciting prospect, the opportunity to study the Sapient A-forms first hand."

With a shout of triumph, Winters spun and rushed out of the room. "Hey, Vonn!" he shouted. "They're okay! And guess what? misterbob says he's going to come with us!"

The barrage of scent and sound that followed only reminded misterbob that there was still much to be learned about this new species.

19

Nine hours later the *Hergest Ridge* limped into orbit around Council 5. Three of the blockading ships had made it in ahead of them with lifepods in tow, so an official escort was there to meet them, along with a handful of UTE Fleet tugs. O'Hearn stayed on the bridge the entire time, until the ship had safely been grappled by the tugs and was headed for the Fleet's orbital refitting platform. It was only when she was told that one of the UTE Fleet representatives had boarded the *Hergest Ridge* and was waiting for her to show him the damage to the liner that she relinquished command to Junnell and left the bridge, stopping to request Captain May's company for the lift ride down.

The doors to the lift slid shut and it started coreward. With a sigh of exasperation, O'Hearn reached over and stopped the car between decks.

"What's wrong?" May asked.

"I am torn," she said. "Very torn. I don't know if I should thank you or kill you."

May swallowed. He could feel the temperature rising in the small lift. "Dare I admit that I don't understand?"

"That's typical. You never understand. You just do what pleases you, and if it makes anyone else happy, then it worked out fine." O'Hearn put her hands on her hips. "I'm sorry. I didn't mean to pick at a sore. I'd just like you to appreciate my situation. On one hand, I couldn't have made it through all of this without you."

The statement was a baited stick just waiting for May to grab it. He remained silent.

"On the other hand, your presence only exacerbated the problem. I honestly don't know which is worse. For example, if Vonn hadn't come on board, I'm sure I would have lost the Arcolian delegation to the kidnappers—"

"No," May said. "The failed logic board would've prevented that."

"That's a moot point. If Vonn hadn't gotten in deep and intervened, I would have gone by the UTE Fleet book, which means I would have arrived at Council 5 with a full-blown hostage situation. That would not have looked good on my record.

"Instead, I can say that Vonn independently went undercover to disrupt a plot to kidnap the Arcolians. He did what he had to do in order to maintain his cover. Certain regrettable events did take place, and Vonn was officially in your employ, but the record will show he was secretly on our payroll, and he will be paid accordingly."

"Incredible," May said.

"Believe it. He picked up on something that the Fleet's security department had missed. If I was shipboard security, I'd be fearing for my job, but as commander, I can only comment on their lack of efficiency."

"You're not really going to tell your superiors that, are you?"

"I'm going to tell them exactly what they want to hear. Played right, there's a great PR angle here, one that would overshadow rescuing you and your crew. Can't you see it? 'Only the UTE Fleet puts undercover agents on each ship to make your trip safer!' I'm in the remarkable position of being able to save my commission, the UTE Fleet's name, and your anonymity with one fell swoop.

"But that's only the good news," O'Hearn continued. "The bad news is what Duke did to the starboard transgear bay. I can only hope the goodwill from saving the delegation can offset that."

"Duke wants to do what's right," May said. "He's offered—"

"And the Arcolians will be livid if we lift a finger against him, May. They refuse to press charges against him, and protocol says that I shouldn't even slap him with a token punishment for fear of offending them. Besides, misterbob seems to have an understanding of Duke that surpasses anything our science can come up with. In spite of the fact that it saw Duke assault redbutler, it remains convinced of Duke's innocence. I can't touch him. He could volunteer for lifetime exile on Sol 3 and it wouldn't mean a thing."

"All because of Eric Dickson," May said. "I'm sorry—"

"Save it," she snapped. "The way I see it, there's a way out of it, but I'm not happy with it. Again, it means deviating from the truth for the sake of an official version."

"Maggie, you don't have to do this for my sake—"

"I'm not doing this for your sake," she said sharply. "At this point I wouldn't lose one nanosecond of sleep if they tied a rope to your neck and dropped you down a gravity well. If I can save the UTE Fleet's good name out of this, then I can save my commission."

"You're going to blame it on Bachman."

She nodded. "I'm sure Vonn will be happy to corroborate the story if it means not going to jail."

"But Duke was found in the area—"

"Duke is from an agrarian world," O'Hearn countered. "Your big defense of him was the fact that he was a harmless nobody. If you took your evidence to the UTE Fleet yourself, that's all they would come up with. Under the circumstances, that's all they'll *want* to come up with. It's a sad substitute for the truth, but the truth stands to cost us billions in lost passenger fares."

"What about the Essence—"

She put her finger to her lips. "Not another word on that. It's not substantive evidence because according to you, that stuff has never been properly tested on another human. Am I correct?"

"More or less."

"If you're intent on staying alive after you collect the reward, your anonymity must be guaranteed. If you go hauling Duke in before the UTE Fleet, not only are you betraying him, you're betraying Winters and Vonn and Roz and the others who died bringing that stuff out of the Cosen system.

"As far as I'm concerned, Duke was in the lower deck area because he and Roz were going to secure the *Angel's Luck* for the blockade run. He may even have been acting under instructions from misterbob. We don't know for sure, do we?"

"I'd better not," May said.

"My point exactly. Case closed." With a grim look on her face, she reached over and shook the merchant's hand. "Thank you, Captain May," she said curtly. "I couldn't have done it without you."

"You did all right in spite of me, Maggie."

She gave a slight shrug. "I mean for supporting me at the right moments. That was something you were always so good at. Even when I wanted—'' She stopped and looked away for a moment. ''Even when I decided that I wanted to go back to the academy. You wouldn't give someone the time of day, but when it came to me you gave until you were hurting.''

''Don't start,'' May said quickly, not returning her gaze.

''You were ready to eject the *Angel's Luck* to help me out. Giving up your ship, that's an awfully big offer.''

''I did give my ship up.'' May sighed. ''It belongs to the UTE Fleet now.'' He gave a sad smile. ''In the end you managed to get that part of me, too.''

''Don't go into a pout,'' O'Hearn growled. ''You're going to get your way, just like you always have. The situation will be rectified.''

''Another official version?'' May said weakly.

''One that's already on the books,'' she said sternly. ''Company policy states that if a legitimate, registered claimant can be found for the salvaged materials, they can be purchased—''

May groaned.

''—for a price determined as reasonable by a person in authority. That happens to be me.''

''The price?''

''Enough to recover the costs of filing the paperwork and the annoyance to the clerk who inputs the data. That would come to . . .'' She did a quick mental calculation. ''That would come to approximately one hundred credits.''

May gave his ex-wife a sideways stare. ''Why are you sticking your neck out for me like this?''

''I'm not sticking my neck out for you,'' she snapped.

''Right.'' He nodded. ''You're doing this for yourself.''

''You're damned right. I'm doing this to get you back out of my life. I'm hurting too much as it is, James . . . *Captain*.''

May stuffed his hands in his pockets. ''Forgive me. I'm a little short of cash right now.''

''I'll loan it to you,'' O'Hearn said.

''I'll pay you when—''

"You can lase it to me in care of the Fleet."

"But I've got cash for—"

"You don't understand," she blurted, too loud. "Always you don't understand, Captain."

May studied her. She was almost standing at attention, arms at her sides, looking straight ahead.

"This lift stops on my requested deck. I get off to meet the company reps. You stay in the car. The door closes, and we do not see each other again. Ever. *Now* do you understand?"

"I understand," May said.

He was relieved when O'Hearn leaned forward and started the lift again. Cool air flooded in, and he used it as an excuse for his trembling.

Maybe I could talk to misterbob, he thought, and get a little bottle of that pheromonal whatever he used on us in the brig . . .

The car stopped and the doors opened. Without looking back, Commander Margaret O'Hearn stepped off and started down the hall.

No, May decided as the doors closed. It wouldn't be right. It would be just another case of me getting my own way.

He drew a deep breath, held it, and leaned with closed eyes against the wall.

"Excuse me," a polite voice said.

May opened his eyes. The lift was empty.

"I hate to interrupt," the voice said, "but I need to know your destination. Where would you like me to take you?"

"Back," James May said. "About twenty-five years."

20

"Some damage," Duke said, looking out the window of the lift. "It's a miracle we didn't shake apart."

May stared at the battered luxury ship as it shrank into the background. "They're built to take it," he said. "Like the *Angel's Luck*."

Duke put his hand on the merchant's shoulder. "Are you going to be all right?"

May nodded.

"Okay." Duke cleared his throat. "Listen, May, there's something I need to talk to you about before we get to the shuttle."

"I didn't pick one named *Angel's Luck* if that's what you're talking about," May said. "We're not even flying *Sky Subway*. How's that for taking care of you?"

"Fine," Duke said, scratching his head. "But that's—"

"I don't know how long we'll be planetside," May continued. "It'll be at least a month before I get all the contract estimates on refitting the *Angel's Luck*. As soon as I get the work started, we'll go to the Essence people and collect our money. After what we've been through, we deserve it."

"But that's not—"

"And we'll have the Essence people look at you, too. Don't worry, they won't dare raise a fuss over you borrowing some of their product, not after hearing what you did to save it. Besides, they should be happier than hell to know that it works."

Duke sighed, and the tone on the lift sounded. A voice gave instructions for them to disembark to the shuttle and beware of low gravity, then the door slid open.

"May, listen—"

"And we'll have your arm checked to see if you need a new cast. Are you sure that you only took a bump on the head from our run-in with the tanker? You look kind of pale." May pushed off the wall and started to drift through the access tunnel.

"The medical section turned me loose," Duke said, following, "but that's not the point . . ."

May turned the corner into the body of the shuttle. "Vonn, you old dog! We made it, didn't we? We're going to be rich!"

Duke turned the corner. The merchant and the mercenary were embracing.

"May—"

May broke from Vonn and gave Roz a big hug. "How's that friend of yours, Peter Chiba?"

"Fine," Roz said quietly. "He's already been sent planetside."

"I heard you saved Duke. And then he turned right around and saved you. What a trip it's been!"

Vonn cocked his head at Duke. His expression was one of concern. "Did you break the news to him?"

Duke shrugged. "I haven't been able to get a word in edgewise."

"Winters!" May called as he moved down the narrow body of the shuttle. He pumped the big man's hand and nodded. "Always there when we need you. I heard you pulled Vonn out of a pretty nasty scrape." He threw his arm around Winters and turned back to the others. "And we're all together. I'm so happy that all of us could be here."

"Yesssss," a voice cracked. "It will be most interesting."

May spun and drifted into a chair. A hulking figure was haphazardly belted into it.

"misterbob," he said, jaw dropping. "What are you doing here?"

"That's what I've been trying to tell you," Duke said. "He's asked to come with us."

"I invited him," Winters said proudly.

May looked at the Arcolian, eyes narrowing. "What the—what for?"

The Arcolian purred. "The Sapient A-forms at Council 5 are pleased to be our hosts and will make certain that everything is perfect. However, this is a disadvantage to the xenologist wishing to study your race on a detailed level. Travel with you will allow assembly of information not presented by our hosts."

"In other words, you want to see us in our natural form, not some snooty image served up by—"

"Watch how you say it," Duke advised.

"But you can't," May protested.

"Sure he can." Winters beamed. "That's why there was five of them."

"The others are quite capable of carrying on diplomatic duties while I make this pilgrimage of study."

"Yeah," May said, slack-jawed.

"Please do not scent of confusion, jamesohjames. This will be an important time in our cultures. There is much information to be shared. Our blended scents should be most unique."

"Unique." James Theodore May sighed. "Indeed."

About the Author

Once upon a time there was a young advertising major named Joe Clifford Faust. While sitting in class one day, he decided that writing novels would be infinitely more fun than writing toilet paper commercials. Rather foolishly, he left college and started to write.

Along the way he got married, started a family, and was confronted with handfuls of bills that arrived on a monthly basis. He paid them by working as a disc jockey, a newsletter editor, a salesman of wire and cable, and a film critic. He also worked as a sheriff's dispatcher and was certified to teach law enforcement officers in the state of Wyoming.

Mr. Faust currently makes a precarious living by writing the novels he dropped out of college to write. Against the advice of his lawyer, he now resides in the state of Ohio.

THE HEECHEE SAGA

an epic galactic trilogy
by
FREDERIK POHL